Prologue

Caleb Walker sat at the small round table in the corner of a downtown Wichita, Kansas, hotel bar, staring at the two men seated across from him. Not even the blond waitress giving him an interested smile and the fact that he hadn't had sex in a month of Sundays diverted his attention from the matter at hand.

All of his life, he'd been a man without siblings and with no idea who his father was. But not more than an hour ago, in a plush executive office at the corporate headquarters of Emerald, Inc., all that had changed. Caleb had learned that his father was none other than globe-trotting playboy and heir apparent to the Emerald, Inc. empire, Owen Larson. The late Owen Larson.

Now Caleb was having to come to terms with the fact not only that he knew who his father was, but that the man had gone and gotten himself killed in a boating accident off the coast of France before Caleb had had the chance to confront him for making Caleb's mother pregnant and leaving her without so much as a by-your-leave. He'd also learned that his grandmother was the indomitable Emerald Larson and that the two men sitting across from him were his half brothers.

"I can't believe we've been under that old bat's surveillance all of our lives." A muscle jerked along Hunter O'Banyon's tanned jaw. "She knew everything there was to know about us and didn't do a damned thing to fill us in on the big mystery until now."

"That 'old bat' is our grandmother. And I'd say she's done plenty." Nick Daniels took a swig from the long-necked bottle in his hand, then set it on the table with a thump. "Hiring P.I.s to report our every move from the time we were out of diapers while keeping us in the dark about it takes balls."

"The size of watermelons," Caleb added. His gut still churned with anger that Emerald Larson, founder and CEO of one of the nation's most successful female-owned and operated conglomerates, had denied them all the right to know who they were for so long. "I'm having a problem with her blackmailing our mothers with the threat of cutting us out of inheriting any part of Emerald, Inc. just to keep them silent about her worthless son being the jerk who got them pregnant." He shook his head in disbelief. "I'll give her this much, the old gal's a master at manipulation."

Nick nodded. "I can understand why our moms went along with her. They were hoping to ensure a better life for us. But they paid a hell of a price for it."

"I don't give a damn about inheriting any part of Emerald Larson's little self-made empire." Hunter shook his head. "Hell will freeze over before I dance to her tune."

"So you're going to turn down her offer?" Caleb asked.

If they accepted Emerald's conditions, they'd each be given one of her companies. She'd assured them there were no strings attached and she wouldn't interfere with the way they ran the businesses. But Caleb wasn't fool enough to believe it. It looked like his brothers weren't either.

"I haven't flown a chopper in the past five years." Hunter's mouth thinned to a menacing line. "What business would I have trying to run an air medevac service?"

"Well, it makes more sense than sending a desk jockey to run a cattle ranch in Wyoming." Nick's scowl deepened. "I've lived in a condo in St. Louis for the past twelve years. The closest I get to any kind of livestock these days is the Clydesdales when they pull a beer wagon down Market Street during a parade."

Caleb had to agree that what Emerald Larson was asking them to do was ludicrous. He'd excelled in the business courses he'd taken in high school, but that had been a good number of years ago. He didn't particularly like the idea of making a fool of himself when it became apparent he was in way over his head.

"Well, how do you think I feel?" He shook his head at the thought of what the old gal had in mind for him. "I'm a Tennessee farmer with nothing more than a high-school education. Emerald couldn't have come up with anything more ridiculous than me taking over a financial consulting firm."

Hunter reached for a pretzel from the bowl in the middle of the table. "You can bet that old girl has more up her sleeve than giving us part of Emerald, Inc. out of the goodness of her heart."

"No doubt about it," Nick said, nodding.

Caleb wasn't sure exactly what Emerald Larson had in mind, but he knew just as surely as the sun rose in the east each morning that whatever it was, she'd purposely chosen the business she wanted each of them to run. "It's my guess she wants us to prove something."

Nick looked surprised. "Like what? That we don't know what we're doing?"

"Beats me. But you can bet Emerald Larson has a reason for everything she does." Caleb shrugged as he swallowed the last of his beer. "The way I see it, we have two options. We can either turn the old gal down and walk away, making the sacrifices our mothers made to ensure our futures a total waste of time. Or, we can accept Emerald's offer and show her that she doesn't know beans from buckshot about who we are and where our talents lie."

Hunter looked thoughtful. "I kind of like the idea of showing up the high-and-mighty Mrs. Larson."

"It would serve her right when we all fall on our faces," Nick said, still looking reluctant.

"But if we're going to do this, we at least have to give it our best shot." Caleb stood up and tossed a couple of dollar bills on the table. "It's not in me to do anything half-assed."

"Me neither," the other two said in unison as they rose to their feet and added money to pay for their drinks.

"Then I guess all we have left to do is give Emerald our answer." Caleb suddenly felt as if he was about to step out onto a tightrope without a safety net.

But as he led the way out of the bar and down the street toward the corporate offices of Emerald, Inc., he couldn't help but feel a bit of nervous anticipation begin to build. He'd always enjoyed a challenge. And as unbelievable as it was, he was actually looking forward to taking over Skerritt and Crowe Financial Consultants. His only regret was that he didn't have the education or the slightest idea of how to go about doing the job right.

One

Approaching the reception desk outside the executive offices of Skerritt and Crowe Financial Consultants, Caleb plastered on the professional smile he'd been practicing for the past week. "I'm here to see A. J. Merrick."

"Do you have an appointment, sir?" the older, gray-haired receptionist asked as he started toward the doors behind her desk.

"I'm Caleb Walker." He gave her a conspiratorial wink. "I believe Merrick is expecting me."

"Hold it right there, Mr. Walton," she said, rising to block his way.

"Walker." He frowned. Hadn't Merrick let the other

employees know about his taking over as president of the firm?

The woman shrugged. "Walker, Walton, it doesn't matter what your name is. You're not going in there without an appointment."

Apparently, no one had bothered to inform this woman. "Tell you what—" he glanced at the nameplate on her desk "—Geneva. After I talk with your boss, I promise I'll come back and introduce myself."

"My *boss* is busy and doesn't want to be disturbed." Geneva pointed to a row of chairs lining the wall across the room. "If you'll have a seat, I'll see if I can work you in."

At six feet four inches tall, he towered over the woman by at least a foot, but she wasn't acting the least bit intimidated by it. From the look on her face, she was just as determined to keep him out of the office as he was determined he was going inside.

It was all he could do to keep a straight face. Geneva reminded him of a little banty hen his grandpa used to own—all bluff and ruffled feathers. And if her defiant expression was any indication, he had no doubt that he'd be sitting in the reception area until hell froze over before she picked up the phone and announced his arrival.

"There's no need to go to all that trouble, Geneva." Chuckling, he sidestepped the woman as he reached for the polished knob on the mahogany door with A. J.

Merrick engraved on a brass plaque. "Take my word for it, Merrick is going to want to meet with me right away."

"I'll call security," Geneva threatened, rushing over to the phone.

"You do that," Caleb said, nodding. "I'd like to meet with them, too."

"Oh, you will, buster," she promised, stabbing her finger at the phone's keypad.

Without waiting to see if Geneva reached the security desk, Caleb opened the door and stepped into the spacious office. His gaze immediately zeroed in on the young woman seated behind a huge walnut desk in front of a wall of floor-to-ceiling windows.

With her dark auburn hair pulled back in a bun tight enough to make his grandma Walker proud and a pair of oversize black plastic-framed glasses, she looked more like a headmistress at one of those hoity-toity private all-girl schools in Nashville than a modern corporate secretary. And if her disapproving expression was any indication, she was just as unyielding and strict about rules and protocol as one of those overly uptight teachers, too.

But as he sauntered over to stand in front of the desk, he thought he saw a hint of uncertainty about her—a vulnerability that, considering the image she was obviously trying to project, he hadn't expected. "Excuse me. I'm looking for A. J. Merrick."

"Do you have business here?" she asked, her voice cool enough to freeze ice.

Rising to her feet, she pushed her glasses up her pert little nose with a delicate hand, inadvertently drawing attention to her brilliant blue eyes—eyes that sent him a look that would have probably stopped a lesser man dead in his tracks. It didn't faze Caleb one damned bit. On the contrary. He wasn't sure why, but for some reason he found something quite intriguing about her intense blue gaze.

"I'm—"

"If you're looking for personnel, it's down the hall," she said, cutting him off before he had a chance to introduce himself. Pausing, she arched one perfectly shaped eyebrow. "Was Mrs. Wallace at her desk?"

The woman's no-nonsense tone couldn't quite mask the soft, melodic quality of her voice and had Caleb wondering why the sound seemed to bring every one of his male hormones to full alert. Wondering what the hell had gotten into him, he decided it had to be the fact that he hadn't been with a woman in the better part of a year. That alone was enough to make any normal, healthy adult male feel as though he was about to jump out of his own skin. It also made him overly conscious of every move a woman—any woman—made.

Satisfied that he'd come up with an explanation for his interest in the less-than-friendly secretary, he jerked his thumb over his shoulder. "As far as I know, Geneva's still out there." He chuckled. "Although I'm not real sure she didn't break one of her fingers punching in the number for security."

"Good."

"Good that she might have broken a finger? Or good that she was calling security?" he asked, grinning.

"I didn't mean—" Frowning, she stopped short and it was clear that for a split second, he'd thrown her off guard. "Good that she's summoning security, of course."

"Hey, lighten up. Life is too short to be so uptight."

The woman rounded the end of the desk, her expression anything but welcoming. "I don't know who you think you are or why you're here, but you can't just walk in and—"

The sound of the door crashing against the wall stopped the young woman in midsentence.

"That's him."

Caleb glanced over his shoulder to see the receptionist charge into the office with a defiant glare. Two middle-aged, potbellied uniformed men followed close behind.

"I see you got hold of the security guards, Geneva." He glanced at his watch, then nodded his approval. "Their response time wasn't bad, but I think we could work on improving it, don't you?"

Geneva managed to look down her nose at him despite the difference in their heights, then turned her attention to the woman with the remarkable baby blues. "I'm sorry, Ms. Merrick." She eyed Caleb like she didn't think his elevator went all the way to the top floor. "*He* wouldn't take no for an answer."

Caleb raised an eyebrow. This was A. J. Merrick?

Interesting. She definitely wasn't what he'd expected. Emerald had led him to believe that Merrick was a stodgy old gent, not a twentysomething woman with incredible blue eyes.

As they stared at each other like opponents in a boxing ring, his neglected libido noticed that A. J. Merrick wasn't dressed like most women her age. Instead of her black suit caressing her body and showing off her assets, it hung from her small frame like an empty tow sack. But if her delicate hands, slender neck and what he could see of her long, perfectly shaped legs were any indication, he'd bet his grandpa's best coonhound she was hiding some pretty incredible curves inside all that baggy black linen.

"It's all right, Mrs. Wallace." Ms. Merrick treated Caleb to a triumphant smile that did strange things to his insides and made him feel as if the temperature in the room had suddenly gone up ten degrees. "I'm sure you'll understand that applying for a job now would be a waste of time for both of us." To the guards coming to stand on either side of him, she added, "Please show this gentleman to the parking lot."

"That's mighty unfriendly of you," Caleb said, shaking his head.

Allowing the men to demonstrate how they would

handle the situation if he'd been a real threat, Caleb almost laughed out loud when they clumsily grabbed his arms and attempted to pull them behind his back. He immediately decided that they not only needed to work on their response time to a situation, but could both benefit from a refresher course in methods of restraint. If he'd been of a mind to, he could have broken their hold without doing much more than flexing his biceps.

"I'm not here to apply for a job." He smiled. "I already work here."

"Oh, really?" Ms. Merrick tilted her head curiously. "Since I do the final interviews for all new employees, would you care to refresh my memory and tell me what your name is, when we hired you and just which area of Skerritt and Crowe you think you work in?"

"I got the job a week ago and I intend to work in the office next to yours." Chuckling, he decided he was going to enjoy sparring with A. J. Merrick. "The name is Walker. Caleb Walker."

He could tell from the widening of her baby blues behind those ridiculous glasses that his answers were *not* what she'd expected. But she quickly recovered her composure and motioned toward the two guards. "Mr. Norton, Mr. Clay, please release Mr. Walker immediately."

"But Ms. Merrick—"

"I said, let him go," she repeated. She lifted her stubborn little chin a notch. "Mr. Walker is the new president of Skerritt and Crowe."

From somewhere behind him, he heard Geneva gasp at the same time as the two guards dropped their hold on him.

"Sorry about that, Mr. Walker," one of the men said, clumsily trying to straighten Caleb's shirtsleeve.

Silence reigned for several tense seconds as Caleb and the woman in front of him stared at each other. In a lot of ways she reminded him of another woman and another time.

He took a deep breath. That had been a while back and he'd learned a lot in the few years since. He was no longer a naive farm boy with lofty dreams and a trusting heart. He was a grown man who'd learned his lessons well.

"If you'd give Ms. Merrick and me a few minutes, I'd surely appreciate it," he finally said as he continued to meet her intense gaze. When he heard the quiet click of the door being pulled shut behind the three, Caleb smiled. "What do you say we start over?" He stuck out his hand. "I'm Caleb Walker. It's nice to meet you, Ms. Merrick."

When she hesitantly placed her hand in his, the feel of her soft palm against his sent a shock wave all the way to his toes. She apparently felt the same jolt of electric current because she dropped his hand faster than the high-school football captain's pants hit the floor on prom night. He barely managed to keep from laughing out loud.

"I know I'm earlier than you all expected, but don't you think it would have been a good idea to inform the employees about me? After all, Emerald Larson called you several days ago to tell you I'd be here at the end of this week."

"Mrs. Larson indicated that you'd be here on Friday."

"I'm only a day early," he said, breathing a bit easier when A.J. didn't refer to Emerald as his grandmother.

He'd purposely asked Emerald not to mention their relationship when she called Skerritt and Crowe, and it appeared that she'd respected his wishes. He didn't want or need the added prejudices of being the owner's grandson when he took over.

"It was my intention to introduce you to everyone tomorrow at the directors' meeting," she said, sounding extremely efficient.

"Well, I can guarantee you the cat's out of the bag now," he said, grinning. "I'll bet Geneva and her two sidekicks are spreading the word like fire through a hay field."

To his amazement, she didn't even crack a smile. "I'm sure they are."

Her calm demeanor had Caleb wondering if A. J. Merrick ever let herself lose control. Something told him that it didn't happen often. But he also sensed that when she did let go, it would be a hell of a sight. What he couldn't figure out was why he'd like to be there to see it when she did.

She waved her hand at one of the burgundy leather armchairs in front of her desk. "Please have a seat, Mr. Walker."

Sitting down, he watched her walk around the desk to lower herself into the high-backed executive chair. "Since we're going to be working together, why don't we ditch the formalities?" he asked, wondering what made A. J. Merrick tick. "Call me Caleb."

"I'd rather not, Mr. Walker," she said, straightening some papers on her desk.

"Why not?" He wasn't at all surprised by her insistence on formalities. However, he was dismayed by his own persistence in getting her to let down her guard.

She stopped fussing with the documents to give him a pointed look. "It will only complicate things when the time comes for you to let me go."

Now where had that come from? To his knowledge, he hadn't given her any reason to feel threatened or to believe he'd be firing her, or anyone else for that matter. But she was acting like it was a done deal.

He sat forward. "Where did you get the harebrained idea that I'd be letting you go?"

"Any time there's a change in upper management, the result is always the same. The new president or CEO brings in his or her own people for the top positions and the old regime is history." She shrugged one slender shoulder as she met his gaze head-on. "Since I'm the operations manager over all the departments here at

Skerritt and Crowe, mine will be one of the first heads to roll."

He wasn't sure, but he thought he detected a slight tremor in her voice. But as she continued to stare at him like he was lower than the stuff he scraped off his boots after a trip through the barnyard, he decided he'd imagined the sound. A. J. Merrick was way too professional to show the slightest bit of emotion. What shocked him more than her steely control was his sudden desire to see what lay beneath that cool facade, to discover what she was so obviously trying to hide.

"Let me put your fears to rest right here and now. I'm not getting rid of you or anyone else," he said, forcing his mind back to the matter at hand. She had no way of knowing, and he wasn't about to tell her that he didn't have a clue about running a firm of financial consultants or that he'd have to rely heavily on her and others' experience in order to keep from falling on his face. "Your job is just as safe today as it was before Emerald, Inc. bought this firm."

She pushed her glasses back up her nose with a brush of her hand. "You say that now, but it's a well-known fact that within six months of any takeover there's always a shake-up."

"That might happen with a hostile buyout, but Emerald Larson bought this company with Frank Skerritt and Martin Crowe's blessings. They both wanted to retire, but neither of them had family members who wanted to take the reins of the firm."

As he watched her nibble on her lower lip while she considered his words, he found himself wondering if her perfectly shaped lips were as soft and sweet as they looked. Swallowing hard, he decided that he'd better keep his mind on business and off the fact that Ms. Merrick had the most kissable mouth he'd seen in a very long time.

"I'll be—" he stopped to clear the rust from his throat before he continued "—making a few small changes here and there. But as far as I'm concerned, the only way any of the employees will lose their job is if they up and quit."

"We'll see," she said softly.

Her expression was completely neutral and gave no indication of what she was thinking. But Caleb knew she wasn't buying his assurances for a minute.

Deciding that he'd probably have more luck convincing a pack of wolves to become vegetarians than he would getting A. J. Merrick to believe her job was secure, Caleb took a deep breath and stood up. "I think I'll mosey on out of here and introduce myself to a few of our people."

"But what about the meeting I have set up for tomorrow morning at ten, Mr. Walker?" she asked as she rose from her chair.

Was that a hint of panic he detected in her wide blue eyes?

Interesting. It appeared that any break with tradition threw A. J. Merrick for a loop. He'd have to remember that.

"The name's Caleb." He shrugged. "The meeting is still on. I'll just use it to outline a few of the policy changes I intend to make and explain my plan of action."

He noticed the white-knuckled grip she had on her ink pen and, without thinking, reached across the desk to place his hand on hers in a reassuring manner. But the moment his palm touched her satiny skin, a charge of electricity zinged up his arm and quickly spread throughout his chest. Her startled gasp told him that she felt it, too.

Quickly moving his hand, he tried to appear nonchalant about the gesture. But considering his insides were still tingling like he'd grabbed hold of a 220-volt wire, that was mighty damned hard.

"Relax, Ms. Merrick," he said, wondering what the hell had gotten into him. Surely he didn't need to get laid so badly that he'd started getting turned on by merely touching a woman's hand. "Not only do you have my word that your job's safe, I promise that what I have in mind will improve employee morale and increase productivity."

At least, that's what he hoped to accomplish. Considering he didn't know beans from buckshot about running this or any other company, he'd just have to operate on the trial-and-error system, refer to the management manual he'd picked up at a bookstore and hope for the best.

She defensively folded her arms beneath her breasts and simply stared at him. "I suppose I'll have to take your word on that."

"I guess you will," he said, walking toward the door. He needed to put some distance between them in order to regain his perspective. He was here to take over the consulting firm, not try to figure out why this woman's reluctance to believe him bothered the hell out of him. Or why he was starting to get turned on by staring into her pretty blue eyes. "I'll see you tomorrow morning, Ms. Merrick."

"C-Caleb?" She stumbled over his name, but the sound of it on her soft voice did a real number on his neglected hormones.

His hand on the doorknob, he turned back to face her. "Yes, Ms. Merrick?"

"I suppose since you insist that I use your first name, you might as well call me A.J."

"Okay, A.J." He smiled. Maybe they were making progress after all. "I'll see you first thing in the morning."

A.J. watched the door close behind Caleb Walker a moment before her trembling legs folded and she collapsed into her leather executive chair. Why was her heart racing? And why did her skin still tingle from his touch?

She removed her glasses and buried her face in her hands. What on earth had come over her? She never had been, nor would ever be the type of woman who let a handsome man divert her attention from what was important. At least not since the fiasco with Wesley Pennington III. He'd taught her a valuable lesson, and one that she couldn't afford to forget—mixing business with pleasure was a fool's game, one that ultimately led to disaster.

Normally, it wasn't even an issue. Since losing her heart, her virginity and her first job due to her naiveté, she'd made it a point to do everything she could to appear as professional as possible. It kept things simple and helped to reinforce her strict policy of keeping coworkers at arm's length. And it had worked well.

Most people, and especially men, were put off by her all-business demeanor and didn't bother taking a second glance at her. And that suited her just fine. But Caleb Walker had not only looked twice, he'd focused his disturbing hazel gaze on her from the moment he'd walked into her office.

A tiny tremor coursed through her. He had a way of looking at her that made her more aware of her femininity than she'd ever been in her life. And that was what made him dangerous.

Shaking her head, she tried not to think about the wild fluttering in her lower stomach that she'd experienced when Caleb had smiled at her, and concentrated on the fact that he was her new boss. He was here to take over Skerritt and Crowe and eventually replace her with one of his own people. And even though he'd assured her that wasn't the case, she knew better. Everything she'd worked to achieve in the past five years was about to go down the drain and she was powerless to stop it.

She put her glasses back on and swiveled the chair

around to stare out the plate-glass windows. Blindly watching the late-June sun bathe downtown Albuquerque with its warm afternoon rays, she fought the urge to cry. She had a feeling that Caleb Walker was going to turn her structured, well-ordered world upside down. And there wasn't a thing she could do to stop him.

There was no telling what kinds of changes he intended to implement or just how quickly he'd decide she was dispensable. And the most upsetting aspect of all was the fact that all she could think about was how intense his hazel eyes were, how his light brown hair hanging low on his forehead made him look more like a rebel than a businessman. And how the combination of his deep baritone and sexy Southern accent made her insides hum.

"Don't be a fool," she muttered, turning back to her desk.

She wasn't interested in Caleb Walker any more than he was interested in her. But as she stared at the documents on her desk, she couldn't stop thinking about how broad his shoulders looked in his chambray shirt, how his jeans fit him like a second skin or how her hand still tingled where he'd touched her.

When a tiny moan of frustration escaped, she quickly stuffed the pile of accounting reports she'd been reviewing into her briefcase, grabbed her purse from the bottom drawer of the desk and headed for the door. "I'll be out of the office for the rest of the day," she told Geneva as she rushed past her.

A.J. didn't wait for the startled receptionist's reaction to her atypical behavior. She didn't have time to worry about that now. She needed to get to her apartment before the cool persona she'd perfected over the years slipped away and she revealed what only her parakeet, Sidney, knew about her.

Alyssa Jane Merrick wasn't the cold, emotionless automaton everyone at Skerritt and Crowe thought her to be. She was a living, breathing woman who collected whimsical figurines, shed buckets of tears over sentimental or touching moments, and feared failure more than anything else.

As she walked across the parking lot, she quickened her steps and trotted the distance to her sensible black sedan. She was less than a split second away from doing one of two things. She was going to either let loose with a scream loud enough to wake the dead or start crying like a baby. Neither one was acceptable behavior for her professional image.

Unlocking the driver's door, she threw her briefcase inside, slid behind the steering wheel and closed her eyes. She counted to ten, then twenty as she struggled with her emotions. For the first time in five years, she was close to losing the tight grip she had always held on herself whenever she was at work. And that was something she simply couldn't afford to let happen.

She had never, nor would she ever allow any of these people to see her lose control. Not only would it be a

serious breach of her professionalism, but her late father would come back to haunt her for doing something
so typically female.

From the time she'd been old enough to listen, her
career-military father had stressed how important it was
not to let her enemies see any sign of weakness. And
there was no doubt about it, Caleb Walker posed a serious threat to her professional demeanor. But he was
also the best-looking enemy she'd ever seen.

Two

"The first thing I want to do this morning is assure all of you that your jobs are secure," Caleb said, addressing the directors and department managers. He made it a point to look directly at A. J. Merrick. "Contrary to standard corporate practice, I have no intention of letting anyone go in favor of bringing in my own people. The only way you're going to lose your job is if *you* make the decision to quit."

The doubt he detected in her blue gaze stated quite clearly that she still didn't believe him. What he couldn't figure out was why it mattered to him that she trust him. If their collective sigh of relief was any indication, the rest of the occupants in the room did. What made her opinion of him so damned important?

Deciding not to dwell on the mystery of why her doubts bothered him, Caleb turned his attention back to outlining his plans for the company. "I've reviewed the quarterly reports for the last fiscal year and although growth is slow, it has been steady." He grinned. "And as my grandpa Walker always said, 'If it ain't broke, don't fix it.' That's why I won't be making changes in the daily operations of the company." *At least not until I can take a few business courses and figure out what the hell I'm doing.*

"I like the way your grandpa thinks," Malcolm Fuller said, nodding.

Caleb chuckled. "I'm glad that meets with your approval, Malcolm." He'd met the older man the day before and they'd instantly hit it off. Malcolm reminded Caleb of Henry Walker, his late grandpa—filled with country wisdom and more than willing to speak his mind.

When Caleb noticed several raised eyebrows and the exchange of curious glances between the other department heads seated at the big oval conference table, he frowned. Apparently all of the employees at Skerritt and Crowe were as unaccustomed to the laid-back, informal approach to management as A. J. Merrick was.

Taking a deep breath, he figured there was no time like the present to shake things up and see how receptive the management team was to the changes he did have planned. "Although I don't intend to adjust the operating procedures, I do plan to make a few improvements to the work atmosphere around here."

"What did you have in mind, Mr. Walker?" Ed Bentley asked, looking more than a little nervous.

"The first thing we're going to do is drop the formalities." Caleb gave them all a smile he hoped would put their minds at ease. "Don't you think it's pretty silly to work with someone eight hours a day, day in and day out and not use their given name?" Before they could react, he went on. "We'll naturally continue to give our clients the respect they deserve and address them in a formal manner. But I want you all to feel free to be on a first-name basis with me, as well as each other."

The men and women at the table began to smile. Everyone, except A.J. Her clasped hands resting on the table in front of her had tightened into a white-knuckled knot, indicating that she strongly disagreed with his decision.

Why would she object to doing away with an outdated tradition? Hadn't she learned in college that a more relaxed environment encouraged teamwork and raised productivity? Hell, he'd found that little tidbit of information on the Internet, so it couldn't be that big a secret.

"You want us to call you Caleb?" Maria Santos asked hesitantly.

Grinning, he turned his attention to the director of the payroll department. "That's my name, Maria."

"What other changes do you have planned…Caleb?" one of the other men asked.

"Effective immediately, there's an open-door policy

between upper management and the workers on the floor." He paused to let them digest his statement. "I want every employee we have, no matter what their position, to feel comfortable with bringing problems and complaints to our attention, as well as sharing ways to improve morale and bring in new clients."

"You've got a lot of good ideas," Joel McIntyre, the head of the billing department, said, nodding his approval. "Is there anything else?"

"As a matter of fact there is, Joel." Caleb smiled. He was sure the last couple of changes he was about to announce would be welcomed by everyone, including A. J. Merrick. "Since most of our business is conducted over the phone and through the Internet, I don't see any reason why we can't relax the dress code around here. I'll still expect you to dress accordingly when you meet with one of our clients, but from now on you're all free to wear whatever you like." He chuckled. "That is, as long as it's decent and doesn't look like something you'd put on to clean out the barn."

He laughed out loud when several of the men immediately reached up to remove their ties and unfasten the top button of their shirts. "I guess this means everyone is in favor of doing away with the dress code."

When he glanced at A.J. his smile faded. *Well, almost everyone.*

"Is that all?" she asked tightly. She stared straight at him and it was as clear as a cloudless sky that she wasn't happy.

None of the other department heads seemed to notice that the operations manager was even in the same room with them, let alone less than enthusiastic about his ideas. But Caleb had been aware of her presence from the moment she'd sat down in the chair at the far end of the conference table. He'd hoped that once she heard what he had planned she'd find his ideas to be innovative or at least be open to giving them a chance.

Unfortunately, she looked even more unhappy than she had yesterday afternoon when he'd walked into her office and announced who he was. But more troubling than her lack of enthusiasm was his reaction to her reluctance. He had an almost uncontrollable urge to walk over to her, take her in his arms and reassure her that the changes he planned to make would be of benefit to everyone.

He shook his head, as much to dispel his disturbing thoughts as to let her know he had more plans in the works. "I have one more announcement before I let you all get back to work." Tearing his gaze from A.J., he forced his attention to the others seated around the table. "On Monday, there will be a seminar for all managers to learn team-building techniques. Then, once a month, the firm will pick up the tab for you and all of the people in your department to take a Friday off and put what you've learned into action."

"This is where we go on picnics, play golf and things like that to build communication skills and encourage interaction with our coworkers, isn't it?" Joel asked, sounding excited by the possibilities.

"That's the plan," Caleb said, nodding. At least others could see his objective, even if A.J. couldn't. "There's no reason we can't have fun while we develop a tight, efficient team." Smiling, he pushed his chair back and rose to his feet. He'd given them enough to digest for one day. In the next week or so, he'd shake things up a little more. "Now, what do you say we all get back to work and make some money."

As the meeting broke up and her coworkers surrounded Caleb to express their enthusiasm for the changes he'd be making, A.J. escaped to the sanctuary of her office. Closing the door behind her, she leaned up against it as she struggled to breathe. She felt as if she were about to suffocate on the myriad of emotions racing through her. In less than an hour, Caleb Walker had single-handedly destroyed every reason she had for working at Skerritt and Crowe. And he didn't even realize it.

He thought he was doing everyone a favor by improving the quality of their work atmosphere. And she had to admit that what he planned would probably motivate the employees and breathe new life into the firm.

But she'd purposely chosen to accept the position

with Skerritt and Crowe, instead of at a more modern financial group, because of the formalities and old-fashioned approach to management. It enabled her to focus all of her attention on her job and kept the people she worked with at a safe distance.

Pushing away from the door, she walked around her desk and sank into the high-backed leather chair. Although she wasn't antisocial by nature, she'd learned the hard way to keep her coworkers at arm's length. It was the only sure way to guard herself against betrayal and the emotional pain that accompanied it.

But what frustrated and confused her more than anything else was her reaction to Caleb. The entire time he'd been outlining the ways he intended to destroy her safety net, all she'd been able to think about was how handsome he was and how his deep Southern drawl made her insides hum.

Barely resisting the urge to let loose with a scream that was sure to send Geneva Wallace into cardiac arrest, A.J. turned to her computer screen and opened the file containing her résumé. There was no longer any question about it. Her days as operations manager at Skerritt and Crowe were numbered and she'd do well to start looking for another job.

"A.J., could you come in here?" Caleb's voice invading her office through the intercom caused her stomach to flutter wildly. "I have something I need to talk over with you."

What could he possibly want now? Hadn't he done enough in the past hour to turn her world upside down?

Sighing, she depressed the talk button. "I'm working on something at the moment. Could we postpone the discussion until this afternoon?" He didn't need to know that she was updating her résumé or that she planned on finding another job. When silence reigned, she pushed the button again. "Mr. Walker? Caleb?"

She gasped when the door connecting their offices opened and he strolled into the room.

"Sorry if I startled you, but I'm a face-to-face kind of guy," he said, grinning. "I like to look a person in the eye when I'm talking to them."

The sound of his voice and his sexy grin sent a shiver streaking up her spine and had her wondering what else he liked to do face-to-face. Her breath caught and she did her best to hide her shock at the direction her wayward thoughts had taken.

"What did you want to discuss, Mr.—"

He raised one dark eyebrow at the same time he cleared his throat.

Resigned, she closed the computer file containing her résumé. "What did you want to discuss…Caleb?"

He smiled his approval. "I think I've come across another way to improve employee morale."

Just what she wanted to hear, she thought disgustedly, another cockamamy idea that would no doubt increase her anxiety level.

She trained her gaze on his forehead to keep from looking directly into his startling hazel eyes. "What did you have in mind?"

"I'm thinking about turning the break room into a 'family room.'"

A.J.'s mouth dropped open and her gaze flew to his. "Excuse me?"

"Better watch that." He chuckled. "You might catch a fly."

She snapped her mouth shut. Didn't he take anything seriously?

"Would you care to explain what you mean when you use the term *family room?*" she asked, rubbing at the sudden pounding in her temples.

"I'm thinking couches, coffee tables and a big-screen TV," he said, looking thoughtful. "When our employees take their breaks, they should be able to relax and enjoy the few minutes they have away from the job."

"If you make it too comfortable, they'll go to sleep," A.J. said before she could stop herself.

She hadn't meant to be so blunt. But facts were facts and he might as well be aware of them right up front.

He grinned. "Nothing wrong with a little power nap now and then. Studies have shown that it gives most people a second wind."

She'd seen the research and couldn't argue with the findings, but that didn't mean she agreed with them.

"Are you wanting to know what I think of the idea?" she asked cautiously.

"Not really." He gave her a smile that warmed her all the way to her toes. "But I would like your help putting the project into action."

Her first inclination was to refuse his request. But to her amazement, she found herself asking, "What do you want me to do?"

"I'd really appreciate your input on what colors and style of furniture to use." His expression turned sheepish. "I'm not real up on this decorating stuff."

Oh, he was good. He knew just when to turn up the wattage on that smile and use his boyish charm to get exactly what he wanted. Fortunately, she was immune to such tactics.

"What makes you think I'm any better?"

"I don't." He shrugged. "But I need a woman's perspective. The room needs to be comfortable for both men and women. If I try to do it entirely on my own, it'll end up looking like a sports bar."

"Why don't you get Mrs. Wallace to help you?" A.J. hedged. "I've heard her say she never misses that television show where friends redecorate each other's rooms."

"I have Geneva busy heading up another project," he said, grinning.

"You do?" Good Lord, what on earth had he charmed their stodgy sixty-year-old secretary into doing?

"I've given her a five-thousand-dollar budget for uniforms and equipment and put her in charge of organizing our sports teams."

A.J. couldn't believe what she was hearing. "You've got to be joking."

"Nope." His smile intensified. "Depending on the amount of interest among the employees, we're going to have bowling and volleyball teams this winter and a softball team next summer."

"You do realize this consulting firm is comprised of accountants and financial analysts, don't you?" She shook her head in disbelief. "That's not exactly the material jocks are made of."

He shook his head. "I don't care if we have winning teams. I'm more interested in creating an overall sense of unity among the employees." Rising to his feet, he stretched and started walking toward the door to his office. "You've got the weekend to give some thought to what we can do to the break room, then we'll go over your ideas next week."

As she watched him close the door behind himself, A.J. groaned. From the time she'd been old enough to understand, her father had preached the military mantra of structure and order. He'd said they were essential for a successful life. Captain John T. Merrick had believed it, had lived by it and had insisted that his daughter adhere to it. He'd even chosen the boarding school she'd attended after the death of her mother because of its strict code of conduct and rigid set of rules. And the one and only time she'd deviated from the path her father had set her on, she'd ended up in the middle of a humiliating workplace scandal.

But she'd survived because that's what her late father would have expected her to do. It had been extremely difficult, but she'd picked up the pieces of her shattered pride, became a born-again virgin and found her present job at Skerritt and Crowe. And she'd been—if not happy—content for the past five years.

Unfortunately, it seemed that contentment had come to an end with the arrival of Caleb Walker. When he'd strolled into her office yesterday afternoon with his good-old-boy attitude and devastating good looks to announce he was taking over the firm, she felt as if she'd been tossed into a vortex. He represented everything in life she'd been taught to approach with caution, if not avoid altogether. He was innovative in the way he approached management and his ideas were unorthodox and, unless she'd missed her guess, for the most part spontaneous.

So why did her pulse pound and air feel as if it were in short supply whenever they were in the same room? Why did his sexy Southern drawl send sparks of electric current over every nerve in her body? And why did the sight of his wide shoulders and slender hips cause her body to hum with a restlessness like she'd never known before?

Biting her lower lip to stop its trembling, she hastily reopened the computer file containing her résumé. There was absolutely no question about the matter. She had to find another job as soon as possible or risk losing what little sense she had left.

The following Tuesday afternoon, Caleb sat at his desk, wondering what on God's green earth Emerald Larson had gotten him into. He didn't have the vaguest idea of how he was supposed to deal with one of Skerritt and Crowe's best clients. His night classes at the University of New Mexico weren't scheduled to start until the end of next month. He somehow doubted the business administration courses he'd signed up for would start out covering the interaction with clientele, anyway.

He drummed his fingertips on the desk's polished surface. He hadn't been able to find anything on conducting meetings with clients in the management manual, either. The damned thing only covered supervising employees and ways to improve their work environment. It was completely useless for learning how to deal with clients.

But whether Caleb knew what he was doing or not, it didn't change the fact that Raul Ortiz wanted to meet with him. Caleb had taken over running the financial consulting firm that had helped Ortiz Industries create one of the best employee investment plans in the state, and he suspected that Ortiz wanted to make sure Caleb passed muster.

When he heard A.J.'s voice through the door connecting their offices, Caleb's spirits lifted. The woman might be driving him crazy trying to figure out what made her tick, but he'd read her personnel file. She really knew her stuff when it came to financial planning and marketing analysis. He'd also discovered that she'd graduated from high school at the age of fifteen and had acquired her master's degree in investment banking and business administration by the time she was twenty.

If he took her with him when he drove down to Roswell, surely the meeting with Ortiz would work out. He was good with people and A.J. was a whiz at anything to do with accounting and financial planning. Together they should make a hell of a team.

Caleb took a deep breath and rose to his feet. He hated feeling inadequate at anything. But he had decided up front that he was going to have to rely on the people working for him until he took courses and got a basic understanding of the business Emerald had given him. It looked as though that reliance was going to have to start sooner than later.

Opening the door between their offices, he smiled when A.J. glanced at him over the top of her computer screen. "I just got a call from a man down in Roswell," he said, walking over to slump into the chair in front of her desk. "He claims to be our most satisfied client."

"That would be Mr. Ortiz," she answered, nodding. "He's one of our most valued patrons."

"That's what he said." Caleb chuckled. "I get the idea he's also one of our most outspoken clients."

"I've never known him to mince words," she said, pushing her glasses up her pert little nose. The action drew attention to her remarkable eyes and Caleb had to remind himself that he'd entered her office for a reason other than staring into her baby blues.

"So you've dealt with him before?"

She nodded. "Mr. Skerritt took care of Ortiz Industries' employee investment program, but he assigned me to advise Mr. Ortiz on his own personal retirement package. Why do you ask?"

"He wants me to drive down to Roswell tomorrow for a get-acquainted meeting." Trying to sound nonchalant, Caleb added, "I've decided I'll take you with me."

"Me?" Her eyes widened behind her oversize glasses and the panic he saw in their depths reminded him of a deer caught in the headlights of a car. Was the thought of spending time with him that upsetting?

"Is there a problem, A.J.?"

"Why? I mean, I can't possibly—" She suddenly closed her mouth and simply stared at him.

As he returned her gaze, Caleb did his best to keep his attention on the issue at hand and off her perfectly shaped lips. "I realize this is on the spur of the moment, but I don't see that we have any other choice. Since I've just taken over here, I don't know diddly-squat about Ortiz or our business with him. And until I'm up to speed on the individual accounts of our clients, I'd rather not run the risk of losing them."

His argument made sense to him. He just hoped it sounded reasonable to her.

Watching her nibble on her lower lip as she mulled over what he'd said, it was all he could do to keep from groaning. Why did he suddenly find her mouth so damned fascinating? Hadn't he learned a damn thing about professional, career-minded women?

"What time is the meeting?" she asked.

Was it his imagination or was there a slight tremor in her voice?

"Ortiz wants to give me a tour of the manufacturing plant tomorrow afternoon, then have dinner around six or seven."

"It would be too late for us to drive back tomorrow evening and I have two phone meetings early the next morning." She sounded extremely relieved when she added, "I'm sorry, but I really think my going with you would be impossible. We've been courting these potential clients for several months and there's the possibility of losing them if I reschedule the calls."

He wasn't about to give up that easily. "Where are they located?"

"Mr. Sanchez is in Las Cruces and Mrs. Bailey is in Truth or Consequences." Her eyes narrowed. "Why?"

"If I remember my high-school geography, those two places aren't that far from Roswell," he said, thinking fast. "Call and tell them we'll be in their area day after tomorrow and that we'd like to meet with them in person. It'll show that we'd really like to work for them, as well as free you up to go to Roswell with me. Then we'll drive back after dinner Thursday evening." Deciding to beat a hasty retreat before she could find another excuse, he headed for the door. "I'll come by your place around ten in the morning."

"Th-that won't be necessary," she said, stopping him. When he turned back, she added, "I have to come in tomorrow morning to tie up a few loose ends. We can leave from here."

Caleb could tell she wasn't happy, but that couldn't be helped. He wasn't particularly proud of having to rely on her expertise to keep from looking like a fool in front of a client.

"Fair enough," he said, nodding. "I'll have Geneva make a reservation for tomorrow night in Roswell."

"That should be reservations—plural—as in two rooms."

"Of course."

Heading out the door to speak with their secretary, Caleb couldn't help but grin. He clearly made A. J. Merrick as nervous as the parents of a four-year-old talking to the preacher after Sunday services.

The next two days had the potential to prove ex-

tremely interesting and in a way he hadn't counted on.
Not only would he get to see how A.J. dealt with clients, he had a feeling he just might see that cool self-
control of hers slip, as well.

Three

After an uneventful drive down to Roswell, a tour of Ortiz Industries and a highly successful dinner meeting with Mr. Ortiz, all A.J. wanted was the solitude of her motel room and a nice, hot, relaxing bath. Thoroughly exhausted from tossing and turning the night before, she'd spent the entire day in Caleb's disturbing presence and she was more than ready to put a bit of distance between them.

"Why don't you check in for us while I get the bags from the back of the truck?" he asked as he stopped the pickup in front of the motel entrance.

She opened the passenger side door. "I assume the rooms are under the firm's name?"

"Yep. Geneva said she reserved the last two rooms

in Ros—" He stopped abruptly when a family of glow-in-the-dark aliens with oval-shaped heads and big, un-blinking eyes walked past the front of the truck and got into a blue minivan.

"This is festival week," A.J. explained. She couldn't help but laugh at the incredulous expression on his hand-some face. "You'll probably see a lot of that sort of thing."

"I saw the banners when we drove through town." He shook his head. "But I didn't realize they went to ex-tremes with the alien thing."

Getting out of the truck, she nodded. "It's the anni-versary of the Roswell Incident. People from all over the world converge on the town the first part of July to at-tend seminars, share the experiences they've had with extraterrestrials and participate in a variety of activities, including a costume contest."

Caleb chuckled when another alien, this one with tentacles and silver eyes, waved as he drove past in a yellow Volkswagen Beetle. "Sounds like we're lucky Geneva found rooms for us."

"I'm really surprised she did on such short notice."

A.J. closed the truck door and, breathing a sigh of re-lief that she'd soon have a little time to herself, entered the motel lobby and approached the desk clerk. "I'm with Skerritt and Crowe Financial Consultants. I believe you have a couple of rooms for us."

The smiling teenage girl behind the counter snapped her gum, then blew a bubble as she checked her computer screen. "Actually, we have you down for one room with a couple of beds."

"There must be a mistake," A.J. said, shaking her head. She knew Geneva Wallace was far too capable to make that big of an error. "Could you please double-check the reservations?"

Shrugging, the girl keyed in the information again. A moment later, she looked up, shaking her head. "It shows only one room reserved for the Skerritt and Crowe folks. But like I said, it does have two beds."

A.J.'s temples began to throb. "Do you have another room available?"

The girl smiled apologetically. "Sorry. This week's been booked solid for months. In fact, if we hadn't had a late cancellation, we wouldn't have had this room for you." Snapping her gum, she looked thoughtful. "I'd say the closest motel with rooms available would probably be down in Artesia. And that's real iffy."

"Is there a problem?" Caleb asked, walking up to stand beside A.J.

"Apparently there's been a mix-up and they only have one room for us." She suddenly knew how Dorothy must have felt when the tornado picked her up and she came over the rainbow, crashing down in the land of Oz. "With the festival going on there aren't any rooms available for miles. It looks like we'll have to drive on to Las Cruces tonight."

To her astonishment, Caleb shook his head. "It's al-

ready dark, we're both tired and some of the roads between here and there are two-lanes. Driving in unfamil-
iar territory under those conditions wouldn't be a good
idea."

Desperation began to claw at her insides. Had he lost
his mind?

"We can't stay in the same room."

"You can have the bed and I'll sleep on the floor." He
made it sound so logical.

"The room has two double beds," the teenage girl
spoke up helpfully.

"We'll take it," he said, setting their overnight cases
down to reach for his wallet.

If she thought she'd felt desperate before, A.J. was a
hairbreadth away from an all-out panic attack. Tugging
on his arm, she led him over to the seating area of the
lobby for a private discussion.

"You can't be serious."

"We don't have a choice."

"What happens when the employees at the firm find
out that we spent the night in the same room?"

He shook his head. "Unless one of us tells them,
they'll never know."

"Don't fool yourself. What do you think is going to
happen when you turn in the receipt to accounts payable?" she asked, knowing that once word got out there
was only one room on the bill, the gossip and speculation would run rampant.

"I'll put it on my credit card instead of Skerritt and Crowe's." He sounded so darned reasonable, she wanted to stomp.

"But—"

He reached out and put his hands on her shoulders. "I agree, it's a major pain in the butt that we can't have our own rooms. But we're both adults, A.J. We can handle this." Before she could stop him, he removed his wallet from his hip pocket and handed a credit card to the girl behind the counter.

Her heart did a backflip. Maybe he could deal with the situation, but she wasn't so sure about herself. Spending the entire day with him, first in the close confines of his pickup truck, then in the meeting with Mr. Ortiz, had more than taken its toll.

From the moment they'd left the Skerritt and Crowe offices that morning, her senses had been assaulted by the man. The scent of his woodsy aftershave, the timbre of his deep voice and the occasional brush of his arm against hers when he opened doors for her had charged every cell in her being with a restlessness she refused to define. If she had to spend an entire night in the same room with Caleb only a few feet away, there was a very real possibility she'd be a raving lunatic by morning.

As he sat on the side of the motel bed, Caleb took off his boots, then picked up the television's remote control and absently flipped through the channels. He had to get his mind off the woman changing clothes in the bathroom.

Glancing at the closed door, he shook his head. He'd put in a hell of a day listening to her soft voice and watching her move with a catlike grace that he found absolutely fascinating. But it was the few times they'd brushed against each other that had him feeling like he was about to jump out of his own skin. What was there about A.J. that sent his hormones racing through his blood like the steel balls in an pinball machine?

She was the consummate professional and gave every indication that she was totally immersed in her career. And he'd learned the hard way to avoid her type like a bachelor avoids a widows' convention. So why was she all he'd been able to think about from the moment he'd laid eyes on her? What was there about her that he found so damned compelling?

Her clothes certainly weren't provocative or meant to entice a man. And although she was far from homely, A.J. sure didn't wear makeup or style her hair in a way to make herself look anything but plain.

He frowned. It was as if she was doing everything she possibly could to keep from attracting attention to herself.

That's what he was having the devil of a time trying to figure out. A.J. didn't look or act like an executive. Leslie Ann Turner, the woman he'd been involved with a few years back, had been the perfect example of a corporate climber and taken great pains to look attractive at work, as well as when they'd gone out on the town. They'd met by accident when he'd attended a farm symposium at one of the downtown Nashville hotels and she'd stopped by the lounge after work for drinks with her girlfriends. He'd asked her out and that had started their two-year affair. She'd been a junior executive then and hadn't yet developed a thirst for power and position, nor had she looked down on him because he'd had nothing more than a high-school education.

But as time had gone on and she'd gotten a few promotions under her belt, that had changed. She'd stopped asking him to attend corporate parties with her and had adopted the attitude that the measure of a man was determined by the number of diplomas he held. And it really hadn't come as a big surprise when she'd dumped him like a blind date on a Saturday night.

However, as hard as it had been to face the fact that she apparently thought he wasn't good enough for her, he did have her to thank for a lesson well learned. A career woman wasn't anyone he wanted to become involved with, no matter how compelling her baby blues were.

But A.J. didn't seem to possess the same barracuda instincts, the same do-whatever-it-takes-to-get-ahead attitude that Leslie Ann had. Hell, there were a couple of times when he'd been outlining the policy changes, then later when he'd asked her to help with the break room renovations, that A.J. had almost looked unsure and vulnerable.

As he sat there pondering his uncharacteristic fascination with A.J., the bathroom door opened. Looking up, Caleb's jaw dropped and he felt like he'd been blindsided by a steamroller. With her owlish glasses off and her long, auburn hair down around her shoulders, A. J. Merrick was a knockout.

He swallowed hard as she walked past him to the other bed. Her emerald silk pajamas and robe enhanced the red highlights in her hair and were the perfect contrast to her flawless porcelain complexion and baby-blue eyes.

"The bathroom's all yours," she said with a wave of her delicate hand.

She still hadn't looked his way and he was damned glad. He'd been staring at her like a teenage boy stared at his first glimpse of a *Playboy* centerfold and there was no doubt in his mind that she'd think she was sharing a room with some kind of nutcase.

Suddenly feeling as if the walls were closing in on him, Caleb stood up. "I'm not all that tired," he lied. "I think I'll go down to the restaurant and get a cup of coffee." Edging toward the door, he asked, "Do you want me to bring something back for you?"

"No, thank you."

"Will you be okay here alone?"

She turned her incredible baby blues on him. "Sure. Why do you ask?"

He wasn't about to tell her that she looked prettier

and more feminine than he'd ever imagined. Nor did he want to admit that he felt like a prize jackass for running like a tail-tucked dog.

"Just checking."

She hid a huge yawn with one delicate hand. "I'll probably be asleep before you make it downstairs."

The thought of what she might look like with her long silky hair spread across the pillow, her dark lashes resting on her creamy cheeks like tiny feathers, made his body tighten and had him reaching for the doorknob in less than two seconds.

"Night," she called.

"Uh, yeah, night," he muttered, closing the door behind him. He was halfway down the hall before he realized his boots were still sitting on the floor beside the bed in their room.

He stopped dead in his tracks. "Well, hell."

"Flashback?"

Turning, Caleb found a tall, skinny man, with what looked like a piece of tinfoil molded to his bald head, standing behind him. "Excuse me?"

"I asked if you were having a flashback from your last encounter with *them*," the man said, pointing toward the ceiling. "Some of us have flashbacks from time to time. Especially if the encounter was a really close one."

When Caleb caught on that the gentleman was referring to E.T., he shook his head. "No. This was more like a first-time sighting."

"I can totally relate. It can be a pretty disconcerting experience the first time you see *them*." Grinning, the man reached up to adjust his foil skullcap. "But as time goes on you'll find yourself looking forward to it and even hoping for an encounter of the third kind."

Caleb nodded. He was already anticipating how soft and feminine A.J. would look when she woke up tomorrow morning. And just the idea of a close encounter with her of any kind made him hard as hell.

When the man continued on down the hall, Caleb turned and walked back toward the room. "You have no idea, buddy. No earthly idea at all."

The moment the door closed behind Caleb, A.J. collapsed onto the side of the motel bed. She'd felt his gaze follow her across the room when she'd walked out of the bathroom and her knees still felt as if they were made of rubber. How on earth would she be able to close her eyes, let alone get a wink of sleep?

All she could think about was what he'd wear to bed and how he'd look first thing in the morning when he woke up. And just knowing that he'd be sleeping a few feet away sent shivers up her spine and made breathing all but impossible.

A.J. glanced around the room in near panic. She needed to get her mind off her disturbing boss. In desperation, she picked up the remote control and switched the television to a classic film channel. It would definitely be in her best interest to try losing herself in the plot of an old movie. Maybe then she'd be able to forget that she was about to spend the night in the same room as the sexiest man she'd ever known.

When she realized the film was *An Affair to Remember,* she took off her robe, pulled back the covers and crawled into bed. Even though she'd seen the movie at least twenty times and always ended up sobbing her heart out, it was one of her all-time favorites.

Settling back against the pillows, she managed to forget about her current situation as she braced herself for the movie's ending. And sure enough, when the hero discovered why the heroine had failed to meet him at the top of the Empire State Building, A.J.'s tears began to fall.

Unfortunately, Caleb chose that very moment to return to the room. "I forgot my—" He stopped abruptly. "Are you crying?"

Mortified that he'd caught her in a less-than-professional moment, she stared at the television screen. "N-no."

To her horror, he walked over to the side of her bed and sat down. "Yes, you are." He took her hands in his. "What's wrong, A.J.?"

"N-nothing." She'd known he'd be returning in a short time. Why on earth had she chosen to watch a movie that never failed to make her cry buckets?

"Look at me, sweetheart." The gentle tone of his voice caused her tears to fall faster. Why wouldn't he just go away and leave her alone?

"I…can't." Dear God, could the day get any worse?

It had been years since she'd allowed anyone to see her shed a tear. But here she was crying like a baby. And in front of her new boss, no less. She'd never been more humiliated in her entire life.

Why couldn't he find what he'd forgotten and leave? At least, long enough for her to pull herself together.

He cupped her cheek and turned her head until their gazes met. "I'm sorry, sweetheart. I didn't realize you were this upset by the situation. Please don't cry. I'll sleep in my truck if it will make you feel better."

His sincerity touched her deeply and for reasons she didn't care to analyze, she couldn't allow him to think her emotional display was because they'd be spending the night in the same room. "It's…the movie."

Glancing over his shoulder, he turned back to smile at her a moment before he reached out and took her into his arms. "That one always does a number on my mom, too."

"W-what are you doing?"

"It's all right, Alyssa."

The sound of his deep voice saying her name with such tenderness sent a shock wave straight to her core and she didn't even think to push away from him. "How did you…know my name?"

"It's in your personnel file." He pulled her to him, then smoothed his hands down her back in a comforting manner. "And don't go getting any ideas about me replacing you. I reviewed all of the managers' files."

"Why?" God help her, but with his strong arms wrapped around her and her cheek pressed to his wide chest, she wasn't sure she cared why he was going through hers or anyone else's file.

"I was trying to decide what team-building activities would best serve each manager and their department." His warm breath stirred her hair and sent shivers streaking up her spine. He hugged her close. "Cold?"

Unable to form a coherent sentence, she nodded. Even if she could have found her voice, she wasn't about to tell him the real reason she trembled.

But when he pulled back to look down at her, she knew he wasn't buying her excuse for a minute. "Are you sure?"

With his intense hazel gaze holding her captive, she wasn't sure of her own name, let alone what he'd asked her. "W-what was the question?"

"It doesn't matter, Alyssa." His sexy drawl caused her insides to feel as if they'd been turned to warm pudding and as he slowly lowered his head, she couldn't for the life of her remember why it should.

As his mouth brushed over hers, her heart skipped several beats. She should call a halt to this insanity and send him outside to spend the night in his truck. But for reasons she couldn't begin to explain, she wanted Caleb's kiss, wanted to feel his hard body pressed to her. And when he settled his lips more fully over hers, she threw caution to the wind and melted against him.

As he explored her with a tenderness that stole her breath, tiny electrical impulses skipped over every nerve in her body and she couldn't have stopped him if her life depended on it. Didn't even want to.

His kiss was slow and thoughtful and warm tingles filled her when he traced the seam of her mouth with his tongue. He was asking permission to deepen the kiss and without so much as a thought to the consequences, she parted to give him access to her tender inner recesses.

A heady warmth began to swirl through her veins when he slipped inside to caress and coax her into a response. She knew she was playing with fire, but as he teased her with featherlight strokes, temptation never tasted as good as Caleb's masterful kiss.

When he lowered her to the mattress, her stomach fluttered with the first stirrings of need and her nipples tightened in anticipation at the feel of his hand cupping her breast through the fabric of her silk pajamas. She wanted his hands on her body, wanted to feel his hair-roughened flesh pressed to her sensitive skin.

Tugging at the collar of his shirt, she was startled out of the sensual haze in her addled brain by a feminine moan of frustration. Had that sound really come from her? Dear heavens, what was she doing?

Embarrassed beyond belief, Alyssa pushed against him. "I can't. Please stop."

Caleb looked as dazed as she felt. "It's…all right,

sweetheart." He cleared his throat and sat up. "It stops right here." Rising to his feet, he smiled. "I think I'll go get that cup of coffee. Are you sure I can't bring something back for you?"

It appeared that he was going to act as if nothing had happened between them. Unsure whether she was disappointed or relieved, she decided to take his lead and ignore the fact that they'd been making out like a couple of hormone-crazed teenagers.

She shook her head. "N-no, thank you. I think I'll turn in for the night."

He stared at her for several seconds before he reached down and lifted her chin with his forefinger. "I'll try not to disturb you when I return."

"I sleep pretty sound." His touch was doing strange things to her insides and she sounded as if she'd run a marathon. "I doubt that you'll make enough noise to wake me."

"I didn't say anything about making noise, sweetheart." His deep chuckle and mischievous grin sent her pulse racing. "There's a big difference."

Alyssa felt as if her heart suddenly dropped to her stomach, then bounced back up to pound at her ribs when she realized what he meant. Before she could find her voice, Caleb gave her a quick kiss on the forehead, then picked up his boots and walked across the room and out the door without a backward glance.

Staring at the closed door, she had to force herself to

breathe. Now she knew for certain that she'd landed on the other side of the rainbow. Either that, or she and Caleb had both been taken over by aliens. After all, they were in Roswell, where the unexplained was not only accepted, it was expected.

But as she reached up to turn off the bedside lamp, she shook her head. She knew what had gotten into her and it had nothing whatsoever to do with friends from a faraway galaxy. From the moment Caleb Walker had strolled into her office, she'd fought it, tried to ignore it and even denied its existence. But the truth was, she was attracted to her new boss.

She burrowed deeper into the bed and pulled the covers up to her chin. What on earth was she going to do now?

In the past few minutes, she'd abandoned the two most important rules she'd set for herself. She'd allowed one of her coworkers to witness her emotional side and she'd practically thrown herself at him when he'd offered her comfort.

She sighed heavily. There was no way around it now. Her departure from Skerritt and Crowe was not only inevitable, it was imminent.

Closing her eyes, she tried not to think of the damage she'd done to her professional reputation and willed herself to relax. She probably wouldn't be able to sleep, but at least she wouldn't be sobbing like a baby when Caleb returned this time.

What seemed like only a few minutes later, the ringing phone roused her. Who on earth could be calling at this time of night?

She grumbled about wanting to hurt whoever was on the other end of the line as she switched on the light and snatched up the receiver before it could ring again. "Hello?"

Dead silence greeted her.

"Is someone there?" she asked impatiently.

"Who is it?" Caleb asked, sounding groggy.

She sucked in a sharp breath as she glanced over at the other bed. Apparently she'd been asleep longer than she'd realized. He'd not only returned to their room, but he'd been sleeping as soundly as she'd been.

"Ms. Merrick?"

"Yes." She looked at the digital alarm clock on the nightstand. "Who is this and why are you calling at two in the morning?"

"This is Clarence Norton, A.J....Ms. Merrick. I'm sorry to wake you," the security guard from Skerritt and Crowe said apologetically. "The motel operator was supposed to connect me with Mr. Walker's room."

"Is there a problem?"

"The firm's silent alarm went off at the police station about an hour ago," he explained. "They called me to come down and let them in so they could do a thorough search of the building."

Fully awake, she asked, "Was there a break-in?"

"No," Clarence assured her. "But the alarm system shorted out and—"

"What's going on?" Caleb threw back the sheet and sat up on the side of the bed. "Give me the phone."

Alyssa held up her finger to silence him, but it was too late. Clarence had already heard Caleb's voice.

"I-Is that Mr. Walker?" From the tone of his voice, the security guard was shocked right down to his big flat feet.

With Caleb reaching for the receiver and Clarence stammering on the other end of the line, she surrendered the phone without another word.

Her worst nightmare had just been realized. Clarence Norton was the biggest gossip in Albuquerque. By the time she and Caleb returned to the office the day after tomorrow, everyone at Skerritt and Crowe would know that they'd spent the night together.

Four

Caleb set the cruise control, then glanced over at the silent woman seated on the passenger side of the truck cab. Other than answering direct questions, Alyssa hadn't said more than a handful of words to him since the kiss they'd shared the night before. She'd been congenial and outgoing enough when she'd discussed financial options and outlined plans for the two potential clients they'd met with in Las Cruces and Truth or Consequences. But whenever they found themselves alone, she clammed up.

"I'm pretty sure we've picked up Mr. Sanchez and Mrs. Bailey as clients," he said, trying once more to draw her out.

She nodded. "It looks that way."

"Are you going to handle their accounts personally or turn them over to someone else?"

"I'll probably turn them over to Richard Henshaw or Marla Davis."

When she let the discussion drop once again, he released a frustrated breath. "Talk to me, Alyssa. Tell me why I'm getting the silent treatment. Is it because of what happened last night?"

Nodding, she stared straight ahead. "I can't stop thinking about Clarence's phone call and the rumors that I'm sure were being passed around the office today."

"You're worried about what's being said at the office?" he asked incredulously. He hadn't given much, if any, thought to the phone call. His mind had been occupied with that kiss. To say she'd damned near knocked his socks off was an understatement.

"Aren't you concerned?" She looked at him like he'd sprouted horns and a tail. "Clarence Norton is the biggest gossip this side of the Mississippi and he's not going to let something like my being in your room at two in the morning go by without putting his spin on it. By now, I'm sure he's told everyone who will listen that we slept together last night."

"Technically, we did sleep together," Caleb said, grinning. "Just not in the same bed." The cab of the truck was dark, but he'd bet every last dime he had that her cheeks had colored a pretty pink. He wished like hell he could see them.

"I suppose that's true. But do you honestly think anyone will believe that?" she asked.

"Maybe." He shrugged. "But the way I see it, our only option is to tell the truth. After we explain things, it'll be up to everyone else to draw their own conclusions."

"You know what that will be." She glared at him like she thought he might be a little simpleminded.

"We can't control what others think or say about us, Alyssa." He gave her what he hoped was an encouraging smile. "But even if they are talking about us now, this time next week someone else will be the topic of conversation around the water cooler."

"I hope you're right."

"I'm sure—"

He stopped short when he noticed steam rolling out from under the truck's hood. Glancing at the temperature gauge on the dash, he said a word that would have had his mother washing his mouth out with soap if she'd heard. It was a dark, moonless night and they were miles away from the last gas station.

"Why is your truck smoking?" she asked, clearly alarmed.

"It's my guess we have radiator problems."

"That's not good." She pushed her owlish glasses up her nose with a brush of her hand—a gesture he'd come to recognize as a sign of her nervousness. "What are you going to do?"

"I'll have to find a place to pull over so I can check

it out." He'd no sooner gotten the words out than they passed a sign indicating a rest area less than a mile ahead. "Looks like we're in luck. At least it will be well lit and I can see what I'm doing."

Ten minutes later, Caleb stood in the parking lot of the rest area with Alyssa peering around his arm at the truck's steaming engine. "The radiator hose is busted," he said when he noticed her questioning expression.

"Do you think you can fix it?"

He shook his head, stepped back and slammed the hood. "I'll have to call roadside assistance." Pulling his cell phone from the clip on his belt, he asked, "Is there another town between here and Socorro?"

She looked anything but happy. "No. This rest area is about halfway between Socorro and Truth or Consequences. And I'm sure that everything in either direction is closed by now."

Pushing the button with the auto club's preprogrammed number, Caleb gave their location and the nature of the problem, then waited for the customer-service representative, identifying himself as Jason, to contact the nearest associate. When the man came back on the line, the news wasn't what Caleb wanted to hear.

"What do you mean they can't get to us until tomorrow morning?" he demanded.

Alyssa cringed. "They won't be here until morning?"

"I'm sorry for the inconvenience, sir. We have only

one associate garage in that area and the mechanic is out on a call," Jason apologized. "After that he has three more to take care of before he can get to you."

Thinking fast, Caleb asked, "Could you send someone with a rental car?"

"Just a moment, please."

"What did he say?" she asked anxiously.

"He's checking." Caleb smiled. "I'm sure we'll have a car here in no time." At least, he hoped they would.

"Sir, your rental car will be delivered to your location by four in the morning," Jason said, sounding as if he'd accomplished something wonderful.

"Four!" Caleb checked his watch, then shook his head. "Five hours is unacceptable, Jason. Even if the car is coming from Albuquerque, it shouldn't take more than a couple of hours."

"I'm sorry, sir," Jason said, beginning to sound like a broken record. "The agencies in both Truth or Consequences and Socorro are closed, the one in Las Cruces has all of its cars rented right now and the one in Albuquerque is having to call someone in to drive the car down to you."

Caleb glanced over at Alyssa. She looked fit to be tied.

"So that's the best you can do?" he asked the young man.

"I'm afraid so, sir," Jason answered. "If there's anything else we can do for you, please let us know."

Caleb snapped the phone shut as he turned to Alyssa.

"I guess you've figured out by now that we aren't going anywhere until around four tomorrow morning."

Looking more pale than she had a few minutes ago, she nodded and started for the passenger door. "I think one of us must be related to Murphy."

"Who the hell's Murphy?"

"I'm not sure, but his law has plagued us throughout this trip."

"Ah, yes. Anything that can go wrong, will go wrong, and at the worst possible moment." He helped her into the truck. "Well, things could be worse."

She looked at him like he had spit for brains. "How on earth could things be any worse?"

He grinned. "We could have broken down before or after we got to the rest area."

"Small consolation," she said, settling herself on the bench seat. "We're still stranded."

"Yes, but at least we're stuck at a rest area with vending machines." He hooked his thumb over his shoulder. "I'm going to see if they have bottled water. Do you want one?"

She nodded. "Thank you."

As Caleb walked the short distance to the row of vending machines, Alyssa took one deep breath, then another. How much anxiety could one woman handle before she lost her mind?

She'd been stressed enough over her behavior when he'd kissed her. Then, after the phone call from the security guard, she'd spent the rest of the night tossing and turning as she'd thought of the office gossip that would surely be spreading like wildfire. Now, she was having to spend another night in Caleb's disturbing presence.

Watching him get bottles of water from the machine, then start back toward the truck, she shivered. He looked darned good in his sports jacket, dress shirt and jeans. On some men, the combination just wouldn't work. But on Caleb, it was sexy beyond words. And she had to admit that spending more time with him wasn't an unpleasant thought. He wasn't just devastatingly handsome, he was intelligent, easy to talk to and had a nice sense of humor. And boy, oh boy, could he kiss.

Her cheeks heated and she had to force herself to breathe. The more time she spent with him, the more she wanted to know about him, the more she wanted him to kiss her again. And therein lay the problem.

For heaven's sake, they worked together. She shouldn't want to spend more time getting to know him. And she definitely shouldn't want his kiss. She knew all too well from past experience that becoming friendly with a coworker spelled disaster with a great big capital *D*.

But the choice had been taken out of her hands. Fate had stepped in and taken over—first with the room mix-up and now with a broken radiator hose.

When he opened the driver's door, he handed her two bottles of water and a package of cookies before removing his sports jacket. Tossing it on the seat between them, he rolled up the sleeves of his white dress shirt, then slid in behind the steering wheel.

Her breath caught and she decided she was in real trouble if all it took to make her insides hum was the sight of his bare forearms. But as he turned up his shirt sleeves, the movement drew attention to the play of muscles and sent her pulse into overdrive.

"I thought you might get hungry while we're waiting on the rental car," he said.

She glanced down at the package of cookies. It was only a stale vending-machine snack, but his thoughtfulness touched her more than she could have imagined. No one, including her father, had ever shown her a lot of consideration. She'd always been the bookish nerd who blended into the background, no matter where she went or who she was with. There had even been times after her mother had died that she'd suspected her father had forgotten she existed.

"Thank you," she said, barely able to get the words past the lump clogging her throat.

"Are you all right?" He reached out to put his arm around her, then, moving his jacket out of the way, pulled her to the middle of the seat. "I know being stuck here is upsetting, but—"

"I'm fine. Really." Wanting to change the subject before she made a complete fool of herself, she asked, "Do you really think going on picnics and getting closer with the employees is going to make Skerritt and Crowe a more efficient consulting firm?"

He nodded. "Let me ask you this. How much do you know about the people who work under you?"

Thinking hard, she shook her head. "Not much."

"Exactly." Twisting in the seat to face her, he leaned back against the driver's door. "Would you say Geena Phillips has been working up to her potential lately?"

She didn't have to think twice about the matter. The woman had been late several times in the past couple of weeks. "No. Lately, she's seemed distracted and I've been meaning to talk to her about it."

"Don't," he said, shaking his head. "A disciplinary talk will only add to the problem."

"I take it you know something I don't."

His mouth flattened into a grim line. "She's battling a case of morning sickness. It's her first pregnancy, she doesn't know where the father of her baby disappeared to and she's scared witless that she won't be able to handle things by herself."

Alyssa was shocked. "I had no idea Geena was going through anything like that."

"That's because in the past it's been company policy to check your private life at the door when you come to work." He shook his head. "Geena's a good accountant who's hit a rough patch in her life. She needs our support and assurance that she's not going to lose the job she'll need to support herself and the baby. That kind of encouragement from an employer can go a long way to instill loyalty in an employee, as well as inspire them to work harder for the company."

She could see where a change was definitely in order in that area. "I'll talk to her about coming in a couple of hours later until she starts feeling better."

Yawning he nodded his approval. "Now you have the right idea." It seemed that he'd no sooner gotten the words out than he was sound asleep.

As she leaned her head back against the seat and tried to get comfortable, she had to admit that Caleb's approach to management made a lot of sense. *By the book* wasn't necessarily the best way to handle employees.

But the idea of letting her employees know her better still made her extremely nervous. The more someone knew about you, the more they could use against you. At least, that was the philosophy her father had preached to her for as long as she could remember.

She sighed. If she stayed at Skerritt and Crowe, becoming friendly with those around her was definitely going to take some getting used to.

Reluctant to open her eyes and end the dream of having two strong arms holding her securely to a wide masculine chest, Alyssa burrowed deeper into her dream lover's embrace. It felt wonderful to be held while she slept and she wanted to enjoy it for as long as she could, even if it was just a dream.

"Good morning."

Her eyes flew open and she started to pull away. Dear heavens, she wasn't dreaming. She was lying on a very real Caleb Walker, who, at the moment, seemed intent on keeping her right where she was.

"I—I'm sorry," she stammered, trying once again to extricate herself from his hold.

He tightened his arms around her and his deep chuckle beneath her ear vibrated all the way to her soul. "Don't be sorry. I'm not. You were comfortable and I thought I'd let you sleep."

Her heart did a funny little flip. "It was nice of you to think of me," she said, straightening her glasses. She managed to put a little space between them to look up into his twinkling hazel eyes. "But—"

"Sweetheart, I think about you more than you realize." He gave her the sexy grin that never failed to curl her toes as he drew her closer, then rested his forehead on hers. "In fact, you're about all I've been able to think of since night before last."

Shivers skittered up and down her spine from the mere memory, but the only way she'd been able to face him had been to tell herself that she'd dreamed it. "Nothing happened," she insisted.

He chuckled. "Then I must have a real vivid imagination, because after that kiss, I walked out of the motel room hotter than a two-dollar pistol at a skid-row pawnshop."

Alyssa felt as if her heart had stopped completely and even if her vocal cords hadn't suddenly become temporarily paralyzed, she couldn't think of a thing to say.

Leaning back, he gazed at her for several long seconds. "You want to know something else?"

"I—I'm not sure," she said, feeling extremely short of breath.

"I want to do it again." He removed her glasses, then placed them on the dash. "Do you want me to kiss you, Alyssa?"

Mesmerized by his remarkable gaze and promising smile, she didn't even hesitate. "Yes."

He removed first one, then another of the pins holding her hair up. "You have beautiful hair. You should wear it down more often."

"I've always hated my hair," she said honestly.

"Why?" Running his fingers through it, he cupped the back of her head and started to draw her forward. "It feels like strands of silk."

Unable to breathe, much less think, Alyssa's eyes drifted shut as she allowed Caleb to nibble at her lips, then cover them with a kiss so tender it made her feel as if she were the most cherished woman on earth. What was there about this man that she couldn't resist?

She'd never had trouble rejecting advances from other men. But when Caleb touched her, rational thought seemed beyond her capabilities. All she wanted was to feel his big, hard body pressed to hers, to taste the desire on his lips and hear his sexy Southern drawl as he said her name.

When he used the tip of his tongue to coax her to open for him, she decided it didn't matter that she had no will of her own where he was concerned. The truth was, she liked the way he made her feel when he kissed her and the last thing she wanted him to do was stop.

As Caleb slipped his tongue inside, Alyssa met him halfway in a sensuous game of advance and retreat and he felt like his heart would pound a hole right through his rib cage. He'd tried to tell himself to leave well enough alone, that Alyssa Jane Merrick was off-limits.

For one thing, she was a career woman and, considering his history with them, he should be running as hard and fast as his legs would carry him in the opposite direction. And for another, he was having to rely on hers and the other managers' experience at Skerritt and Crowe to keep the firm running until he could get some business courses under his belt. He didn't need an emotional involvement added to the mix. It would only complicate things and increase the possibility of one of them getting hurt.

But whether it was wise or not, he hadn't been able to resist the temptation of holding her soft body against his, of once again savoring her perfect lips. He'd spent a hell of a day yesterday and an even worse night reliving that kiss and he needed to know if she was as fantastic as he remembered.

When she lightly stroked his tongue with hers, the sweet, shy response aroused him so fast it made him light-headed and he immediately decided that if anything, his memory had been more than a little faulty. He'd never in all of his thirty years been this turned on by simply kissing a woman.

Slowly tugging her blouse from the waistband of her skirt, he slipped his hand under the beige silk. Her smooth skin felt like satin beneath his palm as he slid it over her ribs to the underside of her breast. Cupping the soft mound, he gently caressed her as he nibbled his way from her lips down the slender column of her throat.

Her tiny moan of pleasure sent a fresh wave of heat straight to his groin. But when he realized that she'd unbuttoned the first few buttons on his shirt and was doing a little exploring of her own, his body tightened with an intensity that quickly had him shifting to relieve the pressure in his suddenly too-tight jeans. Just knowing she was as turned on as he was sent his blood pressure skyrocketing.

At that moment, he wanted her more than he wanted to draw his next breath. He wanted to lay her down and discover all of her secrets. And he wanted to share all of his with her.

"Hey man, get a room."

Glancing through the windshield, Caleb noticed a group of grinning teenage boys walking past the truck on their way to the information center.

Damn! His timing couldn't have been worse. The front seat of his truck in a rest area with God and everybody strolling past wasn't exactly the place for the pleasurable kind of exploring he had in mind.

He took in some much-needed oxygen as he rearranged Alyssa's blouse. "Sweetheart, there's nothing I'd like more than to continue kissing you and a hell of a lot more. But if we keep this up, somebody's going to call the cops. And I'm not real keen on the idea of our being arrested for lewd conduct in a public place."

She made no comment as she stared at him, but the heightened color on her cheeks indicated that she'd forgotten where they were, the same as he had.

"It's daylight," she said, looking around. "What time is it?"

Checking his watch, he shook his head to clear it. "It's a little past eight."

"Where's the rental car?" She slid over to the passenger side of the seat. "I thought it was supposed to be here by four."

Caleb shrugged. "They're late."

"No kidding." She tucked her blouse back into the waistband of her skirt. "Have you called them?"

"The driver thought we were in the rest area north of Socorro," he said, nodding. "When he didn't find us there, he turned around and went back to Albuquerque instead of calling roadside assistance to get a verification on our location."

He didn't add that he wasn't all that sorry the guy was incompetent. Whether it was smart or not, he'd enjoyed holding her while she'd slept.

"Are they sending another car?"

He shook his head. "I told them not to bother."

"You did what?" If looks could kill, he'd be dead in about two seconds flat.

"The mechanic from Truth or Consequences should be here any time with a new radiator hose." He stretched to relieve a few of the kinks in his muscles. "I didn't see the need for a car when he'll have the truck fixed in less than fifteen minutes."

"I suppose that makes sense." She frowned. "But I was hoping we'd be back at the office well before everyone arrived for work. I wanted to run home for a quick shower and to change clothes." She glanced down at her wrinkled suit. "I'm a mess."

"Don't worry about it. We won't get there until mid-morning." He gave her his most reassuring smile. "Everyone will be busy and you can get your car without anyone being the wiser."

She looked more than a little doubtful. "I hope you're right."

He didn't tell her, but he hoped like hell he was, too.

Five

When Caleb steered the truck into his reserved parking space, Alyssa immediately noticed that something was wrong with her car. Instead of sitting level, it was tilted to one side. So much for making a quick getaway before someone in the office saw her disheveled appearance.

"Looks like you have a flat tire," Caleb commented when he got out of the truck and came around to open the passenger door for her.

"Great. Just what I wanted to do before I go home," she said, wondering what else could go wrong. "I get to change a tire."

He frowned. "You're going to do it yourself?"

She nodded. "I've been changing my own tires since I learned to drive. My father insisted on it."

"You don't have an auto service plan?"

"No."

He held out his hand. "Give me the keys."

"Thanks, but I'll take care of it," she said, removing her suit jacket.

"Not while I'm around." He took the keys from her, then motioned toward the building. "Why don't you go inside and get out of this heat?"

She nibbled on her lower lip. The temperature was rising, but so was her apprehension that someone would see her.

"I'd rather not."

She could just imagine the stares if she walked into her office looking the way she did. Her clothing couldn't have been more wrinkled from spending the night in the truck and her hair was hanging down her back like a limp mop because Caleb had lost most of the pins when he'd taken it out of her usual chignon.

"Don't be silly." He opened the trunk of her sedan. "It's already in the nineties and—"

"No need for you gettin' all hot and dirty, Caleb," Ernie Clay called as he hurried out of the building toward them. The security guard stopped in front of them, then, grinning like a Cheshire cat, he nodded at her car. "Clarence noticed Ms. Merrick's tire was flat and had me call my brother-in-law. He owns a garage and tow-ing service and should be here in a few minutes to take care of it."

"Thanks, Ernie." Caleb placed his hand at the small of her back and started urging her toward the entrance. "We'll be in our offices. Let us know when your brother-in-law has the tire changed."

The last thing Alyssa wanted to do was walk into the office looking the way she did. But before she had a chance to protest, Caleb ushered her through the building entrance and over to the elevators.

When the elevator door slid shut, she looked down at her clothes. "I'm a complete mess."

He frowned. "You look fine to me."

She shook her head. "My hair is down, my pantyhose has a huge run and I look like a raccoon from the mascara smudges under my eyes."

Removing her glasses for a closer look, he shook his head. "Just one little place under your left eye."

Her jacket fell to the floor as she was thrown off guard by his unexpected touch, and she braced her hands on his chest to keep from falling when the elevator came to a halt on their floor. "I'll take care of—"

The doors opened at that very moment and to Alyssa's horror, Malcolm Fuller and the entire public-relations department observed her clinging to Caleb as he used his thumb to wipe gently at the tender skin below her eye. From the looks on their faces, she could tell exactly what they were thinking.

"Well, hello there," Malcolm said, not even bothering to hide his ear-to-ear grin. "We're headed out to our first team-building picnic. Would you two like to join us?"

"No, thank you," she said before Caleb could get them into something else that would no doubt cause her further humiliation. "But have a good time."

Her cheeks burned with embarrassment as she picked up her jacket, then brushed past the group and headed straight for her office. She didn't wait to see if Caleb followed, nor did she care that he still had her glasses. She'd spent two and a half nerve-racking days with him and she needed some space.

Although her father would strongly disapprove and probably come back to haunt her for being such a coward, all she wanted to do was hide out in her office until her car was fixed. After that, she had every intention of going home, climbing into bed and sleeping the entire weekend. Hopefully, when she woke up Monday morning, she would escape the nightmare she'd been trapped in for the past week.

But even as she mourned the loss of her well-ordered work environment, she couldn't deny that her body still hummed from Caleb's touch. And just the memory of his steamy kisses was enough to leave her aching for things she had no business wanting.

As she walked down the hall toward the conference room to meet with a client, Alyssa finally began to relax.

It had been a week since she and Caleb had returned from the Roswell trip and it appeared that he'd been right about the gossip dying down once they'd told the whole story. To her immense relief, she hadn't heard a single word about them spending the night together or being caught in a compromising position in the elevator. Other than a few smug smiles and knowing looks from a couple of her male coworkers, it had been business as usual around the office.

"Has anyone seen them together since Friday?" Alyssa overheard someone ask as she approached the door to the break room.

The hushed voice stopped her dead in her tracks.

"No. I think they're probably trying to be a little more discreet about their affair." The woman laughed. "I mean really, getting caught in the elevator like that, then trying to convince us that he was looking at her eye. How dumb do they think we are? I heard that half of her clothes were on the elevator floor and she was tearing at his shirt when the doors opened."

A chill raced through her and it felt as if ice water had replaced the blood in her veins. She wanted to scream that they were wrong in their assumptions, that it really was just as Caleb had told them. But she knew it was useless.

"You know there's a door connecting their offices," she heard a third voice chime in. "There's no telling how many times during the day they get together for a little tête-à-tête."

The laughter that followed the erroneous statement made Alyssa nauseous. Feeling as if her world had just caved in on her, she retraced her steps and headed back to her office. She'd heard enough to know that her professional reputation at Skerritt and Crowe had gone down in a blaze of glory—and that there was nothing left but cinders.

"Please call Geena Phillips and have her meet with Mr. Holt in the conference room," she said, placing the client file on Geneva's desk.

"Is something wrong?" the older woman asked, her obvious concern reflected in the tone of her voice. "You don't look like you feel well."

"I don't." That was the understatement of the year, Alyssa thought as she walked into her office and closed the door.

She'd been a naive fool to think that people weren't talking about her and Caleb. How could she have been so stupid? The employees weren't going to discuss their thoughts on the issue in front of the two people involved.

Walking straight to her desk, she sat down at her computer and began drafting her resignation. She'd hoped to have another job lined up before she quit, but the choice had been taken out of her hands. There was no way she could stay at Skerritt and Crowe now. By close of business this afternoon, she'd be unemployed.

"Geneva told me you're sick," Caleb said, walking

into her office without so much as a tap on the connecting door. "Do you need to see a doctor?"

"No." Alyssa should have known their secretary would run to him with her concerns. Geneva, the traitor, had embraced every one of Caleb's ideas and took it upon herself to keep him informed of everything that went on in the office as soon as it happened.

"Are you sure you're all right?" He frowned. "You do look pale. I'll drive you—"

"I'm fine." She glared at him as she keyed in the command to print her resignation. "Now, will you please leave?"

"You don't feel well and you're cranky as hell. But you're fine?" An understanding smile suddenly turned up the corners of his mouth. "That time of month, huh?"

Exasperated, she threw up her hands and sat back in her desk chair. "Why do men automatically think of PMS when a woman wants to be left alone? Did it ever occur to you that I might be tired and just want a little peace and quiet?"

Instead of going back into his office as she requested, he sat down in one of the chairs in front of her desk. "You were on your way to outline a retirement plan that you've been working on for the past week, then all of a sudden you turn the file over to Geena. If you aren't sick, what's the problem?" Before she could answer, he shook his head. "And don't feed me that line about peace and quiet. What's going on?"

Suddenly feeling much too tired to argue, she removed her letter of resignation from the printer, signed it and handed it to him. "I think this is self-explanatory."

He scanned the letter, then shook his head. "You can't resign."

She laughed humorlessly. "I just did."

"I'm not going to accept it." He ripped the paper in half, rose to his feet, then rounded the desk to turn her chair to face him. Placing a hand on each of the chair arms, he had her trapped and she had no alternative but to listen to him. "Talk to me, Alyssa. Tell me what's brought on this sudden decision to bail out of a job I happen to know you love."

His face was only inches from hers and it took every ounce of her concentration to remember what he'd said. "You were wrong," she finally blurted out before she could stop herself.

He frowned. "About what?"

Defeated, she fought to keep her voice even. "The gossip hasn't died down about us. If anything, it's led to more speculation among the employees."

"That's it?"

"Isn't that enough?"

"No."

Caleb's gut churned with a mixture of anger and desperation. He'd known they were still the favorite topic of idle conversation around the office and although he wasn't happy about it, he'd done his best to ignore it. Trying to set the record straight once again would only make matters worse and add more grist to the rumor mill.

Unfortunately, that was only the tip of the iceberg. The possibility of Alyssa leaving the firm was what had him tied in knots. He wasn't proud of having to rely on her without her knowing it, but he needed her expertise to keep things running smoothly until he got a grasp on what he was supposed to be doing.

But as important as her business acumen was to him, the real reason his stomach churned like a cement mixer whenever he thought about her leaving Skerritt and Crowe was far simpler. He'd hated to admit it, even to himself, but he just plain didn't want to face coming to the office without her being there.

Noticing a tear at the corner of her big blue eyes, he removed her glasses and gently wiped it away. "Did you overhear something, sweetheart?"

She nodded. "According to some, you and I are having a grand old time in here." She rolled her eyes. "Several times a day."

He chuckled. "I'm good, but I wasn't aware that I'm *that* good."

Her cheeks turned a pretty pink. "I wouldn't know anything about that. But I do know that I can't effectively supervise when everyone thinks I'm sleeping with the boss."

Lifting her chin with his index finger, he stared at her for several long seconds. God, she was pretty and it tore him up to see her upset like this.

"It's going to be all right, Alyssa. I promise."

"I don't know how."

She looked so dejected, it was all he could do to keep from taking her into his arms. But that would only add fuel to the fire if someone walked into her office and caught them.

As he continued to stare at her, a germ of an idea began to form. It was crazy enough that it just might work.

"I think I have a solution that will stop the tongues from wagging and allow you to keep your job here," he said, smiling.

She looked doubtful. "I'm listening."

"Let's go along with the rumors."

He laughed when she looked at him like he might not be playing with a full deck. "Have you lost your mind?"

"Probably." He took her hands in his, then pulling her to her feet, took her in his arms. "My grandpa used to say that sometimes the only way to put out a fire is to throw kerosene on it."

"In other words, insanity runs in your family?"

Caleb grinned. "Grandpa did have his share of peculiarities, but most of the time his logic made a hell of a lot of sense. Toss a little fuel on a fire and it burns itself out real quick and that's the end of it. Leave it alone and it can smolder for a while, then flare up again and again."

"Would you care to explain how that relates to our current problem?" To his satisfaction, she'd wrapped her arms around his waist and seemed genuinely interested in hearing him out.

"If we come out in the open and tell everyone that we are romantically involved, there won't be anything left to speculate about." He paused as something else came to mind. "In fact, as of right now, we're engaged. Then, in a few weeks, we'll announce that we've changed our minds and decided to just be friends."

"Now I'm sure you've gone over the edge." Pulling away from him, she stepped back and shook her head. "It would never work."

"Sure it will. And the sooner we announce our big news the sooner we'll be back to business as usual." Giving her a quick kiss, he reached over to press the button on her intercom. He wasn't waiting for her to come up with any more arguments why his plan was faulty. "Geneva, call a mandatory meeting of all employees for two this afternoon in the lobby downstairs."

"Consider it done," the secretary answered. "Is there anything else?"

"Nope. That's it. Thanks, Geneva." Turning back to Alyssa, he smiled. She had that deer-in-the-headlights look again. "Relax. In about an hour, we'll make our big announcement and the problem will be over."

She sank into her chair as if her knees would no longer support her. "Or just beginning."

"Trust me, sweetheart. An engagement is just what the doctor ordered to take care of this little problem."

She sighed. "Which doctor would that be? Kevorkian?"

Laughing, he headed back into his office. "Hang on to your sense of humor and everything will work out great. You'll see."

When he closed the door behind him, Caleb walked over to stare out the window behind his desk. A fake engagement? What the hell had he been thinking?

But when Alyssa had shoved her resignation at him, he'd felt like his stomach had dropped to his shoe tops. And it hadn't been entirely due to the fact that he needed her to stay at the firm and keep things running while he took his classes.

The simple fact of the matter was he didn't want Alyssa to leave because he had a case of the hots for her and there didn't seem to be any way he could stop it. Not even reminding himself of his miserable track record with a career woman had lessened her appeal. Since their trip to Roswell last week, all he'd been able to think about was how soft and sweet she'd looked when she slept and how good it had felt to hold her.

He took a deep breath and shook his head in an effort to clear it. If they were going to convince the Skerritt and Crowe employees they were wild about each other, it was going to take some planning.

A slow grin spread across his face. They had an entire weekend to get their act together and he knew the perfect place to hold their strategy session. Now all he had to do was convince Alyssa to go with him.

* * *

"This is never going to work, Caleb," Alyssa said as they walked out of her office into the deserted hall.

"Just follow my lead and act happier than you've ever been in your life." He waited for her to step onto the elevator. "I'll take care of the rest. Did you get your purse?"

She nodded. "Although I can't understand why you think I need it."

"You'll see."

His grin told her that he had something up his sleeve, but she didn't have time to think about what it could be. What was about to take place was foremost in her thoughts and had her wondering if they'd both lost their minds. In just a few short seconds, the elevator doors were going to open and they'd tell the entire Skerritt and Crowe staff they were engaged.

When the elevator came to a halt on the ground floor, Caleb grinned and took her hand in his. "Ready?"

"No."

"Smile," he whispered as the doors swished open.

Stepping off the elevator, instead of looking deliriously happy, she'd bet everything she owned that she looked more like she was about to throw up. The sick feeling intensified when she watched several of her colleagues exchange knowing glances.

"Since our trip to Roswell last week, there's been a lot of speculation about the nature of the relationship be-

tween me and A.J.," Caleb said, getting right to the heart
of the matter. "That's why we've called you all here this
afternoon. We want to end the speculation and set the
record straight, once and for all."

There was no turning back now. She took a deep
breath and trained her unwavering gaze on Caleb. She
wasn't certain she'd be able to get through the next few
minutes if she had to look at anyone else.

"Yes, there's something going on between me and
A. J. Merrick." Her heart skipped several beats when he
looked down at her and smiled. "I'd like to announce that
as of this afternoon, Alyssa and I are engaged."

Stunned silence reigned for several seconds before
the crowd suddenly broke out in a round of enthusiastic applause. But when Caleb pulled her to him and
kissed her like a soldier returning from war, the cheers
were so loud it was almost deafening.

When he raised his head, he announced, "Alyssa and
I are leaving town for the weekend, so don't try calling
us. We'll be busy making…" His pause and suggestive
grin caused several knowing smiles. "Wedding plans,"
he finished. He pointed to Malcolm. "You're in charge
until we return on Monday."

The kiss and Caleb's announcement that they were
going away together had taken her by surprise, but he
shocked her beyond words when he swept her up into
his arms and carried her from the building to the uproar-
ious cheers and applause of the Skerritt and Crowe em-

ployees. Unable to find her voice and not knowing what else to do, she threw her arms around his shoulders and hung on for dear life.

"What in the name…of all that's holy…do you think you're doing?" she finally managed to squeak out as he walked across the parking lot toward his truck.

He laughed. "I'm whisking you away like any white knight worth his weight in beans would do when he's won the hand of his fair maiden."

"Don't you think you're taking this farce just a bit far?" she asked when he opened his truck door and deposited her on the bench seat.

When she started to scoot over to the passenger side, he slid behind the steering wheel and pulled her up against him. "If this is going to work, we have to look like we're wild about each other, right?"

"Yes, but—"

"Don't you think everyone would expect us to spend time together away from the office?" he asked, starting the truck, then backing it from the parking space. "And especially right after we got engaged?"

She sighed. "All right, you've made your point."

He gave her a grin that curled her toes inside her black pumps. "We'll drop by your apartment for you to get some clothes together, then head up to my place to hide out for the weekend."

Feeling as if her life was spinning out of control with no hope of recovery, she gasped. "I beg your pardon.

When did this fiasco escalate to me actually going away with you?"

As he drove the truck out onto the street and headed in the direction of her apartment, he shook his head. "Think about it, Alyssa. Ed Bentley lives in the same complex you do. In fact, he and his wife live in the building across the street from yours. Even if you stayed in for the entire weekend, he'd notice your lights going on and off and know you were home." He gave her a pointed look. "The success of our plan hinges on this, sweetheart."

Her temples began to throb and her stomach felt as if it had been filled with rocks. "Why did I ever let you talk me into this?"

"Because the rumors and gossip were getting to you." He took her hand in his to give it a gentle squeeze. "Besides, we need to map out a game plan for how we'll play our engagement and eventual breakup."

Everything he said made perfect sense, but that did little to lessen the apprehension building inside her as he steered the truck into her apartment complex. She didn't even have a clue where he lived.

As if he'd read her mind, he smiled. "Be sure to bring a jacket. It gets chilly at night."

"You live in the mountains?" Somehow, she wasn't surprised.

"Yep. About twenty miles from here, in the East Mountain area," he said, parking in front of her building. He shrugged. "I never have been much of a city boy."

She took a deep breath and reached for the door handle. "I'll pack accordingly." When he started to get out of the truck, she shook her head. "If you don't mind, I'd like a few minutes alone to collect my thoughts."

He stared at her for a moment before he nodded. "Don't forget to pack your swimsuit. I have a hot tub and pool."

As she entered her small apartment to begin packing a few things for her weekend away with Caleb, Alyssa wasn't sure whether to laugh or cry. Why on earth had she allowed him to talk her into such a ridiculous scheme?

But as she finished folding clothes into her small bag, then made arrangements with Mrs. Rogers to take care of her parakeet, Alyssa knew exactly why she'd gone along with Caleb's plan. She simply didn't want to leave Skerritt and Crowe to find a position elsewhere. Other financial firms might offer the same opportunities to do the work she loved, but there was one thing they didn't have—a handsome CEO with hazel eyes, a sexy as sin grin and kisses that turned her into melted butter.

Six

Opening the wrought-iron gate, Caleb wondered what was going through Alyssa's pretty little head as he led her across the courtyard to the front door. The farther out of the city they'd driven, the more silent and speculative she'd become.

"If you're worried about the sleeping arrangements, don't," he said when they entered the house. He set her small case down to punch the deactivation code into the security system. "There are three extra bedrooms. You can take your pick."

"I really hadn't given where I'd be sleeping much thought." When he turned to face her, she gave him a sheepish grin. "I've been mentally calculating how much stucco homes cost and what the investment potential in real estate is on this side of the Sandia Mountains. I would think that the equity would build quickly since this area seems to be growing pretty fast."

He chuckled as he picked up her overnight case. "Once an accountant, always an accountant, huh?"

"Something like that." She gave him an odd look. "With your background in business, wasn't it something you considered when you moved here?"

"Not really." He wasn't about to tell her that the house had been given to him when he'd accepted Emerald's offer to take over the firm or that his background in business started two weeks ago when he'd walked through Skerritt and Crowe's front doors. "I was more interested in the fact that it's fairly secluded and has several acres of land."

She seemed to accept his explanation and, breathing a little easier, he followed her into the great room. But his heart damned near hammered a hole clean through his rib cage when she stopped to stare at a portrait of a middle-aged Emerald Larson and her infamous playboy son, Owen—Caleb's late father.

"Are they your relatives?" she asked, smiling.

The picture was at least twenty-five years old and it was apparent that Alyssa hadn't recognized the pair. Hopefully, she wouldn't.

"That's my grandmother and father," he said cautiously.

Gazing at him a moment, she nodded. "There's a strong family resemblance."

He placed his hand at the small of her back to usher her toward the bedrooms before she had a chance to study the picture closer and figure out who they all were. He hadn't lied to her thus far and he wasn't about to start now. If she'd recognized the Larsons, he'd have admitted to being one of the heirs to the Emerald, Inc. conglomerate. But she hadn't. And although omission of the facts was something he wasn't proud of and continued to struggle with, being outright dishonest was out of the question. It just wasn't his style.

"Feel free to check out the other two bedrooms, then decide which one you want," he said, opening the door to the room closest to his. The room had been done in yellow and green and looked a little more feminine than the other two bedrooms. "They all have their own private bathroom, but this one is the only one besides the master suite that has a sitting area."

"This is fine," she said, glancing around. She walked over to the French doors on the opposite side of the room to look out at the patio and pool. "It's a lovely area and your home is beautiful, Caleb. You must love living up here."

"Thanks." He set her bag on the end of the bed, then walked over to stand behind her. "The terrain is a lot different here than in Tennessee, but I'm getting used to it." He didn't tell her that it was a far cry from the humble farmhouse he'd grown up in or that he was having a hard time thinking of it as his, even though it had been signed over to him when he'd accepted Emerald's offer.

"I'd like to hear about where you used to live," she said, sounding wistful. "I've never been east of the Mississippi, but I've heard the southern states are quite beautiful."

"They are. Back home when I look at the mountains, I'm used to seeing them covered with trees, and everything is green. Here it's just as pretty, but in a different way. There aren't as many trees and everything is shades of tan, brown or orange." Without thinking, he slipped his arms around her waist and drew her back against him. "I'll have to take you to see the eastern mountains sometime."

He heard her soft intake of breath a moment before she turned to face him. "Caleb, what are we doing?"

Staring down at her, he wondered the same thing. She was the type of woman he'd vowed to steer clear of, yet there was something about Alyssa Jane Merrick that he couldn't resist. He wanted to show her where he'd grown up, wanted her to know who he was and what had molded him into the man he'd become, and he wanted to know all about her. And that scared the living hell out of him.

Suddenly needing to put a little space between them in order to figure out what the hell had gotten into him, he kissed her forehead then, releasing her, started for the door. "While you get your things put away and freshen up, I'll go see what I can scare up for supper."

As Alyssa watched him leave the room, she sighed

heavily. It hadn't been lost on her that he'd avoided answering her question. Could he be as confused about what was going on between them as she was? What *was* happening between them?

She certainly wasn't an expert at affairs of the heart, but it was evident there was something drawing them together. They couldn't be in the same room for longer than five minutes without being in each other's arms.

What was there about Caleb Walker that made her forget the lesson she'd learned five years ago at the hands of a man just like him? Hadn't she suffered enough humiliation when she'd learned that men weren't above using women to achieve their own goals or advance their careers?

Sitting on the side of the bed, she thought about Wesley Pennington III, the man who'd taught her just how cutthroat the business world could truly be and the lengths that some men were willing to go to in order to get ahead. Handsome and charming, Wesley had swept her off her feet about a year after they'd both started working at the prestigious financial group of Carson, Gottlieb and Howell. And right up until the end of their six-week affair, she hadn't had a clue that he'd been using her to gain information about a potential client.

But as she mentally compared Caleb to Wesley the weasel, she had to admit there were very few, if any, similarities. Wesley wouldn't have been caught dead in a pair of jeans and boots, nor would he have chosen to live in a secluded house in a quiet rural area over his ultramodern uptown condo. And that was just scratching the surface of how the two men differed.

Wesley had been a polished sophisticate and tended to act superiorly with anyone below him on the corporate ladder. But Caleb wasn't anything like that. His casual, down-to-earth personality immediately put everyone at ease and he not only treated those who worked for him as his equals, he seemed to genuinely care about them as well.

That was something she knew firsthand to be beyond Wesley's capabilities. He didn't care about anyone but himself and he wasn't above stepping on those who posed a threat to, or got in the way of, his lofty ambitions. He hadn't thought twice about using her affections for him to gain information that had led to his obtaining a coveted corporate account and ultimately the promotion that rightly should have been hers. When she'd confronted him about it, he'd readily admitted that he'd only started dating her for the purpose of getting ahead. But the most devastating blow had come when she'd overheard her coworkers gossiping about the whole sordid mess. That's when she'd decided she had no alternative but to look for another job and had found her present position at Skerritt and Crowe.

But she was certain Caleb would never stoop to that level, would never take credit for her or anyone else's accomplishments, even if he wasn't already the head of

Skerritt and Crowe. Nor would he publicly humiliate her. On the contrary. He'd come up with the pretend engagement and had her spending the weekend with him because he was trying to squelch the rumors and gossip that she found hurtful.

Sighing, she put the last of her clothes in the dresser drawer, then changed into a pair of baggy camp shorts and a T-shirt. She'd tried every way in the world not to like Caleb. But the truth of the matter was, she trusted him more than she had anyone in a very long time. And whether it was smart or not, she might as well admit it—if she hadn't already fallen for him, she was well on her way.

"Thank you for a delicious dinner. You're a very good cook."

"Not really." Caleb grinned. "Throwing something on the grill and fire roasting a few vegetables is about the only thing I know how to fix, besides frying bacon and scrambling eggs."

"Well, I thought it was scrumptious." Her sweet smile did a real number on his insides. "And I'm glad you suggested we eat out here on the patio." He watched her look past the pool at the valley below. "The view is absolutely gorgeous."

He couldn't agree more; the view was beautiful. But he wasn't looking at the cedar trees or the valley. The woman seated at the table with him was far prettier than anything he'd ever seen.

Rising to his feet before he did something stupid like take her in his arms and kiss her senseless, he gathered their plates. "I like sitting out here after the sun goes down. Other than an occasional coyote howling, it's pretty quiet."

"Let me help with those," she said, standing up.

He shook his head. "I'll take care of the cleanup."

"That's not fair," she protested. "You cooked. I should clear the table."

He started toward the house with the dishes. "While I'm doing this, why don't you change? I don't know about you, but I could use some time in the hot tub before I turn in for the night."

"That does sound wonderful, but are you sure I can't help you first?"

Damned if she didn't follow him into the kitchen. Taking a deep breath, he shook his head. He was about two seconds away from kissing her until they both needed CPR or carrying her to his bedroom to make love to her for the rest of the night. But he couldn't tell her that. She'd probably belt him a good one, then run as hard and fast as she could back to Albuquerque.

"I'll just put these plates in the dishwasher, then meet you in the hot tub in ten minutes," he said, surprised that his voice sounded fairly steady. Considering his state of mind and the changes his body was going through at that very moment, he figured it was nothing short of a miracle he could talk at all.

"Okay." She gave him a smile that caused his blood

pressure to shoot up a good fifty points. "But I'm cooking breakfast tomorrow morning."

"You've got yourself a deal, sweetheart." He'd agree to just about anything as long as she left the room and let him get a grip on his runaway libido.

But as he watched her walk away, his heart stalled and his body tightened so fast it left him feeling lightheaded. Even though her khaki shorts and pink T-shirt looked to be a couple of sizes too big, it couldn't disguise the sexy sway of her shapely hips or the fact that her long, slender legs looked like they could wrap around a man and take him to heaven.

Caleb closed his eyes and forced himself to breathe. What the hell had he been thinking when he'd suggested they get in the hot tub? If just watching her walk made him hard, what would happen when he saw her in a swimsuit?

The mental image his overactive imagination conjured up made his knees wobble and sweat pop out on his forehead and upper lip. Leaning against the kitchen counter for support, he groaned. How on God's green earth was he going to keep his hands to himself for the next two days?

When the phone rang, he was grateful to whoever was on the other end of the line for interrupting his disturbing thoughts. "Thank you."

"You're welcome. Now, do you want to tell me what I did?"

"Hey, Hunter." Once he and his brothers had learned

about each other, they'd all, by unspoken agreement, stayed in touch. And Caleb was happy with the bond they were forming.

"What's up with answering the phone the way you did?"

"Just thinking out loud," Caleb said, hoping his oldest brother forgot about his slip of the tongue.

"How's the financial world? Any new advice on how I can turn my savings account into a fortune?"

"If you want to build your money, the best advice I can give you at this point is to leave it where it's at," Caleb said dryly.

Hunter snorted. "You sound about as sure of yourself at this financial stuff as I feel about running an airambulance service."

Caleb smiled. "How's the EMT course going?"

There was a pause before Hunter finally answered. "I've been in that damned class for almost two weeks and I still get light-headed whenever I see a needle."

"At least you've stopped passing out at the sight of them," Caleb said, laughing.

"Just barely." Obviously wanting to change the subject, Hunter asked, "Are you going to attend Emerald's birthday party at the end of the month?"

It was Caleb's turn to snort. "I don't think we've been given a lot of choice about going. The invitation read more like a summons than a request to help her celebrate her seventy-sixth birthday."

"It sounds like the one I got." Hunter laughed humorlessly. "I knew that old gal was going to yank our chains every chance she got."

"Have you talked to Nick lately?" Caleb asked.

"He called me last night and suggested we all meet for a beer before we attend Emerald's party."

"That's a good idea." Caleb chuckled. "Maybe if we have a buzz going, it'll make the evening more tolerable."

"I like the way you think."

Finalizing plans to meet before the party, Caleb hung up and headed for his bedroom to change. He was looking forward to seeing Nick and Hunter again. And his only regret about finding out that he had two brothers was that he hadn't learned of their existence sooner.

But he really had no room to complain. He'd had a great childhood with the love and guidance of his maternal grandparents and a mother who had been totally devoted to raising him the right way. He'd asked who his father was a few times, but his mother would only smile and tell him to be patient—that one day he'd learn all about the man. After a while he'd given up asking, and if he'd missed having a father, Caleb couldn't ever remember it. His grandfather had taught him everything he'd needed to know, from how to tie a fishing lure to what it meant to be a good, honest man.

But as he pulled on a pair of gym shorts, he decided he couldn't say he'd missed knowing his manipulative paternal grandmother. No matter what she said about not meddling in their lives back then or the way they ran the businesses she'd given them now, he had a feeling she still had their every move under surveillance and would have no problem stepping in to take over if she felt it was warranted.

But when Caleb opened the French doors to step out onto the patio and spotted Alyssa standing by the hot tub, his grievances with Emerald Larson were quickly forgotten. Damn, but Alyssa looked good. Her black one-piece bathing suit clung to her body and enhanced all the curves that he'd been fantasizing about ever since walking into her office the day he'd arrived to take over the financial firm.

He swallowed hard. He'd been right about her legs, too. They were long, sleek and perfect for holding a man close while he made love to her.

"I'm sorry." Walking over to her, he had to clear his suddenly dry throat. "It took longer than I planned. One of my brothers called."

"I heard the phone ring." She smiled wistfully. "It must be nice to have siblings."

"You're an only child?" He wasn't ready to tell her that a little less than a month ago, he hadn't even known his brothers existed.

Nodding, she took off her glasses and, laying them on a nearby chair, started to climb the steps to get into the hot tub. "I always wanted a brother or sister to share memories with, but it wasn't meant to be."

Caleb took hold of her arm to help steady her as she stepped into the bubbling water, but the second his fingers touched her satiny skin, a jolt of electric current zinged straight up his arm and exploded in the pit of his belly. Climbing into the hot tub on shaky legs, he sat down beside her and tried to think of what they'd been talking about.

"I, uh, haven't always been close with my two brothers."

"Is there a big age difference between you?" she asked, sounding genuinely interested.

"No, we're all about the same age." He knew he was walking a fine line, but he wanted to be as truthful with her as possible. "We had the same father, but different mothers." Deciding it was time to change the subject before he revealed more than he intended, he smiled. "Could you tell me something, Alyssa?"

"It depends on the question and whether or not I know the answer," she said, looking a little apprehensive.

"Why do you go by your initials at work, instead of your given name?" He'd wanted to know the answer since reviewing her personnel file. "It's very pretty." *Like you.*

She shrugged one slender shoulder. "That's what my father always called me. I think it was his way of pretending I was the son he always wanted, but never had."

Reaching out, Caleb traced his index finger along her porcelain cheek. No matter what kind of hell he'd have to go through, he couldn't seem to stop touching her. "I'm sure he loves you more than you realize, sweetheart."

She remained silent for several long moments before nodding. "I suppose it was possible that he cared for me, but it's something I'll never know. He died on a mission in the Middle East during my junior year in college."

Caleb felt like a complete jerk for bringing up an obviously painful subject. Without thinking twice, he lifted her onto his lap and did his best to ignore how her shapely bottom felt pressed to his rapidly hardening body.

She stared at him for several long seconds. "Caleb, this isn't a good idea."

"Hush." Cradling her to his chest, he held her close as the water bubbled around them. He tried to tell himself that he was offering her comfort, but the truth was she felt so right in his arms, he couldn't bring himself to let her go. "I'm sorry, Alyssa. I didn't mean to pry."

"It's all right." He felt her begin to relax against him. "I've never had any illusions about it. My father and I didn't have a great relationship."

He kissed her temple. "What about your mom? Are you close to her?"

"Mother passed away when I was eight." She sighed. "That's when I started attending school at the Marsden Academy for Girls."

"Your dad sent you to a boarding school?" Anger burned at his gut. How could Merrick have done that to his only child? Caleb could only imagine how lonely and scared she must have been. At that moment, he despised the man for abandoning her when she'd obviously needed him most.

"Actually, Dad didn't have a lot of choice about sending me to Marsden," she said softly. "He was a navy SEAL and never knew when his team would be called out on a mission."

"Couldn't you have stayed with a relative?"

He wondered why her grandparents hadn't stepped forward to take her in. There was no way in hell his grandparents would have ever turned their grandchild away. They'd stood by his mother when she'd found herself pregnant and alone, and had helped her raise him, even though it hadn't been as socially acceptable then as it was now for a single woman to have a child.

Alyssa shook her head. "I've never even met my grandparents. My dad was raised in the foster-care system and my maternal grandparents didn't think he was good enough for their only child. When my mom eloped with him on graduation night, her parents more or less disowned her."

Alyssa had no idea why she was telling Caleb about her family or, more accurately, her lack of one. Normally, she didn't share any details about herself with anyone. But he was easy to talk to and his compassion made her feel at ease and free to discuss it for the first time in years.

"What about you?" she asked, enjoying the feel of

his wide bare chest against her arm. "What was your childhood like?"

"It was pretty average," he said, shrugging. "I grew up on a farm in central Tennessee—"

"If you hadn't told me before that you were from the South, I'd have never known," she said dryly.

He chuckled. "You can take the boy out of the South, but you can't take the Southern accent out of the boy."

"Something like that," she said, laughing. Wanting to hear more about his childhood, she asked, "What was it like growing up on a farm?"

"I guess it was pretty much like growing up anywhere else," he said, thoughtfully. "I did most of the things other kids my age did—played Little League baseball, helped Grandpa around the farm and went skinny-dipping in the creek every chance I got." His mischievous grin curled her toes. "Still do."

Her insides fluttered. "You swim in the nude?"

He nodded. "I don't even own a pair of swim trunks. The only reason I'm wearing gym shorts now is to protect your tender sensibilities."

She suddenly felt a warmth course through her that had nothing to do with being in the hot tub. "I've never gone swimming without a suit."

His grin caused her to feel as if the water temperature rose a good ten degrees. "You should give it a try sometime."

She'd never been good at sexy banter and, unable to

think of a suitable comeback, she asked, "Where did you go to school?"

His muscles tensed slightly before he answered. "No private academies for me. I went to public schools."

"University, too?"

"There's no other team like the University of Tennessee Vols."

"Vols?"

"Short for Volunteers," he said, smiling. He pulled her closer. "But I don't want to discuss schools or sports teams right now." He brushed his lips over hers as he slid his finger under one of the straps of her swimsuit. "Do you have any idea how great you look in this little black number?"

She'd purposely ignored the fact that she was still sitting on his lap, but suddenly several things became quite apparent. They were alone in the semidarkness; their water-slick bodies were pressed together and his muscular thighs under her bottom weren't the only things that were hard.

Her eyes widened and a breathtaking charge of need filled every cell in her being. "I think…I'll move over to the seat."

"I like you right where you are." With one arm around her waist, he held her in place as he slid his hand from her shoulder down her upper arm, taking her swimsuit strap with him. "Your skin feels like silk, Alyssa."

Desire so hot she felt scorched by its intensity washed over her and, closing her eyes, she sighed. "This is insanity."

"Do you want me to stop?" he asked, his voice so low and intimate it caused goose bumps to shimmer over her skin.

God help her, but she didn't want him to stop. She wanted him to kiss and hold her. She wanted to feel his strong hands caressing her body. And if she was really honest with herself, that's what she'd wanted since their trip to Roswell.

She shook her head as she opened her eyes to meet his questioning gaze. "That's what's insane. I don't want you to stop. I should. But I don't. And that's what's so confusing. I've never been the type of person to throw caution to the wind." A shiver streaked up her spine when he cupped her cheek with his palm and she had to take in some much-needed air before she could finish. "But being with you, I find that I don't want to analyze every move I make. I don't want to be sensible. And living for the moment suddenly sounds so very tempting."

"It's up to you, Alyssa. All you have to do is tell me what you want and I promise to respect your wishes." He smiled. "But if it's left up to me, I'll take this suit off of you and show you just what temptation is all about."

His sexy drawl made her insides hum and all of her

secret places pulse with a hunger stronger than anything she'd ever experienced. "I want you to make me feel alive. I want you to touch me and…" She took a deep breath. "More."

Seven

As he gazed at her, Caleb wondered if he'd lost every ounce of sense he'd ever possessed. He had an incredibly desirable woman sitting on his lap, telling him that she wanted him. And what he was about to say could very well end things before they ever got started.

But his sense of honor wouldn't allow him to proceed without giving her the chance to call a halt to it right here and now. He had a feeling it was going to be one of the most meaningful nights of his life and he didn't want her regretting one minute of what they would share.

"Alyssa, I'm going to tell you something and I want you to think about it very carefully."

She looked apprehensive. "Okay."

He took a deep breath and went on before he had a chance to change his mind. "If I continue, I'm not going to stop. I'm going to take this bathing suit off and kiss every inch of your beautiful body. I'm going to touch you in places that will make you moan with pleasure. I'm going to do things to you that will drive you crazy and have you calling my name when you find your release. And then, when you think I'm finished, I'm going to start all over again."

To his immense relief, instead of the small spark of desire in her luminous blue eyes dimming, it grew to a hunger that matched his own. But he needed to hear her say the words, needed for her to tell him that she wanted him to make love to her.

"Is that what you want, Alyssa?"

"Yes." There wasn't a moment's hesitation in her simple answer, nor a hint of reservations in her steady gaze.

Groaning, Caleb covered her mouth with his, then traced her perfect lips with his tongue. If she'd told him no, he'd have had a hell of a time finding the strength to walk away. But she hadn't. And just knowing she wanted him enough to let down her guard made him hot in ways he'd never imagined.

Her contented sigh encouraged him and he took advantage of her acceptance to slip inside and once again explore her sweetness. As he tasted and coaxed her with strokes that mimicked a more intimate union, he decided that kissing Alyssa was quickly becoming as addictive to him as any drug.

The way she held on to him, the way she responded to his kiss was all any man could dream of and proved what he'd thought from the moment they'd met. She wasn't the emotionless woman she tried to lead her coworkers to believe. She was warm, affectionate and, if her enthusiastic response to his kiss was any indication, passionate as hell when she let herself go. He just thanked the good Lord above that he was going to be the man holding her when that happened.

As he worshipped her with his mouth, he moved his hands over her shoulders and down her arms to slide the top of her swimsuit out of the way. He wanted to feel her soft body melting into the hard contours of his. But when he pulled her more fully against him, nothing could have prepared him for the reality of having her firm breasts pressing into his chest, their pebbled nipples scoring his skin.

"You feel so damned good," he rasped as he kissed his way from her mouth to the tender skin just below her ear.

Shuddering against him, she whispered close to his ear, "Please…don't stop."

Turning her to face him, he lifted her until her breasts cleared the surface of the warm water. "Sweetheart, there's not a chance in hell of that happening."

Slowly moving his lips over her creamy skin, he made his way from her shoulder down the slope of her breast to the hardened tip. Taking the tight bud into his mouth, Caleb sipped the water droplets from her puckered flesh, savored the sweetness that was uniquely Alyssa.

As he sucked and teased her nipples, a moan of pleasure escaped her parted lips and, raising his head, he asked, "Does that feel good?"

"Mmm." Threading her fingers through his hair, she held him close. "It's wonderful."

Suddenly needing to feel all of her against him, Caleb quickly shoved her swimsuit down her hips and legs, then tossed the wet black spandex over the side of the hot tub. His gym shorts quickly followed.

Reaching for her, he pulled her to him and the feel of smooth female skin against his hair-roughened flesh sent a flash fire to every nerve in his being. He wanted to take things slowly, to do all the things he'd promised, but his body was urging him to stake his claim and make her his.

"Alyssa, I want you so damned bad I can taste it," he said through gritted teeth. "I think we'd better get out of here and—"

"Please, Caleb," she said, wrapping her arms around his shoulders. Her eyes were glazed with hungry need when she added, "I need you inside. Now."

At her throaty plea, a shaft of longing rushed through him at the speed of light and white-hot desire enveloped him. With his mind clouded to anything but the need to possess her, he sank to his knees and lifted her to him.

Determined to enter her slowly, he clenched his back teeth together so hard it would probably require surgery to separate them. But as he guided himself to her, she proved his other theory about her when she wrapped her long, slender legs around his waist and her body consumed his in one smooth motion. He definitely felt like he was in heaven.

But her quiet gasp, the tightness surrounding him, penetrated the haze of passion. If he'd caused her any discomfort at all, he'd never forgive himself.

"Did I hurt you? You're really tight, sweetheart."

"It's been a…while." She nibbled at his neck and damned near caused him to have a coronary when she whispered, "You feel absolutely wonderful right where you are."

Crushing her coral lips beneath his, he kissed her until they both gasped for breath. "I'm so hot right now…" He closed his eyes in an attempt to slow down. "I think I might just spontaneously combust."

She touched his cheek with one wet finger as she moved her lower body. "Make love to me, Caleb."

Her request and the motion of her body unleashed the hungry need he'd been trying to hold in check and, groaning, he began to thrust into her. He'd never had a woman hold his body quite so perfectly or respond to him in ways that, until tonight, he'd only imagined in his wildest fantasies.

But as ideal as the moment was, the warm water bubbling around them enhanced the spirals of fiery passion binding them together and he could feel her body straining for the same mind-shattering release that he'd been trying to forestall from the moment they'd become one. All too soon her feminine inner muscles held him captive, then quivered as he felt the tight coil inside her let go. The sound of her whispering his name and the amazing sensation of her pleasure triggered his own release from the tension gripping him. Groaning, he thrust into her one final time and held her to him as he emptied himself deep inside of her.

With their energy completely spent, they clung together for several long moments before reality began to clear his passion-fogged brain. Saying a word that he usually reserved for smashed thumbs and drivers who cut him off in traffic, he eased away from her.

"What's wrong?" she asked, clearly alarmed by his harsh curse.

He ran an unsteady hand across the tension gathering at the back of his neck. "Tell me you're on the pill or patch or some kind of birth control."

"N-no. It hasn't been an issue for several years." As she stared at him, her eyes suddenly grew wide. "We didn't—"

He shook his head. "I'm sorry. There's no excuse for me not taking precautions."

She nibbled on her lower lip for a moment. "I probably don't have anything to worry about."

"We," he said, placing his hands on her shoulders. "I want you to know that we're in this together, Alyssa. If you do become pregnant, I'll be right there with you every step of the way."

"I'm tired," she said suddenly. "I think I'll take a shower and turn in."

Caleb didn't try to stop her when she climbed out of the water, wrapped herself in one of the towels and, grabbing her glasses, hurriedly disappeared through the doors into her room. They both needed time to come to terms with what they'd shared and the possible consequences of his carelessness.

He couldn't believe he'd been so thoughtless. Where the hell had his mind been, anyway?

In the past, he'd never failed to use protection. Even before knowing who his irresponsible father was, Caleb had been determined not to be anything like the man who had impregnated Caleb's mother, then left her to face things on her own. He'd always made it a point never to get so carried away that he lost sight of what an unexpected pregnancy could mean for him or his partner.

But he'd been so turned on, so mind-numbingly hot for Alyssa, the thought of protection hadn't even crossed his mind. All he'd been able to think about was how perfectly she fit within his arms, how soft her body was and how her sweet kisses warmed him to the depths of his soul. His body hardened at the very thought of how amazing their lovemaking had been and had him wanting nothing more than to go inside and make love to her for the rest of the night.

Cursing a blue streak, he splashed out of the hot tub and made a beeline for the pool. When he dove into the much cooler water and started swimming laps, his muscles protested, but he didn't care. He had to get himself under control.

When he reached the end of the pool on his tenth lap, he stopped to catch his breath and, glancing toward the French doors, shook his head. His body still throbbed with a need that left him dizzy and he had a feeling he could swim from now until his dying day and not even come close to easing the burning ache to make Alyssa his once again.

Climbing out of the pool, he wrapped a towel around his waist and, picking up his gym shorts and her swimsuit, headed for his room. He had a feeling one of two things was going to happen this weekend. Either they were going to make love again or, first thing Monday morning, he was going to be seeking medical attention for a perpetual erection.

Alyssa stared at the ceiling as she thought about what had happened in the hot tub. She still couldn't believe what had taken place when Caleb had touched her, nor did she understand it. It was as if she'd been taken over by a shamelessly uninhibited wanton who not only lived for the moment, but threw caution to the wind and didn't even consider the possibility of the consequences.

She'd never in all of her twenty-six years acted that way before. Not even when she and Wesley had been seeing each other and she'd thought she was in love had she experienced a total loss of control. And that scared her as little else could.

But all it took was one kiss, one touch of Caleb's hands and she lost all sense of herself. It was as if she became part of something larger than either of them, emotionally as well as physically. If his reaction was any indication, he'd experienced it, too.

The best thing she could do for her own well-being and peace of mind would be to have him take her back to Albuquerque tonight. Then, first thing Monday morning, insist that he accept her resignation, effective immediately.

She knew their coworkers would question why their "engagement" was off and why she no longer worked at Skerritt and Crowe. But that couldn't be helped. Caleb could tell them whatever he liked about the matter. She wouldn't be there to hear their comments and speculation on what might have happened between them.

Tossing the sheet aside, she climbed out of bed and pulled on her robe. The sooner she got back to the safety of her apartment, the better. Not only could she finish updating her résumé, she needed to check her personal calendar. Until she did that, she really wasn't certain whether she needed to worry about an unplanned pregnancy.

"Caleb?" She tapped on his bedroom door. "Are you still awake?"

When there was no response, she turned to go back to her room. She'd only gone a couple of steps when the door opened.

"Did you need something?"

The sight of him standing in the doorway in nothing but a pair of white cotton briefs rendered her temporarily speechless and all she could do was nod.

When they'd gotten into the hot tub there hadn't been enough daylight left to see the details of his body, then, when he'd removed his gym shorts, they'd been in the water. But the light from his bedside lamp cast just enough light now to enhance the ridges and ripples of his well-defined muscles and drew attention to the fact that Caleb Walker was perfection and then some.

His heavily padded pectoral muscles, bulging biceps and sculpted shoulders were proof that he'd spent years doing a lot more on that farm than just going skinny-dipping. Her gaze drifted lower and her pulse sped up.

Caleb's stomach had so many ripples it resembled a washboard. But it was everything below the waistband of his white briefs that had her gulping for air. The stretchy cotton hugged him like a second skin and outlined the size and heaviness of his sex. The lack of a tan line on his long, muscular legs was confirmation that he did, in fact, swim in the nude.

"You look a little shook up."

Why wouldn't she be? He was standing there practically naked and didn't seem the least bit self-conscious about it.

Taking a step toward her, he placed his hand on her shoulder. "Are you all right?"

Nodding, she tried to remember why she'd knocked on his door, but the feel of his warm palm touching her through her thin robe made it extremely difficult to breathe, let alone think.

He stared at her for several long seconds before he smiled and lightly touched her cheek with his index finger. "We need to talk, sweetheart."

Her insides fluttered wildly and she couldn't seem to catch her breath. "I…agree. I have something I need to ask you."

He stepped back and motioned toward his open door. "Let's go into my room and sit down."

She shook her head. "I'm not sure that's a good idea."

"I think it is." Before she could stop him, he grabbed her hand and tugged her into his bedroom. "I have something I need to do."

"Caleb—"

"It's all right, Alyssa." Leading her past the bed to the sitting area by the French doors, he sank into one of the armchairs, then pulled her onto his lap. "I want you to listen to me before you say anything. Will you do that?"

"Y-yes."

Why was she allowing him to take command of the situation? Why wasn't she demanding that he immediately take her back to Albuquerque before something else happened? But with all of the bare male skin surrounding her, she found she was too distracted to do much of anything but go along with what he wanted.

"Good." He gently stroked her hair as his hazel gaze held hers captive. "I want to apologize for the way I acted earlier and set the record straight. I wasn't upset with you, Alyssa. I was mad as hell at myself for letting you down. I know that's no excuse. But the truth of the matter is, I failed you, then acted like a real bastard about it. And I'm sorry, sweetheart."

Her conscience wouldn't let him shoulder all of the responsibility. "You weren't in that hot tub alone. I'm just as much to blame as you. I should have thought—"

He stubbornly shook his head. "It's a man's place to protect a woman."

"I beg to differ. Both partners should share the responsibilities of prevention." When he looked like he was going to protest, she reached up to place her finger to his lips. "But I'm not going to argue that with you now. I think it's safe to say we both got a bit carried away."

"You're right about that, sweetheart." His sexy grin sent waves of heat coursing through her. "I was so hot for you, I'm surprised we didn't cause the water in the hot tub to boil."

His candor and the sound of his low drawl caused her to feel as if the blood in her veins had been replaced with warm honey. Deciding it would definitely be in her best interest to move before she lost sight of what she needed to ask him, she started to stand up.

"Hey, where are you going?" he asked, holding her in place. He brushed his lips over hers in the gentlest of kisses. When he raised his head, he asked, "Didn't you say you had something you wanted to ask me?"

With every cell in her body tingling and her heart skipping every other beat, how was she supposed to think? Why had she knocked on his door? For the life of her, she couldn't remember.

But Caleb didn't seem to mind that she had temporary amnesia. Giving her a promising smile, he lowered his head again to kiss her with such tenderness it brought tears to her eyes. As he used his tongue to trace her lips, spirals of desire slowly swirled to every part of her and a shiver of excitement skipped up her spine. All he had to do was touch her and her will to resist melted away like mist under an early summer sun.

As he teased her to open for him, then dipped his tongue inside to explore her inner recesses, she was shocked at her own eager response. Boldly stroking him, she wrapped her arms around his shoulders and pressed closer.

His groan of pleasure rumbled up from deep in his chest and the vibration against her breasts sent a flash of heat streaking through her at the speed of light. When he broke the kiss, his lips seared a path from her neck to her collarbone, making her feel as if she were about to go up in flames.

He pushed her gown and robe aside to continue a blazing trail of nibbling kisses to the valley between her breasts and Alyssa was certain she'd been branded by the intensity of it. The ribbons of need flowing through her began to wind their way to the pit of her stomach, forming a coil of hungry desire deep in the most feminine part of her.

Seated on his lap, she knew immediately when his body began to change, to grow hard with the same passion that was overtaking her. Right or wrong, wise or not, she wanted to be warmed by the heat of his desire, to once again have him claim her body and soul.

"Please, Caleb."

"I want you again, sweetheart." His drawl sounded rough and impassioned. He raised his head to give her a look that seared her all the way to her soul. "Do you remember what I told you in the hot tub?"

"I—I'm not sure." She was about to burn to a cinder and he wanted her to recall something he'd said earlier?

The wicked grin he gave her sent a wave of goose bumps shimmering across her skin. "I promised you that I was going to kiss you all over. That I was going to touch you in all of your secret places and make you cry out with pleasure. Then, when you think I'm finished, I'm going to start all over again."

His suggestive words caused the coil in her stomach to tightened to an empty ache that robbed her of breath.

"And I have every intention of keeping that promise." His intense hazel gaze made her feel as if she'd melt right then and there when he added, "I'm going to love you the way you deserve to be loved. Right here. Right now."

Alyssa's pulse pounded in her ears and without a moment's hesitation, she nodded that she wanted that, too.

It fleetingly crossed her mind that she was playing with fire and there was a very real possibility that she'd end up being burned. But she didn't want to think about that now. She wanted to be held and touched and loved by the man who had stolen her heart.

Eight

If Caleb had given her time, Alyssa might have panicked at the realization that she'd fallen in love with him. But he was already taking matters into his own hands. Lifting her as if she weighed nothing at all, he stood up with her in his arms and walked over to his king-size bed.

Setting her on her feet, he held her gaze with his as he slowly untied her robe and slid it from her shoulders. "This time we're going to take things slow and easy. I want to savor every inch of you and by the time I'm through, there won't be a doubt in your mind about how special I think you are."

With every word he spoke, her limbs felt a bit weaker

and the restlessness deep inside her grew stronger. "I'm going to hold you to that," she said, wondering if that sultry female voice was really hers.

He slid his palms along her arms, then, taking her hands in his, he lifted them to kiss each one of her fingertips before placing them on his shoulders. "I'd rather you hold *me* to you."

She threaded her fingers through the hair at his nape, then, drawing his head down for her kiss, she pressed herself to his hard frame. "There are a few things that I want to do to you, too. Holding you against me is just one of them."

If she'd thought about it, she might have been appalled at her shamelessness. But it was as if she shed every one of her inhibitions when Caleb took her in his arms. And, for the first time in her life, she felt free to explore her own sexuality.

His smile increased the humming in the very core of her as he gathered her nightgown in his hands and slowly pulled it up over her head. "Let's get the rest of these clothes off."

Tossing the peacock-blue silk to join her robe on the floor, he ran his hands along her sides to her hips, then, hooking his thumbs in the elastic waistband of her panties, slowly pushed them over her hips and down her thighs. Once she kicked them aside, he stepped back to strip himself of his briefs. Her breath caught and an ache of pure need filled her at the sight of him.

She'd been right. Caleb's body was sheer perfection. Hard and lean, there wasn't a spare ounce of flesh anywhere on him.

But it was the sight of his strong arousal that caused her heart to skid to a stop, then take off at a gallop. He was above average in height and it appeared that other things about him were above average as well. If she hadn't already experienced the power of his lovemaking, she might have been a bit apprehensive. But she trusted Caleb implicitly. Although he'd been as excited for her as she'd been for him, he'd taken great care not to hurt her when they'd made love in the hot tub.

"You're beautiful." His voice was so reverent, so filled with awe that she had no doubt that he meant what he said.

"I was thinking the same thing about you," she said softly. "You're perfect."

As he took a step toward her, his deep chuckle made her feel as if the temperature in the room had suddenly risen several degrees. "I'm not perfect, sweetheart, but you know what they say about practice."

She felt color flood her cheeks. "I didn't mean—"

"I know. But I intend to spend the rest of the night making sure our lovemaking is perfect for *you*," he said, reaching for her.

If his words hadn't sent her into total meltdown, the feel of his hard male flesh against her softer female skin would have. A shudder ran through his big body and she knew he felt the same scorching heat she did.

Closing her eyes, she reveled in the differences between a man and woman—the contrast of hard ridges to soft curves. "I love the way your body feels pressed to mine."

As he lowered his head, his slow grin held a wealth of promise. "I like the way I feel inside you more."

Her knees wobbled and, feeling as if she'd melt into a puddle at his feet, she sagged against him. Opening her eyes to gaze up at him, she whispered, "I do, too."

Without warning, he swung her up into his arms, placed her in the middle of his bed, then stretched out beside her and pulled her to him. "Keep talking like that, sweetheart, and I'll go off like a Roman candle on the Fourth of July."

Before she could respond, he captured her lips with a desperate hunger that sent a flash fire streaking all the way to her soul. But when he broke the kiss to nibble his way from her collarbone down the slope of her breast, then took the tight bud into his mouth, she felt as if she'd burn to a crisp. His gentle sucking, the feel of his tongue on her sensitized nipple caused the spiraling heat to increase the tension building deep in her womb.

A moan escaped as she held his head to her. The delicious sensations Caleb created with his erotic teasing were driving her absolutely wild.

"Do you like that?" he asked, kissing her abdomen.

Nodding, she shivered from the exquisite feeling of his warm breath whispering over her. "Please…"

He dipped his tongue in the indention of her navel as he ran his calloused hands along her sides. "Tell me what you want, Alyssa."

"M-more."

"Are you sure?"

There was an underlying tone, a warning of sorts in his quiet question. He was asking for her trust, asking for permission to take her places that no man had taken her before.

"Yes!" If he didn't do something soon she was going to die from wanting.

Without another word, he raised his head and the blazing passion she saw in his hazel eyes stole her breath. Sliding his hands over her hips, then down her legs, he held her captive with his heated gaze as he caressed the insides of her thighs. Her heart pounded hard beneath her breast as inch by slow inch he came closer to the nest of curls at the apex of her thighs. When he finally reached his goal, pleasure radiated throughout her body at his featherlight touch.

"Oh, my!"

"Does that feel good?" he asked as he continued to drive her mad.

"Yes."

"More?" His deep drawl was as seductive as the feel of his hands on her.

"P-please!"

His kiss on the inside of her thigh sent a tingling excitement straight to her core. Clenching her eyes shut, she gripped the sheet with both hands. "I feel like…I'm on fire."

"Easy, sweetheart. It's only going to get better." He'd no sooner gotten the words out than he lowered his head and gave her the most intimate kiss a man can give to a woman.

Shock waves of pure ecstasy raced through her and she couldn't stop a moan from escaping. "C-Caleb, please…I need—"

Kissing his way back up her body, he nibbled at one of her aching nipples. "What do you need, sweetheart?"

"You. Now."

"Why?" he asked, treating the other taut nub to the same sweet torture.

"I can't…take…much more."

"Open your eyes, Alyssa." When she did as he commanded, he shook his head. "Remember what I told you?"

"N-no." He expected her to think at a time like this?

His promising grin sent another wave of heat flowing through her veins. "I told you that just when you think I'm finished, I'm going to start all over again."

If she could have found her voice, she'd have told him that much more and she'd go stark-raving mad. But before she had the chance, he lowered his head and held true to his promise.

Worshipping her body with his hands and lips, Caleb took her to the crest again and again. But just when she thought she'd find the peace of sweet release, he'd pause just long enough for the tightening inside her to ease a bit, then he'd start all over again.

"I can't take…another second…of this." The tension inside her was so great that it made her feel as if she were coming apart at the seams. "Please…make love to me, Caleb. N-now."

His kiss was so tender it brought tears to her eyes. "Just a minute, sweetheart." He slid open the bedside table to remove a foil packet. "I'm not going to let you down a second time," he said, rolling the condom into place.

With their protection arranged, he took her into his arms, then, nudging her knees apart, held her gaze with his as he moved to cover her. Her pulse thundered in her ears as he slowly, carefully sank himself deep inside her welcoming body.

When he was completely immersed within her, she watched him close his eyes and she knew he was fighting for control. "I think…I've died…and gone to heaven," he said, the strain of his struggle evident in his husky voice.

Tilting her hips, she felt him sink into her a fraction more. "Take me to heaven with you, Caleb," she whispered close to his ear.

His big body shuddered and a groan rumbled up from deep in his chest a moment before he opened his eyes to stare down at her. The hungry need in the hazel depths matched her own and as he eased himself back, then forward, she wrapped her arms around him and joined him in the wondrous dance of love.

Holding her gaze with his, he set a slow pace that tightened the pit of her stomach and made her feel cherished in a way she'd only dreamed of. He must have realized the delicious sensations within her were building to a crescendo because he strengthened his thrusts and Alyssa found herself straining to reach the summit.

She was suddenly there and, as the coil inside her burst free, she cried out his name as she shattered into a million shards of brilliant light. Tightening her arms around him, she tried to absorb him into her very soul as she rode the waves of utter and complete fulfillment. No more than a second later, she felt Caleb tense, then heard him call her name as he found his own release from the storm.

When he collapsed on top of her, she held him close as her heart filled with an emotion like nothing she'd ever felt before. She'd done her best to resist. But in that moment, she knew beyond a shadow of doubt that she'd done the unthinkable. She'd fallen in love with Caleb Walker.

The following Friday afternoon, Caleb sat at his desk tapping his ink pen on the polished surface as he stared off into space. As far as work went, he hadn't been worth a damn all week. All he'd done was sit around with a sappy grin on his face and think about how fantastic the past weekend had been and how totally amazing Alyssa was.

Her response to his touch had been everything a man could ever dream of, and he'd been just as hot for her. They'd spent the entire time making love, falling asleep in each other's arms, then awakening to make love again.

When his lower body tightened, he took a deep breath and willed himself to relax. All he had to do was think about her and he got aroused so fast it made him dizzy.

But his desire to be with her wasn't just physical. Once he'd gotten to know the real woman behind those baggy suits and owlish glasses, he'd found that she was warm, compassionate and had a great sense of humor.

He grunted. How on God's green earth had he ever thought her to be anything like Leslie Ann?

Even if he hadn't checked the personnel records and found her employee evaluations, he would have figured out that Alyssa had used her brains and education to get where she was with Skerritt and Crowe. She'd worked her cute little tail off and hadn't had to step on anyone's toes to get the promotion to operations manager six months ago.

But Leslie Ann had taken the easy way to the top. She'd done anything and everything to climb the corporate ladder. Hell, he could even remember a couple of times when she'd bragged about taking credit for the hard work of those working under her. And her barracuda instincts hadn't stopped there. He had no doubt that she'd have crawled off her deathbed just for the chance to attend a party where she could schmooze with the big boys. Nor was she above kissing a few executive rear ends along the way to get what she wanted.

Disgusted with himself for wasting two years chasing after such a selfish, self-absorbed woman, he shook his head. Leslie Ann had never been, nor would she ever be half the woman Alyssa was. And somewhere between walking into her office that first day and sitting here thinking about their weekend together now, he'd fallen for her.

His heart stalled and he felt like he couldn't breathe. When had Alyssa gotten past his defenses? Why hadn't he seen it coming?

He sat for several long minutes feeling as though he'd just been run over by the Tennessee Titans' entire defensive line. His timing couldn't have been worse. He'd barely taken over running Skerritt and Crowe and he hadn't attended one of his classes at the university, let alone earned a degree.

Propping his elbows on the desk, he buried his head in his hands. Now that he'd found Alyssa, he wasn't about to let her go. But what could he do about the situation? There was no way in hell they could build a relationship unless he came clean and told her who he was and that he didn't have anything more going for him than a high-school education.

He raised his head to stare blindly out the plate-glass window at downtown Albuquerque. He'd boxed himself into one hell of a corner.

How was he going to tell her that he was a fraud, that he wasn't really qualified to run a financial consulting firm? And how would she react when she found out that he was one of Emerald's grandsons?

"Caleb, you have a call on line one." Geneva's voice coming through the intercom broke into his unsettling thoughts.

He depressed the talk button. "Take a message, Geneva."

"It's Mrs. Larson," Geneva said, as if in awe of Emerald.

Great. Just what he needed right now—a conversation with his manipulative grandmother. "Thanks, Geneva. I'll take the call."

Taking a deep breath, he picked up the phone. "Hello, Emerald."

"Caleb, darling, how are you?" Emerald Larson might be at least three-quarters of a century old, but she looked and sounded like a much younger woman.

"I'm tied up with something pretty important right now." At the moment, his newly discovered feelings for Alyssa and trying to figure out what he was going to do about them took top priority. "Could I call you back this evening?"

"Of course. You have the number at the mansion, don't you?"

"It's on speed dial at the house."

"Good. I retire around ten," she added. "I'll expect your call before that."

Before he could say another word, she hung up. "Well, goodbye to you, too," he muttered, replacing the receiver.

He briefly wondered what Emerald wanted, but he quickly dismissed the call when Geneva's voice once again came across the intercom. "Caleb, you're needed in the break room."

"Can't it wait?"

When Geneva failed to answer, he impatiently walked over to open the door to the outer office. The secretary was nowhere in sight.

"Did you just get a page from Geneva to go to the break room?" Alyssa asked, walking out of her office.

He nodded. "Did she tell you what was going on?"

"No." She looked around the deserted office. "Where is everyone?"

Shrugging, he walked over to take her in his arms. "Beats me."

As he gazed down at her, he didn't think he'd ever seen her look more beautiful. Since their weekend together, she'd started wearing her hair down and she'd replaced her baggy dark suits with pastel silk blouses and linen slacks. Today she wore pink and tan and looked so damned lovable she took his breath away.

"Have I told you how incredible you look today?" he asked, kissing the tip of her nose.

Her breathless laughter sent a shaft of longing straight to the region below his belt buckle. "I was thinking the same thing about you."

"We need to talk," he said suddenly. He wasn't sure how she'd react when he told her everything about himself and the reason he'd taken over the firm, but he knew for certain there couldn't be any secrets between them. "Come home with me for the weekend."

"I'm not sure—"

"I am," he said, nodding. "Remember, we're supposed to be planning our wedding. Don't you think we'd be expected to spend our weekends doing just that?"

"My poor parakeet will think I've abandoned him," she said, laying her head against his chest.

He wasn't about to let a bird keep him from being with the most desirable woman he'd ever known. "We'll take him with us."

"Are we going to discuss my ideas for the break room?"

"Among other things," he said, distracted by the feel of her softness.

"There you are," Geneva called from down the hall. She looked extremely flustered. "Please hurry. We need you both in the break room. It's an emergency."

"What's wrong, Geneva?" With Alyssa hot on his heels, Caleb jogged down the hall. But when he entered the room, he stopped dead in his tracks. "What the hell?"

"What's going on?" Alyssa asked, bumping into his back.

"Congratulations!" the entire Skerritt and Crowe staff shouted in unison.

Shocked to see all of the firm's employees crammed into the break room, it took a moment for Caleb to figure out what was going on. He and Alyssa were the guests of honor at a surprise engagement party.

"Oh, my dear heavens." Alyssa's cheeks colored a deep rose and her baby-blue eyes were round with disbelief.

"We wanted you two to know how happy we are for you," Geneva said, dabbing at her eyes with a lacy handkerchief.

Caleb put his arm around Alyssa's shoulders to draw her to his side. "I think I speak for both of us when I say we really didn't expect you all to do this."

"I…we truly don't know what to say," Alyssa added, leaning against him as if her knees were about to buckle.

"Well, I do." Grinning from ear to ear, Malcolm Fuller stepped forward and handed them each a champagne flute. "Since I'm the oldest employee here at Skerritt and Crowe, I have the honor of being the first to toast the happy couple." Clearing his throat, he held his own glass high. "It's with great pleasure that I have the opportunity to celebrate Caleb and Alyssa's happiness. May your engagement be brief and your wedding perfect, and your honeymoon go on for a lifetime." His voice grew gruff. "Congratulations, kids. You make a beautiful couple."

As they listened to several others express their good wishes, Caleb realized that was exactly what he wanted—a long and happy life with Alyssa at his side. He wanted to make love with her every night and wake up with her in his arms each morning for the rest of his life.

When she glanced up and smiled at him, he knew he'd walk through hellfire and back just to make her happy. And if she'd let him, he had every intention of making their pretend engagement real.

Nine

Nine

After a leisurely swim, Alyssa sat between Caleb's legs on a lounge chair by the pool, watching the shadows of evening fade into the dark of night. What were they going to do now? she wondered. The surprise party had been a wonderful gesture and she really appreciated their coworkers' thoughtfulness, but it had also greatly compounded an already complicated situation.

She and Caleb couldn't break off their "engagement" right away. It would look far too suspicious and without a doubt, everyone would know that it had been a sham from the beginning.

Unfortunately, continuing their pretend commitment posed an even bigger problem for her. The more time she spent playing the role of Caleb's loving fiancée, the more she found herself wishing their engagement was real.

"You're mighty silent tonight, sweetheart." Caleb's whispered drawl caused a wave of goose bumps to shimmy over her skin as he pulled her back against him to wrap his arms around her.

She sighed. She wasn't about to tell him the real reason for her pensive mood. "I like watching the shadows cover the valley as the sun goes down."

His low chuckle seemed to vibrate right through her. "Besides the scenery, is there anything else you like about being here?"

"Hmm, I really like the pool," she teased.

He nuzzled the side of her neck. "Anything else?"

She closed her eyes as a wave of need swept over her. "The hot tub…is very…nice."

"Yes, it is," he murmured against her skin. "It's very relaxing." He nibbled her earlobe. "It's really wet." He nipped her shoulder. "It's definitely hot." Slipping the top of her swimsuit down, he covered her bare breasts with his warm palms as he kissed her temple. "And it's a great place to make love."

Her heart thumped her ribs and her breathing grew shallow. "If I remember correctly, that's what you said about the pool, your bed, the sofa in the great room, the—"

He nodded. "Anywhere is a good place to make love with you, sweetheart."

"We proved that last weekend." With his hands caressing her breasts and his growing arousal pressed to her bottom, Alyssa felt as if her insides had been turned to warm pudding. Closing her eyes as her temperature rose, she added, "I think we made love in every room in the house, as well as out here by the pool and in the hot tub."

Shaking his head, he chafed her nipples with the pads of his thumbs. "There's one place we haven't made love." He kissed the nape of her neck, then set her away from him. Rising from the lounge chair, he held out his hand. "And I think it's high time we changed that, don't you?"

Without so much as a moment's hesitation, she placed her hand in his and let him pull her to her feet. As they walked through the French doors to his bedroom, she reminded herself that she should resist temptation, run as hard as she could back to her apartment and protect what was left of her heart.

But when he led her into the master bathroom and turned her to face him, she realized that she didn't have a choice in the matter. Staring up into his intense hazel eyes, she knew it was far too late to save herself. Her heart was no longer her own. It belonged to Caleb, and it had from the moment he'd swaggered into her office the day he'd arrived to take over Skerritt and Crowe.

Smiling, he peeled her damp swimsuit away, then tossed it aside. "Your body is way too beautiful to cover up with clothes."

She grinned. "Even at work?"

As he lightly slid his hands from the swell of her breasts down to her hips, the wicked gleam in his eyes stole her breath. "I don't share. Seeing you this way is for my eyes only, sweetheart."

"That street goes both ways," she said, tugging his wet gym shorts from his lean hips. "I love the way your body looks, too. But I wouldn't want any other women appreciating it the way I do."

He took her into his arms as he lowered his head. "Only for you, Alyssa. Only you."

He fused his mouth with hers then, and the promise in his gentle kiss, the feel of his muscular body surrounding hers caused her pulse to race and stars to dance behind her closed eyes. The warmth of need that she only experienced in Caleb's arms flowed through her—heating her blood, filling her with passion so strong it made her weak in the knees.

His arms tightened around her as he slipped his tongue inside to entice her with the taste of his hunger, and a fluttering swirl of desire began to form in the very core of her. But when he ran his hands down her back to cup her bottom and lift her closer, the feel of his hard arousal pressed to her lower belly caused an answering tightness deep within her and a delicious ache to commence in all of her feminine places.

Lost in the sensations he'd created inside her, she vaguely realized that he was moving them into the large tiled shower, closing the door and turning on the water. He tightened his arms around her once again to pull her to him and the feel of his wet skin against hers sent ribbons of excitement twining to the most interesting places.

Sliding his hands along her sides, then back up to cup the heaviness he'd created in her breasts, he lowered his head to sip the trickling water from her aching nipples. He teased first one hardened tip, then the other and by the time he raised his head to kiss her, she tingled all over.

Caleb's gaze held her spellbound as he reached for the soap, then ran it over her shoulders, her breasts and down her abdomen. His slick hands touched her everywhere, sliding over her skin, sending tiny sparks of electricity skipping over every nerve in her body and it took all of her concentration just to remember to breathe.

Determined to treat him to the same sensual massage, she smiled as she took the soap from him. Lathering her trembling hands, she smoothed them over his wide chest, rippling stomach and lean flanks. She wanted to give to him as he'd given to her and, taking him in her palms, she slid her fingers along his taut skin, measured his length and the strength of his need for her.

He closed his eyes and a deep groan of pleasure escaped his parted lips. "Sweetheart, if I die right now, I'll leave this world a happy man."

"But I don't want you to be just happy," she said, wondering if she had the nerve to take her exploration to the next level. "Open your eyes, Caleb." When he did as she commanded, she waited until the water had rinsed away the last traces of soap. "I want you to be fulfilled."

Caleb's heart stalled and he didn't think he'd ever breathe again as he watched Alyssa sink to her knees in front of him. "Sweetheart, you don't have to—"

At the feel of her sweet lips on his heated body, he stopped abruptly and clenched his teeth together so hard he'd probably end up with a broken jaw. Her intimate kiss was sending liquid fire streaking though his veins at the speed of light and he wasn't altogether sure how much longer his legs were going to support him.

Placing his hands on her shoulders, he lifted her to her feet. "If you keep that up much longer, fulfillment won't be an issue."

She smiled. "You don't like what I was doing?"

"I didn't say that." He drew some much-needed air into his lungs and shook his head. "The problem is, I like it too much. But I want both of us to be there for the grand finale. And I fully intend to be inside you when that happens."

He lowered his head to swirl his tongue around one beaded nipple, while he chafed the other one with his thumb. Teasing her with his teeth, then sucking the tight tip into his mouth, he slid his hand down between them to find the sensitive nub at the apex of her thighs. She trembled against him as he gently stroked her and he decided that he'd like nothing better than to spend the rest of his life bringing her pleasure.

By the time he raised his head to gaze at her beautiful face, her porcelain cheeks were painted with the rosy glow of passion and her baby-blue eyes sparkled with deep longing. Her heightened excitement fueled his own and Caleb suddenly needed to possess her body and soul.

"Do you want me, Alyssa?"

"Yes."

"Now?"

"Yes."

Somehow he found the strength to step back and momentarily leave the shower. When he returned with their protection in place, he turned her away from him, then wrapped his arms around her and pulled her back against his chest.

"Caleb?" Her uncertainty was evident in the tone of her voice.

"Do you trust me, Alyssa?" When she nodded, he kissed her shoulder. "I'm going to caress your body while I make love to you."

He supported her weight as he lifted her to him and in one smooth motion entered her from behind. Her soft moan of pleasure mingling with his deep groan sent waves of hot, urgent desire coursing from the top of his head all the way to the soles of his feet and he had to struggle to retain what little control he had left.

The feel of her holding him deep inside, her inner muscles clinging to him as she adjusted to his size almost sent him over the edge. But, determined to ensure her pleasure above his own, he covered her breasts with his hands then, kissing her shoulder and the slender column of her neck, slowly began to rock against her.

Their water-slick bodies moving in perfect unison caused the pulse in his ears to roar and, wanting her to find the same release that was rapidly overtaking him, he slid his hand down to touch her intimately. Stroking her with a rhythm that matched the movement of their bodies, he felt her inner muscles constrict, then gently caress him as she found the culmination they both sought. Her release triggered his own and, holding her to him, he shuddered as he followed her over the edge and gave up his essence to the woman he loved.

When his mind began to clear, Caleb carefully lowered Alyssa to the tiled floor, then turned her to face him. Even with her hair hanging wet and limp around her shoulders, she was the most beautiful woman he'd ever had the privilege to lay eyes on and he had every intention of making her his—permanently.

But he couldn't do that until he'd told her everything—who he was, why he'd been sent to run the financial firm and that he lacked the credentials to do the job right. He just hoped liked hell she'd forgive him for not telling her about himself from the beginning.

"We need to talk, sweetheart."

Wrapping her arms around his waist, she grinned. "Here?"

He smiled as he shook his head. Standing buck naked in the shower wasn't exactly the best place for the kind of confessions he'd be making. "Let's dry off and get in bed."

"I like the sound of that."

Taking her by the hand, he pulled her out of the shower. "I'm going to make sure you like doing it even more."

The next morning, when Alyssa woke to the sound of Caleb warbling an off-key version of a popular country song, she couldn't keep from smiling. She found his habit of singing while he showered quite endearing. But in the few short weeks they'd known each other, she'd come to realize there wasn't anything about him that she didn't find completely irresistible.

He was outgoing and compassionate and when they made love, he never failed to ensure her pleasure before finding his own. And even though she'd had serious doubts about him taking over Skerritt and Crowe, she had to admit he was an absolute genius in his approach to management. Since his arrival, employee morale had been greatly improved, productivity was on the rise and they'd signed several new clients.

But as she lay there thinking about all the reasons she'd fallen in love with him, she couldn't help but wonder what he wanted to discuss with her. He'd mentioned before the party, then again in the shower last night that they needed to talk. But when they'd toweled each other dry, their insatiable hunger had taken over and, after making love again, they'd immediately fallen asleep.

Had he decided their role-playing posed too great a threat to his peace of mind? Was he wanting to discuss how they were going to handle breaking off their pretend engagement?

Her stomach clenched painfully at the thought of never being held in his strong arms, of never tasting his need for her in his tender kiss. She'd given her heart to him, but she had no idea how he felt about her.

Deciding that she had a few questions of her own that needed to be answered, she tossed the covers aside and got out of bed. She grabbed his shirt from one of the chairs and quickly pulled it on. Sleeping with him in the nude was wonderful, but they needed to talk without being distracted again.

She got halfway across the room, but the ringing phone stopped her. Glancing at the clock, she wondered who on earth would be calling this early on a Saturday morning. She frowned when she read the words *No Data* on the caller ID.

As she stood there wondering if she should let the machine pick up the call, Caleb stopped singing. "Could you get that, Alyssa?"

"Sure." She picked up on the third ring. "Hello?"

There was a moment of silence, then a commanding female voice demanded, "Who am I speaking with?"

Alyssa frowned at the censure in the older woman's voice. "Who are you wanting?"

"My grandson, Caleb Walker. Is he there?"

"He's unavailable at the moment. Could I take a message?"

"Is this Ms. Merrick?" the woman asked, suddenly sounding much more pleasant.

"Yes, it is." How on earth had the woman known who she was?

"Emerald Larson here. I thought I recognized your voice. How have you been? I don't think we've had a chance to talk since I called to let you know Caleb would be taking over the firm."

Alyssa felt as if her stomach had dropped to her feet. Emerald Larson, one of the most successful business-women ever and the first female to break into the Fortune 500 top ten, was Caleb's grandmother?

"I must thank you for everything you've done for Caleb, my dear. I've heard the two of you make a great team," the woman went on. "Considering Caleb's lack of education, making the transition from simple country farm boy to running a financial firm the size of Skerritt and Crowe was a major challenge. But I'm not surprised that he's been successful. He has the Larson genes, after all."

"Of course," Alyssa said, feeling more sick inside than she'd ever felt in her life.

"I'm sure that once he gets a few college courses

under his belt, he won't have to rely so heavily on you to run things. But rest assured, my dear, I'll see that you're well compensated for your efforts."

Alyssa had to get off the phone before her fragile composure shattered into a million pieces. She'd done it again. She'd fallen for a man who only wanted to use her to accomplish his goal. The only difference this time was that she'd fallen hopelessly in love with Caleb.

"I really need to go, Mrs. Larson. I'll tell Caleb to call you."

Before the woman could respond, Alyssa broke the connection. When she looked up, Caleb was walking through the bathroom door as he secured a towel around his waist.

"Who was that?"

"Your grandmother." Walking over to place the cordless phone in his hand, she fought to keep her voice even as she looked into his incredible hazel eyes. "Emerald Larson. She wants you to call her."

When he reached for her, Alyssa successfully side-stepped his touch. "Please, don't."

His expression stoic, he took a step toward her. "Let me explain, Alyssa."

"I think your grandmother explained things quite clearly. You've been using me to keep the firm running while you played at being the successful businessman." A sudden rush of emotion threatened to choke her and she had to take a deep breath before she could finish.

"You know, I never paid much attention to the tabloid headlines about Owen Larson and his nefarious escapades." She laughed humorlessly. "I should have. Maybe I'd have recognized the same traits in his son and avoided making a fool of myself."

"Alyssa—"

Shaking her head, she impatiently wiped a tear from her cheek. "I can only imagine how pathetically desperate for a man I must have appeared to you. The frumpy numbers cruncher whose entire life revolved around her job." Straightening her shoulders, she drew on a lifetime of being taught to face the enemy with courage and grace. "But that no longer matters. Please tell your grandmother that I don't want, nor do I need, the compensation she mentioned."

His scowl deepened. "Compensation?"

"I'm certain she was unaware that you had devised your own way of appeasing me."

He shook his head as he quickly stepped forward to place his hands on her shoulders. "It's not like that, sweetheart."

"Don't call me that." Jerking from his grasp, her shaky voice rose considerably as she fought to keep her emotions in check. "Don't ever call me that again."

"Dammit, Alyssa, listen to me."

"Why should I? You haven't been honest with me thus far, why should I believe you now?"

"You have to calm down and see reason."

Struggling to keep the torrent of tears in check just a few moments longer, she glared at him. "I don't *have* to do anything but leave, Mr. Walker. And that's exactly what I intend to do."

Her legs felt as if they might not support her as she walked over to pick up the small overnight case she'd packed when they'd stopped by her apartment the evening before. Heading down the hall, she stopped at the first bedroom she came to, quickly changed out of his shirt and into her own clothes, then called a cab.

When she walked out into the hall, Caleb was waiting for her. He'd changed into a chambray shirt, worn jeans and scuffed boots.

If he thought reverting to his good-old-boy persona would make a difference, he was sadly mistaken. "Excuse me," she said, starting to walk past him. "I'll wait outside for my ride."

He stood stock still. "I'll drive you back to Albuquerque."

"No, you won't."

Folding his arms across his wide chest, he looked dubious. "Then how do you expect to get back home?"

"If I have to, I'll walk." She brushed past him. "But that's no longer any of your concern, Mr. Walker."

"Don't be so damned stubborn that you do something foolish," he said, following her down the hall to the front door.

When she turned on him, her body trembled with a

combination of anger and emotional pain. "We've already established that I cornered the market on foolishness."

Opening the door, she walked out and slammed it behind her. As she hurried down the driveway, she remembered that she'd left Sidney's cage in the family room. But she couldn't go back for the parakeet. She'd have to call later and request that Caleb bring the bird to the office.

Right now, she needed to put as much distance as she could between herself and Caleb. If she went back, he'd realize that she'd fallen hopelessly in love with him. And that was something she'd rather die than have him do.

Caleb stood watch until Alyssa got into the cab, then, turning away from the window, he walked out onto the patio. Everything inside him shouted for him to go after her, to bring her back and make her listen to reason, to convince her to hear what he had to say. But she was hurting right now and just knowing that he was the cause of it tied him in knots.

He'd had every intention of telling Alyssa about himself last night. But when they'd gone into the bedroom, he'd been so hot for her again that they'd made love until they'd both fallen asleep from complete exhaustion. Then he'd planned as soon as he finished his shower to serve her breakfast in bed, tell her everything, then ask her to make their engagement real.

But, Emerald had beaten him to it. That complicated

matters greatly, but it didn't mean he was ready to throw in the towel.

Alyssa needed time to calm down. And he needed time to make a few plans.

If there was one thing he'd inherited from his paternal grandmother, it was her determination. The old gal hadn't gotten where she was today without it and he fully intended to use her legacy to win back the only woman he'd ever love.

Ten

Alyssa sniffed back a fresh wave of tears as she sat on her couch, staring at her apartment walls. She'd expected Caleb to call on Monday after finding her resignation on his desk, along with a request that he leave Sidney in Geneva's care. But by close of business Wednesday, she realized that he didn't care about her leaving Skerritt and Crowe. And it was apparent he didn't intend to return her bird.

"The least he could have done was give Sidney back to me," she muttered miserably.

When the doorbell rang, she sighed. It was probably Mrs. Rogers again. The older woman had been sweeping her walk Saturday morning when Alyssa had gotten out of the cab and, taking one look at Alyssa's red-rimmed eyes, the woman had decided to lend moral support. She'd been over at least twice a day since, and today it appeared that she was going to make it three times.

Getting up from the couch, she walked over to open the door. "I'm fine, Mrs.—" She stopped abruptly. "You aren't Mrs. Rogers."

The red-haired, freckle-faced young man in a white courier's uniform grinned and shook his head. "Afraid not." He glanced at the clipboard in his hand. "Are you Ms. Alyssa Jane Merrick?"

"Yes."

"I have an express for you," he said, handing her an envelope marked Urgent. "Could you please sign on line twenty-four?"

Signing where the young man indicated, she started to thank him, but he was already halfway back to his delivery truck. When he squealed the tires as he pulled away from the curb, she decided that he took the company's claim of being the speediest delivery service in the world a little too seriously.

As she closed the door, she glanced at the return address. Who on earth did she know in Wichita, Kansas?

Her heart suddenly stopped, then started hammering at her throat. Emerald, Inc.'s headquarters were in Wichita.

Her hands shook as Alyssa pulled the tab to open the thin cardboard packet. If Emerald Larson had sent anything but a final paycheck, she'd get it back so fast she'd wonder if it had ever left her office.

But when Alyssa pulled the papers out of the envelope and thumbed through them, her mouth fell open. It was her letter of resignation, along with a handwritten note from Emerald Larson, herself.

Dearest Alyssa,

In order for your resignation as operations manager of Skerritt and Crowe Financial Consultants to be effective, you'll need to deliver it to me in person. I've arranged for a car to pick you up at your apartment tomorrow morning at eight. Please be prompt. The corporate jet will be waiting to fly you to Wichita, then return you to Albuquerque later in the day.

Yours truly,

Emerald Larson

Suddenly feeling as if her knees were made of jelly, Alyssa sat on the couch to stare at the letter. She'd never heard of anyone having to hand deliver their resignation. Why would the woman do that? Was it even legal for Emerald Larson to require that of her?

Alyssa wasn't sure. But she'd go to Wichita if that was what it took to divorce herself from Skerritt and Crowe, Emerald, Inc. and the fiasco with Caleb. Then she'd spend the rest of her life trying to forget the only man she would ever love.

"Who's your mole at Skerritt and Crowe, Emerald?" Caleb sat in the executive office of Emerald, Inc., staring across the French provincial desk at his indomitable grandmother. "And don't tell me you don't know what I'm talking about. You had to have someone at the firm feeding you information. Otherwise, you wouldn't have mentioned that Alyssa and I make a good team."

To her credit, she didn't even try to pretend that she didn't know what he was talking about. "Does it matter, darling?"

"Yes, it does." He wasn't about to let her get away with playing her little mind games. "You told me, Hunter and Nick that we'd have free reign in managing the companies you gave us—*without* your interference."

"I haven't interfered with the way you're running the financial firm." She smiled. "I just wanted to keep track of how you're doing, that's all."

"Did it ever occur to you to ask me?"

She patted a platinum hair back into place. "I wanted an unbiased opinion."

Caleb sat forward. "Let me assure you. If I'm about to land on my ass, I'll let you know so you can send in one of your ace managers to clean up the mess before it's too late. I'm not about to let the employees at Skerritt and Crowe pay the price for my screwups. They're good people and I don't want to see them hurt by your little experiment."

Instead of being offended by his statement, the old gal looked as pleased as punch. "All right."

"And I'll tell you something else." If she thought he was finished, she was sadly mistaken. "If I find out you're playing any more of your little games with me or the firm, I'm out. I'll go back to Tennessee and you can forget offering me any more of your sweet deals because I'll turn them down flat."

To his surprise, she grinned. "I would expect no less from a grandson of mine." She glanced at the diamond-encrusted watch on her left wrist. "Alyssa should be arriving in just a few moments. Are you sure you don't want me to stay? I might be able to clarify the facts about your father."

He shook his head. "You're getting her here was enough. I'll handle it from here on out."

She stood up and walked toward the door. "If you need me—"

"I won't." Too keyed up to remain seated, he rose to his feet. If he had any chance of a future with Alyssa, he had to be completely honest with her. And the information about himself would have to come from him, not his rich-as-sin grandmother. "I got myself into this. I'll get myself out."

Emerald nodded approvingly. "I hope your young

woman realizes what a good man you are, Caleb. Best of luck, son."

Caleb stared at her for several long moments. There was a sincerity in her voice that he hadn't expected. "Thank you…Grandmother."

When Alyssa stepped off the elevator on the sixth floor of Emerald Towers, a distinguished-looking gentleman of about fifty was waiting for her. "Ms. Merrick, please follow me. I'm Mrs. Larson's personal assistant, Luther Freemont. I've been instructed to take you directly to her private office."

As she followed the man down a long hall, Alyssa clutched the folder containing her resignation. She wasn't nervous, but she was eager to get her meeting with Emerald Larson over with. Once she'd done that, she could work on rebuilding her life.

Mr. Freemont stopped in front of a set of tall, ornately carved mahogany doors. Holding one of them open for her, he stepped back. "I hope your meeting turns out to everyone's satisfaction, Ms. Merrick."

"Thank you."

Why would the man tell her something like that? Was Mrs. Larson going to try to talk her out of resigning?

If so, the woman was in for a disappointment. There was no way Alyssa could continue working at the firm as long as Caleb was there.

But when she walked into the office, her heart felt as

if it had dropped to the floor. Instead of finding Emerald Larson in the plush executive office, she saw Caleb looking out the plate-glass window.

When he turned to face her, he looked so devastatingly handsome that her breath caught and a shaft of longing went straight to her soul. His low-slung jeans emphasized his lean waist and muscular thighs, while the knit fabric of his navy polo shirt drew attention to the well-developed muscles of his upper body, reminding her of how strong he was, how easily he'd held her when they'd made love in the shower. His light brown hair was slightly mussed as if he'd recently run his hand through it, but it only added to his appeal.

"Good morning, Alyssa."

"Where's Mrs. Larson?"

He shrugged. "I suppose she's around the offices here somewhere."

His smile and the sound of his deep Southern drawl caused a wave of emotion so strong it threatened to bend her double, to sweep through her. She turned to leave. "I can't do this," she whispered.

"Wait, Alyssa." He quickly crossed the room to take hold of her upper arms. "Please, I need for you to hear what I have to say. Then, if you still want to resign, I promise I won't try to stop you."

"Is this the only way you'll accept my resignation?" she asked, already knowing his answer.

"I'm afraid so, sweetheart." He turned her to face

him, then stepped back and motioned toward a sitting area by the doors. "Have a seat."

"I'd rather not."

"This may take a while."

She shook her head. "Caleb, I don't really think there's any point in—"

He folded his arms over his wide chest. "I do."

Suddenly feeling completely defeated, she walked over to sit down on the edge of one of the overstuffed armchairs. She stared at the folder on her lap. "Please make this quick."

He was silent for a moment and she could tell he was waiting for her to look at him. But she couldn't. If she did, she knew without question she'd fall apart.

"Everything I told you about myself is true, Alyssa," he said quietly. "I grew up on a farm in central Tennessee and I have two brothers—Hunter O'Banyon and Nick Daniels." He hesitated as if he didn't like what he had to say next. "I've never lied to you. But I am guilty of omitting a few facts."

"B-but you did lie to me," she said, hating that her voice shook with emotion. She looked at him directly. "You told me you went to the University of Tennessee."

He smiled sadly and shook his head. "I said there was no other team like the UT Vols. I never said I attended classes there."

"But you knew what I'd think."

Nodding, he ran his hand over the back of his neck.

"I'm not proud of that. But it was easier to let you draw your own conclusions than it was to admit that I have nothing more than a high-school education."

His expression grim, he sat on the end of the coffee table in front of her. When she noticed their knees were almost touching, she scooted back in the chair. If he touched her in any way, she feared she'd lose the tenuous hold she had on her feelings.

She watched him prop his forearms on his thighs and stare down at his loosely clasped hands. "I had an academic scholarship to go to UT at Knoxville, but I had to turn it down. Grandpa got sick that summer and I was needed at home to keep the farm going. Then later on, it was a matter of economics."

There was deep regret in his tone and she could tell that his lack of a postsecondary education bothered him a lot. "There's still time to get your degree."

He shrugged. "I'm enrolled in night classes for the fall semester."

She frowned. Something didn't add up. "Now, hold it. Emerald Larson is your grandmother. Why couldn't she have helped you out with school?"

"It wasn't until last month that my brothers and I learned about each other and that we're the product of the late Owen Larson sowing his wild oats." He laughed humorlessly. "Until then, we didn't have a clue who our father was or that we were related to one of the richest women in the world."

"You're kidding."

"I wish I was joking," he said, shaking his head. "But unfortunately, I'm not."

She couldn't begin to imagine what a shock that must have been for the three men. "How did you find out?"

"Luther Freemont showed up at the farm one day to tell me that I was needed in Wichita." He looked as if he still had trouble believing it himself. "When I asked him who was making the request and why, he said he wasn't at liberty to tell me. So, I told him to go to hell and went back to working on my tractor."

"I take it he didn't give up?"

Caleb shook his head. "My mom stepped in and told me that it was time to learn about my father and that she wanted me to go."

"I don't understand," Alyssa said, wondering why it had been such a big secret. All things considered, she shouldn't care. But she could see that he'd been deeply affected by what had taken place and she couldn't stop herself from asking, "Why hadn't she told you who your father was?"

"That's where it gets complicated." Taking a deep breath, he added, "Emerald Larson knew about all of us, practically from the moment we were conceived. But she didn't want us turning out like her son—our father."

"So she didn't acknowledge any of you until recently?" Alyssa couldn't understand how Emerald Larson could live in the lap of luxury while denying her grandsons the opportunities that would have made their lives easier.

He shook his head. "She told us that she knew she'd made a lot of mistakes when she gave Owen everything he wanted, instead of giving him the time and attention he needed from her. She said she also knew that we'd have a better chance of turning out to be decent men if our lifestyle was more down-to-earth and we were raised by mothers who taught us the values that she'd failed to teach Owen." He smiled. "As crazy as it sounds, Emerald was actually trying to protect us."

Alyssa thought about it for a moment. "I guess, in a strange way, that makes sense." She shook her head. "But it doesn't explain why your mother failed to tell you about your father."

His expression turned dark. "I'm still having a problem with this part of the whole sordid mess. Mom worked at one of the luxury hotels in Nashville. She was a young, naive country girl and Owen swept her off her feet. Then after he left town, Emerald contacted Mom through a private investigator while she was pregnant and arranged to support us with a modest monthly allowance. The only requirement was that Mom couldn't tell anyone—including me—who my father was. Emerald even went so far as to have Mom sign a legal agreement stating that if she divulged who had gotten her pregnant that I would be cut out of inheriting any part of Emerald, Inc. and the Larson fortune. She did the same thing with Hunter's and Nick's mothers."

Alyssa could understand Mrs. Larson's not wanting the boys to turn out like their father. No one in their right mind would want to see a child grow up to be a hedonistic, irresponsible adult, which she'd heard Owen Larson had been before the boating accident that had claimed his life six months ago. But what Caleb was describing that Emerald Larson had required of the women sounded suspiciously like blackmail.

"And in all that time, your mother never told anyone who your father was?"

His intense gaze met hers. "No. She felt that she was ensuring a better future for me than she could ever give me on her own."

Alyssa couldn't help but be a bit envious. Her mother had loved and doted on her when she'd been alive, but after her death, Alyssa hadn't felt that she'd been loved by anyone.

They remained silent for several long moments before he took a deep breath. "When we all arrived in Wichita and Emerald explained about our father and that she was going to give each of us one of her companies to run, I fully intended to turn her down because I didn't feel qualified to run a place like Skerritt and Crowe."

"What changed your mind?"

"I thought about my mom's dream of giving me a better life and I knew I had to give it a try." He shrugged.

"So I started reading books on management and went on the Internet to search for everything I could about creating a better work atmosphere and unity among the workers. Then I remembered seeing a report on one of the news shows a year or so back about companies using innovative ways to keep employees motivated. I bought a couple of books, did a little more research on the computer and the changes I've made at Skerritt and Crowe are the result."

"It worked." Her conscience wouldn't allow her to say otherwise. "Everyone at the firm is a lot happier than they were under the old management."

He shrugged. "I also figured if I made it a nice place to work, left everyone alone to do their jobs and let you make the business decisions, I'd be okay until I could take some administrative courses and get an idea of what I was really supposed to be doing."

His admission caused her chest to tighten and she wasn't sure she'd be able to draw her next breath. Thinking he'd been using her was one thing, but hearing him put it into words hurt more than she could have ever imagined.

"I—I really need…to go." She quickly stood up and shoved the file containing her resignation into his hands. If she didn't get out of there soon the floodgates were going to open. "G-good luck with…the firm."

Rising to his feet, he tossed the folder to the floor and pulled her into his arms. "I haven't told you the most important detail of all, Alyssa."

He cradled her close and the feel of his strong arms folded around her, the wide expanse of his chest pillowing her head, and the tender way he stroked her hair caused her heart to break even more. Just knowing that once she walked out the door she'd never again be held by him or know the softness of his kiss was almost more than she could bear.

"C-Caleb, p-please—"

"Don't cry, sweetheart. It tears me apart to see you cry." His chest rose and fell beneath her ear as he took a deep shuddering breath. "Do you want to know what happened when I arrived at Skerritt and Crowe?"

"N-no."

"I fell in love with a beautiful, intelligent woman who tried to hide how wonderful she is behind baggy suits and oversize glasses." Leaning back, he cupped her face with his large hands and the sincerity she saw in his incredible hazel gaze caused her heart to skip several beats. "Yes, I let you call the shots at the firm. But I never used you. I never took credit for anything."

As she stared up at him, she realized that what he'd said was true. The main reason everyone at Skerritt and Crowe was so happy was the fact that Caleb left them alone to do their jobs and didn't try to micromanage their every move.

"I—I'm sorry that I jumped to conclusions." She took a deep, steadying breath. It was suddenly important that he understand why she'd refused to listen to him that morning, how she'd let fear blind her to the facts. "Before I came to work at the firm, I made a huge mistake by getting involved with a coworker who used our relationship to gain information about a client I had been hoping to sign. He took all the credit for the research and winning the account, then got a promotion for all of *his* hard work."

"The jerk should be shot for doing that to you." Caleb shook his head. "No wonder you thought I'd been using you to make myself look good."

"I suppose in a way, I was looking for it to happen." Her voice caught. "I guess I expected for you to hurt me the same way he had."

His intense gaze held hers. "Do you still feel that way, Alyssa?"

"No." Caleb may have omitted a couple of important facts, but he had told her as much as he could about himself without revealing who his grandmother was and that he didn't have the credentials to run Skerritt and Crowe.

Caleb kissed her temple. "I love you, Alyssa Jane Merrick. Never doubt that. And I'd never do anything to hurt you, sweetheart."

"I know that now." Her eyes filled with moisture, but this time they were tears of joy. "I...love you, too, Caleb. So very much."

He crushed her to him, kissing her until they both gasped for breath. "I want to spend the rest of my life proving to you just how much you mean to me, sweetheart." Stepping back, he pulled a small velvet box from his jeans pocket and removed a diamond-and-sapphire ring from inside. Then, dropping to one knee, he took her left hand in his. "Alyssa, will you marry me?"

Her heart filled with so much love it felt as if it would burst. "Yes."

Slipping the ring on her finger, he rose to take her into his arms. "I intend to spend the rest of my life making sure you never regret becoming my wife, sweetheart."

She wrapped her arms around his waist. "I could never regret marrying the only man I'll ever love."

"God, I missed you," he said, kissing her eyes, her cheeks and the tip of her nose. "And I wasn't the only one."

"I missed you, too." She leaned back to look at him. "What do you mean you weren't the only one?"

Caleb laughed. "Sidney missed you, too."

Grinning, she asked, "Why didn't you return him?"

His sexy grin caused her stomach to flutter. "I had every intention of holding him hostage for as long as it took to get you to say yes."

"There was no way I would have said otherwise." She glanced at the ring on the third finger of her left hand. "How did you know what size of ring I wear?"

He shook his head. "I don't know how Emerald does it, but after I picked out the ring I wanted to give you, she told me she'd take care of having it sized."

"But we'd only spoken on the phone, she's never met me. How did she know?"

"I'm not sure, but she has her ways. Now, let's introduce the two of you, then head for the airport." He took her hand in his and led her to the door. "We have something waiting for us back at my house."

"And what would that be?"

Caleb's sexy grin sent waves of heat coursing through every cell in her body. "A hot tub."

"I like the way you think." Raising up on tiptoe, she kissed his lean cheek. "I love you with all my heart, Caleb Walker."

His tender smile lit the darkest corners of her soul. "I love you, too, Alyssa Jane Merrick. Now, let's go home and I'll get started on that lifetime promise of showing you just how much."

Epilogue

"How much longer?" Caleb asked, walking over to gaze out the farmhouse window.

"I swear to God if you don't stop pacing, Hunter and I are going to tie you down," Nick said, laughing.

Hunter checked his watch. "You have approximately fifteen minutes of freedom left, bro." Grinning, he slapped Caleb on the shoulder. "There's still time to make a run for it."

Caleb shook his head. "No way. Alyssa's everything I've ever wanted."

"You're one lucky son of a gun," Nick said, smiling. "She's a great girl."

"Nick and I both wish you the best," Hunter added

as they headed for the door. "When is she taking over the reins at the financial firm?"

"Right after we get back from our honeymoon in the Bahamas." Caleb led the way toward the meadow down by the creek. "Our plan is for her to keep things going until I get my business degree, then we'll run it together."

"And Emerald is okay with that?" Nick asked, looking doubtful.

"She's the one who suggested it," Caleb said, taking his place beside the preacher from the local Methodist church.

As he gazed over the small crowd seated in white folding chairs under the shade of the oak tree he'd climbed as a boy, he noticed that several of the Skerritt and Crowe employees had made the trip from New Mexico to Tennessee for the wedding. His smile widened when his gaze drifted to his mother and grandmothers. On opposite sides of the aisle, they were chatting congenially. All things considered, he'd have never believed it was possible, but his mother, his grandma Walker and Emerald had become fairly good friends.

His heart swelled with love for the women in his life. When he'd brought Alyssa home to meet his mother and grandmother, they'd immediately accepted her as the daughter and granddaughter they'd never had. Then, to his surprise, his mother had called Emerald and the four of them had had a grand old time planning the wedding together.

But when the string quartet that Emerald had insisted on hiring started playing "Here Comes the Bride" and the crowd rose to their feet, Caleb turned his attention to the woman being escorted down the aisle by Malcolm Fuller. Alyssa was dressed in a long, white, satin-and-lace wedding gown, and he'd never seen her look more beautiful. Her gaze never wavered from his and, when Malcolm put her hand in Caleb's, her radiant smile lit the darkest corners of his soul.

"I love you, sweetheart. Are you ready to become Mrs. Walker?"

"I've been waiting for this moment my entire life," she whispered.

"They make a very striking couple," Emerald murmured, watching Caleb raise Alyssa's veil.

"Quite," Luther Freemont agreed.

As she watched her handsome grandson kiss his lovely bride, Emerald smiled. She'd been right to pair Caleb with Alyssa. From the first time she'd spoken on the phone with the young woman, Emerald had been impressed with her intelligence and business acumen. Then, after a discreet check into Alyssa's background, she'd instinctively known each was exactly what the other needed. Caleb was a natural-born leader and Alyssa a sensitive intellect. They were a perfect match and together they would be a major force to contend with in the financial world, not to mention producing beautiful, intelligent heirs.

Extremely pleased with the results of her first endeavor, she turned her attention to her other two grandsons. Hunter and Nick were going to be a challenge. Both of them had pasts that would have to be overcome before they could find their happiness.

But she wasn't worried. She and Luther had done their research and had put their plans into action. In the months to come, she fully expected everything to turn out to her satisfaction with Hunter and Nick as well.

When Caleb and Alyssa walked down the aisle as husband and wife, Emerald turned to Luther with a smug smile. "One down and two to go."

* * * * *

REUNION
OF REVENGE

BY
KATHIE DeNOSKY

For Charlie, Bryan, David and Angie,
for loving me in spite of my eccentricities.

From the desk of Emerald Larson, owner and CEO of Emerald, Inc.

> To: My personal assistant, Luther Freemont
> Re: My grandson Nick Daniels
>
> My grandson, Nick, will be leaving at the end of the week to take over running the Sugar Creek Cattle Company in Wyoming. Please be advised that he won't be particularly happy when he discovers that his ranch foreman is the woman he was to have married thirteen years ago. To ensure the success of my plan and to avoid the fallout of his displeasure, I am instructing you to intercept all calls from him until further notice.
>
> As always I am relying on your complete discretion in this matter.
>
> *Emerald Larson*

One

"**D**rop that roll of wire and back away from your truck."

Nick Daniels took a deep breath and tried to ignore the jolt of awareness that shot from the top of his head all the way to his feet. It had been thirteen long years since he'd heard that soft, feminine voice. But if he lived to be a hundred, he knew he'd recognize it anywhere, anytime. The melodic sound had haunted his dreams and left his body aching with unfathomable need too many nights for him to ever forget.

"I told you to put that down and step away from the truck."

At the sound of a shotgun being pumped, Nick slowly lowered the coil of barbed wire to the tailgate of his new truck and raised his gloved hands to show he was complying with her command. Then, turning to face the reason he'd left Wyoming one step ahead of the law, he smiled sardonically. "It's been a long time, Cheyenne."

The widening of her eyes and the slight wavering of the double-barrel shotgun she pointed at him were the only indications that she was the least bit surprised to see him after all this time. "I don't know what you think you're doing out here, Nick Daniels, but I'd advise you to get in your truck and go back to wherever you came from. Otherwise, I'll call the law."

He took a deep breath as he stared at her. Damned if she wasn't more beautiful now than she'd been at sixteen. Her long brown hair, streaked with golden highlights, complemented the healthy glow of her sun-kissed skin and her aqua-green eyes to perfection.

His gaze drifted lower. Her pink tank top caressed her torso, fascinating the hell out of him and giving him more than a fair idea about the size and shape of her breasts. He swallowed hard as his gaze drifted even lower. She'd always been a knockout in a pair of jeans, but the well-worn denim hugged her hips and thighs like a second skin and emphasized how long and shapely her legs were.

He diverted his gaze back to the gun in her hands. He'd do well to forget how good she looked after all this time and concentrate on the fact that she was ready to blow his ass to kingdom come.

"Go ahead and call the sheriff. Last time I heard, it wasn't against the law for a man to mend a fence on his own property."

"It's not your land. It belongs to the Sugar Creek Cattle Company. And you're trespassing."

He shook his head as he took a step toward her. "No, I'm not."

"I swear I'll shoot you if you don't stop right there, Nick."

"That wouldn't be very neighborly of you, sweetheart."

"Don't call me that." She released the safety on the shotgun when he moved forward.

From the sharp edge he'd heard in her voice, he knew he'd hit a nerve. He inched a little closer. "You used to like when I called you sweetheart."

She shook her head. "That's past history. Now, get in your truck and disappear like you did thirteen years ago."

"Why would I want to do that? This is my home." With the gun barrel still pointed at the middle of his

chest, he wisely chose not to point out that her father
had been behind his disappearing act back then, or
that he was damned tired of a Holbrook trying to run
him off his own land. "If you'll remember, the Sugar
Creek ranch has been in my family for over a hundred and twenty-five years."

"If *you'll* remember, you gave up the right to this
land a long time ago." Was that bitterness he detected
in her voice?

"That's where you're wrong, Cheyenne." Easing
forward a bit more, he was almost close enough to
reach the shotgun. "I still own this place, lock,
stock…" He lunged forward and, grabbing the shotgun, shoved it away with one hand at the same time
he reached out to wrap his arm around her waist.
"…and barrel," he finished, pulling her to him.

"Turn me loose." She pushed at his chest as she
tried to wiggle from his grasp.

"Not until we get a few things straight." The feel
of her soft body squirming against his was heaven
and hell rolled into one shapely little five-foot-two-
inch package. He did his best to ignore it. "When you
point a gun at a man, you'd better be prepared to use
it, sweetheart."

"I was." She sounded breathless and if he didn't
know better, he'd swear he felt a slight tremor pass
through her.

Shaking his head as much in answer to her statement as in an attempt to clear his mind, he whispered
close to her ear, "You and I both know you could
never shoot me, Cheyenne."

"Let me have my gun back…and I'll show you."
There was no doubt that she shivered against him this
time.

He couldn't resist teasing the side of her neck
with his lips. "Not until you calm down."

Her labored breathing quickly reminded him of
the changes in her body since the last time he'd held
her. At sixteen, Cheyenne Holbrook had had a figure
that sent his hormones racing around like the steel
bearings in a pinball machine. But that had only been
a hint of the woman she would become. Her breasts
were fuller now and her hips had a slight flare that
promised to cradle a man and take him to paradise
when he sank himself deep inside her.

When his lower body tightened, he cursed himself
as the biggest fool God ever blessed with the breath
of life. He wasn't an eighteen-year-old kid anymore.
He was a thirty-one-year-old man and should have
mastered at least a modicum of restraint.

"Turn me loose."

When she pushed against him this time, he let her
go, but held on to the gun. He shook his head when she
reached for it. "I'll hang on to this for a while longer."

"Suit yourself." She reached for the cell phone clipped to her belt. "It's not going to stop me from calling Sheriff Turner and having you arrested for trespassing."

"You do that."

Her finger hovered over the phone's dial pad as she glanced up at him. "You aren't worried about being arrested?"

"Why should I be? I own the Sugar Creek." He shrugged as he placed the shotgun on the tailgate of his truck, well out of her reach. "You, on the other hand, are on my land." He stopped short of adding that her father and the sheriff would have a hell of a time getting him to leave again.

"I don't think so." She impatiently brushed a silky strand of hair from her cheek as she glared at him. "Emerald, Inc. is the corporation that bought your ranch after you and your mother left."

"The hell you say." He removed his leather work gloves, then, tucking them into the waistband of his jeans, he folded his arms across his chest. "And just how would you know that?"

She looked hesitant a moment before taking a deep breath and defiantly looking him square in the eye. "I'm the foreman of the Sugar Creek Cattle Company. Don't you think I'd know who my employer is?"

Nick couldn't believe it. Cheyenne's father, the judge, had actually allowed his precious daughter to work? And at a job where she might actually get her hands dirty? Interesting.

It appeared that Emerald Larson had omitted a couple of important details when she told him she was his grandmother and gave him back the ranch. She'd explained her reasoning behind having his mother sign documents stating that the identity of his father would remain a secret until she deemed he was ready to learn the truth. She'd even solved the mystery of who had tipped his mother off about his impending arrest the night they left Wyoming when she told him that she'd had a private investigator reporting his every move from the time he was born. But she hadn't mentioned anything about Cheyenne Holbrook being the ranch foreman. And as soon as he went back to the house, he was going to call Wichita and find out what other surprises the old gal had in store for him.

"I know this is going to come as a shock to you, but I really am the owner of this spread," Nick said.

Cheyenne paled, then stubbornly shook her head. "I don't believe you. When Luther Freemont from the corporate office called me just last week to discuss my quarterly report, he didn't mention anything about Emerald, Inc. selling the Sugar Creek."

Nick wasn't surprised to hear the name of Emerald's personal assistant. She trusted the man implicitly and relied on him to be the liaison between her and most of the managers of the companies she owned.

"I'll tell you what, Cheyenne." He picked up the shotgun and emptied the shells from its chamber before handing it to her. Then, pocketing the ammunition, he pointed to the truck she'd parked several yards away. "Why don't you go back to your father's ranch and give old Luther a call?"

"Don't think I won't," she said, raising her stubborn little chin a notch.

"After you hear what he has to say, we'll go from there." Nick pulled his work gloves from the waistband of his jeans and prepared to finish mending the section of fence he'd thought looked weak before he went back home to call Emerald. "Be over at my house tomorrow morning at nine."

"Why?"

She didn't look at all happy about having to see him again. And he knew as surely as he knew his own name that she didn't for a minute believe he was telling the truth about owning the Sugar Creek.

"We'll have to discuss the terms of your contract." He grinned. "And the last I heard, it's pretty common for a rancher and his foreman to work together running a ranch."

In an obvious test of wills, she glared at him for

several more seconds before turning to stalk back to her truck.

As Nick watched her leave, he couldn't stop himself from noticing the gentle sway of her delightful little backside as she walked away. She still had the ability to take his breath away with her beauty and with no more than a touch she could make him harder than hell in less than two seconds flat.

But he'd do well to remember that her father was the mighty Judge Bertram Holbrook, the most ill-tempered, acrimonious son of a bitch on two legs. A man who had half the county officials in his pocket and the other half scared to death he'd turn his wrath their way.

And if Holbrook had his way about it, Nick would still be rotting away in jail, simply because he'd tried to marry the man's only daughter.

The next morning, as Cheyenne drove the five miles between the Flying H and the Sugar Creek ranch houses, she wondered for at least the hundredth time what she could do about the situation. When she'd talked to Luther Freemont after her confrontation with Nick, she'd developed a splitting headache. He'd confirmed everything Nick had told her and, feeling as if her world had once again been turned completely upside down, she'd ended up lying awake the entire night, reliving the past and worrying about what the future held for her and her father.

It had taken her years to get over the devastation when Nick walked away from their relationship—from her—without so much as a backward glance, and seeing him after all this time had shaken her more than she could have ever imagined. But when he'd grabbed her to take away her gun, she couldn't believe the awareness that coursed through her traitorous body. At the feel of his rock-hard muscles surrounding her, she'd grown warm from the top of her head all the way to her toes and drawing her next breath had taken supreme effort. It had also scared her as little else could.

When they'd been teenagers, she'd thought the sun rose and set around Nick. He'd been two years ahead of her in school and the best-looking boy in the county. With his dark blond hair, charming smile and tall, muscular build, he'd been every sixteen-year-old girl's dream and every father's worst nightmare. Her pulse sped up as she remembered the heart-pounding excitement she'd felt the first time Nick had turned his sky-blue eyes and charming smile her way. She'd instantly fallen head over heels in love.

But her father wouldn't hear of her having anything to do with Nick. He'd told her the boy was nothing but bad news and a heartache waiting to happen. He'd never explained why he felt that way about

Nick, but unfortunately, she'd found out the hard way that her father had been been right.

When he and the sheriff had stopped her and Nick from getting married the summer between her junior and senior year of high school, Nick had disappeared that very night. She'd waited for months, hoping for a phone call, a letter—anything that would explain why he'd abandoned her. But there had been no word from him at all and she'd finally come to the conclusion that just as her father had said, Nick Daniels was trouble with a great big capital *T*. He hadn't even had the common courtesy or the courage to face her and tell her it was over between them.

But now he was back. And worse yet, he was her boss. How could fate be so cruel?

Seeing him again had been more than a little disturbing. But when he'd announced that he owned the Sugar Creek Cattle Company, the situation had become downright impossible.

She'd hoped when she questioned Mr. Freemont he would tell her that it was all a lie and that she had corporate's blessing in having Nick thrown off the property. But without elaborating on the details, Luther Freemont had verified that Nick Daniels did indeed own the Sugar Creek and that, in accordance with her contract, she was locked into working for the cattle company for the next four years, no matter who the owner was.

Parking her truck at the side of the big, white two-story Victorian house, she swallowed around the lump clogging her throat. She hadn't dared tell her father about the latest development. He wasn't well and hearing about Nick's return would only upset him and possibly cause more problems. And until she figured out what she could do about the situation there was no reason to worry him unnecessarily. Besides, she was doing enough stressing for the both of them.

As she grabbed the manila folder on the seat beside her and got out of the truck, she prayed for a miracle. She didn't really expect one, but at this point, divine intervention seemed to be her only hope of escaping the current mess she found herself in.

When she climbed the steps of the wide wrap-around porch and knocked on the door frame, instead of Nick, a heavy-set woman of about sixty opened the screen. "You must be Cheyenne Holbrook." She stepped back for Cheyenne to enter the foyer. "I'm Greta Foster. My husband, Carl, and I have been the caretakers here at the Sugar Creek for several years, but I don't believe we've had the pleasure of meeting."

Cheyenne wasn't surprised that they hadn't met. Before Nick left, her father had forbidden her to go anywhere near the place. And after she'd become the ranch foreman a little over six years ago, she hadn't ventured this far onto the Daniels property because it only reminded her of the shattered dream she'd had when she was sixteen.

She was supposed to have been Nick's wife and lived here with him and his mother in this big, wonderful house. While he ran the ranch, she was going to teach school and together they were going to raise a houseful of children and live happily ever after.

Removing her red ball cap, she shook her head to dispel the last traces of her troubling thoughts. "I've talked to Carl on the phone several times to let him know some of the men I supervise would be working close by, but I've never actually been here."

"Well, now that you have, you'll have to drop by more often." Greta's smile was friendly as she motioned toward a closed door across from the great room. "Nick's waiting for you in his office. Would you like something to eat or drink? I just took an apple pie out of the oven and made a fresh pot of coffee."

"No, thank you." Cheyenne smiled and raised her hand to knock on the office door. "I'm hoping this meeting won't take long." At Greta's surprised expression, Cheyenne hastily added, "I need to make a trip to the feed store for some supplies before Harry closes for lunch."

Apparently satisfied with her explanation, Greta nodded. "If you change your mind, I'll be in the kitchen."

As the woman moved down the hall toward the back of the house, Cheyenne took a moment to settle her jangled nerves. The last thing she wanted to do was go through with this meeting, but the choice had been taken out of her hands.

Before she could change her mind and run as far away as her old Ford truck could take her, she knocked, then opened the door. "Nick?"

He was sitting at a large oak desk, talking on the phone. "I'm glad to hear that you and Alyssa had a good time on your honeymoon in the Bahamas." Nodding for Cheyenne to come in and sit in the chair in front of his desk, Nick laughed at something the person on the other end of the line said. "Let me know when you hear more from Hunter about his E.M.T. courses. Talk to you later, Caleb."

When Nick hung up the phone and turned his attention on her, his easy expression faded. "I take it you spoke with Luther Freemont?"

Unable to relax, she sat on the edge of the leather armchair and pushed the folder across his desk. "Mr. Freemont told me that you were the owner of the Sugar Creek now and that I should discuss the terms of my contract with you."

His expression unreadable, he stared at her for several tense seconds before he picked up the file and flipped it open.

Cheyenne's cheeks grew increasingly warmer the longer he scanned the contents of the file. When she'd signed the contract to work for the cattle company, Mr. Freemont had assured her that the terms of their agreement would be handled with complete discretion and only a handful of people would know the real reason she'd signed away ten years of her life.

When Nick finally looked at her, his questioning expression had her wishing the floor would open up and swallow her. "Would you like to explain all this, Cheyenne?"

Humiliated beyond belief, she bit her lower lip to keep it from trembling. When she felt in control enough to get the words out, she proudly raised her head to meet his gaze head on.

"I think it's pretty self-explanatory." She took a deep breath. "Not only do you own the Sugar Creek, you own my father's ranch, as well."

Two

Nick couldn't have been more shocked if he'd been zapped by a juiced-up cattle prod. How ironic that the eighteen-year-old boy Judge Bertram Holbrook had tried his best to ruin all those years ago had not only returned to reclaim his ranch, he owned the good judge's ranch as well. If what the man had tried to do to him hadn't been so low and vindictive, Nick might have laughed out loud. But one look at Cheyenne's pretty face told him there was more behind the story than met the eye.

"All this contract tells me is that I own the Flying H and you have four more years left on a ten-year work agreement." Shoving the folder aside, he sat back in the leather desk chair. "Why don't you fill me in on the details?"

He could tell that was the last thing she wanted to do. But when she raised her eyes to meet his, there was a defiant pride in their aqua depths that he couldn't help but admire.

"Daddy had a stroke six years ago. He's been partially paralyzed on his left side and in a wheelchair ever since."

"I'm sorry to hear that, Cheyenne."

Nick knew how much she loved her father and how hard that had to have been for her. And no matter how much he despised the man, Nick didn't like to hear of anyone's suffering.

She glanced down at her hands. "When I dropped out of school to come home to care for him—"

"You had to quit school?" She'd always wanted to become a teacher and he hated that she'd had to give that up.

"I only had a couple of semesters left, but Daddy needed me more than I needed to finish school." She shrugged, but he could tell it still bothered her. "There wasn't any money for my last year at the university anyway."

Nick frowned. Bertram Holbrook had always been one of the wealthiest, most powerful men in the county. Or at least, that's what he'd always led everyone to believe.

"Surely—"

"No." Obviously embarrassed, she suddenly rose to her feet and walked over to the window between the floor-to-ceiling bookshelves. "Do I have to spell it out for you? We're broke. The only thing keeping us from being homeless is that contract."

He didn't know what to say. As far as the judge was concerned, Nick couldn't have cared less. But Cheyenne didn't deserve the burden of having to pay for the sins of her unscrupulous father or be forced to give up her dreams.

"What happened?" he asked, when he finally found his voice.

Her shoulders sagged as if the weight of the world rested on them a moment before she finally turned to face him. "Daddy had made some ill-advised investments and when the stock market took a nosedive, he was too incapacitated from the stroke to sell before he lost most of his portfolio."

"He had a lot of Web site stocks?" Nick guessed, remembering the crash of the Internet stocks several years back.

"What was left wouldn't even cover our utility bills for a month," she said, nodding. "Then, when the doctors told us he couldn't work any longer, things went from bad to worse."

"What about insurance and a pension? He should have had the same paid benefits that other county and state officials have."

Something didn't ring true about the whole situation. Either the judge had been an extremely poor planner or his thirst for money and power had finally backfired on him. Nick suspected it was the latter that had finally brought the man down.

She walked back over and sank into the chair. "After Daddy had the stroke and couldn't work, there wasn't enough money to keep up the premiums on the insurance and he'd withdrawn everything in his pension fund to invest in the stocks."

Nick would have thought the judge had more sense than to deplete every resource he had. But then, greed could do that. And if there was ever a more greedy, power-mad human being than Bertram Holbrook, Nick had never met him.

"You didn't know any of this?"

"No." She rubbed her forehead with a trembling hand. "Daddy never discussed finances with me. He always told me that I'd never have to worry about those things."

Nick would bet every dime he had that finances weren't the only things the man had kept her in the dark about. "I'm sure it all came as quite a shock when you found out."

She nodded. "I had no idea what we were going to do. Fortunately Emerald, Inc. contacted me about buying the Flying H right after I came to the conclusion there was no alternative but for us to file for bankruptcy." Her cheeks colored a deep rose. "Then, when it became clear there wasn't enough money from the sale of the ranch to pay off Daddy's medical and rehabilitation bills, Mr. Freemont told me the corporation would pay off the rest of our creditors, allow us to stay in our home and pay me a modest salary if I signed a ten-year contract to be the ranch foreman of the newly formed Sugar Creek Cattle Company. At the end of that time, our debts will be considered paid in full and I'll be free to renegotiate my contract or move on."

If Nick had thought things were strange before, they'd just taken a turn toward bizarre. But the more he thought about it, the more it sounded like Emerald had learned of the Holbrook's money problems and, in the bargain, seized the opportunity to mete out a bit of revenge for the judge's treatment of him and his mother all those years ago.

Unfortunately it wasn't Bertram Holbrook who was having to pay the price for Emerald's retaliatory actions. Cheyenne was the one who'd practically sold herself into servitude to bail the old man out of his financial woes. And it didn't sit well with Nick one damned bit that his indomitable grandmother had obviously been taking advantage of Cheyenne.

"Do you mind if I keep this for a couple of days to look over?" he asked, picking up the contract. If there was a way to get them both out of this mess, he intended to find it. "I need to figure out if you owe me or Emerald, Inc."

She shrugged one slender shoulder as she rose to her feet. "You might as well, since it appears that I work for you now, instead of Emerald, Inc."

"Where are you going?"

From the look on her face, she couldn't wait to end their meeting. "Unless you have something more you want to discuss, I've got work to do."

He did, but first he wanted to talk to Emerald. "I'll go over this and see what the exact wording is, then we'll discuss it tomorrow afternoon while we inspect the herds."

"Can't you do that on your own?" She sounded close to going into a panic at the thought of spending time with him.

Nick smiled. "I could, but it's standard practice for the foreman to show the new owner around. Besides, I'm sure I'll have a few questions about the way you've been running the operation."

Clearly unhappy, she hesitated a moment before she nodded. "Fine." Walking to the door, she turned back. "I'll be here tomorrow after lunch. Be ready."

"I'll have the horses saddled."

"The truck would be faster."

"I'd rather ride."

She glared at him for several long seconds before she finally nodded. "All right…boss." Then, opening the door, she walked out into the hall and slammed it shut behind her.

Once he was alone, Nick inhaled deeply. He hadn't drawn a decent breath since Cheyenne had walked into the room. He wouldn't have believed it was possible, but she was even prettier today than she'd been yesterday. Her turquoise T-shirt had brought out the blue-green of her eyes and the sun shining through the window behind her when she'd turned to face him had accentuated the golden highlights in her long brown hair.

His temperature soared at the mental image and shaking his head at his own foolishness, he did his best to ignore the tightening in his groin. But then, it had always been that way with Cheyenne. From the first moment he saw her at the homecoming dance his senior year, he hadn't been able to think of anything but making her his wife and living out the rest of his days trying to prove himself worthy of her.

Thinking back on that summer after his high school graduation, he still couldn't get over how naive they'd been. He and Cheyenne had gone steady throughout his senior year, even though her father had forbidden her to have anything to do with Nick. Neither of them had understood the judge's intense dislike of Nick, but they'd managed to sneak around to see each other at school functions and met in town every Saturday afternoon to hug and kiss their way through a double-feature matinee at the movie theater. And despite Bertram Holbrook's concentrated efforts to keep them from seeing each other, by the end of the summer they'd fallen in love and were desperate to be together.

Nick couldn't remember which one of them had hatched up the plan to run away and get married. Truth to tell, it really didn't matter. It was what they'd both wanted and they'd heard that for a couple of hundred bucks the clerk over in the next county would issue a marriage license to anyone, whether they were of legal age or not. So he'd worked at the feed store on weekends and saved every dime he could until he had enough to make Cheyenne his bride.

Then, one hot night in late August, he'd picked her up at the house of one of her friends and they'd driven across the county line to get married. But just before they were pronounced husband and wife, the judge and his cohort, Sheriff Turner, had shown up to stop the ceremony.

Nick rubbed the tension gathering at the back of his neck. Until yesterday afternoon, his last remembrance of Cheyenne had been watching her sob uncontrollably as her father led her away from the little church to his car.

But things had a way of working out for the best. Marrying his high school sweetheart had been the lofty illusion of an eighteen-year-old boy with more hormones than good sense. He was a grown man now and no matter how alluring he found Cheyenne, there was no danger of falling under her spell a second time.

Besides, after discovering that his father was an irresponsible player who had thought nothing of walking out on not one, but three women he'd impregnated, who was to say that Nick hadn't inherited the same "love 'em and leave 'em" gene? After all, he was the one who'd lost interest in every relationship he'd had since leaving Wyoming.

Picking up the contract, he scanned the contents of the document a little closer. There had to be a clause concerning termination of the agreement—a way to free them from having to work together.

His frown turned to a deep scowl when he found it. In the event that Cheyenne quit or her position as foreman was terminated for any reason, the balance of the money immediately became due and payable to Emerald, Inc. No exceptions.

He should have known Emerald would cover all the bases. She hadn't gained the reputation of being an invincible force in the boardroom or become one of the richest, most successful businesswomen in America by accident.

As he dialed his grandmother's private number, he took a deep breath to control his anger. Although he no longer had feelings for Cheyenne, he didn't like the idea of Emerald taking advantage of her or circumstances that were beyond her control.

Instead of Emerald, Luther Freemont answered. "I'm sorry, Mr. Daniels. Your grandmother is unavailable at the moment. May I take a message?"

Nick could tell the man had him on the speakerphone and knew the old gal was probably sitting right there at the desk listening to every word he said while her assistant ran interference for her. "Maybe you can help me, Luther. I have a few questions about Cheyenne Holbrook's employment with the Sugar Creek Cattle Company."

There was a long pause before the man spoke. "What would that be, sir?"

"I'd like some more information on Ms. Holbrook's salary, the balance on what she owes Emerald, Inc. and if she's my employee or Emerald's."

Another long pause signaled that the man was most likely looking to Emerald for direction. "I'm not at liberty to say, sir. I'm afraid you'll have to discuss that with Mrs. Larson."

Irritated with the entire situation, Nick muttered a pithy curse. "Tell Emerald to give me a call as soon as possible."

"I'll be sure to do that. Is there anything else I can help you with, sir?"

Nick couldn't resist teasing Emerald's stiff and formal personal assistant. "As a matter of fact, there is, Luther."

"Yes, sir?"

"You sound like a robot. Loosen up and stop being such a tightass."

"I'll take that under advisement, sir," the man said with a hint of laughter in his voice.

Nick grinned when he heard the definitive sound of a woman laughing in the background a moment before the connection ended.

"Daddy, I have to go up to the summer pastures to check the herds this afternoon," Cheyenne said as she put their lunch plates in the dishwasher. "Will you be all right until I get back?"

Her father nodded as he backed his wheelchair away from the table. "I'll be fine, princess. Gordon called this morning to tell me he's going to stop by for a while." He chuckled. "I'm sure he's got some hot piece of gossip he'd like to share."

Cheyenne smiled wanly. She'd never cared for Sheriff Turner, but he and her father had been friends for over twenty years and her father always looked forward to his visits.

She kissed her father's cheek. "There's some lemonade in the refrigerator and peanut butter cookies in the cookie jar if you two get hungry."

Smiling, he patted her arm. "What would I do without you, princess?"

"I'm sure you'd do just fine, but that's something you won't ever have to worry about." Checking her watch, she gave him a quick hug, then grabbed her truck keys from the counter. "You and Sheriff Turner stay out of trouble."

Her father laughed. "Now what could a county sheriff and a crippled old judge possibly do to get themselves in hot water?"

"Let me think." Tapping her index finger on her chin, she acted as if she had to give it a lot of consideration. "I'm sure you'll turn down the extra cigar that Sheriff Turner just happens to bring with him?"

"Of course I'll turn it down. Just like I always do." Her father's eyes twinkled mischievously. "I wouldn't think to do anything else, princess."

They both knew he was telling a fib. The sheriff always tried to time his visits to coincide with her working on another part of the ranch in order for her father to smoke a cigar—something his doctors had advised him to cut out. But he had very few pleasures left in life and she decided the occasional cigar he enjoyed once or twice a month while he visited with his best friend wasn't going to do that much harm.

Smiling, she opened the door to leave. "Just remember, if the sheriff wants to have a cigar there's no smoking in the house. You'll both have to go out onto the back porch."

Her father waved for her to leave. "You just be careful out there in the pastures. You might run across a wolf, or worse."

Cheyenne's stomach twisted into a tight knot. She wouldn't encounter a wolf somewhere along the way, she'd be riding right along beside one.

Nodding, she ducked out the door before he had a chance to see the guilt she knew had to be written all over her face. It had been three days since she'd run across Nick repairing that section of fence and she still hadn't found the courage to tell her father about him being back in the area or that he owned the very house they lived in.

For one thing, she wasn't sure how her father would react. He'd already had one stroke. She certainly didn't want to run the risk of him having another when he learned that she was working for Nick. And for another, she didn't want or need to listen to him tell her how disreputable Nick was or that she'd do well to steer clear of him. She knew firsthand how unreliable Nick was.

Cheyenne sighed heavily as she climbed into her truck and drove the five miles to the Sugar Creek ranch house. She really didn't have a lot of choice in the matter. Even if they figured out who held the promissory note—Emerald, Inc. or Nick—heaven only knew she didn't have the money to repay it in order to get out of the work agreement.

Ten minutes later, when she pulled into the ranch yard and got out of the truck, the first thing she noticed was the bay and sorrel geldings standing saddled and tied to the corral fence. They were waiting for her to take Nick to see the cattle company herds—his herds. But he was nowhere in sight. And that suited her just fine. The less time she had to spend with him the better off she'd be.

Walking over to the horses, she patted the sorrel gelding's neck. She'd been more humiliated than she'd ever been in her life during their meeting yesterday when she'd had to tell him that she and her father were practically destitute. But that hadn't stopped her from noticing that the boy she'd once loved with all her heart had grown into a devastatingly handsome man or that whenever he turned his deep blue eyes her way, her chest tightened with an ache she'd thought she'd long ago gotten over.

"You're late."

Her stomach did a little flip at the sound of Nick's deep baritone and, turning around, she found him standing with one shoulder propped against the edge of the barn door, his arms crossed over his wide chest. She swallowed hard and tried not to notice how his chambray shirt emphasized the width of his shoulders or how his worn jeans hugged his muscular thighs and rode low on his narrow hips. As he pushed away from the barn and walked toward her, her pulse sped up and she felt as if she couldn't breathe.

"I had things to do," she said, hating the breathless tone of her own voice. "Besides, this shouldn't take long. Both herds are pastured within a few miles' ride of each other."

He nodded as he untied the two horses, then handed her the sorrel's reins. "I need to be back before supper."

"We'll be back well before then," she said, mounting the gelding.

"Good. I have plans."

Cheyenne couldn't believe the twinge of disappointment coursing through her. She couldn't care less if he had a date. She really couldn't. As long as he left her alone, he could date and bed the county's entire female population and it wouldn't bother her one bit.

"If you'd like to postpone checking the herds, it won't bother me. I have other things I need to be doing anyway."

He effortlessly swung up onto the bay and rode up beside her. "No, I want to see what we've got so that when I go to the auction tomorrow night, I can compare what we have to what's being sold. Then I'll have a fair idea of how much I can get when I sell our cattle."

"You're selling out?"

Panic sent a cold chill snaking up her spine and caused her stomach to twist into a painful knot. If he sold everything, how was she supposed to pay off the remainder of her debt?

"Don't worry, you'll still have a job," he said as if he'd read her mind. "I'm starting a new breeding program that will make the Sugar Creek a major force to contend with in the beef industry. And I can't do that with the cattle we have now."

"You're not going to start raising some obscure breed that no one has ever heard of, are you?"

"Not hardly." Laughing, he shook his head as they

nudged the horses into a slow walk. "The Sugar Creek has always raised Black Angus and we always will. The same as the Flying H. But they're going to be free-range cattle. No more supplements, growth hormones or commercial cattle feed. We're starting an all-natural operation."

Relieved to hear that she wouldn't have to worry about finding a way to pay back money she didn't have—at least for now—she nodded. "Free-range stock of all kinds are becoming very popular."

"It's getting bigger by the day and we're missing out on a fast-growing market." When he turned his head to look at her, he adjusted the wide brim of his black Resistol so that their gazes met. "The way I figure it, between the two ranches there's a little over a hundred and fifty thousand acres of prime grazing land and plenty of good grass to cut for hay to feed the cattle in the winter months."

He definitely had her interest. It could take several years for an operation like that to reach its peak. Maybe if he was busy planning how many acres he'd use for graze, how many for hay and where and how to market the beef, she'd be free to do her job and get through the next four years of her contract without having a lot of contact with him.

"When are you going to start selling off the herds and bringing in the new stock?"

"Within the next couple of weeks. I'm going to talk to the auction house tomorrow night about selling off the cattle in lots of ten to fifteen. I think I'll get more out of them that way."

She frowned. With the cold Wyoming winter just around the corner, it seemed like a bad time to be bringing in a new herd. "When will the new stock arrive?"

"Next spring."

Glancing over at him as they rode across the pasture behind his house, she couldn't help but wonder where she fit into the equation. With no stock to feed or any need to chop ice for the cattle to get water from the ponds and streams this winter there really wasn't going to be any work for her to supervise.

When they reached a gate at the back of the pasture, she started to dismount, but Nick was quicker and jumped down from the bay to open it. "I'm betting you're wondering what you'll be doing with your time this winter."

She led the bay as she rode the sorrel through the opening into the next field. "Well, now that you mention it, it did cross my mind."

He chuckled. "Don't worry. There'll be more than enough work for both of us." Taking the bay's reins, he swung back up into the saddle. "After the herds are sold, we'll be busy planning how many acres per head of cattle we'll need, how we intend to rotate them and how many acres of hay we'll need to cut in the summer to get them through the winter."

Her heart skipped a beat. "We? Why can't you do that yourself?"

He stared off across the Sugar Creek Valley at the Laramie Mountains in the distance. "I'm changing your job description. From now on, you'll be working in the office and I'll be out supervising the men and managing the daily operation."

"Excuse me?" She reined in the gelding at the edge of the creek the ranch had been named for. "What office are you talking about?"

Stopping the bay, he shrugged. "My office at the Sugar Creek."

Cheyenne felt a chill travel from the top of her head to the soles of her feet. How on earth was she going to keep her distance from him if she had to work in his office? In his home?

"You mean until the new cattle arrive in the spring?"

He shook his head. "From now on. I've missed being out in the fresh air and feeling like I've actually accomplished something when I go to bed so tired that I'm asleep before my head hits the pillow."

She couldn't help it, she laughed out loud as she urged the sorrel across the slow moving, shallow water of Sugar Creek. "Give me a break. You can't tell me you'd rather be out in weather so cold your breath freezes on your lips or so hot that you feel like your brains are baking inside your hat."

"I'm serious, Cheyenne." He rode up the bank on the other side of the creek. "I've been stuck being a desk jockey for the past eight years and I'm tired of it."

It wasn't any of her business nor did she care what he'd been doing for the past thirteen years, but curiosity got the better of her. "What kind of job did you have?"

"I developed software for a bank's online customers to pay bills and transfer funds from one account to another."

"You graduated from college." She couldn't keep from sounding wistful.

"Yep. I have a degree in software development and computer applications."

"And you gave up all that to come back here to shovel manure and cut yourself to ribbons stringing barbed wire fence? Are you nuts?"

He grinned. "Put that way, it doesn't sound real smart, does it?"

Laughing, Cheyenne shook her head. "I'll bet your mother is very proud of you for earning your degree, but fit to be tied that you won't be using it. She always wanted you to go to college." It suddenly occurred to her that she hadn't asked about his mother. "By the way, how is she doing?"

His smile faded and stopping his horse at the top of a rise, he gazed out over the herd of sleek black cattle grazing in the shallow valley below. "Mom died about a year after we moved to St. Louis. She never knew that I went to college, let alone graduated."

"Oh, Nick, I'm so sorry. I didn't know." She'd always liked Linda Daniels and hated to hear of the woman's passing. "Had she been ill?"

Cheyenne knew from experience how hard his mother's death had to have been for Nick. She'd lost her own mother when she was very young and had it not been for the love of her father, she wasn't sure she would have survived. But Nick hadn't had anyone to lean on. His mother had never married and it had always been just the two of them.

"Mom knew she didn't have long to live when we left here," he said quietly.

"Was that why you went to St. Louis? I think I remember you mentioning that your mother had a cousin there."

Nick turned to stare at Cheyenne. The sincerity in her blue-green eyes convinced him that she didn't have a clue why he'd run away in the middle of the night like a coyote with a backside full of buckshot. And that had him wondering just what the good judge had told her about his disappearance the night they were to have been married.

"That's where we went to live," he said, turning his attention back to the herd of cattle in the valley below. "But that wasn't the reason we left here."

He could tell from her intense stare that she was baffled by his answer, but she didn't pursue the issue further. Instead she reined her horse toward the path leading down into the meadow. But the gelding balked, then gingerly held his front hoof off the ground as if it might be injured.

"I think we have a problem," Nick said as they both dismounted to examine the sorrel's left front leg. Bending down, he gently examined the inside center of the animal's hoof. "The sole looks swollen."

"It's probably a stone bruise."

Straightening, he nodded. "That would be my guess. Looks like we'll have to ride double."

She shook her head as she patted the gelding's neck. "It's only a few miles. You go ahead and I'll walk him back."

"I don't think so, sweetheart." He took the reins from her. "There's no way in hell I'm going to ride back to the house and leave you out here alone with a lame horse."

"You can go faster without me." She took a step back. "You said yourself that you have a date tonight and I certainly don't want to be the cause of you being late."

Nick stared at her for several long seconds. Had there been a bit of sarcasm in her voice?

He knew he should let it go, but some part of him had to know. "Does it bother you that I might be seeing someone, Cheyenne?"

"Not at all." Her laughter was as hollow as the old bee tree out behind his barn. "I don't know why you'd wonder something like that. I gave up caring what you do a long time ago."

He knew she was lying and for reasons beyond his comprehension, he wanted her to admit the truth. "You never could lie worth a damn, sweetheart."

"I'm not lying."

"Yes, you are." He stepped forward and putting his arm around her waist, drew her to him. Lowering his voice, he whispered close to her ear. "You don't like caring, but you do."

"D-don't flatter yourself, Nick Daniels. What you do or who you do it with is none of my concern."

"Is that so?"

"Absolutely."

The breathless tone of her voice and the tremor he felt pass through her slender body belied her words and, unable to stop himself, Nick pushed the brim of her ball cap up out of the way and lowered his head. "Let's just settle the issue here and now."

Three

When Nick covered her mouth with his, Cheyenne's heart began to pound like she'd run a marathon and every cell in her body tingled to life. She tried to remain unaffected, tried to fight the heat filling every fiber of her being. She didn't want to feel anything for him but contempt.

This was the man who had broken her young heart all those years ago, the man who had left her behind without a word or even a backward glance. He'd proven what her father had said about him to be right on the money—there wasn't anything more to Nick Daniels than a handful of empty promises and a boatload of heartaches. But try as she might, she couldn't stop the honeyed warmth flowing through her veins or the overwhelming need to kiss him back.

At eighteen, Nick the boy had kissed her with the soft, innocent reverence of youthful love. But as his lips moved over hers now, then urged her to open for him, she found that Nick the man kissed her with a thoroughness that caused her head to spin and made every bone in her body feel as if it had been turned to rubber.

When he tightened his hold and she felt the hard contours of his body pressed to her much softer curves, her pulse throbbed and she gave up all pretense of resisting. His breathtaking exploration of her tender inner recesses stole her breath and wiped out all thought of the past, present or future. At the moment, all she wanted to do was savor the delicious sensations flowing from the top of her head all the way to her curled toes inside her scuffed boots.

With her hands trapped between them, she had to grasp his shirt in order to keep her balance. But the flexing of his rock-hard pectoral muscles beneath the fabric sent her pulse racing and caused her knees to give way completely. Moving his hands from her back to cup her bottom, he positioned his leg between hers to help support her.

Cheyenne's heart stopped, then took off like a

runaway train at the feel of his strong thigh wedged against the most feminine part of her. A flash of unexpected need, so strong it sent shivers up her spine, streaked through her and caused her to moan from the sheer pleasure of it.

The uncharacteristic sound shocked her back to reality and pushing against him, she shook her head. "No. Stop."

He immediately set her away from him, then stepping back gave her a look that sent her temperature up at least ten degrees. "I guess we settled that, didn't we, sweetheart?"

His confident comment and knowing smile were as effective as a bucket of ice water and chased away all traces of desire. "I suppose we did." She took the sorrel's reins and, leading the injured animal, started walking back the way they'd come. "I'm sorry to disappoint you, Nick, but you're going to have to face facts. That spark we used to have between us is long gone."

Before she'd gone two steps, his hand on her arm stopped her. "Is that why you were clinging to me? Or why you brought up my going out on a date in the first place?"

Cheyenne stared at his large hand wrapped around her upper arm a moment before she pulled away from his grasp. "I merely pointed out that you'll be late if you insist that we ride back to the house together." She gave him a smile that she hoped with all her heart set his teeth on edge. "You're the one who seems to think it should matter. Not me."

"Whatever you say, Cheyenne." Grinning, he shook his head as he took the sorrel's reins from her and dallied them to the bay's saddle horn. "Come on. We're wasting time."

She wasn't looking forward to walking three miles in boots, but it was preferable to riding double with him. Especially after that kiss.

"You go on. I'll walk."

"This isn't negotiable."

Mounting the bay, Nick held his hand out to help Cheyenne up onto the horse. She didn't look any happier about the situation than he was, but, grasping his arm, she allowed him to pull her up to sit behind him on the gelding's broad back.

They rode in silence for some time and it wasn't lost on him that she held on to the back of the saddle instead of wrapping her arms around his waist. And that suited him just fine. The less physical contact they had, the better.

What the hell had he been thinking when he'd taken her in his arms, anyway? Why had it been so imperative that he make her admit it bothered her to think of him with another woman?

He'd acted like some kind of macho jerk out to

prove a point. And the only thing he'd succeeded in doing was proving to himself that he was more like his father than he wanted to admit.

From everything Nick had heard about Owen Larson, he'd been the kind of man who used the steamroller approach with women—overpowering them with his charm, seducing them in order to prove to himself that he could. And although Nick hadn't kissed Cheyenne with seduction in mind or because he wanted to prove his virility, he had wanted to overwhelm her and make her admit that she still cared for him.

As they crossed Sugar Creek and started up the bank on the other side, he felt as if he'd been struck by a bolt of lightning when Cheyenne had to put her arms around him for a more secure hold. The warmth of her body and the feel of her breasts pressed to his back did strange things to his insides and had him struggling to draw his next breath.

He'd gotten over her years ago and he had absolutely no interest in rekindling anything they'd once shared. But that didn't stop his body from responding to her in a way that made sitting astride a horse damned uncomfortable, if not dangerous.

Deciding he needed to put a little space between them or risk emasculating himself, he pulled his horse to a stop. "We'll let the sorrel rest a bit before we go on."

"I think that's a good idea," she said, sliding from the back of the bay.

After he let the horses get a drink, Nick ground-tied them to graze, then joined Cheyenne, sitting under the shade of a large cottonwood tree. Wanting to ease the tension between them, he searched for a neutral topic.

"Catch me up on all that's happened around here since I've been gone."

"There hasn't been much." She shrugged as she plucked a blade of grass to twirl it between her slender fingers. "Your friend, Tom Little Bear, is making a career in the Marines. He married a North Carolina girl while he was stationed at Camp Lejeune and the last I heard, they had four children and another one on the way."

Nick laughed. "That sounds like Bear. He always said he wanted a big family."

Cheyenne smiled. "His sister, Marleen, has eight children."

"What about your friends?" he asked casually. "Did Sally Hanley finally convince Doug Carson to take a trip down the aisle?"

"Yes, but they couldn't make it work. They divorced after three years and Sally ended up marrying Gerald Reynolds. They run the Bucket of Suds Bar and Grill in Elk Bluff."

They sat in silence for some time as Nick assimilated all the changes that had taken place in the thirteen years he'd been gone. But as he sat there pondering everything Cheyenne had told him about their friends, he couldn't help but wonder if she'd found someone special.

The thought caused a burning in his gut and had him wondering if he'd lost his mind. It was none of his business who she'd seen after he left. He'd forfeited that right a long time ago.

Standing up, he offered his hand to help her to her feet. "Are you ready to go?"

When she nodded and took his hand a charge of electricity streaked up his arm, then spread throughout his chest. She must have felt it too because once she stood up she dropped his hand so fast he was surprised she didn't end up hurting her wrist.

"You're not the only one who needs to get home," she said, checking her watch.

Grinning, he teased, "Got a hot date?"

She gave him a smile that sent his blood pressure sky high. "As a matter of fact, I do."

He instantly stopped grinning and the burning in his gut that he'd experienced earlier at the thought of her with another man returned with a vengeance. "Then we'd better get going." He caught the horses and mounting the bay, he pulled her up behind him.

"When you see loverboy tonight, tell him that you won't be available tomorrow evening."

"Why?"

"You'll be working."

Her glare could have melted metal. "And just what will I be doing?"

Traditionally, ranchers gave their hired help Saturday night off. But for reasons he wouldn't even allow himself to consider, he didn't want Cheyenne available to anyone but him.

"I've decided to take you to the stock auction with me."

As Nick watched the Cardinals shut out the Diamondbacks, he struggled with his insistance that Cheyenne accompany him to the stock auction tomorrow night. He hadn't originally intended to take her along. So what the hell had gotten into him?

He'd found it rather humorous when she'd mistakenly thought his plans for the evening included a woman. But her admission that she had a date tonight had tied him up in such a knot that it had damned near knocked him to his knees. And for the life of him, he couldn't figure out why.

What they'd once had together was past history and it would be completely unreasonable for him to expect her not to have moved on with her life. He had. And although he wasn't overly proud of the fact that he hadn't been able to sustain a relationship for longer than a few months without losing interest, it wasn't like he hadn't had his share of women in the years since they'd parted ways.

But whether it was rational or not, just the thought of Cheyenne in the arms of another man sent a searing pain straight to the pit of his belly and had him ready to punch something or somebody.

Taking a swig of beer from the longneck bottle in his hand, he shook his head as he blindly stared at the ball game. He had a feeling he knew exactly what his problem was. When he and Cheyenne had been kids sneaking around behind her father's back to be together, he'd never crossed the line with her, never taken her virginity and truly made her his. Not that he hadn't wanted to or that she wouldn't have been willing. But Nick had been determined not to be anything like the man who'd gotten his mother pregnant, then left her high and dry to face the consequences. And that meant not making love to Cheyenne until he'd done the right thing and made her his wife.

He took a deep breath. He didn't expect her to still be a virgin at the age of twenty-nine, but the thought that some other man had touched her and taken her innocence was enough to turn him wrong side out. That was supposed to have been his claim, his right as her husband. But that was no longer an issue after all this time.

Shaking his head, he closed his eyes and leaned his head back against the chair. Thirteen years ago, his obsession with her and her father's unexplained hatred of him damn near cost him a prison sentence and he wasn't about to jeopardize the chance Emerald had given him to reclaim what was rightfully his. But the truth of the matter was, he still wanted Cheyenne physically. He wasn't happy about wanting her. But he did. It was just that simple.

As he questioned his sanity, a thought suddenly occurred to him. He was no longer that green as grass kid he'd been back then and Cheyenne was no longer jailbait. And although he had no intention of becoming emotionally involved with her or any other woman, he couldn't think of one good reason why they couldn't enjoy a satisfying physical relationship.

He knew for certain she was as attracted to him as he was to her. And as long as they kept it all in perspective and their emotions in check, there shouldn't be a problem.

Now, the uppermost question on his mind was how to go about convincing Cheyenne that it was the best way for both of them to get each other out of their systems once and for all.

* * *

Cheyenne kept her head lowered as she preceded Nick through the crowded auction barn and up the bleachers to find a couple of empty seats. She wasn't the least bit happy about being seen out in public with him. Nearly all of the ranchers and ranch foremen attending the sale knew her and her father and she was positive that several of them remembered Nick. And although he'd changed a lot in thirteen years, she had no doubt that someone would recognize him.

Normally that wouldn't be a big deal. She was Nick's employee and there was absolutely nothing going on between them. But she'd yet to tell her father that Nick was back in the area, let alone that he was the new owner of the Sugar Creek. What if one of her father's acquaintances mentioned that they'd seen her at the auction with Nick before she found a way to break the news of his return?

Slumping into one of the chairs, she pulled the bill of her ball cap a little lower and prayed that the first lot of cattle would be herded into the arena soon. Once the auctioneer started the bidding, everyone's attention would be focused on the action in the ring and off the matter of who was in attendance.

"You're awfully quiet," Nick said as he settled into the seat beside her.

"I'm just waiting for the sale to start." She glanced

around to see if anyone noticed them. Breathing a little easier when she found that no one seemed interested, she asked, "Did you talk to the manager? Is he agreeable to auctioning off lots of ten to fifteen head of cattle at a time?"

Nick nodded as he looked over the sale bill. "I called earlier today and he said he'd be more than happy to accommodate my request."

She frowned. "If you've already made the arrangements, then why are we here?"

"Prices. I want to see what the going rate is so that I can calculate what I think we'll get for the herds."

"You could have done that yourself."

"I wanted company," he said, shrugging.

Glaring at him, she folded her arms beneath her breasts and without thinking, muttered, "You could have asked your date from last night to accompany you. I'm sure she would have been a lot happier to be here than I am."

Nick's slow smile made her warm all over, but just as he opened his mouth to comment on her ill-chosen words, the auctioneer welcomed everyone to the night's event and instructed the gate man to let the first animals up for bidding into the arena. It appeared that she'd been saved from having to explain herself, at least for the time being.

Over the next few hours, she began to relax a bit as she watched a procession of cattle, horses and sheep herded into the arena—some individually, some in lots. Surely by the end of the auction Nick would forget that she'd mentioned his date again.

What she couldn't understand was why she kept bringing it up. She didn't care that he was seeing another woman. She really didn't. And maybe if she kept telling herself enough times, she might even start to believe it.

But when the gavel came down for the final time and Nick took her hand to keep them from being separated in the crowd departing the auction barn, his smile told her that he not only hadn't forgotten her slip of the tongue, but he had every intention of commenting on it.

"Would you like to know what my plans were last night, Cheyenne?" he asked as they walked the short distance to his truck.

"No." She didn't particularly want to hear the details, even if she didn't care that he was seeing someone.

"Are you sure?"

"Yes." Why was he being so persistent?

"I'll tell you about my evening, if you'll tell me about yours."

His eyes lit with mischief and she could tell he

wasn't going to let the matter drop. "Oh, good heavens! Tell me and get it over with."

Opening the passenger door to his truck, he smiled. "Ladies first."

Thinking quickly, she smiled. "I took Sebastian MacDougal to bed with me and spent the entire evening with him."

Nick's expression turned dark. "Who the hell is this Sebastian character?"

"Just someone I know," she said, shrugging as she climbed into the truck.

"Is he from around here?"

"Not that it's any of your concern, but no. He's not from around here." Smiling, she buckled her shoulder harness. "He's from the United Kingdom."

She almost laughed out loud at the deep scowl on Nick's handsome face. If only her evening had been as exciting as what she'd just described. But she wasn't about to admit that the man in question was the hero in a suspense novel she'd been reading.

"What about your evening?" she asked when he walked around the front of the truck and slid in behind the steering wheel. "I've told you about mine. Now it's your turn."

"Mine wasn't anywhere near as wild as yours." He gave her a look that made her warm all over as he started the truck's engine. "I stayed home and watched the Cardinals kick the Diamondbacks' butts, then I went to bed. Alone."

"What happened?" she asked before she could stop herself. "Was your date canceled?"

"No. I did exactly what I intended to do. I watched the ball game."

"But you said—"

He shook his head as he put the truck in gear and steered it from the parking lot. "I told you I had plans and that I wanted to get back home before supper. You were the one who insisted that I had a date."

His evening hadn't included a woman? No wonder he'd been amused when he asked her if she was bothered by the thought of him seeing someone. Her reaction had confirmed that it did.

"Why didn't you correct me?" She wasn't about to take all the blame for the misunderstanding. After all, he hadn't made the slightest attempt to set the record straight.

He smiled. "I had my reasons."

Not wanting to listen to him tell her how transparent she'd been, she decided it would be in her best interest to change the subject. "Did you find out who I owe in the event I find myself without a job at the Sugar Creek?"

"I'm still waiting on a call from Emerald, Inc. for clarification, but the best I can decipher from your contract, you're in the clear as long as you continue to work for me." He shook his head. "If you're worried about being out of a job—don't. I have no plans to replace you or anyone else."

On the one hand, it was a relief to know she wouldn't have to come up with the thousands of dollars it would take to pay off the debt. But on the other hand, it appeared there was no way out of working for Nick for the next several years.

"It doesn't make sense to me how I can work for you and the Sugar Creek Cattle Company and still owe Emerald Inc. I would have thought that when you bought the cattle company, you'd have also gained control of my contract." She stared out the windshield at the brilliant display of stars dotting the midnight sky. "Is it just me, or is there something about this whole deal that doesn't add up?"

Unwilling to admit that the Sugar Creek had been given to him or that the mighty Emerald Larson was his newfound grandmother, Nick made no comment. Hell, he hadn't gotten used to the idea himself. Besides, he needed to talk to Emerald before he discussed things with Cheyenne.

On the surface, it did look like she and her father should owe him the balance of the loan. But Nick had a feeling that Emerald fully intended to retain control of Cheyenne's contract until it was completely paid off. What he couldn't figure out was why. And until he talked to his domineering grandmother, it would be best to keep quiet.

When he steered the truck into the yard and parked beside the house, he started to get out and open the passenger door, but Cheyenne beat him to it. She was already halfway to her truck when he managed to stop her.

"Would you like to come in for a while?"

"I don't think that would be a good idea," she said, shaking her head.

Without thinking, Nick reached out and loosely circled her waist with his arms. "What's the matter? Are you afraid Sebastian will find out?"

She placed her hands flat on his chest, but instead of shoving him away, her fingers seemed to caress his chest muscles through the fabric of his shirt. "M-maybe."

"How serious are you about this Sebastian character?" he asked, wondering how far she'd take the ruse.

"Why do you care?" She sounded slightly winded.

"I don't." Pushing the wide brim of his Resistol back, he lowered his head to nuzzle the satiny skin along the column of her neck. "When are you going to admit that Sebastian is the lead character in Baxter Armstrong's latest mystery novel?"

To his immense satisfaction, she shivered against

him. "Wh-what makes you think that Sebastian's fictional?"

He laughed. "I read the book a couple of weeks ago."

"Then why—"

Kissing the frown from her forehead, he smiled. "I wanted to see just how far you'd go with your little story."

She shook her head. "It wasn't a story. I told the truth. I took the book to bed with me and woke up this morning with it on the mattress beside me. I can't help that you assumed I was having a wildly erotic night with someone."

Nick knew that he should let well enough alone and drop the matter. Instead he found himself pulling her closer. For reasons he'd rather not dwell on, he wanted to wipe out the memory of the men in her past, to make her forget anyone but him.

"This is insane, Nick." He felt a slight tremor pass through her at the contact of her body pressed closely to his. "What we had between us is ancient history."

"You're right, sweetheart." Tightening his arms around her, he lowered his head to brush her mouth with his. "I'm not concerned with the past. It's the present that I want to explore."

As his mouth settled over hers, he could tell she was trying to remain impassive, trying to deny the myriad the sensations coursing between them. But when he coaxed her to open for him, she readily complied and melted against him.

Encouraged by her response, Nick savored the taste of her and the feel of her soft body pressed to his. Her breasts crushed to his chest, the nipples taut with longing scored his skin through the fabric of his shirt and caused a flash fire to race through every fiber of his being.

But when she wrapped her arms around his waist and shyly stroked his tongue with hers, the heat gathering in the pit of his belly tightened his groin with an intensity that robbed him of breath. He wanted her. And if the way she was clinging to him was any indication, she wanted him just as much.

Moving his hands from her back, then up along her sides, he slid them to the underside of her breasts. Her impatient whimper and the tightening of her arms around his waist when he paused assured him that she wanted his touch. Cupping the soft mounds through the layers of her clothing, he gently caressed and teased the tight tips until she moaned with pleasure.

The sound of her own passion seemed to startle her, and he knew from the sudden rigidity of her slender frame that the moment was over.

Nick eased away from the kiss, then stepping back, he smiled down at her. "Be here first thing

Monday morning. We need to start making decisions about dividing up the herds."

She blinked, then propping her fists on her shapely little hips, gave him a look that would have dropped a lesser man dead in his tracks. "I don't know what game you're playing here, Nick Daniels. But you can count me out."

If he'd ever seen a more beautiful woman, he couldn't remember when. Even with her ponytail threaded through the back of an old red ball cap and a frown marring her pretty features, she could easily win the top title in a beauty contest.

"I don't play games, sweetheart."

"Then what was that all about?" she demanded, sounding out of breath.

He smiled. "I was just telling an old friend good night."

She shook her head. "Good night is a handshake, a pat on the shoulder or a 'see you later.' It is not a kiss hot enough to blister paint."

Grinning, he rocked back on his heels. "So you thought my kiss was that hot, huh?"

"I didn't—" She stopped, then glaring at him, shook her head. "Stop trying to turn this back on me. You were the one who—"

Before she could get a good head of steam worked up, he took her back in his arms and kissed her until they both gasped for breath. When he raised his head, he was pleased to see her scowl had been replaced by a slightly dazed expression.

"Good night, Cheyenne. Drive carefully on your way home."

She stared at him for several seconds before she turned and without a word walked the distance to her truck.

As he watched the taillights of her truck disappear into the dark night, Nick took a deep breath and willed himself to relax. It appeared that convincing Cheyenne they could have a satisfying physical relationship was going to be easier than he'd first thought.

Turning toward the house, he climbed the steps and headed upstairs to a cold shower. He wasn't proud of the fact that he was consciously planning to seduce her. That really made him no better than his philandering father.

But his need for Cheyenne was a weakness that was too strong to resist. And as long as he made sure neither of them developed an emotional attachment, there was no chance of either of them getting in over their heads or being hurt.

Four

"You were out pretty late last night, princess." Bertram Holbrook rolled his wheelchair up to his place at the head of the kitchen table. "Did the auction run longer than usual?"

Cheyenne nodded as she opened the refrigerator to take out a carton of eggs substitute and a package of bacon. "There was a lot of stock being sold." She wasn't about to tell him that she'd also been detained at the Sugar Creek Ranch after the auction, who had detained her or why.

"Is the company looking to buy some more cattle?" he asked conversationally.

Unable to meet her father's questioning gaze, she busied herself arranging strips of bacon in a skillet. "I've been told that we're going to sell off these herds and bring in all new stock."

Her father frowned. "What's wrong with the cattle we have? Aren't Black Angus good enough for those corporate bigwigs?"

"There's nothing wrong with our stock." She turned to put bread in the toaster. "We'll still be raising and marketing Black Angus beef. But our herds will be free-range cattle."

"That's going to cost a small fortune to replace all those cattle. Why in the name of Sam Hill does the company want to do something like that?" He shook his head. "It looks to me like it would make more sense to use the stock they've got and just stop feeding them store-bought feed."

"There's a lot more to it than that, Daddy." She finished making their breakfast, then, setting a plate at each of their places, she poured them both a cup of coffee and sat down at the table across from him. "Besides, it's not my place to question what's planned for the Sugar Creek. My job is to follow orders and put the plan into action."

"That's the problem with these corporations trying to play around at being cattle ranchers," he said disgustedly. "They jump on the bandwagon every time something new comes along. Then they wonder why they aren't making money."

She shrugged. "Actually I think it's a good move. The market for free range beef is really growing right now and it doesn't look to stop any time soon. More people than ever are wanting their food to be raised naturally and that includes beef free of growth hormones and supplements."

He smiled. "You do make a pretty good argument, princess. If you think it's a good idea, then I'm sure it is."

They fell into silence as they ate and Cheyenne tried to think of a way to break the news to him that Nick Daniels was not only back in the area, he was the new owner of the Sugar Creek Cattle Company and the one responsible for changing the status quo. She knew that the longer she put off telling her father, the harder it would be.

For one thing, he wasn't going to be the least bit happy that Nick had returned. And for another, he was going to resent that she hadn't told him about it immediately. But his blood pressure and the possibility of another stroke had to be considered, too. If her father got upset, it could very well cause him more problems.

Lost in thought, it took a moment for her to realize that he'd asked a question. "I'm sorry. What was that, Daddy?"

"I asked if you saw anybody you knew at the sale barn last night."

Feeling more guilty by the second, she rose to her feet to clear the dishes from the table. "I wasn't all that happy about having to be there, so I really didn't pay that much attention. But I suppose the usual crowd was there."

Her father was silent for a moment before he quietly said, "I'm sorry, princess."

She turned to face him. "What for?"

"You shouldn't have to work so hard or be going places you don't want to go." The sadness etched in his once handsome face and the regret in his faded blue eyes broke her heart. "If I hadn't had the stroke, you'd be a schoolteacher instead of working off a debt that isn't yours."

Tears burned her eyes as she walked over and knelt down beside his wheelchair. "Oh, Daddy, please don't blame yourself. You couldn't help that you got sick. And I really don't mind ranch work." She smiled through her tears. "Remember what you told me when I was younger? You always said that I was the best cowboy you ever saw."

He put his arms around her shoulders and hugged her as close as the wheelchair would allow. "You're the best of everything in my life, princess. I don't know what I'd do without you."

She hugged him back. "I don't want you worrying about that because it isn't an issue. I'm taking care of everything."

Later that evening, as Cheyenne went about the task of feeding her gelding and Mr. Nibbles, the pony she'd had since she was five, then checked on a couple of calves she'd isolated because they'd shown signs of pink eye, she thought about what she had and hadn't told her father. She'd tried to be as honest as possible without telling him a lie. But dancing around the truth was getting more difficult with each passing day. And if that wasn't enough to have to contend with, the guilt of not telling him about Nick was weighing on her like a ton of bricks.

Sitting on a bale of hay outside her horse's stall, she weighed her options. Her father's health was frail at best and she didn't want to cause him any more problems. But she had four years left to work for Nick or Emerald, Inc. or whoever held her contract. And there was no way she could avoid telling him about Nick for that long.

She took a deep breath and started walking toward the house. Her father was having a fairly good day and the news might not affect him as badly as she feared, as long as she stressed there was no danger of her falling for Nick again. The only problem was, she wasn't sure who she'd be trying to convince of that fact—her father or herself.

But when she entered the kitchen, her heart plummeted. She could tell from the accusing expression on his face that he knew.

"I can't tell you how disappointed I am in you, princess. Why didn't you tell me that Daniels bastard is back?"

Instead of the remorse she expected, a huge sense of relief washed over her. "I'm sorry, Daddy. I didn't want to upset you and I wasn't sure how to tell you without doing that."

Her father sadly shook his head. "I would've rather heard it from you than learn about it from J. W. Schaefer."

"Was he at the auction last night?" she asked, not at all surprised that one of her father's acquaintances had seen her and Nick. Being a judge in a small county, Bertram Holbrook was well-known by nearly everyone, and so was his daughter.

"He was sitting a couple of seats away from you," her father said, nodding. "But that's not important. What I want to know is why Daniels is back here. And why were you with him? After the way he left here like a thief in the night thirteen years ago, I can't understand why you'd want to have anything to do with him."

Cheyenne hated having to tell him the rest of the

news. He was upset enough and she certainly didn't like the idea of upsetting him even more. But there was no way around it. He had to know everything.

"Nick is the new owner of the Sugar Creek Cattle Company, Daddy. He's my boss now. I don't have a choice."

He stared at her for several long seconds, then to her dismay, her father suddenly seemed to be much more calm. "Really? I wonder how he came up with the money for that?" He shook his head. "Did he give you any explanation about why he high-tailed it out of here all those years ago?"

Before she could answer that she had no idea, the phone rang. Answering on the second ring, she wondered how much worse her day could get when she discovered Nick on the other end of the line.

"Cheyenne, I know this is your day off and I'm really sorry about asking you this. But I need you to get over here right away." The urgency in his voice alarmed her.

"What's wrong?"

"I've got a mare in labor and she's showing signs of distress."

"Of course I'll help. Have you called Doc Connors? He's the veterinarian we've been using since Doc Haywood retired."

"Yes, but he's tied up at the McIntire ranch with

a possible outbreak of bovine tuberculosis and he's not sure when he'll be able to get here."

There was no hesitation in her answer. An animal was in trouble and it was her job as ranch foreman to see that it got the help it needed. "I'll be there in fifteen minutes or less."

When she hung up the phone, Cheyenne turned to her father. "I have to go help Nick with a pregnant mare having trouble giving birth."

Looking a bit distracted, he nodded. "Go ahead and do what you have to do, princess. I've been thinking about giving Gordon and a couple of my other cronies a call to see if they wanted to play cards this evening anyway."

As she gathered the first-aid kit she kept for animal emergencies around the ranch, her father proceeded to call Sheriff Turner and set up a game of poker. She thought it was a bit odd that her father had so readily dismissed the subject of Nick's return, considering how much he'd always disliked Nick. But Cheyenne didn't have time to speculate on her father's abrupt turnaround. The lives of a mare and her unborn foal were dependent on her doing her job. And that's exactly what she intended to do.

While Nick waited for Cheyenne to arrive, he got the agitated mare up and walking around the large birthing stall. He'd seen this type of problem before in other horses and although it had been a long time, he still remembered what to do when a foal's head failed to appear with both forelegs.

Sometime during the stage two phase of labor the foal had failed to position itself properly for the delivery. By getting the mare to walk, it would hopefully stop her from pushing and reduce the pressure on the foal. With any luck, the fetus would fall back into the womb enough to reposition itself for a normal birth.

"What seems to be the problem?" Cheyenne asked in a soft, low tone as she slowly approached the stall.

"We have a retention of the head," Nick answered just as quietly. Keeping the mare calm was crucial and any loud noise or sudden moves could increase her anxiety and cause more problems.

Easing into the stall, Cheyenne asked, "How long have you had her up and walking?"

"About forty-five minutes." He stopped the mare to check her hindquarters. "If the foal repositions, I think we'll be okay and have a normal birth. But if it doesn't present properly, I may have to reach inside and help."

Cheyenne stepped up to take hold of the mare's halter. "I'll keep her walking while you wash your arms with disinfectant."

As he walked down the wide center aisle of the

barn, Nick was thankful for Cheyenne's tranquil presence. She'd always had a way with animals and he was going to have to depend on her to help keep the mare calm in the event something intrusive had to be done.

When he stepped into the stall a few minutes later, Cheyenne was patting the horse's sweat-soaked neck and crooning to her softly. "She's tried to lie down several times, but I wanted to wait until you returned, in case she needs our help."

He nodded. "Let's get her down and see how it goes."

Without any encouragement from the two humans, the mare immediately lay down on her side on the thick bed of straw and began pushing to bring her colt into the world. Within minutes, first one tiny hoof, then the other emerged.

Nick found himself holding his breath, waiting to see if the foal's head presented as it should. When it did, he had to force himself not to let out a loud whoop of joy.

But his jubilation was short-lived when the mare suddenly relaxed as if her job was complete. Kneeling down beside her, he laid his hand on her belly. The contractions had stopped after the emergence of the foal's shoulders.

"Damn! I was afraid something like this would happen."

"She's too tired. I think you're going to have to help her." Worry was written all over Cheyenne's pretty face as she continued to pat the animal's sweat-soaked neck and he could tell she feared they'd lose both the foal and the mare. The same as he did.

He hadn't wanted to intervene if he didn't have to. But it appeared that the matter had been taken out of his hands. Nature wasn't going to take its course and he didn't have a choice.

Sitting behind the exhausted mare, Nick braced his boots flat on the floor of the stall for traction and, grasping the foal's fetlocks, slowly began to pull. He hoped the steady pressure of his efforts would restart the mare's abdominal contractions. But when it became apparent that it wasn't working, Cheyenne moved into position beside him without having to be told what to do and took hold of one of the foal's front legs.

"Ready?" he asked through gritted teeth.

When she nodded, they worked together and, careful not to injure the animal, they slowly began the arduous task of pulling the foal from the mare. Working for what seemed like hours, but in fact was only a matter of minutes, they finally succeeded and the new baby slid out onto the soft bed of straw.

While Cheyenne caught her breath from the physical exertion, Nick quickly cleared the bluish-white amniotic sac away from the foal's nose and muzzle. To his relief, the colt immediately moved its head and started breathing without further assistance, then rolled to its sternum to make the job a little easier. Turning his attention to the mare, Nick was further relieved to discover that, although exhausted from her ordeal, she appeared to be fine.

"We did it," Cheyenne said, throwing her arms around him.

They were still on their knees in the straw and her exuberant reaction damned near knocked him over, but he didn't care. He felt the same as she did. They'd seen the mare through the crisis and had good reason to celebrate.

"We sure did." Wrapping her in a bear hug, he pulled her close. "We make a hell of a team, sweetheart. If I hadn't had your help, I'd have probably lost both of them."

As he drew back to stare down at her, the feel of her soft body against his and the emotional bond they shared from having weathered the crisis together was too strong a connection to resist. Without thinking twice, Nick lowered his head to capture Cheyenne's lips with his.

Tunneling his hands through her glossy hair, the golden-brown strands flowed over his tanned skin like silk threads and the instant his mouth touched hers, an electric current traveled all the way from the top of his head to the soles of his feet. A need stronger than anything he'd ever experienced overtook him. He wanted her, wanted to lose himself in her sweetness and forget that they'd spent thirteen years apart or that they'd never have a future together. All that mattered was here. Now.

He leisurely savored her lips as he reacquainted himself with their softness. When Cheyenne splayed her hands across his back and pressed herself closer, the feel of her lush breasts crushed to his chest sent a shock wave straight to the most sensitive part of his anatomy.

She sighed at the contact and he instinctively knew she was experiencing the same intense need he was. Her acceptance of his kiss encouraged him and he slipped inside to taste the sweetness that was uniquely Cheyenne. Stroking her tongue with his, he teased and coaxed her into exploring him, but when she returned the favor, his heart thumped his ribs like a bass drum and the blood flowing through his veins felt as if it had been turned to liquid fire.

As she tentatively acquainted herself with him, it took everything Nick had in him not to take charge of the caress. But he sensed that she needed to feel in control, needed to come to terms with what he'd already accepted. They were going to make love. And, if their inability to keep their hands off of each other was any indication, it was going to be soon. The thought sent his hormones into overdrive and not only was his arousal immediate, the intensity of it left him feeling light-headed.

Unable to remain passive any longer, he tugged the tail of her T-shirt from the waistband of her jeans, then ran his hands along her sides to cup the underside of her breasts. When they were kids, he'd never taken the liberty of exploring her body, never touched her in any way that could have been considered inappropriate. But they were no longer teenagers and as far as he was concerned, there was nothing out of line between two consenting adults.

When he used his thumbs to tease her taut nipples through her lacy bra, her moan of pleasure vibrated against his lips and sent heat streaking to every cell of his being. "Does that feel good, Cheyenne?" he whispered.

She nodded. "We shouldn't be doing this."

"Do you want me to stop?"

"No."

He chuckled. "I shouldn't be touching you. But you don't want me to stop?"

"Yes…no…" She shivered against him. "I…can't think."

"It's okay, sweetheart." He rose to his feet, then pulled her up to stand in front of him. Staring at her upturned face, he smiled at the rosy blush of passion painting her porcelain cheeks. "I'm not going to lie to you. I want you, Cheyenne. I want to kiss every inch of your body, then sink myself deep inside you and watch you come apart in my arms when you find your release." He touched her satiny skin as he shook his head. "But I can't promise you anything beyond the pleasure. I'm not looking to start a relationship with you, nor do I want a commitment from you."

His lower body tightened further when her little pink tongue darted out to moisten her perfect lips. "In other words, you want sex with no strings attached?"

Put in such basic terms it sounded cold and calculating and he'd like nothing better than to deny it. But his conscience was stronger than his desire to finally claim her body.

"I didn't want to phrase it that way, but yes. That's exactly what I want."

Five

Even though she'd gotten over Nick years ago and the very last thing she wanted to do was become involved with him again, Cheyenne couldn't believe the level of desire that filled her at his admission that he wanted her. "I think I'll be going now. You should be able to handle things from here with the mare and colt."

He stared at her for several long moments before he nodded and stepped back. "Thanks for coming over to help. I really appreciate it."

Thankful that he wasn't going to pressure her, she shrugged as she knelt to repack the first-aid kit. "No need to thank me. Taking care of the Sugar Creek livestock is part of my job description." When she stood up and walked to the stall door, he started to follow her, but she shook her head. "There's no need for you to show me out. I know the way."

Needing to put distance between them, but unwilling to let him see how tempted she'd been by his confession, she forced herself to walk slowly from the barn and over to where she'd parked her truck. She felt Nick's gaze following her as she put the first-aid kit in the back, then opened the driver's door and climbed in behind the steering wheel.

As she started the engine and drove from the ranch yard, she had mixed emotions about what Nick was proposing. On the one hand, she didn't want a relationship with him any more than he wanted one with her. She'd suffered the sting of his rejection once. She certainly didn't want to spend years trying to get over him again. But on the other hand, whether she liked it or not her body craved his touch and she wanted him as badly as he wanted her.

She slowed the truck to a stop and, taking a deep breath in an effort to settle her frayed nerves, stared out the windshield at the quiet, starless night. She couldn't believe she was even considering his outrageous suggestion. But the truth of the matter was, she was tired of always doing the right thing, of always being the person someone told her she should be. Just once she'd like to throw caution to the wind and do something completely out of character, simply because it was what she wanted to do, instead of what everyone expected of her.

But could she have an affair with Nick without endangering her heart in the bargain? Was it possible for a woman to share her body with a man and not become emotionally attached? Did she even have the courage to try?

Cheyenne wasn't sure how long she sat there waging her internal debate or when she came to a decision. But before she had the chance to change her mind, she steered the truck back onto the road and drove back to the Sugar Creek ranch.

What she was about to do was the most impulsive, insane thing she'd ever done in her entire life. But it was too late to back out now. When she pulled her truck to a stop, Nick was still standing in the open doorway of the barn and from his seductive expression she could tell he knew exactly why she'd returned.

Suddenly unable to find the courage to get out of the truck, she was aware that he had started walking toward her. The closer he got, the faster her pulse raced and when he opened the door and took her hand in his to help her down from the seat, her heart skipped several beats.

Neither spoke as they walked the short distance to

the house and climbed the porch steps. But when they entered the foyer, Cheyenne stopped.

"Your housekeeper and her husband—"

"Live in the foreman's cottage down the road." He gently cupped her cheek with his callused palm and gave her an encouraging smile. "I promise we're alone, Cheyenne."

A tiny shiver coursed through her at the sultry look in his hooded blue gaze as he once again took her hand in his and led her upstairs to his bedroom. But instead of stopping beside the bed, he led her into the master bathroom.

"We're going to take a shower together," he said, removing her ball cap, then the elastic band holding her ponytail. He threaded his fingers through her hair as he lowered his head to hers. "Then I'm going to give you more pleasure than you've ever imagined."

Tender and soft, his kiss warmed her to the depths of her soul and as his mouth moved over hers, she refused to think of the possible consequences of her actions or that she was playing a fool's game with a man she couldn't trust. At the moment, all she wanted to do was feel his hard body pressed to hers and taste the passion on his firm male lips.

When he coaxed her to open for him, she readily complied and the feel of his tongue stroking hers sent a flash fire racing to the pit of her belly and caused every cell in her being to tingle to life. Wanting to get closer to him, she wrapped her arms around his waist and splayed her hands over the firm muscles of his broad back.

It didn't matter that Nick was the last man she should be kissing or that her decision could very well be the biggest mistake of her life. She was too caught up in the feel of his strength surrounding her, his hands molding her to him and his strong arousal pressed to her lower abdomen.

Her heart pounded against her ribs and her mind began to spin when he broke the kiss and, holding her gaze with his, slid his hands from her back to her sides, then up under the tail of her T-shirt to pull it over her head. He tossed it to the floor, then made quick work of unfastening her bra.

His gaze never wavered as he drew the straps from her shoulders and she shivered in anticipation of his touch. Heaven help her, but she wanted to feel his hands on her, wanted him to explore her in ways that she'd never experienced before.

But just when she thought he was going to caress her heated body, he took a deep breath and knelt to remove their boots and socks. When they were both barefoot, he reached to unbuckle her belt. He seemed to be devoting his total concentration on each task and not once did he look at her body.

Once he had the leather strap unfastened, he pushed the button through the buttonhole, then slowly eased the zipper down. Her heart pounded so hard, she was surprised it didn't leap out of her chest when he hooked his thumbs in the elastic at the top of her panties and eased them and her jeans down her legs.

When he straightened, his blue gaze seemed to touch her everywhere and instead of feeling the self-consciousness she'd expected, she felt more feminine than she'd ever felt in her life. "You're even more beautiful than I imagined, Cheyenne." Smiling, he guided her hands to the snaps on the front of his chambray shirt. "Your turn, sweetheart."

Her fingers trembled as she slowly opened each one of the metal closures and when she finally parted the garment to push it from his wide shoulders, her breath caught. When they'd been teenagers, she'd seen him without a shirt and thought he had a nice physique. But the lanky body of the eighteen-year-old boy she'd known had grown into the impressively muscular body of a man. And he was absolutely gorgeous.

As she unbuckled his belt and reached for the snap at the top of his jeans, the sight of his bulging fly had her hastily amending her assessment of him. Not only did Nick have an impressive body, but he was the perfect specimen of a thoroughly aroused

man in his prime. The room suddenly felt several degrees warmer and she couldn't seem to get her fingers to work.

"I think you'd better do this," she finally said, surprised that her voice sounded a lot more steady than
she felt.

The sexy sound of his low chuckle sent a wave of
longing straight to the pit of her belly and made her
knees feel as if they had been turned to rubber.
"You're probably right. Metal zippers can be damned
dangerous to a man in my condition."

Watching Nick carefully pull the zipper down,
then push his jeans and white cotton briefs down his
muscular thighs caused tiny sparks of electric current
to skip over every nerve in her body. When he kicked
his clothes aside and she caught a glimpse of his
magnificent body, her heart stalled. His chest wasn't
the only impressive part of his superb physique.

"You're perfect," she said aloud.

He shook his head and pulled her into his arms.
"Not as perfect as you."

The contact of feminine skin with hard male flesh
and the feel of his strong arousal pressed to her soft
lower belly sent the tingling sensation racing to her
very core.

"You feel so damned good, sweetheart." His deep
voice was rough with desire and caused an answer-

ing shiver of compelling need to slide over every inch of her.

When she finally managed to draw a breath, she nodded. "So...do you."

Caught up in the delicious sensations swirling throughout her body, she wasn't sure when Nick turned on the water and moved them under the warm spray. But the feel of water sliding over her sensitized skin helped restore some of her sanity.

She'd never in her life showered with anyone and until that moment, she'd never considered how intimate it could be. If he'd given her the opportunity, she might have even been a little embarrassed by how truly exposed she was. But Nick didn't give her the chance.

Turning her away from him, he poured a dollop of shampoo into his hands and began to work it into her long hair. His fingers felt wonderful massaging her scalp and any traces of apprehension she might have had disappeared immediately.

When he rinsed her hair, he gave her a quick kiss before washing and rinsing his own. Then, taking a bar of soap, he worked it into a lather and began to slide it over her shoulders and collarbone. Placing it in the built-in soap dish, he slowly ran his soapy hands up along her ribs to cover her breasts. The friction of his palms caressing her, the calluses chaf-

ing her pebbled nipples sent ribbons of desire threading their way throughout her body.

As he leisurely smoothed his hands over her upper
torso, Cheyenne closed her eyes and reveled in the
delicious sensations coursing through her. Massaging
her everywhere he touched, Nick created a need
within her like nothing she'd ever known before. And
by the time he reached her lower belly, she was certain she'd go completely mad from the intense longing building deep inside of her.

"You're making me crazy," she said, turning and
bracing her hands on his wide chest.

"Trust me, sweetheart. It's only going to get better."

His mouth came down on hers with an urgency
that stole her breath and she eagerly returned his kiss
with a boldness that might have shocked her if she'd
been able to think about what she was doing. But
with the tantalizing fog of passion clouding her mind
and his hands slowly skimming the insides of her
thighs, all she could do was feel.

At the same time as he slipped his tongue inside
to stroke her tender inner recesses, he placed one
arm around her back to steady her, then used his
other hand to part the delicate folds of her femininity. Sparkles of light danced behind her closed eyes
and her knees threatened to give way at the exquisite
tightening in her womb.

Just when she thought she'd go into total meltdown, he gently broke the kiss and, putting a bit of space between them, handed her the soap. "I scrubbed your back, now it's your turn to scrub mine."

Cheyenne realized that in slowing down his sensual exploration, he was actually heightening her anticipation of things to come. Taking a deep breath, she smiled as she ran the bar of soap over his heavily muscled chest and rippling stomach.

"I don't know how to tell you this, cowboy. But you need a lesson in female anatomy if you think that was my back."

His sexy grin caused her stomach to flutter. "I'll tell you what. I'll teach you about the male body, if you'll teach me about a woman's."

Her heart skipped several beats when he took the soap from her. She'd bet her next paycheck that he knew a lot more about the female form than she knew about a man.

"Lesson number one," he continued, guiding her hand to him. "This is what you do to me, how much you make me want you."

At the same time as her fingers encircled his engorged flesh, Cheyenne watched his jaw tighten and his eyes close a moment before he shuddered against her. An overwhelming sense of feminine power overtook her as she explored his body. Testing the strength and weight of him, she had no doubt about the depth of his desire for her.

He suddenly opened his eyes and caught her hands in his to hold them to his chest. "I think we'd better dry off and take this to bed while I still have the strength to walk."

Turning off the shower, he dried them both with fluffy towels, then giving her a kiss so tender it brought tears to her eyes, he picked her up and carried her into the bedroom. When he set her on her feet beside the bed, she pulled the comforter back and lay down while he turned on the bedside lamp and removed a foil packet from the nightstand.

She caught her lower lip between her teeth to keep it from trembling as she watched him place the condom under his pillow. She was nervous, but her anxiety had nothing to do with having second thoughts and everything to do with her inexperience. But when Nick stretched out beside her, then gathered her to him, her apprehension was quickly forgotten as the feel of his strength overwhelmed her.

His mouth touched hers in a feathery kiss. "I wanted to take this slow, but I'm so damned hot for you, I'm not sure that's going to be an option."

Before she could respond, his lips claimed hers and his need, the taste of his passion sent pleasure racing to every cell of her being. As his tongue swept over her mouth, then darted inside to stroke her, she savored his hunger and reveled in the excitement building deep within her.

When he slid his callused palm along her side, then caressed her breast, a heavy coil of need settled in the pit of her stomach and she couldn't stop a frustrated moan from escaping on her ragged sigh. Wanting to touch him, to explore his incredible body the way he was exploring hers, Cheyenne placed her hands on the thick pads of his pectoral muscles. His flat male nipples puckered in response and his groan of pleasure rumbled up from deep in his chest.

He nibbled kisses along the column of her throat to her collarbone, then down the slope of her breast, causing her breath to come out in tiny little puffs. But as his mouth closed over the hardened peak, the sensation of his warm, wet tongue on her sensitized skin had her wondering if she would ever breathe again.

"You're so soft...so sweet," he murmured as he slowly moved his hand down her abdomen to the juncture of her thighs.

She gasped when he parted her, then teased her with a gossamer touch. The tightening deep inside her lower belly increased tenfold and she couldn't seem to lie still.

"Nick, please!"

"Easy, sweetheart," he whispered as he continued

to tease the tiny nub of intense sensation. "I'll take care of you."

A tremor passed through her and she caught her breath at the empty ache forming in her lower body. "I need...please—"

His kiss was so tender, so poignant she felt as if she would melt. "Do you want me, Cheyenne?"

"Yes."

"Now?"

"Yes."

"Where?"

She was quickly losing her mind and all he could do was ask questions?

"Please...I need you...inside."

He raised his head and gave her a smile filled with the promise of things to come before he reached beneath the pillow for the foil packet. Her heart raced and her breathing became shallow as she watched him arrange their protection.

But when he nudged her knees apart, then settled himself over her, she closed her eyes and braced herself for whatever happened next.

"Look at me, Cheyenne."

When she did as he commanded, he held her gaze with his as he guided himself to her, then slowly, carefully pushed his hips forward. The exquisite pressure she felt as her body stretched to accommodate him was indescribable and instead of the pain she expected, her entire being hummed with a longing to be completely filled by him.

Nick could have never in his wildest dreams imagined the incredible degree of hunger that Cheyenne instilled in him. It was as if he'd finally found the other half of himself when he fitted his body to hers to make them one.

But as he savored the feeling, his heart suddenly stalled and he went completely still at the barrier he met within her. "What the hell—"

The unusual tightness surrounding him, the unexpected resistance and the flash of pain clouding her aqua eyes could only mean one thing. Until that moment Cheyenne had never been with a man.

"You're a virgin," he said, careful to hold his lower body perfectly still.

"Not…anymore." She gave him a tremulous smile. "I'm pretty sure…you just took care…of that…issue," she said breathlessly.

"But you're twenty-nine."

"And you're thirty-one." She grinned. "But I don't think either of us is ready for social security just yet."

"You've never done this before." He knew he wasn't making a hell of a lot of sense. But he was having the devil of a time believing that in the past thirteen years she hadn't found someone she wanted to be with. At least once.

"Does that make a difference?" she asked, suddenly sounding defensive.

Gathering her to him, he smiled as he kissed her stubborn little chin. "No, sweetheart. It doesn't make a damn bit of difference. I just wish that you had told me, that's all."

"Why?"

"Because if I hadn't been trying to take things slowly and make this last, I could have hurt you more than I did."

His body demanded that he complete the act of making her his, but he gritted his teeth and did his best to ignore it. Cheyenne needed time to adjust to the changes caused by his invasion.

She reached up to touch his cheek with her delicate hand. "I'm fine. Really."

"Are you sure?" Her eyes had softened and her body had relaxed some, but he needed to make sure.

When she nodded, he slowly pulled back, then moved forward, ever watchful for any sign of her discomfort. Detecting none, he set a slow pace and all too soon he felt himself climbing the peak of fulfillment.

Unwilling to complete the journey without her, Nick reached between them to lightly caress her feminine secrets. Her immediate tightening around him indicated that she was reaching for the summit and, deepening his strokes, he held himself in check as she found her pleasure and came apart in his arms.

Only then did he unleash the tight control he'd struggled to maintain and give in to his own release. He hoarsely whispered her name as he thrust into her one final time and felt the triumphant of completion as he emptied himself deep inside her tight body.

Several moments later, when he found the strength to lever himself away from her, he rolled to the side and gathered her into his arms. "Are you all right?"

"I can't believe how incredible that was." The awe in her soft voice reassured him that she hadn't found the experience as unpleasant as he'd feared it might be after learning it was her first time.

"I promise that next time will be even better," he said, kissing the top of her head.

She snuggled closer. "I don't see how that's possible."

Chuckling, he leisurely ran his hands over her satiny skin. "Just give me a minute or two to recover and I'll show you."

They lay in companionable silence for several long moments before she raised up to glance at the clock on the nightstand. "Oh, dear heavens! I didn't realize it was so late."

She started to pull from his arms, but Nick held her close. "What's your hurry, sweetheart?"

"I need to get home."

He brushed his lips over hers. "Spend the night with me, Cheyenne."

"I can't. I have to get home to see about my father. He'll be worried." When she tried to get up a second time, Nick let her go.

As he watched, she scurried into the bathroom and when she emerged a couple of minutes later she was fully dressed.

Rising from the bed, he removed a fresh pair of jeans from his closet and pulled them on. "I'll walk you out to your truck."

"There's no need." Her expression was unconcerned as she shrugged one slender shoulder. "That's the beauty of a 'no-strings' arrangement. You don't have to observe the conventions of a relationship."

"Maybe so, but that doesn't mean a man shouldn't be a gentleman about things," he growled. It was completely ridiculous, but her words irritated the hell out of him. "Besides, I want to kiss you goodnight."

Her smile sent his blood pressure soaring. "A simple kiss was what got all this started in the first place."

Placing his arm around her shoulders, he walked her down the stairs and out onto the front porch. "If

I kiss you again, will you reconsider spending the night with me?"

"No."

He kissed her until they both gasped for breath. "You're sure?"

She looked a little dazed as she started down the porch steps. "Right now, I'm not even sure of my own name."

"Good night, *Cheyenne*," he said, laughing.

As he watched her truck disappear down the lane, Nick leaned his shoulder against the newel post and stared up at the night sky. Nothing would have pleased him more than to spend the night with her, then wake up tomorrow morning with her in his arms.

When his body tightened at the pleasant thought, he shook his head to clear it. "That doesn't sound like a no-strings affair," he muttered, suddenly disgusted with himself.

Walking back into the house, he headed straight for the bathroom and a cold shower. How the hell could he still burn for her after the most incredible sex of his life?

But some time later, as he lay shivering in his empty bed, Nick was still having a problem wrapping his mind around the idea that up until a couple of hours ago, Cheyenne had still been a virgin. Surely she'd had other boyfriends after he left Wyoming— if not in high school, at least in college.

Why had she waited until now to lose her virginity? Hadn't she found a guy in the past thirteen years that she'd had special feelings for?

When they'd been teenagers, she'd certainly given every indication that she'd thought he was that special. But out of respect for her and not wanting to be anything like the man who'd spawned him, Nick had been determined to make Cheyenne his wife first.

With his heart racing, his body jackknifed and he sat straight up in bed. Had she waited all this time because she hadn't felt as close with any other man as she had with him? Did she still feel that way?

His mind reeled from the implications. Earlier, in the barn when he'd laid his cards on the table and told her up-front that he didn't want a relationship with her, but that he did want them to have sex, she hadn't been able to get away from him fast enough. But not fifteen minutes later, she'd come back and accepted his terms. Then, after honoring him with the gift of being the first man to touch her, of making the most amazing love with him, she'd reminded him theirs was a no-strings affair.

Collapsing back against his pillow, Nick shook his head. How the hell was a man supposed to understand what was going on when he was getting such mixed signals? And why was he letting it get to him?

He hadn't come back to Wyoming to take up

where he left off with Cheyenne Holbrook, nor did he want to. Unbeknown to him, his mother had requested that after her death Emerald hold his land in order for him to reclaim it when she decided he was ready. That's why he'd returned and that's exactly what he intended to do.

Besides, he and Cheyenne were two different people now and it was best the way things had turned out. The likelihood of them sharing anything more than a few laughs over old times and some really amazing sex was slim at best.

After all, he was Owen Larson's son and he'd proven time and again that relationships weren't his strong suit. It was probably just a matter of time before he lost interest in Cheyenne and the last thing he wanted to do was hurt her.

He frowned as he stared up at the ceiling. But she seemed to be doing all right with their arrangement—maybe even better than he was. He couldn't believe the level of irritation that ran through him when she'd told him that he didn't have to walk her out to her truck. But that was probably due to her inexperience with the dynamics of a no-strings affair. She didn't realize that whether emotions were involved or not, after a woman shared her body with a man, she deserved to be treated like a lady.

Satisfied that he had it all figured out and once

again had his priorities straight, he turned to his stomach and concentrated on getting a good night's sleep. But instead of ways to improve the ranch or the new free-range program he intended to start, his last thoughts before he went to sleep were of making love to a beautiful girl with long golden-brown hair and aqua eyes named Cheyenne.

Six

"Daddy, did you hear anything unusual after I got home last night?" Cheyenne asked her father as she came in from outside.

When her father looked up from the crossword puzzle he'd been working, he shook his head. "No, why, princess?"

"Because I have four flat tires on my pickup truck." Walking straight to the phone, she punched in the number for the county sheriff's office. "And it looks like someone used an ice pick to puncture holes in the side walls."

His expression indignant, he slapped his puzzle

book down on the table. "Who in tarnation would have the nerve to come onto my property and do such a despicable thing?"

Cheyenne held up her index finger to silence his outburst when the county dispatcher picked up on the other end of the line. "Wilma, this is Cheyenne Holbrook. Could you please send a patrol car out to the Flying H Ranch? I'm afraid we've had some trouble with vandals."

"Cheyenne, honey, are you and your dad all right?" the woman asked anxiously.

"We're fine. But I can't say the same for my truck." Cheyenne sighed. "I have four tires that resemble Swiss cheese."

"I'll send Gordon out right away to take your statement and fill out a report."

Cheyenne cringed at the sound of the sheriff's name. She'd never liked Gordon Turner and the less she had to do with him the better. "That's not necessary, Wilma. Just send one of the deputies."

"Good heavens, Cheyenne. Are you looking to get me fired? Gordon is going to insist on taking care of this himself since it happened out there at the judge's ranch."

The woman immediately turned away to radio the sheriff. When she came back on the line, Wilma announced, "He says he'll be there in about twenty minutes."

Sighing, Cheyenne thanked the woman, then hung up the phone. For the sake of her father's pride very few people knew that they were no longer the owners of the Flying H. She supposed having to deal with Sheriff Turner was a small price to pay to keep her father's dignity intact.

"Is Gordon on his way?" her father asked, backing his wheelchair away from the table.

She nodded. "Wilma said he should be here in a few minutes."

Her father waved his hand toward the door. "Push me out onto the back porch. I want to make sure he knows who to question about this trouble."

She pushed his wheelchair out onto the covered porch, then locked the wheels. "We've never had this kind of problem before. Why would you think you know who punctured my tires when I can't think of a soul who would do something like this?"

"Think about it, princess. We've never had trouble like this before." He pointed to the west. "But Nick Daniels moves back into the area and in sight of a week you have four flat tires. Didn't I always tell you he was nothing but bad news?"

Shocked by his vehemence, she shook her head.

"No, Daddy. I don't think so. What would Nick gain by vandalizing my truck?"

"He could be trying to get you to quit your job." Her father sounded a little less passionate, but no less convinced that Nick was guilty of the crime.

"If he didn't want me working for him, I'm certain Nick would tell me so and terminate my contract with the Sugar Creek Cattle Company."

"I'm not so sure about that," her father said stubbornly. "That boy was up to no good thirteen years ago and you can bet he's up to no good now. Once a troublemaker, always a troublemaker."

Cheyenne patted his shoulder in an effort to calm him down as they waited for the sheriff to arrive. She wasn't about to tell him that unless it was some kind of bizarre mating ritual no one ever heard of, she seriously doubted that Nick would flatten all four of her tires after making love to her so tenderly only a few hours before.

"Whatever you say, Daddy."

"I mean it, Cheyenne." He took hold of her hand. "There are things about that Daniels boy you don't know anything about."

His insistence and the earnest expression on his face unsettled her. "What are you talking about, Daddy? I don't remember—"

"You know I'm not at liberty to talk about the aspects of past cases, princess," he interrupted. "But believe me when I tell you, that boy is no good and never will be."

"Nick?"

Looking up from the ranch records, he smiled. "What can I do for you, Greta?"

"Cheyenne's here."

"It's about damn time. She's over three hours late."

At first, he'd wondered if she'd overslept. But the later it got, he'd started to worry that he might have hurt her more last night than she'd let on.

Standing up, Nick walked around the desk, but something about his housekeeper's frown stopped him dead in his tracks. "What's up?"

"Sheriff Turner is with her. They're in the great room." Greta lowered her voice. "Do you want me to call Carl?"

Nick had no idea why he was being paid a visit by Gordon Turner, but he was no longer an inexperienced teenage boy. He could fight his own battles and he damned well wasn't going to let the man run roughshod over him again.

"There's no need to call Carl, Greta. I can take care of whatever the sheriff wants."

He waited until the woman started back toward the kitchen before he crossed the hall into the great room.

"Sheriff Turner. Cheyenne." He nodded a greeting. "I'm guessing this isn't a social call."

Turner grunted. "Not hardly. Just where were you last night, Daniels? And what were you up to?" The sheriff's sanctimonious expression was meant to intimidate, but only served to make him look like a puffed-up bullfrog.

"I've already told you that Nick and I had to help a mare with a difficult birth," Cheyenne said, turning on the man.

Sheriff Turner shook his head. "I want to hear where he was after you left here to go home. And I want to hear it from him, not you, Ms. Holbrook." Turning back to Nick, he narrowed his eyes. "I'm waiting, Daniels."

Nick met the man's accusing glare head on. "I was right here all night."

"Is there someone who can verify that?"

"No. After Cheyenne left, I was alone the rest of the evening." Nick didn't like the sheriff's condescending attitude or the direction his questioning was headed. "Why do you ask?"

A vein began to throb at the man's temple. "I'm the one asking the questions here. All I want from you is answers."

"Oh, for heaven's sake. It's not like it's a state secret, Sheriff." Cheyenne looked angry enough to bite nails in two. "Someone punctured all four of my truck tires last night," she said, turning to Nick. "I tried to tell him that you had nothing to do with it, but he won't listen."

Sheriff Turner stubbornly folded his arms over his barrel chest. "The judge said to question Daniels here, and that's what I'm doing."

Anger, swift and hot welled up inside of Nick at the mention of the judge. It appeared that disabled or not, His Honor, Bertram Holbrook, still had Gordon Turner dancing to his tune.

"Are you accusing me of having something to do with the vandalism, Sheriff?"

"I didn't say that." Some of the sheriff's arrogance seemed to slip and he couldn't quite meet Nick's steady gaze. "I'm just trying to investigate what happened."

"I was here. Alone." Nick hardened his voice so there was no mistaking his meaning. "And unless you have evidence that says otherwise, I suggest you look elsewhere for whoever caused the trouble, because it wasn't me."

A dull flush colored Sheriff Turner's puffy cheeks. "I'll be watching you, Daniels. Don't think I won't." When he turned to leave, he motioned for Cheyenne to follow him. "Come on, Ms. Holbrook. I'll give you a ride back home."

Cheyenne shook her head. "I'll have Nick drive me home later."

"Your father—"

"Knows that I'll be home later," she said, glaring at the man.

The sheriff looked as if he wanted to argue the point, but when it was clear that Cheyenne was going to stand her ground, Turner wisely chose to leave without her.

"I'm so sorry about this, Nick," she said when they heard the front door close. "I tried to tell my father and the sheriff that I didn't think you had anything to do with the incident, but they wouldn't listen. They insisted that you needed to be questioned about it since you'd been in trouble before."

He frowned. Unless she was talking about the night they tried to elope, he'd never in his entire life done anything to land his ass in trouble with the law. And it didn't set well that after he'd moved to St. Louis he'd been falsely accused of doing things without the benefit of being there to defend himself.

"Would you like to refresh my memory? I don't seem to recall doing anything illegal. Just what was it that I was supposed to have done?"

She looked confused. "I'm not sure. Daddy said he couldn't talk about past cases. But I told him that I was sure if you had done something it couldn't have been anything more than a boyish prank."

Although he'd never been able to figure out why, Nick had always known the judge had no use for him. But he'd never dreamed the man would stoop so low as to make up a pack of lies about him.

More furious than he could ever remember, he chose his words very carefully. "Out of respect for you, I'm not going to call your father a liar, Cheyenne. But rest assured, I have never in my entire life broken the law. Not at eighteen. Not now."

"I don't…understand."

He could tell that his impassioned statement and the intensity in his voice startled her. He regretted that. But it couldn't be helped. It was past time for her to face facts. Everything she'd been led to believe about him had been colored by her father's hatred toward Nick's family.

But as much as he wanted to set the record straight, he needed time for his anger to cool. When he explained why he and his mother had left Wyoming in the dead of night, he fully intended to keep his head about him and his temper in check. None of it was Cheyenne's fault and he didn't want to leave her with the impression that he blamed her.

"Don't worry about it, sweetheart. We'll discuss it later." Taking her in his arms, he pressed a kiss to her forehead. "Do you have any idea how amazing you were last night?"

"Not really." He felt some of her tension ease away as he held her close. "I'm not sure…"

When he nibbled at the delicate hollow behind her ear, her voice trailed off. "Were you sore this morning?"

Her porcelain cheeks colored a pretty pink. "A little."

"I'm sorry, sweetheart." He hated that he'd caused her even the slightest discomfort. But he could damn sure see that it didn't happen again. "We'll have to wait a few days before we make love again."

"Don't you mean *have sex?*"

Leaning back, he frowned. "Same thing."

She shook her head. "Making love carries the connotation of an emotional attachment. Having sex is the coming together of two individuals for the purpose of mutual satisfaction." She pulled from his arms and started walking toward his office. "But I'm not here to argue semantics with you. I'm here to get some work done."

It made absolutely no sense, but Nick had the urge to punch something. What Cheyenne said was true. Theirs was an affair with no emotional involvement. That's what he wanted and that's what she was giving him.

But every time she reminded him of that fact it pissed him off. And for the life of him, he had no idea why.

By Friday afternoon, Cheyenne found it extremely hard to concentrate as she sat in Nick's office staring at the preliminary list of cattle to be taken to auction on Saturday night. She'd spent most of the week thinking about the tire incident and Nick's assurance that he'd had no part in it.

Her father and the sheriff continued to suspect he'd been responsible for the vandalism, but it really made no sense. For one thing, puncturing tires was more of a juvenile act than something a grown man would do. And for another, she couldn't think of a single thing that Nick would gain from it.

Her father insisted that Nick had been in trouble with the law when he was younger, and he'd never lied to her. But Nick had been very convincing when he'd sworn that he hadn't. And unless she counted him telling her when they were teenagers that he'd love her until his dying day, to her knowledge he'd always been truthful with her, too.

So who was she supposed to believe? A father who had always had her best interest at heart? Or the man who had captured her heart when she was sixteen and really never let it go?

Her breath caught and she had to swallow around

the sudden tightening in her throat. Did she still love
him? Was that the reason she'd made the uncharacteristic decision to have an affair with him?

Glancing up, she looked at Nick sitting across the
desk from her. In some ways he hadn't changed since
they were teenagers and in others he seemed to be a
entirely different person than he had all those years
ago. There was an edge to him now, a strength that
she hadn't noticed when they were kids.

When he'd talked to the sheriff, she'd been left
with the distinct impression that Nick wasn't the type
of man to start a fight, but he definitely wouldn't back
down from one. And she'd bet every last thing she
owned that whether it was a physical or verbal battle, he'd be the last man standing once the final punch
had been thrown.

Coupled with the gentle way he'd always treated
her, his commanding presence and take-charge attitude only added to his sex appeal. And it was no
wonder she found him completely irresistible.

Suddenly feeling as if the walls were closing in on
her, she stood up. "I'm going to take a break and get
a breath of fresh air." When he looked up from the
ranch's cattle registries, she added, "I'll be back in a
few minutes."

"I could use a break, too." He rose to his feet and
started around the desk, but to Cheyenne's relief the

phone rang. When he checked the caller ID, he smiled apologetically. "I need to take this call."

"That's fine." Actually, it was more than fine with her. Her sole reason for taking a break had been to spend a few minutes alone to try to sort through her feelings. "I'll be on the porch when you're finished with your phone call."

As she walked out onto the front porch and sat down on the suspended wooden swing, she stared out at the mountains in the distance. What in heaven's name was she going to do?

She was caught in an impossible situation with no way out. She loved Nick—had always loved him. For years, she'd tried to tell herself that she'd gotten over him, that she'd only had a foolish schoolgirl crush she'd mistaken for love.

But now she knew that hadn't been the case. All he'd had to do was kiss her and she was right back where she'd been thirteen years ago. She'd given her heart to him then, and as much as she would like to take it back now, she couldn't. Unfortunately for her, he'd made it clear that he didn't want it now any more than he had back then.

Her breath caught at the futility of it all. If she had the money to pay the balance on the promissory note she'd signed with Emerald, Inc., she'd resign as foreman of the Sugar Creek Cattle Company and move her and her father as far away as possible. But she didn't have enough in her meager savings account to even pay the interest on the loan.

Biting her lower lip to keep it from trembling, she didn't see any way out of the situation. She was trapped for the next four years, listening to her father's constant reminder that the man she loved was no good and couldn't be trusted, and knowing there was no chance of Nick ever loving her in return.

She took a deep shuddering breath. He was, and always had been, her biggest weakness and she'd made a huge mistake in thinking she could settle for anything less than his love.

But was she strong enough to call a halt to their "no-strings" affair, then work with him day in and day out until she'd fulfilled her contract? Would she be able to walk away at the end of the four years without making a fool of herself? More importantly, could she hide her feelings for that long without him finding out the way she felt about him?

Deciding she didn't have a choice, she stood up. If she had any chance of surviving, she knew what she had to do. She had to end their physical relationship now or risk losing what little sanity she had left. And as long as he didn't kiss her, she should be able to carry through on her decision.

* * *

"I'm glad to hear you've finally gotten over passing out every time you see a needle, Hunter." Nick laughed as he listened to his older brother tell about the E.M.T. courses he'd been taking. Until a few weeks ago, he hadn't even known that he had two brothers. But after discovering that his mother wasn't the only woman his father had loved and left to face single motherhood alone, the bond forming between him and his brothers meant more to Nick than anything had in a very long time. "How much longer before you get certified?"

"If I can pass this damned course without having to deal with too many needles, I'll get my certificate in about two weeks. Then I have to get checked out to fly choppers again." Hunter sighed heavily. "I'm still not a hundred percent sure that I want to do this. I just don't trust Emerald not to have something up her sleeve with this medical evacuation service that she's not telling me."

"Yeah, the old gal has a way of omitting details and twisting facts to get us to dance to her tune," Nick said, thinking about the things she'd conveniently failed to tell him concerning the expansion of the Sugar Creek ranch.

"Caleb told me about the mess she's gotten you into. Do you have that straightened out yet?"

"No." Nick released a frustrated breath. "Emerald

hasn't returned my phone calls and old Luther is as noncommittal as ever."

Hunter chuckled. "I'm still wondering where she found that guy. He's definitely not normal."

"Not by a long shot," Nick agreed, laughing.

"I guess I'd better get back to studying about compound fractures," Hunter said, sounding less than enthusiastic. "Good luck getting things straightened out with your foreman's contract."

"Thanks. I have a feeling I'm going to need it." As an afterthought, Nick added, "I can't wait to see what Emerald has in store for you."

Hunter groaned. "If it's anything like what she's gotten you into, I think I'd just as soon quit now and save myself the hassle."

Nick couldn't help but laugh. "And miss all the fun?"

After finalizing plans with Hunter to fly down to Albuquerque in a couple of weeks to surprise their brother, Caleb, on his birthday, Nick hung up the phone and stood to go in search of Cheyenne. She'd probably have to find someone to take care of her father for a few days, but that could be worked out. He had every intention of taking her with him and he wasn't taking no for an answer.

He had no idea why it was suddenly important to him that she meet his brothers. The fact of the matter was, he really didn't want to know. He had a feeling he wouldn't be overly thrilled with what he discovered if he tried to analyze his reasoning.

"Some things are better left alone and this is one of them," he muttered as he opened his office door and walked right into Cheyenne. Catching her by the shoulders to keep her from stumbling backward, he laughed as he pulled her to him. "Whoa, sweetheart. Where were you headed in such a hurry?"

"I…need to talk to you about—"

"We'll talk later," he said, lowering his mouth to hers.

The feel of her petite frame pressed to his chest was more temptation than he could resist. It had been the better part of a week since they'd made love and with each passing day, his need for her had grown into an unbearable ache.

As he moved his lips over hers, blood surged through his veins and a spark ignited in his gut. Her soft, feminine body pressed to his sent heat coursing straight through him and a shockwave of desire directly to the region south of his belt buckle.

Caught up in the feel of her perfect lips beneath his and the rapidly building hunger overtaking every fiber of his being, it took a moment for him to realize that she was pushing against him. "Hey, where do you think you're going?"

"Greta—"

He tightened his arms around her. "Greta left right after lunch. She and Carl are going down to Denver to spend the weekend with their daughter and her family."

"W-we're…alone?" If he didn't know better he'd swear there was a hint of panic in her voice.

Deciding he'd imagined it, he kissed his way from her cheek down the slender column of her neck. When he raised his head to meet her wide-eyed gaze, he smiled. "All alone, sweetheart."

Seven

$\mathbf{A}$ momentary wave of panic swept through Cheyenne when Nick's mouth covered hers. But she quickly ceased thinking of why it was so important that she call a halt to their affair or the risk she was taking of losing what was left of her sanity. Nothing mattered but the fact that she was in his arms once again.

When he eased his lips from hers to capture her gaze with his, the heat in his deep blue eyes caused her insides to hum with an anticipation that robbed her of breath. "I want you, Cheyenne." Low and slightly rough, his voice wrapped around her like a warm velvet cape and sent a wave of goose bumps shimmering over her skin. "I want to sink myself deep inside you and make our bodies one."

She knew she was playing a dangerous game and there was a very real possibility of losing what was left of herself. But if all she could allow herself to have with him was this one final moment, she'd cherish the memory of what they shared, no matter how much heartache she suffered later. Right now, she needed to taste the desire in his kiss and feel the strength of his passion as he claimed her one last time.

"Make love to me, Nick."

Without a moment's hesitation, he swept her into his arms and carried her up the stairs to his bedroom. When he set her on her feet at the side of his bed, his sexy smile chased away the last shadow of her doubts and she knew in her heart she'd lost her internal battle the moment he'd touched her.

After bending to quickly remove their boots and socks, he straightened, giving her a look that threatened to melt every bone in her body. "As much as I want to make love to you, I need to know. Are you still sore, sweetheart?"

Her cheeks heated at his intimate question. "The soreness went away after a day or two."

"Do you have any idea how pretty you are when

you blush?" he asked as he removed the elastic band holding her ponytail.

"I've never associated embarrassment…with feeling attractive." Her pulse sped up and her breathing became shallow when he trailed his fingers down her throat to her collarbone.

"I think you're pretty when you're happy, sad, angry—" he lightly ran his fingers over her shoulders, then down her arms to catch her hands in his "—and I even think you're pretty when you're embarrassed." Smiling he brought her hands to his lips to kiss each one. "When we were young, I thought you were the prettiest girl I'd ever seen. Now that we're grown, I *know* you're the prettiest woman I've ever seen."

Before she could get her vocal cords to work, he placed her hands on his shoulders, then reached down to tug the bottom of her tank top from the waistband of her jeans. Slipping his hands beneath the hem, the calluses on his palms sent waves of delight straight to the core of her as he caressed her ribs and the underside of her breasts.

"Raise your arms for me," he whispered close to her ear.

When she did as he commanded, he swept the lavender garment over her head and tossed it to the floor. Then, cupping her cheek with one hand, he kissed her with a tenderness that brought tears to her eyes as he reached behind her with the other hand to make quick work of unfastening her bra.

"How do men…do that?" she asked, feeling more than a little breathless.

"Do what?"

"Unfasten a bra one-handed faster than most people can snap their fingers."

A frown marred his handsome face as he leaned back to look at her. "How do you know—"

"Girl talk with some of my friends."

His rich laughter made her warm all over as he tossed the scrap of lace on top of her tank top, then nibbled kisses from her ear around to her throat. "Never underestimate the talents of a man on a mission, sweetheart."

At the feel of his lips on her sensitized skin, Cheyenne closed her eyes and let her head fall back to give him better access. A tingling excitement began to course through her veins, heating every inch of her as it made its way to pool in the pit of her belly. When he used his tongue to soothe the fluttering at the top of her collarbone, then kissed his way down her chest to the slope of her breast, she felt as if she'd melt into a puddle at his feet.

Caught up in the delicious sensations Nick was creating deep within her soul, her heart skipped several beats when he took her nipple into his mouth to draw on it deeply. Certain she'd burn to a cinder at any moment, she gripped his shoulders as the pooling of need in her lower body intensified.

"Do you like that?" His moist breath against her breast felt absolutely wonderful.

"Mmm."

"I'll take that as a yes." Turning his attention to her other breast, he treated the hardened peak to the same delightful torture.

Wave after wave of desire washed over her and it came as no small surprise when she realized that Nick had unsnapped her jeans and lowered the zipper without her knowledge. Sliding her jeans and panties down her thighs, he quickly added them to the growing pile of her clothes on the floor.

"This isn't fair. I'm completely naked and you still have all of your clothes on," she said, reaching out to unfasten the metal snaps on his Western-style shirt.

Knowing it would be their last time together, she forced herself to go slowly, to savor and enjoy the exploration of his magnificent body. She wanted to memorize every moment, commit every detail of their lovemaking to memory.

As she unsnapped first one gripper, then another, she kissed every inch of newly exposed skin and by the time she parted his shirt, Nick looked like a man in pain. "I think you're killing me."

"Do you want me to stop?" She grazed his flat male nipples with the tips of her fingers and was rewarded by his low groan of pleasure.

"Hell no, I don't want you to stop."

The hungry look in his dark blue eyes encouraged her and pushing his shirt off of his broad shoulders, she tossed it aside, then placed her hands flat on his bare chest. His warm male flesh felt absolutely wonderful beneath her palms and as she mapped the ridges and planes of his muscular physique, he took several deep, shuddering breaths.

Smiling, she trailed her index finger down the shallow valley dividing his rippling stomach muscles. "Your body is so beautiful, so perfect."

"It can't hold a candle to the perfection of yours, sweetheart," he said, shaking his head as he cupped her breasts with his hands.

The feel of his thumbs lightly chafing her tight nipples as he gently caressed her fullness sent her temperature soaring. He continued teasing her and by the time she unbuckled his belt and reached for the stud at his waistband, her fingers trembled from a need deeper than anything she'd ever experienced. Working the metal button free, she paused as she toyed with the tab at the top of his fly.

"It appears that you might have a bit of a problem."

"You caused me to be like this, sweetheart." The smoldering heat in his cobalt gaze caused the butterflies in her stomach to go absolutely wild and sent a shiver of anticipation up her spine.

Slowly brushing her hand across the faded denim, she smiled when he sucked in a sharp breath. "I'm responsible for this?"

"Yeah." He leaned forward to nibble kisses from her shoulder, up her neck to just below her ear. "Now, what are you going to do about it?"

Carefully lowering the zipper, the sight of his arousal straining against his cotton briefs filled her with an irresistible urge to touch him. Running her index finger along the hard ridge, she felt a moment of panic when he jerked as if he'd been shocked with a jolt of electricity.

"Is that uncomfortable?"

"Sweetheart, if you don't get the rest of my clothes off…it's going to be damned near unbearable. Real quick."

Cheyenne couldn't get over how empowering it felt to know that she'd brought him to such a heightened state of need. "That wouldn't be good."

"No, it wouldn't."

The hunger in his steady gaze encouraged her and, sliding her hands beneath the elastic at the top of his briefs, she slid them and his jeans over his narrow hips and down his powerful thighs. When he stepped out of them, then kicked them aside, the sight of his fully aroused body caused her heart to stall.

Crooking his index finger, he gave her a sexy smile. "Come here."

When she stepped into the circle of his arms, the feel of woman against man, skin against skin from shoulders to knees caused a delicious shiver of anticipation to slide through every part of her. But when he cupped her bottom in his large hands and lifted her to him, a sizzling awareness swirled from the top of her head to the soles of her feet, leaving her slightly dizzy from its intensity.

The honeyed heat deep in the most feminine part of her quickly changed to the empty ache of unfulfilled desire and she couldn't have stopped a moan of frustration from escaping if her life depended on. "I need you. Now."

"Easy, sweetheart." His kiss was filled with pure male passion and awakened a yearning in her deeper than she'd ever dreamed possible.

By the time he broke the kiss, she felt as if she would go up in a blaze of glory at any moment. Nick must have experienced the same sense of urgency because he reached into the bedside table to remove a foil packet and quickly arranged their protection. Then, settling himself on the side of the bed, he guided her to straddle his lap.

"Put your legs around me," he whispered hoarsely as he lifted her to him.

When she did, she reveled in the exquisite stretching of her body as he slowly eased her down onto his aroused flesh. Closing her eyes, Cheyenne felt a completeness that she knew in her heart she could never feel with any other man as he joined their bodies and made them one.

"You feel...wonderful," she said, wrapping her arms around his wide shoulders.

"I was about to say the same thing about you." His voice sounded strained and she could tell he was holding himself in check, making sure she was ready before he continued.

Opening her eyes, she raised one hand to thread her fingers in his thick, dark blond hair. Her heart ached with the need to tell him how special he was to her, how much she loved him. But knowing he didn't feel the same, she swallowed back the words and chose to show him how she felt about him.

"P-please...make love to me, Nick."

His gaze held hers as without a word he guided her in a leisurely rocking motion against him. When he slowly increased the pace, her head fell back as wave upon wave of exquisite pleasure radiated over every cell in her body. His lips caressing the sensitive skin of her throat and collarbone escalated the building tension deep inside her and all too quickly, she felt her body begin to tighten as the coil of need prepared to set her free.

He must have sensed her readiness because he tightened his arms around her. "I've got you, Cheyenne. Let go, sweetheart."

If she'd been able to find her voice, she could have told him that she didn't have a choice, that her body demanded she turn loose and reach for the completion they both sought. But her release from the captivating spell overtook her and she was cast into a vortex of incredible sensation.

Quivering from the waves of satisfaction flowing to every corner of her being, Cheyenne felt Nick's body move within her one final time, then stiffen as he found his own shuddering liberation from the passionate storm. As she clung to him, they both made the journey to a place where they basked in the perfect union of two bodies becoming one heart, one mind, one soul.

Tears filled her eyes and she tightened her arms around him in an effort to make the moment last. But as she slowly drifted back to reality, she knew the time had come to end the madness. She only hoped she had the strength to carry through with her decision and tell him their affair was over.

Nick couldn't believe the myriad of emotions tightening his chest. The possessiveness he'd been battling since seeing Cheyenne the first day of his return to the Sugar Creek ranch had grown into a force he could no longer fight. And it scared the living hell out of him.

He'd been a damned fool to think he could engage in any kind of physical relationship with her and not form some sort of bond. But to his relief, she'd apparently been just as affected by their affair. It hadn't been lost on him that she'd stopped referring to their coming together as having sex and started calling it what it was—lovemaking.

His chest tightened further and he suddenly found it hard to breathe. Had he done the unthinkable? Had he fallen in love with her again? Had he ever really stopped loving her?

Thirteen years ago, he'd been an infatuated teenage boy with a case of raging hormones and an inherent sense of honor. And in his attempt to avoid being anything like his irresponsible father, he'd confused lust for love and decided they had to be married before he made love to Cheyenne.

That explained his feelings for her in the past. But what about the way he was feeling now? Was he once again mistaking lust for something deeper, something far more meaningful?

His heart pounded hard against his rib cage and he had to force himself to breathe. The last thing he needed right now was to complicate his life by falling for Cheyenne again.

Deciding it would be better to sort everything out later when he was alone and could think more clearly, he kissed her satiny cheek and concentrated on the present. "Any discomfort this time?"

She shook her head. "No."

"Good."

They sat holding each other for some time before she started to pull away from him. "What's your hurry?" he asked, tightening his arms around her.

"I need to…get home." The tone of her voice warned him that something had upset her.

He lifted her from his lap to sit beside him on the bed. But instead of snuggling against him, she quickly stood up and started gathering her clothes from the pile on the floor.

"What's wrong, sweetheart?"

Instead of answering, she hurried into the bathroom. When she came out a few minutes later, he was waiting for her. There was no way in hell she was leaving until she explained what the problem was.

Placing his hands on her shoulders, he shook his

head. "You're not going anywhere until you tell me what's going on."

"Nothing…everything."

She looked about two seconds away from crying and it twisted his gut into a painful knot to think he might have caused her distress. "Slow down and tell me what's bothering you."

"I can't do this again." Her voice was so soft and tremulous, he almost hadn't heard her.

His heart stalled. She'd said there was no discomfort, but had he unknowingly hurt her in some way?

"Are you all right?"

"Don't worry about me. I'll be fine." Her sad smile caused his gut to twist.

"Then what's wrong?"

A lone tear slid down her pale cheek. "You can't change what happened any more than I can." She wouldn't look him in the eye when she motioned toward his clothes on the floor. "Will you please put something on? It's very distracting to try holding a conversation with a naked person."

"What do you mean we can't change what happened?" Frowning, he turned her loose to reach for his jeans and briefs. "If I did something that's upset you, I'm sorry."

As he started pulling on his jeans, she walked out

into the hall. Turning back, the sadness in her aqua eyes just about tore him apart.

"It's not what you did, Nick. It's what you can't do."

"Dammit, Cheyenne, wait a minute. You're talking in riddles."

In a hurry to follow her, he struggled to get his fly zipped, then started after her. But the sound of the front door closing behind her stopped him halfway down the stairs.

He had no idea what had just happened or why, but he had every intention of finding out. Turning, he went back to his bedroom for his shirt, then sitting on the side of the bed to pull on his boots, he thought about what she'd said.

For the life of him, he couldn't figure out what she'd been talking about. What didn't she think they could change? And what was it that she thought he couldn't do?

If she'd been referring to what happened thirteen years ago, she was right. He couldn't change the past. But he could damn sure explain what happened that night and why he and his mother had left Wyoming under the cover of darkness.

But as much as he wanted to set the record straight once and for all, he decided to wait until they drove back from the auction tomorrow evening to tell Cheyenne the truth about that night. She was too upset right now to listen to what he had to say and he wanted her full attention when he told her the role her father and the sheriff had played in one of the darkest days of his life.

By the time Cheyenne parked her truck in front of her house, she had her emotions under control. But only just barely. She knew she'd handled the situation with Nick badly. But that couldn't be helped. She'd done the best she could under the circumstances and if he didn't realize that she was ending their affair, he'd figure it out soon enough.

He'd probably wonder why she'd changed her mind. He might even question her about it. But after a time, he'd accept that it was over and move on to find a woman who could keep her emotions in check. Considering that he didn't love her, that shouldn't take too long.

"You look tired, princess," her father said as she let herself into the house through the back door. He was sitting in his wheelchair at the kitchen table with several of his old case files spread out in front of him. Slipping several of the papers into a folder, he stacked them on his lap. "Aren't you feeling well?"

No. She wasn't sure she'd ever feel good again.

"I do have a bit of a headache, but it's nothing. I'll be fine."

His eyes narrowed. "You had to work close to that blackhearted excuse for a human being again today, didn't you?"

"Daddy, please." She rubbed her throbbing temples. "I'm really not up to another lecture on how reprehensible you think Nick is."

His expression hard, he shook his head. "I just hate that you have to work for that illegitimate son of a—"

"Daddy!"

His features softened a bit. "I'm sorry, princess. But you're too good to be anywhere near Daniels, let alone have to work for him."

She knew her father only wanted the best for her and found the entire situation extremely frustrating. But neither one of them could change the fact that she had four more years on her contract with the Sugar Creek Cattle Company and there was no sense in belaboring the issue.

"Please, let's not talk about it now." She moved to take the files from him. "Do you want me to put these in your office?"

To her surprise, he held on to the files and shook his head. "Sit down and put your feet up. I'll put these back in the file cabinet, then we can talk about driving down to the Bucket of Suds Bar and Grill for supper. My treat."

"But I'd planned on making a meat loaf," she said

halfheartedly. She really didn't feel like cooking, but she hated for her father to use what little spending money she gave him each month on her.

"We can have meat loaf another time." He turned his wheelchair around and started rolling it toward his office. "You deserve a night off."

Two hours later, as she and her father sat at a chipped Formica table at the back of the Bucket of Suds, enjoying plates piled high with spaghetti and meatballs, Cheyenne felt as if the world had come to a grinding halt when Nick walked through the entrance. Hadn't she suffered enough turmoil in her life for one day? What on earth was he doing here? And what would her father do if he saw Nick?

As she stared at him, her chest tightened. She loved him so much she ached with it. And seeing him day in and day out without being held by him, loved by him was going to make the next four years drag out like a life sentence.

"Princess, did you hear what I said?"

Turning her attention to her father, she shook her head. "I must have been daydreaming."

"I said we should eat out like this more often." He smiled. "It feels good to get out of the house for a while."

She was glad to see that her father was enjoying his night out. Because of the demands of her job, she didn't have a lot of time to take him places and she knew he had to get bored staying at home all the time. She just hoped that he continued to enjoy himself and didn't recognize Nick. Fortunately the restaurant was packed with the usual Friday night crowd and the chances of that happening were fairly good.

Keeping an eye on Nick sitting at the bar, she did her best not to let on that anything was out of the ordinary. "I don't think our budget will allow us to eat out every week, but I think we can afford to do this once a month," she said, smiling.

Her father nodded. "It's something we can look forward to."

Aware of every move Nick made, Cheyenne knew the second he rose from the bar stool and headed toward their table. She tried to dissuade him with a surreptitious shake of her head, but she could tell by the determined look in his eye her effort was futile.

He nodded a greeting as he passed their table on his way to the jukebox. "Good evening, Judge Holbrook. Cheyenne."

"Who is that young man?" her father asked. "He looks familiar."

Cheyenne took a deep breath. "That was Nick Daniels, Daddy."

Her father's congenial expression quickly changed to a glare. "What's he doing here?"

"Probably for the same reason we are. His house-keeper went to Denver for the weekend and I assume he's here to eat dinner."

She swallowed hard when she recognized the beginning notes of the song she and Nick had always called theirs in high school. Why had he chosen that particular song out of all the ones on the jukebox?

"Housekeeper?" her father interrupted her thoughts. "Where's his mother? Didn't she come back to Wyoming with that whelp of hers?"

"Linda Daniels passed away about twelve years ago, Daddy."

"Linda's gone?" She could have sworn she saw a hint of sadness cross his face. But just as quickly as it appeared, it was gone.

Deciding she'd only imagined the change in his demeanor, Cheyenne nodded. "Nick said she knew she didn't have long to live when they left here to go to St. Louis."

As he walked back toward the bar, Nick stopped at their table. "When you left this afternoon, I forgot to tell you that we'll start loading the cattle we're taking to auction after lunch tomorrow."

Before she could respond, her father slammed his fork down on the table. "It's a damn fool idea to be selling off good stock the way you're doing. Of course, you never did have a lick of sense."

"Daddy," Cheyenne warned. Creating a scene in a public place would make the day go from difficult to unbearable.

"It's all right, Cheyenne." Nick smiled, but it was anything but friendly. "Your father has a right to his opinion." Although he'd spoken to her, his gaze never wavered from her father's.

"If you've said your piece move on, Daniels. You're ruining my appetite." As an afterthought, her father added, "And from now on, unless my daughter is on the clock, I don't want you anywhere near Cheyenne. Is that understood?"

Nick shook his head. "In case you hadn't noticed, she's an adult now, Judge. Who she does or doesn't see is her call. Not yours."

The level of hostility between Nick and her father shocked her. "I think you'd both better calm down. This isn't the time or place to be having a conversation like this."

"I was leaving anyway." When Nick finally turned his attention her way, the heat in his sensual gaze robbed her of breath and sent a shiver of awareness all the way to her soul. "I'll see you tomorrow afternoon, Cheyenne."

As he walked away, her father continued his diatribe, but Cheyenne had no idea what he was ranting about. There had been a wealth of meaning in the look Nick had given her and there was no mistaking his intention.

He had questions and he wasn't going to rest until he had the answers.

Eight

By the time the auction was over the next evening and Cheyenne waited for Nick to collect the money from the sale of the cattle, she felt ready to jump out of her own skin. Her nerves were completely shot, and for good reason.

She and Nick had worked together the entire afternoon to get the cattle loaded in trailers and moved to holding pens at the sale barn, then sat together while the animals were auctioned off to the highest bidders. Neither of them had mentioned the run-in he'd had with her father the night before, nor had he asked her why she'd had a sudden change of heart about their affair. But that was about to change.

They had a little over an hour before they got back to the Sugar Creek ranch and the complete privacy of his truck for their conversation. There wasn't a doubt in her mind what they would be discussing or that it was going to be one of the longest drives of her life.

"Ready to go?"

Lost in thought, she jumped at the unexpected sound of Nick's voice only inches away. "As ready as I'll ever be."

He smiled as he tucked the check he'd received from the auction officials in his shirt pocket, then put his arm around her shoulders to walk her to his truck. "Would you like to stop somewhere for a bite to eat before we head back?"

The feel of his body pressed to her side sent a deep longing straight to her soul. "N-no. I need to get home."

The last thing she wanted was to prolong the time they spent together. The more she was with him, the stronger the temptation became to rethink her decision.

"You've worked hard today." Opening the passenger door for her, he lightly ran his index finger from her ear along her cheek to her lips. "I'm sure you're tired."

Her skin tingled where he touched her and it took every ounce of willpower she had not to lean toward him. "I'm used to it." She forced herself to ignore the longing that streaked through her and got into the truck. "It's my job."

He shook his head. "Not anymore. Remember? You'll be in the office and I'll be out doing the ranch work."

If he thought she was going to argue with him, he was mistaken. She'd worked for six long years out in all kinds of weather and an easier job in the comforts of a heated office in the winter and air-conditioned in the summer didn't sound at all bad. And as long as she was alone in that office, she might even manage to retain a scrap of what little sanity she had left.

When he walked around the front of the truck and got in behind the steering wheel the look in his eye warned her that the conversation she'd dreaded was about to begin. "Your father looked fairly healthy last night, considering that he's had a stroke."

She nodded. "I can't get him to see a doctor as often as he should, but he's recovered everything but the ability to walk."

They rode in silence for some time before Nick asked, "What did your father tell you about the night I left Wyoming?"

His question wasn't what she expected. She'd thought he'd want to know why she'd ended their affair.

"Daddy didn't tell me anything until he received

the news that you and your mother were no longer at the Sugar Creek. Why?"

"I figured as much."

Confused, she turned to look at him as he gunned the truck's powerful engine. "What is that supposed to mean?"

He took a deep breath and she could tell he was doing his best to hold his temper. "Before I tell you what really went down that night, why don't you tell me what happened after your father led you away from the church?"

Cheyenne had expected them to be discussing her father's behavior the night before and her decision to end their no-strings arrangement. She couldn't imagine why Nick wanted to talk about the events of thirteen years ago.

"I don't see the need to drag up the past," she said, shaking her head. "My father broke up our wedding and you left without even telling me goodbye. End of story."

The lights from the dashboard illuminated his face just enough for her to watch a muscle work along Nick's lean jaw. "That's not exactly the way it all unfolded that night, Cheyenne."

She shook her head. "It doesn't matter now."

"Yes, it does."

Sighing heavily, she thought back on the night

she was to have become Nick's wife. "After my father and the sheriff stopped our wedding, Daddy took me home and that was it. We didn't talk about it, until a couple of days later when he told me that you and your mother had left the area."

"What did he say?"

There was no sense mincing words. He was well aware of how her father felt about him. "Daddy pointed out that if you had really cared anything about me, you would have told me where you were going or at the least, told me goodbye."

Nick's particularly nasty oath startled her. "I'll bet he didn't bother telling you why we left, did he?"

"How could he? My father didn't know any more about your leaving than anyone else."

His hollow laughter caused a chill to slither straight up her spine. "That's where you're wrong, sweetheart. Your father and the sheriff had firsthand knowledge of why I left Wyoming."

She was becoming more than a little irritated by his intimations that her father had something to do with it. "Well, since everyone seems to know all about it but me, why don't you fill me in on the big secret?"

Nick stared out the windshield for several long seconds before he finally spoke. "After your father and the sheriff put you in the patrol car and left me standing there on the church steps, I drove home and told my mother what happened. She wasn't any happier about our trying to elope than your father, but for different reasons. She told me if she knew anything about Bertram Holbrook that we hadn't heard the last of the incident." He cast her a meaningful glance. "And she was right."

A cold dread began to settle in Cheyenne's stomach. She could tell by the look on his face that the accusations Nick was about to make against her father were going to be ugly and hurtful.

Swallowing around the lump in her throat, she asked, "Just what was it that my father was supposed to have done?"

She watched Nick's hand tighten on the steering wheel. "Around midnight that evening, my mother received an anonymous phone call, telling her that your father was filing charges and that the sheriff would be out the next morning to arrest me for statutory rape."

Gasping, she shook her head. "I don't believe you. My father would never do something like that."

Nick steered the truck to the side of the road and turned off the engine. When he turned to face her, his anger was evident in the tight lines around his mouth and the sparkle in his deep blue eyes.

"Don't fool yourself, Cheyenne. Your father was a powerful judge, who, for whatever reason, despised me and my mother. And I had taken his underage daughter—his only daughter—across the county line to marry her."

"But—"

"He had the motive, the resources and the hatred to pursue the issue." His gaze caught and held hers. "Face it, Cheyenne. Your father had every intention of seeing that I rotted away in a jail cell for the better part of my life."

Her stomach churned and she felt as if she might be physically ill. "I-if what you say is true, then why didn't you stay and fight the charges?"

"Think about it, sweetheart. Your father knew the law inside and out. And he had plenty of people to see that his goal was accomplished." He smiled sardonically. "What chance do you think I would have had at getting a fair trial with one of your father's colleagues sitting on the bench?"

Her mind reeled from the implications of it all. If what Nick told her had actually happened, it would have ruined his life. But she couldn't believe her father would do something so vile, so vindictive.

Taking her hand in his, Nick shook his head. "You have to believe me. The last thing I wanted to do was leave you behind that night. But as my mother pointed out, I didn't have any other options. I either got the hell out of Wyoming while I could or stay and face a guaranteed prison sentence."

Tears filled her eyes as she struggled with what he'd told her. "Why didn't you call…or write to let me know what had happened?"

"I tried to get in touch with you, but your father made sure that didn't happen." He reached down to release her safety harness, then pulled her to his wide chest. "I called every day for a month, sweetheart. But your father always answered the phone and wouldn't let me talk to you, or the answering machine picked up. I left messages, but it's my guess that he erased them before you heard them. I also sent a few letters, but I doubt you ever saw them, either."

She numbly shook her head. "No."

His arms holding her so securely to him were a comfort, but she felt completely overwhelmed and needed to be alone to sort out everything. "I…" Her voice caught. "P-please take me home."

Apparently sensing her need to come to terms with what he'd told her, Nick kissed the top of her head, then releasing her, started the truck.

As they drove in silence through the quiet night, Cheyenne thought about everything Nick had said. What was she supposed to believe?

The man he had described was nothing like the kind, loving father she'd always known. And until that very moment, there had never been a time in her life that she doubted her father having anything but her best interest at heart.

But as much as she hated to admit it, what Nick said made sense. At the time of the incident, her father did have the power and connections to pursue charges against him. And after seeing her father's hostility toward Nick last night, she couldn't deny that it was a possibility.

Why had her father always had such a low opinion of the Daniels family?

She'd never known anyone nicer than Linda Daniels, and even though the woman had had Nick at a time when it wasn't as socially acceptable to be an unwed mother, no one in the area had seemed to care. No one, that is, but her father.

Could that be the reason her father had such contempt for Nick? Had he viewed Nick as less of a person because his mother hadn't married his father?

But that made no sense. Why should her father be bothered by Nick's illegitimacy when no one else was?

Deciding there were no easy answers, Cheyenne rested her head against the back of the seat and tiredly closed her eyes. She had no idea who or what to believe anymore.

One of the two men she loved with all her heart had deceived her. And it didn't matter whether it was her father or Nick, when she discovered the truth, she knew without a doubt that it was going to break her heart.

Nick cursed his carelessness as he parked his truck beside the house and got out to climb the porch steps. He should have known better than to try to stretch a section of barbed wire fence without both work gloves. But like a damned fool, when he'd driven up to the north pasture that morning and discovered that he'd lost one, he'd gone ahead and tried to do the work without the protection of the thick leather covering his hands. Now he had a deep gash in his left hand and the fence still needed to be repaired.

"Greta, you'd better get the first-aid kit," he called when he entered the house.

"What's wrong?" Cheyenne asked, walking out of his office. She stopped short and her face went deathly pale. "Oh, dear Lord! What happened?"

Glancing down at the bloodstains on the front of his shirt, he held up his hand. "I tangled with some barbed wire."

"Let me see." She gently took his hand in hers and carefully unwrapped the blood-soaked handkerchief he'd wrapped around the wound. Looking up at him, she shook her head. "This is more than a scratch, Nick. Why weren't you wearing your gloves?"

Her soft hands holding his almost made him forget how much the gash hurt. "I could only find one of them and didn't want to drive all the way back here to get another pair."

Rolling her eyes, she shook her head. "You're going to need several stitches to close this."

He tried to pull his hand from hers. "I'll just wash it out with some peroxide and wrap it in gauze."

"No, you're not. You're going to the doctor."

"Am not."

"Yes, you are."

When their gazes locked, he couldn't believe how good she looked to him or how much he'd missed seeing her. For the past week, he'd given her the space he knew she needed and managed to be out of the house each morning before she arrived to work in his office. He'd even postponed taking the rest of the herds to auction in order to give her the coming weekend off.

But standing here staring at her now, he decided that space be damned. He wanted nothing more than to take her in his arms and kiss her until they both needed oxygen.

"Here's the first-aid kit," Greta said as she hurried down the hall. She stopped beside Cheyenne, took one look at his hand, then shook her head. "That's going to need more than anything we can do for you."

"He needs to see a doctor," Cheyenne said stubbornly.

"I couldn't agree more." Greta frowned. "Have you had a tetanus shot lately?"

Nick nodded. "About fifteen years ago."

"You're definitely going to the clinic," Cheyenne said, glaring at him.

Nick cringed when he thought about the injection they'd have to give him to numb his hand in order to stitch the wound shut, as well as the inoculation. Apparently an aversion to needles ran in the family because he suddenly understood why Hunter had had problems passing out every time he saw one.

"I don't like doctors."

"That's tough. You're going." Cheyenne held out her hand. "Give me your truck keys."

"If I go—and I'm not saying that I am—I can drive myself," he said stubbornly. He liked having her fuss over him. But this seeing-a-doctor business was getting out of hand.

"Nick." The tone of her voice warned him that she meant business.

Reluctantly placing the key ring in her outstretched hand, he shook his head. "This is ridiculous."

"Come on, cowboy." She tugged him along by his shirtsleeve. "The ordeal will be over with before you know it."

* * *

Two hours later, as Cheyenne drove them back from the clinic in Elk Bluff, Nick finally began to relax. His encounter with the barbed wire hadn't damaged any of the tendons in his hand and he hadn't humiliated himself by passing out when the doctor brought out the biggest hypodermic needle he'd ever seen to numb his hand.

"Are you in pain?" Cheyenne asked, steering his truck onto the highway leading out of Elk Bluff.

The concern in her voice caused a warm feeling to fill his chest. "Nope. In fact, I can't even feel my hand."

She smiled. "Just wait until the anesthetic wears off. I'm betting you'll feel plenty."

"Well, aren't you just a bright little ray of sunshine?" he said, tempering his sarcasm with a wide grin.

She laughed. "Seriously, you should probably take a couple of days off from working around the ranch to keep from tearing the stitches loose."

"I was thinking I might go down to Colorado this weekend to check out a free-range operation, then drive on to Albuquerque and spend some time there, so that won't be a problem."

"Oh." Pausing, she added, "I…hope you have a good time."

"I'm sure I will." Nick could tell Cheyenne was

curious about where he was going and who he'd be with, but she wasn't going to ask. "I'm going to help a relative celebrate *his* birthday."

"I didn't know that you had family down that way." Was that relief he heard in her voice?

He smiled. "Until just recently, I didn't know about it, either."

"It must be nice to have an extended family," she said, sounding wistful.

"Didn't your mother have a sister down in Laramie?" he asked, thinking back on what she'd told him about her mother.

She nodded as they drove up the lane leading to his house. "Yes, but we lost touch after a while and I haven't heard from her in years."

When she parked his truck and they went into the house, he motioned for her to follow him into the office. Picking up the envelope he'd received the day before from the Emerald, Inc. offices in Wichita, he pulled out a bank draft.

"I guess this answers our question about who you work for." Handing her the paycheck, he added, "But since I won't be here and there isn't any stock to tend, I'm giving you the weekend off."

Her fingers brushed his when she reached for the check and a charge of electric current streaked up his arm, then spread throughout his chest. Without thinking twice, he stepped forward and loosely wrapped his arms around her waist.

"Nick, I—"

"Shh. I'm not pressuring you to do something you can't or don't want to do." He lightly touched his lips to hers. "I just want to give you something to think about while I'm gone."

To his satisfaction as he settled his mouth over hers, Cheyenne melted against him and returned his kiss with a hunger that matched his own. Her sweet taste and the feel of her delicate frame pressed to him from shoulders to knees had the blood rushing through his veins and his body aching to claim her, to make her his once and for all. But he'd made her a promise and even if it killed him, he was going to prove to her that she could trust him.

After the confrontation with her father, then their talk on the way back from the auction, he'd decided she wasn't the only one who needed the space to think over a few things. In the past week, he'd done quite a bit of soul-searching on his own and reached several conclusions. Whatever genes he'd inherited from his irresponsible playboy father, the "love 'em and leave 'em" gene wasn't one of them. And although he'd fought with everything he had in him not to fall for Cheyenne again, he knew now that he'd never really had a choice in the matter.

She was his obsession—an addiction for him from which there was no cure. He'd pledged his love to her thirteen years ago and he knew now that was why he'd been unsuccessful at sustaining a relationship with anyone else. His heart had belonged and always would belong to Cheyenne. And whether she realized it or not, she felt the same way about him.

Breaking the kiss, he smiled as he stared into her beautiful aqua-green eyes. "While I'm gone, I want you to do something for me."

"Wh-what?"

He touched her satiny cheek with his finger. "I want you to think about us. I want you to think about me and how I make you feel. When I get back, we'll talk, sweetheart."

As the gray light of dawn began to chase away the dark shadows in her bedroom, Cheyenne lay in bed staring at the ceiling. She'd spent the entire night thinking about what Nick had said yesterday afternoon when he'd kissed her.

Didn't he realize he'd been all she could think about since finding him making repairs to that fence three weeks ago? Wasn't he aware that when he kissed her, nothing else seemed to matter but that she was in his arms? Or that when he made love to her she lost all sense of herself?

She scrunched her eyes shut to stop the wave of tears threatening to overtake her. She loved him— had never stopped loving him. But he'd made it clear that he didn't want her love and had no intention of returning it. And even if Nick did love her, she wasn't sure she could trust him.

He'd told her so many things about her father that she still had a hard time believing were true. Unfortunately, as much as she'd like to dismiss his accusations, she couldn't.

At the time, her father had been a powerful county judge with an intense dislike for Nick's family. And even though her father had always shown her nothing but love and kindness, she knew that he wasn't the same with others. His reputation of being very rigid and intolerant was legendary. But surely he wouldn't have misused his power to try ruining Nick's life, simply because Nick had tried to marry her.

She'd thought about confronting her father with Nick's accusations, but his blood pressure had been running a little high ever since they'd met up with Nick at the bar and grill. The last thing she wanted to do was run the risk of exacerbating her father's health problems with her questions.

"Cheyenne!"

The sound of her father's voice coming over the intercom system she'd had installed after his stroke caused her to sit straight up in bed. It wasn't unusual for him to rise around dawn each morning, but from the panic in his voice, she could tell something was terribly wrong.

She depressed the talk button on the unit beside her bed. "I'll be right there, Daddy."

"Hurry! The barn is on fire."

Cheyenne's heart pounded and her mind raced as she ran down the stairs. How many animals were in the barn?

The calves she'd isolated a few weeks ago had already been turned back into the herd after she'd successfully treated them for pink eye. But her gelding and Mr. Nibbles were still in the barn.

"Call the county fire department," she ordered as she ran past her father for the back door.

Sprinting down the wheelchair ramp and across the backyard, she ignored the pain of pebbles bruising the bottom of her bare feet as she crossed the gravel driveway. A chill snaked up her spine at the eerie glow she saw illuminating the otherwise dark interior of the barn and she was thankful that in deference to the August heat she'd worn a pair of gym shorts and a tank top to bed the night before. She had to get her gelding and the pony out of there and she didn't need the added encumbrance of her nightgown tangling around her legs.

"I called Gordon," he shouted as he wheeled his chair out into the yard after her. "He's contacting the county's volunteer firefighters."

"They'll never get here in time," she said, running toward the barn entrance.

"Cheyenne, no!"

Her father's panicked voice caused her to pause momentarily, but she continued on. Two animals were depending on her to lead them out safely and she wasn't going to let them down.

Nine

As the sky began to lighten, Nick steered his truck onto the road leading back to the Sugar Creek ranch. He'd left way before daylight to make the drive down to the free-range cattle ranch he'd heard about in Colorado. But the more miles he put between him and Cheyenne, the more he realized that leaving her behind was the last thing he wanted to do. They'd already spent thirteen years apart and as far as he was concerned, one more minute away from her was too damned long.

He had every intention of driving over to the Flying H later in the day, telling her father to get over whatever it was the man had against him and ask

Cheyenne to take a trip with him back to that little church across the county line. Only this time the outcome would be different. Come hell or high water, he was going to make her his wife.

Nick glanced toward the Holbrook place as he drove past and uttered a phrase he reserved for dire circumstances and smashed thumbs. Smoke billowed from the barn's hayloft and flames were visible along the outside wall.

Turning the truck around, he sped up the driveway to come to a sliding halt in the loose gravel. As he jumped from the truck, the sight of Cheyenne running into the burning barn caused fear to grip his insides and his heart to stall.

Bertram Holbrook jumped from his wheelchair surprisingly well for a man who was supposed to be partially paralyzed and began waving frantically toward the barn. "Get her out of there!"

Without thinking twice, Nick ran into the barn after Cheyenne. Catching her around the waist from behind, he spun her around and started pulling her toward the door. "What the hell do you think you're doing?"

She squirmed free of his grasp. "I have to get my horse and the pony."

"You get out of here. I'll get them," he shouted above the crackle of the rapidly spreading flames. "Which stalls are they in?"

She shook her head. "I'll get one while you get the other." Before he could stop her, she ran down the center aisle toward the fire.

Following her, Nick threw open a half door on one of the stalls and took hold of the halter on a fat, little chestnut pony. As he tugged the frightened animal along, he stopped at the stall where Cheyenne tried to catch a large buckskin gelding.

"Take the pony and go out the side door," he yelled, pushing her aside to keep the terrified horse from trampling her as it moved nervously around the stall.

When he grabbed the gelding's halter, Nick felt a sharp pain shoot up his arm as the stitches in his hand broke free, but he did his best to ignore it. Then, leading the panicked animal out into the center aisle, he fought to breathe as the choking smoke swirled around him and the terrified horse.

A loud cracking sound from somewhere overhead caused the gelding to shy away from him and Nick had to use every ounce of strength he possessed to bring the animal under control. Praying that Cheyenne and the pony had already made it to safety, he hurried to get himself and the buckskin out of the burning structure before the loft came crashing down on top of them.

He immediately released his hold on the gelding and let the horse run free when they reached the side

door of the barn and the safety of the outside. Looking around for Cheyenne, relief washed over him
when he spotted her several yards away. He started
toward her, but he'd only gone a few feet when the
sudden throbbing pain in his hand threatened to
buckle his knees. He stumbled and might have fallen
had she not rushed over to help steady him, and together they moved away from the burning building.

"Are you…all right?" he asked between fits of
coughing.

She nodded, tears streaming down her face as she
wrapped her arms around his waist and pressed herself to him. "I was so frightened that I might lose you."

His chest tightened with emotion and forgetting
all about his hand, he held her close. "Why were you
frightened, sweetheart?" He had a feeling he knew
the answer, but he wanted to hear her say the words.

"Because I—"

Her answer was cut short when a heavy hand
came down on Nick's shoulder. "There's no way
you're getting out of this one, Daniels. I've got the
evidence to prove your guilt this time."

Releasing her, Nick turned to face his assailant.
"What the hell are you talking about, Sheriff?"

The potbellied lawman waved a leather glove in
front of him. "This is yours, isn't it?"

Nick nodded as he stared at his missing work

glove. It would take a blind man or a fool not to see that he was being set up. Again.

"I thought as much," Sheriff Turner said, looking smug.

"Where did you find it?" Nick asked calmly. The sheriff had to have taken it from his truck the day he'd questioned Nick about the vandalism to Cheyenne's tires.

"It doesn't matter. It was found on the judge's property and you've already admitted it's yours." The man shook his head. "You should've stuck to misdemeanors. Arson is a felony and mark my words, you'll do time over this."

"Nick didn't set the fire," Cheyenne said, shaking her head.

Sheriff Turner shrugged. "I have proof that says otherwise. Besides, Daniels here left his ranch over an hour ago, then conveniently showed up here to help with the fire."

Nick gritted his teeth as he stared at the sorriest excuse for an officer of the law he'd ever seen. "How would you know that, unless you were watching my place, Sheriff?"

"I was out on patrol," the sheriff said, sounding a little less sure of himself.

"Before daylight?" Cheyenne shook her head. "You have deputies for that."

A dull flush began to spread over the man's face. "Now listen here, little girl—"

"Give it up, Gordon. It's over."

"Bertram, I've got Daniels right where we want him," Sheriff Turner said, reaching for the handcuffs clipped to the back of his belt.

Cheyenne turned to see her father coming toward them. He walked with a limp, but it was nothing that would keep him confined to a wheelchair. Nor were his movements and balance those of a man who was unpracticed at walking.

She felt the blood drain from her face as reality slammed into her like a physical blow. If her father had deceived her about his disability, he was certainly capable of everything Nick had alleged happened all the years ago.

As if sensing that she needed his strength, Nick put his arm around her shoulders. His silent support caused emotion to clog her throat.

"Why…Daddy?" Cheyenne asked brokenly. "How could you…be part of something…like this?"

For the first time in her life, she watched her father's shoulders sag and a look of utter shame to cross his face. "I—"

"Watch what you say, Bertram," the sheriff warned.

"What's the matter, Turner?" Nick's arm tightened around her. "Are you afraid the judge will name you as his accomplice?"

"Keep it up, Daniels, and I'll add resisting arrest to the arson and trespassing charges."

"You're not going to do a damn thing." Releasing Cheyenne, Nick turned on the sheriff. "Before you and the judge hatched up your plan, you should have made sure whose property you were torching. I own the Flying H Ranch."

"You're talking crazy," Turner blustered. "This place has always belonged to the Holbrooks."

"That's where you're wrong, Sheriff." Cheyenne glanced at her father. "Would you like to tell him, or should I?"

Her father suddenly looked ten years older. "I lost the ranch right after I had the stroke. Daniels is the owner of the Flying H now."

"And if there are any charges made, I'll be the one making them," Nick said, his tone leaving no doubt in Cheyenne's mind that he meant business.

She felt as if her heart broke all over again at the thought of her father being arrested. But what he and the sheriff had tried to do to Nick was incorrigible and she couldn't blame him for wanting to make them pay for what they'd done.

Despite a cool morning breeze, sweat popped out

on the sheriff's florid face as he glanced at her father. "If I go down, I'm taking you with me, Bertram."

She watched Nick step to within inches of the man's face. "Because I know how much it would hurt Cheyenne to see her father arrested, I'm going to shoot you a deal, Sheriff. And if you're smart, you'll take it because it's the only way you're going to keep yours and the judge's asses out of jail."

Sheriff Turner nodded. "I'm listening."

Nick pointed toward the remnants of the blazing barn. "This is your last official investigation. You're going to go back to Elk Bluff and file a report that this fire was an accident. Then you're going to turn in your resignation as County Sheriff, effective immediately."

"Now, see here—"

"You'd better think about it, Turner," Nick interrupted. "I've heard that lawmen and judges don't fare too well behind prison walls."

Cheyenne swallowed around the huge lump in her throat. She'd never loved Nick more. Even after all that her father and the sheriff had done to discredit him and set him up to face criminal charges—not once, but twice—he was willing to drop the matter in order to keep from hurting her.

"I think you'd better go, Mr. Turner," she advised the suddenly subdued sheriff. The sound of a distant siren grew closer. "That should be the county's volunteer fire department. I think they can take care of what's left of the barn, while you fill out that accident report and draft your resignation."

As the portly sheriff slunk back to his patrol car, Cheyenne turned to her father. "Let's go into the house for privacy. You owe Nick and me an explanation."

As Nick sat across the table from the judge in the Holbrook's kitchen, his hand throbbed unmercifully. But he wasn't going to drive down to the clinic in Elk Bluff to have the wound repaired until he had answers to the questions that had haunted him his entire adult life.

Before he could ask what the man had against him, Cheyenne must have noticed the fresh blood soaking through the bandage on his hand. "Oh, Nick, you've torn the stitches loose. You need to see the doctor."

He shook his head. "Not until I hear what your father has to say."

She stared at him for several moments, then, taking a deep breath, turned her attention to the silent man sitting on the opposite side of the table. "Why, Daddy? What could Nick have possibly done to you to deserve the way you've treated him?"

The tremor in her voice and the disillusionment in her eyes caused Nick's gut to twist into a painful knot. He felt her emotional pain all the way to his soul and he vowed right then and there that even if it killed him, he would never allow anything to hurt her again.

"I never meant for it to go this far," the judge said, sounding tired. Nick noticed that he kept his head lowered and couldn't quite meet their questioning gazes. "I only wanted to make you look bad. I never wanted anyone to get hurt."

"You're lucky no one did." Nick shook his head. "I think I lost ten years off my life when I saw Cheyenne run into that burning barn."

For the first time since Nick arrived, Bertram Holbrook looked him square in the eye, and for once there was no trace of animosity in the man's steady gaze. "I can't thank you enough for getting her out of there, Daniels. I don't know what I would've done if you hadn't shown up."

"Who set the fire—you or the sheriff?" Cheyenne asked.

"Gordon. But it wasn't supposed to get out of hand." The judge stared at his loosely clasped hands on top of the table. "It was supposed to be minor like the tire incident."

"That still doesn't answer my question. What do you have against Nick, Daddy? Why have you always despised him and his mother?"

The judge was silent for several long moments before he raised his head to look at Nick. "There was a time in my life that I wanted nothing more than to marry your mother. She was my high school sweetheart and I had it all planned out. After I finished college and law school, I was going to marry Linda, practice law and raise a family."

Shocked, Nick searched his memory, but he could never remember his mother mentioning that she and Bertram Holbrook had ever been anything but acquaintances. But before he could find his voice to ask the judge what happened between them, the man went on with his story.

"It all might have worked out, too, if she hadn't made that week-long shopping trip to Denver." The old man tiredly shook his head. "That's when I lost her. Once she met your daddy, she didn't want anyone else. I even offered to marry her and raise you as my own child after that philandering bastard left her alone and pregnant. But she wouldn't hear of it. She never would tell me the name of the man who stole her heart, but I hated him just the same. And I'm ashamed to say that hatred carried over to you."

"But what about Mama?" There was a tremor in Cheyenne's voice that tightened the knot in Nick's gut. "Didn't you love her?"

A lone tear spilled from Holbrook's eye. "Yes, princess. I loved your mother very much."

Tears streamed down Cheyenne's face and Nick moved his chair closer to hers and put his arm around her shoulders. "Then why did you—"

"Looking back over the way I've acted all these years…I'm not proud of it," the man said haltingly. "But I carried a grudge toward you and your mother, boy. And I couldn't stand the thought of you being with my precious daughter."

Nick wasn't sure what to say. For one thing, he was astounded that what little Bertram Holbrook had known about Nick's father was more than he'd known himself. There had been a time when he was young that he'd questioned his mother about who his father was and how she'd met him. But she'd only smile and tell him that the time would come when he'd learn about the man and why she didn't want to talk about him. After a while, he'd accepted her silence and stopped asking. He knew now that his mother's reluctance to talk about his father was due to the affidavit that Emerald had had her sign, requiring his mother's silence and ensuring that he would be an heir to the Larson fortune.

"That explains why you've treated Nick so poorly," Cheyenne sobbed. "But why have you deceived me all these years about your ability to walk? Didn't you know how heartbreaking it was for me to see my once strong father in a wheelchair?"

As Nick watched, Bertram Holbrook seemed to shrink before his eyes. "After I had the stroke I was afraid of losing you, princess. I know I've made a lot of enemies and I don't have many friends in this county." Nick almost felt sorry for the man when he reached for Cheyenne's hand and she moved it away from him. "You've always been the light of my life, princess. Since your mother died, you've been the only one to love me unconditionally and I was afraid of losing that." Tears ran unchecked down the judge's face. "But in my desperation to keep from dying a lonely old man, I only succeeded in driving you away."

"But you're my father. Didn't you realize that I would always love you? That I had enough room in my heart for you as well as Nick?"

Sensing that Cheyenne and her father needed time alone to sort through what was left of their father-daughter relationship, Nick kissed her temple, then rose to his feet. "I think the two of you need some privacy to work this out. I'm going to drive down to the clinic and have the stitches replaced in my hand."

Cheyenne looked torn between going with him and staying to work out things with her father.

Giving her a smile he hoped was encouraging, Nick walked to the door. "Come over to my place this afternoon and bring the copy of your contract. We need to settle a few things of our own, as well as discuss how all this is going to affect your employment with the Sugar Creek Cattle Company."

By the time Cheyenne drove over to Nick's that afternoon, she felt emotionally drained. After a long, tearful discussion with her father, they'd come to an understanding. He'd agreed to enter counseling to help him deal with his propensity to manipulate and control people and situations, as well as work through his fears of being alone. And she was going to make her own choices without his interference.

Parking her truck at the side of the Sugar Creek ranch house, she took a deep breath and reached for the file containing her contract on the seat beside her as she readied herself for her meeting with Nick. She knew he cared for her, but he'd made it clear there was no chance of them having a relationship. And they both knew that made it impossible for her to continue working as the Sugar Creek foreman.

Before he fired her, she was going to do the only thing she could do. She was going to turn in her resignation, move away from the area and find another job to pay back the balance of her debt to Emerald, Inc.

When she got out of the truck and climbed the porch steps, Nick opened the door before she had a chance to knock. "You're late," he said as he took her in his arms, then kissed her until she gasped for breath.

"I…didn't realize you'd set a time for this meeting."

"I didn't."

His hand at the small of her back as he guided her toward his office burned through her clothing and sent a shaft of longing straight to her soul. "Then why did you—"

"Because we've wasted enough time getting things settled between us." He reached for the folder in her hand, then tore it in half. "As of right now, you're no longer my employee or Emerald, Inc.'s."

She opened her mouth to tell him that he couldn't fire her because she was quitting, but he didn't give her the chance.

"And if you're worried about paying back the debt—don't. I've already made arrangements with Emerald Larson."

She shook her head. "I don't want you paying my debts."

"We'll talk about that later." His sexy smile caused her heart to skip several beats. "Right now, we have more important things to discuss."

Backing away when he reached for her, she shook her head. "Nick, I can't do this. I can't continue a 'no-strings' affair with you."

To her surprise instead of being disappointed, he grinned. "That's not what I want from you, sweetheart."

Hope began to blossom deep inside of her, but she

ignored it. She couldn't allow herself to believe that he'd changed his mind.

"What do you want?"

He quickly stepped forward and taking her by the hand, led her over to his desk. Activating the speaker phone, he pushed the speed dial. "I want you to listen in on a phone call I'm about to make. But you have to promise not to say anything until I hang up. Would you do that for me?"

"Okay," she said slowly. She wasn't sure what she expected him to say, but listening in on his phone conversation wasn't it.

When she heard her father's voice on the other end of the line, she started to protest, but Nick held up his index finger to silence her. "Judge Holbrook, Nick Daniels here. I have something I need to ask you."

From the long pause, Cheyenne thought her father was going to hang up. "Go ahead," he finally said.

Nick gave her a smile that she thought would surely melt her bones. "Sir, we both know that you haven't changed your mind about me nor will you ever think that I'm good enough for your daughter. But there's one thing you and I have in common. We both love Cheyenne more than life itself. And if she'll have me, I'd like to make her my wife."

A happiness that she'd never dreamed would be hers again filled her body and soul. Nick didn't want them to continue their affair. He loved her and wanted to marry her.

"Are you asking for my permission?" Instead of the animosity she expected to hear in her father's voice, there was only quiet resignation.

"No, sir." Nick cupped her face with his hand as he stared into her eyes. "I don't need your permission to marry your daughter. Whether or not she agrees to be my wife is going to be her decision. What I want from you is your blessing. We both know how much that would mean to Cheyenne and I want whatever makes her happy."

Leaning forward, Cheyenne kissed his firm male lips. "I love you," she mouthed as they awaited her father's answer.

"You'd better be good to her," her father warned.

Nick's expression turned serious. "Judge Holbrook, you have my word that I'll spend every minute of every day for the rest of my life doing everything I can to make her happy."

There was a long pause, then her father said the words that filled her with such joy she could no longer hold back her tears. "If you're what Cheyenne wants, then I have no objections and I'll accept the marriage with no further protest."

"Thank you, sir. I swear, I'll never let either of you down." Ending the call, Nick brushed his lips over hers. "Cheyenne Holbrook, I love you. Will you do me the honor of becoming my wife?"

"Oh, Nick, I love you, too. So very much." She threw her arms around her shoulders and kissed him. "Yes, I'll marry you."

His kiss was filled with such passion, such love there was no doubt in her mind that he meant every word he'd said about making her happy for the rest of their lives.

When he raised his head, the smile on his handsome face held the promise of a lifetime of love and happiness. "I'd like to get married as soon as possible if that's all right with you, sweetheart. I think we've waited more than long enough to start our life together, don't you?"

She returned his smile. "I couldn't agree more."

"What are you doing next weekend?"

"I'm not sure, but aren't you supposed to go down to Albuquerque—" She stopped short. "Weren't you going to go down to Colorado today, then drive on to New Mexico for your relative's birthday?"

He shrugged. "I got as far as the Elk Bluff city limits before I turned around and headed back." The tenderness in his deep blue eyes stole her breath. "I was on my way back for you."

"You wanted me to meet your relatives?" she teased.

"Well, I do want you to meet both of my brothers, as well as get to know my grandmother better, but the reason I came back was to see if I could settle things with your father and ask you to marry me."

Surprised by his statement, she shook her head. "Whoa, cowboy. Brothers and a grandmother?"

Nodding, he explained, "It turns out my mother wasn't the only woman my father impregnated. My brother Hunter is a year older than I am and my brother Caleb is a year younger."

"How long have you known about them?" she asked, feeling envious. She'd always wanted siblings.

"About two months. I found out about them at the same time I learned Emerald Larson is my paternal grandmother."

"*The* Emerald Larson is your grandmother?" No wonder there was such confusion over who her employer was.

As he explained about Emerald's stipulations that the women tell no one who'd fathered their babies because she'd wanted them to grow up without the temptations that had corrupted their father, Cheyenne nodded. "I can understand that she was only trying to protect you and your brothers, but it would have been so nice for you to have all known each other sooner."

"We're getting acquainted now and finding that

we have a lot in common." He laughed. "We all wonder what our all-knowing grandmother is going to spring on us next. When she gave each of us a company to run, she told us we'd get no interference from her. But we're finding that the old gal still has a few surprises up her sleeve. And I have a feeling that in our case, she was doing a little matchmaking in the bargain."

"I'm glad she did," Cheyenne said honestly. She reached out and cupped his lean cheek with her palm. "It's taken thirteen years, but I'm finally going to marry the love of my life."

"I love you, sweetheart."

"And I love you, Nick Daniels. More than you'll ever know."

He kissed her until they both gasped for breath. "How big of a wedding do you want?"

"I think just family would be nice."

"That might be a problem." He gave her a sheepish grin. "Once Emerald gets wind of our getting married, she's going to jump right in and help. And believe me, sweetheart. She doesn't do anything on a small scale."

"Do you think she'd be content with a small wedding and a big reception?" Cheyenne asked hopefully.

Nick nodded. "As long as you put her in charge of planning it, I think she'll be fine."

Her mind reeled from everything that had happened in the past few hours. "I still can't believe this is finally going to happen."

"Believe it, sweetheart. Nothing is going to keep me from making you my wife."

Happier than she'd ever been, Cheyenne kissed the man she'd given her heart to so long ago. "I can't wait to start our life together."

Taking her by the hand, he led her toward the door. "I can't, either."

"Where are we going?"

His grin caused her entire body to tingle as he hurried her up the stairs and into his bedroom. "To start our life."

Epilogue

"**H**ave Cheyenne and the judge arrived yet?" Nick asked as he checked his watch.

"They just drove up." Hunter laughed. "I didn't think I'd ever see any man more impatient to get married than Caleb. But I swear, I think you have him beat, Nick."

"I've waited a long time to make Cheyenne my wife." Nick checked the pocket of his Western-cut suit. "Do you or Caleb have the ring?"

"And I thought I was nervous when Alyssa and I got married." Caleb laughed as he walked into the room. "If you'll remember, you gave me Cheyenne's wedding band when we got here."

A knock on the door signaled that the wedding was about to begin and, taking a deep breath, Nick smiled at his two best men. "I'll feel a lot better when that ring is on her finger and this is a done deal."

As he walked out of the room they'd used to wait for the ceremony to begin, Nick looked around at the interior of the church. Other than a fresh coat of paint on the walls and a different-colored carpet down the center aisle, it looked much the same as he remembered.

Once he and Cheyenne had gotten around to talking about where to get married, they'd both agreed that the obvious choice for the wedding was the little church where they'd tried to become husband and wife thirteen years ago. But this time things were different. This time, instead of leading her away in tears, her father was going to walk her down the aisle and place her hand in Nick's.

When Nick took his place beside the minister and looked at the handful of people sitting in the pews, his grandmother caught his eye. At first, Emerald had been disappointed that the wedding was going to be limited to family. But when she heard they were turning the reception over to her, she was like a little kid at Christmas. And Nick had no doubt that she'd made poor old Luther Freemont's life a living hell when she made him the liaison between her and the people she'd hired to pull it all together on such short notice.

As the organist began playing "Here Comes the Bride," he turned his attention to the back of the church and watched as the double doors opened and Judge Holbrook escorted Cheyenne down the aisle. When they reached the altar where he stood with his brothers and the minister, Nick stepped forward and her father placed her hand in his.

The judge's eyes were suspiciously moist when he kissed Cheyenne's cheek, then turned to Nick. "Take good care of my princess, son."

As the judge limped over to sit on the front pew, Nick stared into the eyes of the most beautiful woman he'd ever seen. "I love you, Cheyenne. Are you ready for this?"

Her smile was filled with such love it robbed him of breath. "I love you, too, Nick, and I've been ready to become your wife for thirteen years."

"Then let's not wait a minute longer," he said as they turned to face the minister.

"And true love prevails," Emerald whispered as the handsome groom kissed his beautiful bride.

"Inevitably," Luther Freemont agreed.

Theirs hadn't been an easy journey, but in the end Nick and Cheyenne's love had won out and they were finally going to realize their dreams. Nick's idea to turn the Sugar Creek Cattle Company into a free-range cattle operation had been brilliant and Emerald had no doubt that it would be a huge success in the beef industry.

She turned her attention to Cheyenne. If her sources were correct, and Emerald had every reason to believe they were, she would be celebrating the birth of her first great-grandchild early next summer, right after Cheyenne graduated from college with a degree in elementary education.

More than happy with the results of her second matchmaking attempt, her gaze settled on her eldest grandson. Hunter was going to be her biggest challenge of all. His was a deeply wounded soul in need of healing. But she had every confidence that what she had planned for him would be just what he needed to come to terms with the past and move forward with his life.

As the minister introduced Nick and Cheyenne as Mr. and Mrs. Nick Daniels, Emerald leaned over to Luther. "Two down and one to go."

* * * * *

BETROTHED FOR
THE BABY

BY
KATHIE DeNOSKY

This book is dedicated to my editor, Tina Colombo.
Thank you for your unwavering support and
encouragement. You're the very best.

And a special thank-you to my son, Bryan, for his help
with the Spanish in this book.

Te amo, mi hijo.

One

When Hunter O'Banyon glanced over at the pretty little blonde he'd met only moments ago, adrenaline began to pump through his veins. Her porcelain cheeks were flushed with a mixture of heat and excitement, and he could tell from the sparkle of urgency in her violet eyes that he was in for one hell of a ride.

"I hope you don't mind, but this is going to have to be faster than I'd planned," she said, sounding a little breathless.

Grinning, he nodded. "Bring it on. I can take it as fast as you want to go."

"I like the way you think." Her smile caused his

heart to race like a twelve-stroke engine hitting on all cylinders. "Hang on, big guy. This might get a little wild."

Hunter took a deep breath and braced himself. "Burn it, darlin'."

At the same time as she pushed the gas pedal all the way to the floor, she reached out to flip a switch on the dash. Lights and the keening wail of a siren competed with the sound of spinning tires kicking up a huge cloud of gravel and southwest Texas dust as the pickup truck careened away from the tarmac at Devil's Fork Community Airfield.

When Hunter had discovered there was no commercial air service to the little town, he'd wondered why the pilot of the Cessna Skyhawk he'd chartered to fly him to Devil's Fork from El Paso had laughed like a hyena when Hunter had called it an airport. Now he knew why. The entire thing consisted of an asphalt landing strip that he'd bet barely met FAA standards, a storage shed that leaned precariously to one side and a wooden pole with a tattered wind sock attached to the top just above the United States and Texas flags. As far as he could tell, there weren't even any lights for landing at night. He could only hope the Life Medevac operation looked better.

"By the way, I'm Callie Marshall, the flight nurse on the Evac II team," the blonde said conversationally.

Nice name for a nice-looking woman, he thought

as they approached the edge of town. "I'm Hunter O'Banyon."

"Thank God." She grinned. "When my pager went off, I didn't give you time to introduce yourself, and it suddenly occurred to me that you might not be the man I was supposed to meet."

His heart stalled and he had to clear his suddenly dry throat. When she smiled, Callie Marshall wasn't just pretty, she was drop-dead gorgeous.

"What were the chances of anyone else flying into Devil's Fork?" he asked when he finally got his vocal cords to work.

Her delightful laughter was one of the nicest sounds he'd heard in a long time. "Good point," she said, nodding. "I think you're the first person I've heard of flying into Devil's Fork since I arrived two months ago."

"Somehow that doesn't surprise me." He tightened his safety harness when she turned a corner, seemingly on two wheels. "Did you arrive by plane?"

"No way." She shook her head, causing her ponytail to sway back and forth. "I drove over from Houston. I wasn't about to take one of those puddle-jumper flights in here."

As they sped down Main Street, Hunter decided that if he'd blinked, he might have missed the entire town. Besides the fact that Callie was going so fast it wasn't much more than a blur, the business district was only a few blocks long and there wasn't much more than two or three blocks to the residential section.

"Mary Lou, our dispatcher, said you're from the Miami area. It might take a while for you to get used to Devil's Fork. It's about six hundred miles from the nearest beach and not exactly a hotbed of social activity."

"No kidding." He cringed when they sailed through a four-way stop on the opposite end of town without so much as slowing down. "I knew this place was small, but I expected something a little bigger than this."

"I did, too," she agreed. "After I drove through it the first time, I had a hard time believing there was enough of a call for a medevac operation to be based here. But I was wrong."

Hunter thought back to what he'd read in the file he'd been handed on the business his grandmother had given him to run. "The way I understand it, we're the only emergency service available for sections of five different counties."

She nodded. "The population is so sparse in this part of Texas, it isn't cost-effective for communities to have their own ambulance." Shrugging, she steered the truck onto a dirt-packed road leading up to a large aircraft hangar with Life Medevac Helicopter Service painted on the side. "Besides, if they had a ground unit, it would take too long to reach most of the people and even longer to get them to a hospital. We're their best hope for emergency medical care."

When she drove the truck around the side of the building, Hunter breathed a little easier. The Life Medevac base appeared to be in much better condition than the Devil's Fork airfield. Besides the well-kept hangar, there were two brand-new, top-of-the-line Bell EMS helicopters sitting on brightly painted helipads, and the entire area was ringed with what looked to be state-of-the-art lighting for night takeoffs and landings.

"I'll see you when we get back," she said, jamming the gearshift into Park at the same time she killed the engine and threw open the driver's door. "I have a flight to catch."

"Thanks for the ride," Hunter called, getting out of the truck.

Turning, she gave him another one of her killer smiles. "I almost forgot to tell you—beware of Mary Lou's coffee. She'll tell you it's the best you've ever had, but don't believe it." She grimaced. "It's awful."

As he stood there staring at Callie slowly jogging toward the waiting helicopter, he couldn't put his finger on what it was about her, but something bothered him. Aside from the fact that she'd driven the truck through town as though the hounds of hell were chasing them and she now moved as if she had all the time in the world, there was something about the snug way her navy-blue flight suit fit her around the middle that didn't seem quite right.

But when she disappeared inside the cabin space of the chopper and the door slid shut behind her, he quickly dismissed his concerns as Evac II lifted off the helipad. Although Emerald Larson had assured him that she'd seen to it that all the equipment was up-to-date and exceeded state requirements, he intended to order new flight suits in a color that could be more easily differentiated from other first responders that might be on scene when the Life Medevac crews arrived. And he'd make sure everyone wore the right size.

"You must be Hunter O'Banyon, the new boss of this outfit."

At the sound of the female voice behind him, Hunter turned to face a woman he'd judge to be somewhere in her late sixties or early seventies. With curly snow-white hair, a perfectly round face and a pair of narrow reading glasses perched on her nose, she looked as if she could easily play Mrs. Claus in a Christmas pageant.

He smiled as he extended his hand. "That would be me. And you must be Mary Lou Carson."

"The one and only." Grinning, she firmly shook his hand. "Come on in the dispatch room and rest a spell. I'll pour you a cup of the best coffee you've ever had, then I'll show you your quarters."

Reaching into the bed of the pickup truck, Hunter grabbed his luggage and followed Mary Lou out of the late-August heat and into the air-conditioned office of the hangar. When she led him into the dispatch room, he looked around at the framed military medals hanging on the wall beside the door.

"Did these belong to your husband?" he asked conversationally.

"Some of them." Mary Lou walked over to a small kitchen area on the opposite side of the room to stir the delicious-smelling contents of a huge pot on the electric range. "The rest are mine."

When she walked back over to where he stood, she handed him a cup of coffee, then motioned for him to sit in one of several chairs on the opposite side of a scarred wooden desk. "Take a load off, Hunter."

"What branch of the military were you in?" he asked, sitting down.

"Lester and I were both career Navy." She walked between the desk and a built-in counter filled with radio equipment, a computer and several telephones to settle herself into an old wooden desk chair that looked as if it might have been around since World War II. "He was an aircraft mechanic and I was a nurse. He died in an accident onboard an aircraft carrier not long before we were supposed to retire."

"I'm sorry." Hunter knew all too well what it was like to lose someone unexpectedly.

"Don't be sorry," she said, surprising him. "Lester died doing what he loved most—working on fighter jets. That's the best way any of us can hope to go out of this world." Before he could respond, she shrugged. "That's why I'm a dispatcher here. After my arthritis forced me to stop working the floor in a hospital, I took this job. When people call with an emergency, I sometimes stay on the line and talk them through whatever medical crisis they have until one of our crews arrives. It's almost as satisfying as nursing."

Hunter took a sip of coffee as he considered what Mary Lou said. But as the bitter taste spread over his tongue, he had to force himself to swallow. Quickly setting the cup on the desk, he barely controlled the urge to shudder. What Callie had told him about the coffee being awful had been an understatement. The stuff was as thick as syrup and tasted as though it had been made with quinine.

Coughing, he looked up to see Mary Lou watching him expectantly. He could tell she was waiting for him to tell her how good it was.

"You like your coffee strong, don't you?" he asked, trying not to grimace.

She shrugged. "I like my coffee to be just the way I like a man—strong and the best I've ever had."

If he'd thought her coffee was enough to send his system into shock, her outspokenness finished the job. He couldn't have been more dumbfounded if he'd tried. Unable to think of a thing to say, he waited to see what she'd say next. Unless he'd misjudged her, that shouldn't take very long.

Her knowing smile clued him in on the fact that she'd known her statement would render him speechless. "There's a few things about me you might as well know up front, Hunt. I don't mince words. I say exactly what I think because I'm old enough to get away with it and I've never been one to beat around the bush."

"I can respect that." Hunter had no idea where Mary Lou was going with this, but he could tell she had more on her mind.

"I'm glad to hear you say that, because what I'm going to tell you now might not set real well."

"I'm listening."

"I'm going to treat you like I treat everyone else around here because I'm not impressed by much of anything anymore. And that includes you being Emerald Larson's grandson."

Hunter frowned. He'd specifically asked Emerald not to divulge his relationship to her. For one thing, he didn't need the added pressure of living up to someone's expectations. And for another, he still hadn't fully come to terms with being her grandson.

"How did you learn about—"

"Emerald and I go way back. She hasn't always been on the top of the heap. When she was a teenager, she worked behind the soda counter in my father's drugstore." Mary Lou grinned. "She was like an older sister to me, and we've stayed in touch over the years."

Hunter wasn't particularly happy about having one of Emerald's lifelong friends working for him. He didn't like the idea of not being able to make a move without his manipulative grandmother knowing about it.

"If you're worried about me running to Emerald to report everything you do, don't waste your time," Mary Lou said as though she'd read his mind. "I don't carry tales. If she wants to know what's going on with you, she'll have to ask you yourself."

"That's good to hear." Whether he should or not, Hunter believed the woman.

Draining the last of her coffee, Mary Lou placed her cup on the desk and stood up. "Now that we have that out of the way, I'll show you to your living quarters and let you get settled in while I finish up the beef stew I put on for our supper." She pointed to his cup. "Would you like that warmed up?"

He quickly shook his head. "I'm not much of a coffee drinker." He didn't want to hurt her feelings, but if he never drank another drop of the bitter brew, it would be all too soon.

She shook her head. "I don't know what's wrong with you young people. I'm the only one working here who likes coffee."

As Hunter grabbed his suitcase and followed her through a doorway and down a hall toward the back of the hangar, he suspected the others' reluctance to drink Mary Lou's coffee had everything in the world to do with self-defense and nothing to do with not liking coffee.

"This is your office," she said, passing a door on the way to the back of the building. Pointing to a door across the hall, she added, "And this is the on-duty crew's sleeping quarters. We have three crews working rotating twenty-four-hour shifts—two days on duty and four off. Of course, on the outside chance that we get a call while one crew is out, the first two days that a crew is off duty, they're on call."

"What about you? What are your hours?"

"I'm here round the clock. When I'm not dispatching a crew, I'm cooking and handing out advice that nobody seems to listen to." She laughed as she pointed to a door next to the crew quarters. "This is my room. I have a ringer in here that wakes me up when we have a night call or I decide to take a nap."

Hunter frowned. "Who's the dispatcher on your days off?"

She continued walking toward a door at the end of the hall. "On the rare occasions that I take a day off, one of the members of the off-duty crew fills in for me."

"You don't have regularly scheduled time off?" He didn't like the sound of that. Aside from Emerald taking advantage of Mary Lou, he wasn't sure that it was even legal for the woman to be working that much.

"Don't get your shorts in a bunch, Hunter," Mary Lou said as if she'd read his mind. "I don't have family,

and working here at Life Medevac is what makes me
happy and keeps me going. I love what I do, so don't
go getting any ideas about making me take time off on
a regular basis, because I won't do it." She opened the
door to his room, then, stepping back, pointed to his
luggage. "Are all your things in that one suitcase?"

He nodded. "I stored the rest of my things until I find
a place in Devil's Fork."

"Good idea." The woman nodded her approval.
"Now go ahead and get your gear stowed away while
I radio Evac II and find out the status of their patient
and what time they estimate they'll get back to base."

Hunter stared after Mary Lou as she breezed out the
door and down the hall as if her working without
regular days off was a nonissue. But he wasn't so sure.
It wasn't just a question of the labor laws. Her age and
well-being had to be taken into consideration, as well.
She might seem like a dynamo with boundless energy,
but working 24-7 would be hard on a much younger
person, let alone a woman close to seventy.

As he lifted his suitcase and placed it on the edge
of the bed to unpack, he decided there were several
things he needed to do right away. Not only did he need
to order the correct size flight suits for everyone, he'd
have to check into Texas labor laws.

Putting away the last of his clothes, he looked
around. It was a good thing he always traveled light.
The room was barely big enough for the twin bed,

small chest of drawers and bedside table. There was no way he'd have had room for anything but his clothes.

But then, he didn't need a lot of room. For the past five years he hadn't cared how spacious his accommodations had been or even where they'd been located. After working construction so hard each day that he'd been too tired to think or remember, all he'd needed was a place to sleep, shower and change clothes. With any luck, there would be enough work to keep him just as busy at Life Medevac.

At the sound of a helicopter landing outside, he walked down the hall to the dispatch room. "They weren't gone long."

Mary Lou nodded. "Juanita Rodriguez thought she was going to have her baby, but it turned out to be false labor." Smiling, she added, "She's only nineteen and it's her first pregnancy. She and her husband, Miguel, are worried they won't make it to the hospital in time."

"I hear that's a big concern for most first-time parents." A twinge of regret ran through Hunter. Anticipating the arrival of a child was something he would never experience.

But he didn't have time to dwell on the disturbing thought as the flight crew from Evac II entered the dispatch room. Besides Callie, the crew consisted of a sandy-haired man who looked to be in his forties and a fresh-faced kid of about twenty.

"The name's George Smith," the man said, smiling

as he walked over to shake Hunter's hand. Almost as tall as Hunter's own six-foot-three-inch frame, George was built like a heavyweight prizefighter, and if his grip was any indication, as strong as one. "I'm the pilot for the Evac II team." He nodded toward the younger man. "And that kid over there is Corey Timmons, the EMT on our crew."

"It's nice to meet you, Mr. O'Banyon," Corey said, stepping forward to pump Hunter's hand enthusiastically. "We've been looking forward to you taking over."

"Call me Hunter." He wasn't surprised to hear the employees had been looking forward to a change in administration. From the file he'd been given, when Emerald bought Life Medevac, the employees hadn't been paid their wages in several weeks.

Grinning, the young man's brown eyes danced mischievously. "We're glad to see you survived the drive across town with Callie behind the wheel."

Hunter chuckled. "Was there doubt?"

"After flying into Devil's Fork with Crash Jenson at the controls of that little four-seater prop job, we kinda wondered if her driving wouldn't finish you off," George added, laughing.

"If you two keep joking about my driving, I'll stop making those chocolate-chip-oatmeal cookies you love so much," Callie warned good-naturedly as she crossed the room to the kitchen area, where Mary Lou was putting the finishing touches on the crew's dinner.

"We take it all back," Corey said earnestly as he walked over to grab a plate for Mary Lou to fill with a generous helping of stew.

"You bet," George said, nodding vigorously. "We were just joking around, Callie. Whatever you do, don't stop making those cookies." Turning to Hunter, he confided, "You've never tasted anything as good in your entire life as her chocolate-chip-oatmeal cookies."

"I'll look forward to trying them," Hunter said, enjoying the easy banter.

As George moved to get a plate of stew, Hunter watched Callie open the refrigerator to remove a carton of orange juice and once again noticed the way her flight suit fit. The navy-blue fabric was fairly loose everywhere but in her midsection and she looked as if…

A sudden cold feeling of intense dread began to fill Hunter's chest and he had to swallow hard against the bile rising in his throat. Callie Marshall wasn't just carrying a few extra pounds around the middle. She was several months pregnant.

Two

As she walked past Hunter to sit down in one of the chairs in front of Mary Lou's desk, Callie wondered what on earth she'd done to come under such close scrutiny. His intense stare had followed her from the moment she'd walked into the room and caused her skin to tingle as if he'd reached out and touched her.

Shaking her head to clear it, she decided her uncharacteristic reaction to him had to be because her hormones were all out of whack due to her pregnancy. It was the only reasonable explanation she could think of to explain it.

His concentrated stare had probably been nothing

more than the result of noticing her thickening midsection. He was no doubt trying to figure out whether she was just a bit plump or expecting a baby.

Careful to keep her voice low to avoid calling the others' attention to the fact that she'd caught him staring, she smiled as she turned to meet his intense green gaze. "In case you're wondering about my odd shape, I'm four and a half months pregnant."

Running an agitated hand through his dark brown hair, he looked a little uncomfortable. "I...didn't mean to—"

"Don't worry about it." She smiled, hoping to put him at ease. "It's not like it's a big secret. And, as you can see, I'm certainly not trying to hide my pregnancy."

"Your husband is okay with you flying while you're pregnant?" He shook his head. "I'm sorry. It's none of my business."

It was an odd question, but the concern on his handsome face and in his deep voice was genuine. "Don't worry about it. I don't have a husband, so it's a nonissue." She shrugged. "I'm unmarried, uncommitted and quite content to stay that way."

"I didn't mean to pry." He looked more uncomfortable than before.

"It's not a problem. I'm actually looking forward to single motherhood."

He looked as if he intended to say something, but Corey chose that moment to walk over and plop down in the chair beside her. "Have we sucked up enough to get more cookies or do we need to grovel a little more?"

Callie laughed at the likable young EMT. "No, I think you've redeemed yourself enough for another batch of chocolate-chip-oatmeal cookies."

"If you'll excuse me, I think I'll go check out my office," Hunter said suddenly, turning to walk down the hall.

Staring after her new boss, she wondered what had caused his abrupt change. When she'd met him at the airfield, he'd been congenial and outgoing. But within the span of a few minutes his mood had become pensive and troubled. Was he concerned that she would be unable to do her job?

She rose to her feet to follow him into the office and reassure him that she was perfectly capable of carrying out her duties, but the dispatch radio chose that moment to crackle to life.

"Looks like we have another run," Mary Lou said, crossing the room to answer the call.

As Callie listened to the highway patrol officer relay the location of the one-car accident on Interstate 10 and the patrolman's assessment of the driver's injuries, she, George and Corey started for the door. "Tell him we're on the way."

"ETA is fifteen minutes," George said.

"Keep the stew warm," Corey added.

Out of the corner of her eye Callie saw Hunter

reenter the room. His concerned expression reinforced her determination to set his mind at ease. But their talk would have to wait until later. Whether or not he believed she was capable of doing her job, she had an accident victim depending on her for emergency medical attention. And she wasn't about to let her patient down.

Drenched in a cold sweat, Hunter awoke with a jerk and, swinging his legs over the side of the bed, sat up. Propping his elbows on his knees, he cradled his head in his hands as he tried to chase away the remnants of his nightmare.

He hadn't dreamed about the accident in almost six months. But it was just as real now as it had been when he'd lived through it five years ago. He and his fiancée, Ellen Reichert, a second-year resident at the Mount Sinai Medical Center in Miami, had flown into Central America to deliver medical supplies and administer first aid to some of the remote villages hit the hardest by a category-four hurricane. Everything about the trip had been routine and uneventful until he'd circled the landing site for their last stop. That's when all hell had broken loose and the course of his life had changed forever.

The twin-turbine helicopter he'd been piloting had suddenly lost oil pressure, then, before he could get it safely set down, it stalled out. He didn't remember a lot of the details of what happened after that, only that he'd fought the controls with little success. The chopper had ended up tilting precariously in midair, then come down hard on its starboard side.

His first thought had been to make sure that Ellen was all right, then get them out of what was left of the helicopter. But the blood in his veins had turned to ice when he'd called her name and she'd failed to respond. He'd placed his fingers to the side of her neck and, detecting a faint pulse, scrambled to release their seat belts. Pushing the door on the port side of the chopper open, he'd carefully lifted her up through the opening, then carried her a safe distance from the wreckage.

When she'd regained consciousness, they'd both known she didn't have long, and that's when his devastating heartbreak had turned to total despair. She'd told him that she'd been waiting for the perfect time to tell him she'd recently learned she was pregnant. With her dying breath she'd told him how much she loved him and how sorry she was that she had to go, then, closing her eyes, she'd quietly slipped away.

The ensuing investigation into the crash had proven the accident had been caused by mechanical failure and there was nothing he could have done to prevent it. But he'd quit flying that day and struggled for the past five years, feeling guilty because he'd walked away with nothing more than cuts and bruises, blaming himself for living when the woman he'd loved and their future child had died. He'd spent countless hours going over every detail of the accident, wondering if there was something he could have done differently, something that could have lessened her injuries or saved her life. But try as he might, he couldn't think of anything that would have changed the outcome.

He took a deep shuddering breath and tried to relegate the disturbing memories to the back of his mind. There was no doubt why the horrific dream had returned, and he couldn't say he was overly surprised that it had. After discovering that Callie was pregnant, all he'd been able to think about was once again being responsible for the lives of a woman and her unborn child. Even though she wasn't on his flight crew, as her employer it was ultimately his job to see to her safety.

Fortunately her shift had ended right after the Evac II team had returned from transporting the car accident victim to a hospital in El Paso. That meant that he had four days to come up with a convincing argument to get her to ground herself. And unless her crew was called out as backup for Evac III, she and her baby would be safe.

Now all Hunter had to do was figure out a way to keep them that way.

"Give me a second," Callie called when it sounded as if whoever was at her front door would knock it off its hinges with their insistent pounding. Wiping the flour from her hands with her apron, she turned her CD player down and hurried from the kitchen to open the door. "What's so important that—"

She stopped short at the sight of Hunter O'Banyon standing on her tiny front porch. Lord have mercy, but he was one of the best looking men she'd ever seen. He was dressed in a black T-shirt and worn blue jeans. The soft fabrics fit him like a second skin and emphasized the width of his broad shoulders and his narrow hips. When she glanced at his arms, the sight of his bulging biceps stretching the knit sleeves of his shirt sent a shiver of awareness straight up her spine.

Callie gave herself a mental shake. What on earth was wrong with her? And why in the name of heaven was she ogling the man as if he were a fudge-nut brownie with rich chocolate frosting?

"Are you all right?" His expression was one of deep concern.

"Of—" she swallowed hard "—course. Why wouldn't I be?" Other than being embarrassed that her hair was piled on her head in total disarray, her shorts and T-shirt were the oldest things she had in her closet and she was coated with a fine dusting of flour, she was just peachy.

"I knocked for five minutes before you answered the door. I thought something might be wrong." He rubbed his hand over the back of his neck. "Never mind. Do you have a few minutes? We need to talk."

What could he possibly think they needed to discuss? And why did he have to show up after she'd received a phone call from her mother?

At least once a week since telling her mother she was pregnant they'd gone through the same old routine of her mother wanting to know who the father of Callie's baby was and why she was so insistent on keeping the man's identity a secret. Frustrated beyond words with her mother's persistence, by the time Callie had ended the phone call, she'd already measured the ingredients for several dozen sugar cookies and had pulled the box of oats from the cupboard for a double batch of chocolate-chip-oat-meal cookies.

Some women cleaned house when they were upset. Callie baked.

"Do you mind if I come in?" Hunter asked, returning her to the present.

"I'm sorry. Please come in." She stepped back for him to enter her small cottage. "I was just baking some—oh no! My cookies!" Remembering the peanut butter cookies she'd put into the oven just before hearing him pound on the door, she made a beeline for the kitchen with him hot on her heels.

"Damn! When you make cookies, you don't fool around, do you?" he said, looking around.

Taking the baking sheet from the oven, she placed it on the top of the stove, then glanced at the table and countertops. Plates of cookies covered every available surface.

Shaking her head at the sight, she nibbled on her lower lip. She must have been more upset over her mother's phone call than she'd realized.

"Would you like some milk and cookies?" She grinned. "I have plenty."

"No kidding." His deep chuckle caused a wave of goose bumps to sweep over her skin. "What are you going to do with all of them?"

"They won't last long around George and Corey."

She opened a cabinet to get something to store the cookies in, but the feel of Hunter's broad chest pressed to her side as he stepped forward to reach for several of the plastic containers on the top shelf sent a charge of excitement skipping over every nerve in her body. When he handed them to her, then stepped back, she had trouble drawing her next breath.

Unnerved, her hand trembled as she took the containers from him. "Th-thank you."

He gave her a short nod, then moved farther away. "I think I will take you up on that offer of some milk and cookies."

Pouring them each a glass of milk, she set one at the far end of the table and started to sit down at the opposite end. Hunter was immediately behind her, holding the chair, and his close proximity unsettled her so much that she almost turned over her glass.

What in blazes was wrong with her? She not only felt as jumpy as a frightened rabbit, she'd suddenly turned into a major klutz.

When he sat down across from her, he studied the plates of cookies between them. "What do you suggest I start with first?"

"I like the oatmeal cookies, but that's probably because I use chocolate chips instead of raisins," she said, reaching for one of the tasty treats.

He nodded as he took a cookie from one of the plates. "I'm kind of partial to peanut butter myself." Taking a bite, his eyes widened. "Corey and George weren't exaggerating—these are some of the best cookies I've ever tasted."

As they munched on the cookies, Callie wondered what it was he thought they needed to discuss. For the life of her she couldn't think of anything so important that he'd pay her a visit on her day off.

"What did you want to talk to me about?" she asked, hoping the sooner he stated the purpose for his visit, the sooner he'd leave. She desperately needed to regain her composure.

Taking a deep breath, he set his empty glass on the table, then caught her gaze with his. "I'm concerned that your job might be a little too much for a woman in your condition."

She laughed. "Contrary to what you might think, pregnancy is not a disability."

"I understand that," he said, nodding. "But at times I'm sure it's extremely tiring."

"I'm not going to pretend that it isn't." She rose to place their glasses in the dishwasher, then started stacking cookies in the containers for freezing. "But there are also times when we'll go for a day or two without an emergency call and I'm exhausted from sheer boredom. Besides, my obstetrician doesn't have a problem with me working as a flight nurse, so if you're worried that it's too strenuous for me, don't. Corey and George are both very conscientious and won't let me do any heavy lifting. And when we're not out on calls, I make sure to take regular naps."

"Yes, but there's other things to be considered, such as turbulence or pilot error," he said as he handed her plates full of cookies to be stored in the plasticware.

"I trust George. He's a good pilot."

"I'm not saying he isn't."

She snapped the lid shut on the box, then started filling another one. "What *are* you saying?"

He rubbed the back of his neck as if to relieve tension. "Aren't you worried about having to make a rough landing or a possible crash?"

"Not really." She couldn't for the life of her figure out why he was so overly concerned. Every pilot she'd ever known considered flying the safest mode of transportation. "In the event that something like that happens, I'm in no greater danger because I'm pregnant than I would be if I wasn't."

"But—"

"I see no reason why you're so worried about it, but if you think it's that important, why don't you review the employment records and put me on the crew with the best pilot?"

To her surprise, he placed his large hands on her shoulders and turned her to face him. But instead of arguing his point further, he stared at her for several long seconds before he muttered a curse and lowered his head to capture her lips with his.

As his mouth moved over hers in a gentle caress, Callie's pulse raced and her insides began to hum. The last thing she'd expected for him to do was kiss her. But instead of pushing him away as she should have, she reached out and placed her hands on his biceps to steady herself. The feel of his rock-hard muscles flexing beneath her palms sent a shiver of excitement up her spine and caused her knees to tremble.

If she had any sense, she'd put a stop to the kiss right now and demand that he leave. But his firm, warm lips were making her feel things that she'd only read about in women's magazines and romance novels, and she didn't want the delicious sensations to end.

When he wrapped his arms around her and pulled her against him to deepen the kiss, the feel of his superior strength surrounding her sent tiny little sparks skipping over every nerve in her body. Opening for him, she felt her heart skip several beats when he slipped his tongue inside to tease and explore her with a tenderness that made forming a coherent thought all but impossible.

Placing his hand at the small of her back, he urged her forward, but the feel of her round little tummy pressed to his stomach must have brought him back to reality. He suddenly went completely still, then, releasing her, he carefully set her away from him and took a couple of steps back.

"That shouldn't…have happened." He ran an agitated hand through his thick dark brown hair. "I think I should probably leave."

"Don't worry about it."

Embarrassed and more than a little confused by her uncharacteristic behavior, Callie began packing more cookies into the plastic containers. Why hadn't she stopped him instead of clinging to him as if she were desperate for a man's attention?

Hunter O'Banyon might be tall, dark and movie-star handsome, but she was no more interested in him than she was in any other man. But, dear heaven above, could he ever kiss.

Her cheeks feeling as if they were on fire from her sudden wayward thought, she shoved a container of cookies into his hands. "Take these back to the hangar for Mary Lou and the on-duty crew."

"Callie…I—"

If he didn't leave soon, she'd be up all night baking. "It's getting late and I'm sure you need to get back." She walked into the living room and opened the front door. "Thank you for stopping by. I appreciate your concerns and I will give them some thought."

"By the way, I know this is short notice, but I'm holding a staff meeting the day after tomorrow at 10:00 a.m.," he said, looking anything but happy. "Will you be able to be there?"

She shook her head. "I have a doctor's appointment. But I'll stop by after my checkup and someone can fill me in on what was covered in the meeting."

He stared at her for what seemed an eternity before he gave her a short nod. "Good night, Callie," he said, walking out onto the porch.

"Have a nice rest of the evening, Hunter," she said, closing the door behind him.

Walking straight to the kitchen, she stacked the containers of cookies on a shelf in her freezer, then pulled out the ingredients for a batch of brownies. Her phone conversation with her mother had been frustrating and caused her to make several batches of cookies. But Hunter's disturbing kiss was sending her into a baking frenzy, and for some odd reason everything she wanted to make was chocolate.

As she measured cocoa and flour, something she'd heard on a cooking show came to mind and caused her to knock over a cup of sugar. Eating chocolate released the same endorphins in the brain that were released while having sex.

"Not good, Callie. Not good at all."

Hurriedly opening a bag of milk-chocolate chips, she popped a handful into her mouth, and as the rich taste spread over her tongue, she decided that even if chocolate did make her gain too much weight, it was far less dangerous to her peace of mind than Hunter O'Banyon.

As he descended the steps and walked over to the white truck with Life Medevac painted on the side, Hunter shook his head. He didn't blame Callie one damned bit for giving him the bum's rush. Hell, he'd deserved more than that. He'd acted like an oversexed teenager on his first date. But what he was having the devil of a time trying to figure out was why.

Getting into the truck, he started the engine and, backing from the driveway, drove across town. But instead of turning onto the road leading to the Life Medevac hangar, he kept going until the lights of Devil's Fork faded in the distance behind him. He needed to think, and even though he could go into his room for solitude, he'd found that staring at the vastness of a starlit night always helped him put things in perspective.

When he parked the truck and stared out the windshield at the stars above the Apache Mountains in the distance, he couldn't help but wonder what the hell had gotten into him. He'd only stopped by Callie's place to try to talk some sense into her and get her to see the wisdom in grounding herself until after she had her baby. But when he'd placed his hands on her shoulders and looked into her pretty violet eyes, he could no more have stopped himself from tasting her sweetness than he could stop his next breath.

He took a deep breath. Although he wasn't overly proud of it, he hadn't exactly led the life of a monk since Ellen's death. But he'd always been careful to be with women who wanted nothing more from him than mutual satisfaction and had no expectations of their liaison leading to anything more. And Callie Marshall was most definitely *not* that type of woman. Instead of smoke-filled nightclubs, champagne cocktails and a meaningless one-night stand, she was a cozy little cottage, homemade cookies and a long-term commitment.

But come to think of it, he'd been so busy in the past several months that he'd completely abandoned any kind of a social life. And although he was far from being as randy as a seventeen-year-old boy, a man of thirty-two did have certain needs that couldn't be ignored.

He frowned. But he'd never in his entire life found a pregnant woman irresistible.

He stared at a shooting star streaking across the inky sky. He guessed it was only natural that he'd be attracted to Callie even though she was expecting a baby, considering his current state of celibacy. She was a very pretty woman with a killer smile, a delightful laugh and a pair of legs that could drive a saint to sin. Combine all those traits with his neglected libido and it was no wonder he'd felt compelled to kiss her.

Satisfied that he'd discovered the reason for his un-characteristic caveman behavior, he started the truck and headed back toward the Life Medevac base. Now that he had things in perspective, there was no reason that he and Callie couldn't put what happened this evening behind them and move forward as employer and employee. Hell, maybe they could even be friends.

But much later, as he lay in bed trying to will himself to sleep, Hunter couldn't seem to forget the sweet taste of Callie's soft lips or that the blood in his veins had heated considerably when she'd kissed him back. And whether he liked it or not, the very last thing on his mind was friendship.

Three

On the drive back from her appointment with the obstetrician, Callie thought about Hunter's visit and how foolish she'd been. The kiss they'd shared had been very nice, but it didn't mean anything. She knew he'd been frustrated with her refusal to ground herself and he'd been just as surprised by his actions as she had. There had really been no reason for her to get so flustered and read more into it than that.

But she'd spent the rest of the night baking everything from chocolate-fudge-nut brownies to chocolate cake. And by the time she'd gone to bed, the gray light of dawn had begun to chase away the shadows of night.

She shook her head. She hadn't baked that much since she'd discovered she was pregnant.

Thinking back on that day, she could still remember walking out of her gynecologist's office in a total state of shock. She'd always wanted children, but she'd envisioned herself happily married and anticipating the blessed event with the man she loved and who loved her in return. She wasn't supposed to have become pregnant by a man who put social status above a meaningful relationship.

When she'd first met Craig Culbertson, he'd swept her off her feet with his charm and thoughtfulness. But it hadn't taken long for her to discover that he wasn't the man she'd thought he was. He'd hidden his true nature behind a winning smile and charming ways, and by the time they'd parted company, *shallow, self-centered* and *selfish* were the nicest words she could think of to describe the conceited snake.

Then, when she'd discovered she was pregnant a month after their breakup, her disillusionment with Craig had turned to abject fear. One of the deciding factors in her ending their relationship had been the sickening disgust she'd felt when he'd confided in her that at the age of nineteen he'd gotten his girlfriend pregnant and that his twelve-year-old brother was actually his son. He'd told her that once his parents had learned of the pregnancy and discovered the girl wasn't the family's social equal, they'd used their money, as well as their position in Houston society, to gain custody of the baby, adopt him and raise the boy as their own.

A cold chill raced through Callie. She could only imagine the devastation and powerlessness the young mother must have felt at losing all contact with her child. And that was the very reason Callie had made the decision to leave her job as an emergency room nurse at one of the Houston hospitals and take the job as flight nurse with Life Medevac.

If Craig found out about her pregnancy, she wasn't sure he and his parents wouldn't try to do the same thing to her that they'd done to the mother of his first child. Callie hadn't been born into a life of wealth and privilege and therefore would no doubt be considered an undesirable candidate to raise a Culbertson heir. They'd take her to court and she'd come out the loser. She didn't have the kind of money it would take to fight a custody battle against their high-powered lawyers.

She'd come from a middle-class single-parent home where there hadn't been an endless supply of money, and social outings had consisted of making trips to the mall or attending a matinee at the movie theater. And even if her father hadn't been lost at sea during a storm while working on an oil platform in the Gulf of Mexico, her social status wouldn't have been a whole lot different.

As she steered her car onto the lane leading up to

the Life Medevac hangar, she placed her hand on her rounded tummy. She might not have been born with a silver spoon in her mouth, but she loved her little boy with all her heart, and no one was going to take him away from her.

Parking the car, she took a deep breath and forced herself to forget about Houston and the ruthless Culbertsons. She was about to face Hunter O'Banyon and tell him that she'd given a lot of thought to his request that she ground herself. She'd even gone so far as to discuss her physical limitations with her obstetrician, and together they'd concluded there was no reason for her to go on maternity leave for a few more months. Now all she had to do was explain that to Hunter.

"Hi, Mary Lou," Callie said as she entered the dispatch room. "Is Hunter in his office?"

The older woman nodded. "I suspect he's back there compiling a list of everyone's size and the number of new flight suits he's going to order." She laughed. "How do you look in red?"

"We're going to wear red flight suits?"

"That's what he says." Mary Lou looked thoughtful. "Come to think of it, though, our crews will be more easily identified among other emergency personnel at an accident scene."

"It does get confusing sometimes when some of the other services wear the same shade of dark blue that we do," Callie agreed.

"Did everything go okay at the doctor's office?" Mary Lou asked. Since learning of Callie's pregnancy, the woman had taken it upon herself to monitor Callie's progress and well-being.

Smiling, Callie nodded. "The obstetrician did a sonogram and said the baby's size is right on target for a four-and-a-half-month fetus." She laughed. "But I doubt that I can get away with blaming my five-pound weight gain on my son."

"No, that would be due to all those cookies you bake," Mary Lou said, grinning.

As Callie walked down the hall to Hunter's office, she decided that Mary Lou was right. If she didn't stop baking, there wouldn't be a flight suit big enough to accommodate her expanding form, whether she was pregnant or not.

Knocking on Hunter's office door, she waited a moment before entering the office. "Do you have the time to fill me in on what took place at the staff meeting or should I come back later?"

He shook his head and pointed to the brown leather chair in front of his desk. "Have a seat. I've been waiting for you."

"That sounds ominous."

"Not really." His intense green eyes held hers as she lowered herself into the oversize armchair and tried not to notice how good-looking he was or that the sound of his deep voice had caused her insides to start humming. "Before I can order the new flight suits for everyone, I need to know if you've given any more thought to my suggestion that you ground yourself until after your baby is born."

"Yes, I have." She met his questioning gaze head-on. "I even discussed your concerns with my obstetrician this morning."

"And?"

Hunter held out little hope that she'd changed her mind, but since it had been the uppermost thing on his mind for the past two days, he had to know.

"The doctor and I both agreed that as long as I avoid heavy lifting, eat a healthy diet and get plenty of rest, there's no reason that I can't continue as a flight nurse on the Evac II team."

"But—"

"But nothing." Her determined expression warned him that she wasn't going to budge on the issue. "I'm not only capable of doing my job, I need the money I'll make between now and when I give birth to pay for the doctor and hospital."

He had to concentrate hard to keep his mind off the fact that she had the prettiest violet eyes he'd ever seen. "And there's nothing I can say to change your mind?"

"No. But as I told you the other night, if my continuing to fly bothers you that much, pair me with your best pilot. That should eliminate some of your concerns about pilot error."

Hunter took a deep breath, then slowly released it as resignation set in. "I anticipated your decision and I've already made arrangements for you and Corey to be switched to Evac I."

"That's your team." If the dismay on her pretty face was any indication, he'd shocked her.

Not at all happy about the situation, he nodded. "George and Mike—the Evac III pilot—are good, but I'm better."

"Don't you think your assumption that you're a better pilot is a bit arrogant?" She didn't look any happier with his decision than he was.

He shook his head. "Not in the least. It's a matter of experience. I have more flight hours in a Bell helicopter than George and Mike combined. Until he retired from the Air Force a couple of years ago, George flew Sikorskys. And Mike flew Apaches for the Army. I've flown a Bell almost exclusively for the past twelve years." He stopped short at adding that if he'd been behind the controls of a Bell the day of the accident, instead of a reconditioned military chopper given to the hurricane relief organization for aid missions, his fiancée would probably still be alive.

"When does this reassignment take place?"

"Effective immediately." Glancing down at the list of everyone's flight suit sizes, he asked, "What size flight suit do you think you'll need until after you have the baby?"

As he watched her thoughtfully nibble on her lower lip, sweat popped out on his forehead. The memory of Callie's softness and sweet taste when he'd kissed her was doing a real number on his neglected libido.

Giving him the size she thought she'd need to accommodate her advancing pregnancy, she asked, "Was there anything else discussed during the staff meeting that I should know about?"

He sat back in his desk chair. "Mary Lou served your cookies, and everyone agreed that if you ever decide to give up nursing, you should open a bakery shop."

She gave him a half smile as she stood up. "I don't think that would be a good idea. I only bake when I'm…" She stopped suddenly and shook her head. "It doesn't matter. What's my new schedule?"

Hunter rose to his feet. "Instead of coming in this evening, you'll need to be here day after tomorrow."

"At the usual time? Or did you change that, too?"

"Six in the evening," he said, nodding. When she turned toward the door, he said, "By the way, the other night I noticed you have a loose board on one of the porch steps. You'd better have your landlord fix it. You don't want to run the risk of falling."

"If I had a landlord, I'd have him take care of the repair." She shrugged one slender shoulder. "But since I bought the place when I moved to Devil's Fork, I guess I'll have to buy a hammer and a few nails and see what I can do about it myself."

For reasons he didn't care to contemplate, he didn't like the idea of her trying to make the repair herself. "I'll be over this evening to fix the step."

"Don't worry about it." She edged toward the door. "Upkeep is part of a homeowner's job. I don't think hammering a couple of nails into a board will be all that difficult."

Hunter figured he knew what the problem was and, rounding the desk, walked over and put his hands on her slender shoulders. He realized he'd made a huge error in judgment the moment he touched her. An electric charge zinged straight up his arms, and he had to fight an overwhelming urge to draw her closer.

"Callie, about the other night—"

"Please, don't." She shook her head. "It was just a simple kiss and I'm sure it didn't mean anything more to you than it did to me."

Whether it was a matter of stung pride, a bruised ego or the fact that he hadn't been able to forget how soft and yielding she'd been in his arms, her statement hit like a physical blow and he was determined to prove her wrong. "Darlin', that kiss was anything but simple." Slowly lowering his head, he felt as though he just might drown in her violet eyes. "And I think you know it as well as I do."

The moment his lips touched hers, it felt as if a spark ignited somewhere deep inside of him and heat spread throughout his entire body. If he had any sense at all, he'd call Emerald Larson, tell her that he'd changed his mind about taking over the air-ambulance service and put as much distance as he could between himself and Callie Marshall.

But instead of setting her away from him and apologizing for acting like an oversexed teenager, Hunter slid his arms around her and pulled her to him. Callie's soft, petite body nestled against his much larger frame sent blood racing through his veins and caused his heart to pound hard against his rib cage.

When her perfect lips parted on a soft sigh, he took advantage of her acquiescence and deepened the kiss. Slipping his tongue inside, he tasted the sweetness that was uniquely Callie and reacquainted himself with her tender inner recesses.

To his satisfaction, she circled his waist with her arms and melted against him as he gently coaxed her into doing a little exploring of her own. But with each stroke of her tongue to his, the fire that had begun to burn in his belly spread lower and his body tightened with desire faster than he could have ever imagined.

Shocked by the intensity of his need, he eased away from the kiss. Staring at the confusion on her pretty face, he had a feeling he looked just as bewildered.

"I, um, think…it might be a good idea…if we didn't do that again," she said, sounding suspiciously breathless.

"I think you're right." Releasing her, he rubbed at

the tension gathering at the base of his neck. Why did he turn into a Neanderthal every time he was around her? "I'll…see you later this evening…when I come by to repair the step."

She hurried over to the door. "It's really not necessary. I can handle fixing the—"

"I said I'd take care of it." He shook his head. "I can still fly a helicopter with a swollen finger. But if you smash your thumb, you'll have trouble starting an IV or splinting a broken limb."

She stared at him for several more seconds before she nodded, then quickly walked out of his office.

As Hunter watched Callie leave, he closed his eyes and counted to ten, then twenty. Why the hell couldn't he have left well enough alone? What on God's green earth had he thought he was going to prove, besides the fact that he had all the finesse of a bulldozer? Hadn't he sorted through what happened the other night and come to a reasonable conclusion for his attraction to her?

He hadn't been with a woman in almost a year, and that was long enough to make any normal adult male ready to crawl the walls. But even as he thought about finding a willing little lady to help him scratch his itch, he rejected the idea. A one-night stand might help him with his basic needs, but a meaningless encounter couldn't fill the void of companionship in his life.

Shaking his head, he walked back to his desk and sank into his chair. He wasn't looking for any kind of romantic relationship and neither was Callie, but he saw no reason why they couldn't be friends. They were both new in town, alone, and she needed someone to help out with the upkeep on her house from time to time.

Now if he could just keep that in mind and stop grabbing her like a caveman and kissing her until they both needed CPR, everything would be just fine.

As he sat there trying to convince himself that he could do just that, the phone rang. Checking the caller ID, he groaned when he recognized one of Emerald Larson's private numbers.

Switching the speakerphone on, he greeted his grandmother. "Hello, Emerald."

"Good afternoon, Hunter. How is my oldest grandson?"

He almost laughed. He wasn't fool enough to think that the old gal had called him just to say hello and shoot the breeze. Emerald Larson had a purpose behind everything she did. And that included placing a phone call to one of her grandsons.

"I'm doing okay. How are you?"

"Planning a little dinner party for my grandsons and their wives for the end of next month." She paused. "You will attend, won't you?"

"Sure," Hunter said, suddenly feeling more alone than he had in his entire life.

He'd only learned about his brothers a few months

ago, and although they'd formed a bond of friendship that he knew would stand the test of time, Caleb and Nick had both recently married. And that made Hunter the odd man out. Unfortunately he'd always be the odd man out. Marriage and family weren't in the cards for him. Not now. Not in the future.

Loving someone only opened a person up to more pain and heartache than it was worth. His mother had loved Owen Larson and ended up suffering a lifetime of loneliness for her efforts. Owen had run out on her, to leave her facing motherhood alone, and never looked back when he returned to Harvard after sweeping her off her feet during his spring-break in Miami. Then, Hunter had damned near lost his mind from the guilt of surviving the helicopter crash that had taken the lives of Ellen and their unborn child.

No, the emotional investment and risks that went along with loving someone weren't worth the high price a man had to pay.

"Hunter, are you still there?"

"Sorry." He took a deep breath. "What was that you were saying?"

"I said I'm on my way back to Wichita from Houston and I thought I would stop by to see you and my old friend Mary Lou."

He should have known that she wouldn't be able to resist checking up on him from time to time. She'd done the same with his brothers and the companies she'd given them. Why should he be any different?

Even though she'd given him Life Medevac to run as he saw fit, it still came under the umbrella of Emerald Inc., and she hadn't become one of the richest, most successful businesswomen in the world by sitting back and letting others oversee her holdings.

"When will you be here?" he asked, barely resisting the urge to cuss a blue streak.

"My pilot said we should be landing at the Devil's Fork airfield in five minutes."

Rubbing the tension at the base of his neck, Hunter sighed heavily. "I'll be there in a few minutes to pick you up."

"There's no need." He could envision her waving her bejeweled hand dismissively. "I had a limousine service send a car down from Odessa to drive me to the Life Medevac hangar."

"Then I guess I'll see you shortly," he said, resigned to his fate of spending the afternoon with his indomitable grandmother.

Fifteen minutes later, when he met the limousine in the Life Medevac parking lot, Hunter wasn't surprised to see Luther Freemont, Emerald's trusted personal assistant, standing ramrod-straight beside the open back door of a sleek black limousine. "Hey there, Luther. How's it going?"

"Very well, sir," the man answered, as formal as

ever. Once he helped Emerald from the backseat of the limo, he gave Hunter a short nod. "It was nice seeing you again, sir."

When his grandmother slipped her hand in the crook of Hunter's arm and started walking toward the office entrance, he noticed that her assistant got back into the limo. "Do you think old Luther will be all right out here on his own? After all, this place is to hell and gone from a corporate office."

"Poor Luther, he's a proper gentleman and very set in his ways." Emerald laughed. "He doesn't quite know what to make of you and your brothers."

"The feeling's mutual."

"And he's not at all sure what to think of southwest Texas."

Hunter opened the door and waited for her to precede him into the building. "Is Luther always such a tight...uptight?"

As she laughed, her silver-gray eyes twinkled merrily. "Yes, he's always very formal."

"I'll bet he was just a barrel of laughs when he was a kid," Hunter said as he escorted Emerald into the dispatch room.

He introduced her to the on-duty Evac III team as they passed through on the way to his private office, but purposely avoided calling her his grandmother. He still wasn't entirely comfortable thinking of her as a family member, nor did he need the added pressure that went along with others knowing he was her grandson.

"Where's Mary Lou?" she asked, seating herself in the chair in front of his desk.

"When she found out you were dropping by, she decided to run into town to pick up something for refreshments. She'll be back soon."

"Good. I haven't seen her in quite some time and I'm looking forward to catching up."

As they stared at each other across the desk, Hunter couldn't help but think how out of place Emerald Larson looked. She was professional elegance from the top of her perfectly styled silver hair to the soles of her Italian pumps. His office furnishings were light-years away from the opulence she surrounded herself with at Emerald Inc. headquarters.

"A few months ago, when you learned I'm your grandmother and I told you about your father, you weren't as vocal about your feelings as your brothers, Caleb and Nick."

She gave him a look that he had no doubt intimidated the hell out of anyone facing her in a corporate boardroom. But he wasn't one of her loyal lackeys and she was on his turf now.

"I'm here to clear the air once and for all," she said bluntly.

"Do we have to?" he asked before he could stop

himself. He knew for certain she wouldn't want to hear what he thought of her interference in his life.

"Yes." There was a steely determination in her voice, and whether he liked it or not, he knew come hell or high water she was going to have her say. "I'm sure you'd like to know why I insisted that your mother keep her silence about your father's identity until I was ready to tell you myself."

He glared at the woman who until three months ago he'd known only by reading about her in newspapers and national magazines. He hated dancing to her tune. But as his mother had pointed out before he'd left Miami, if he hadn't taken Emerald up on her offer of giving him one of her companies to run, the sacrifices she'd made to ensure his birthright would have been in vain. Keeping his father's identity a secret from her close-knit Irish family had caused a breach that had never been reconciled.

Hunter clenched his back teeth together so tightly his jaw ached. "I'm still having a problem with that. What gave you the right to coerce my mother into signing a paper stating that she wouldn't tell anyone— not even me—who my father was?"

"I know you're bitter about the way I handled everything," Emerald said patiently. "I'd probably feel the same way. But believe me, it was the best for all concerned parties."

Anger, swift and hot, burned at his gut. "For who? You or your son?"

"I never once considered the effect it would have on me or Owen." She shrugged. "My only concern was you and your mother."

"What you did to my mother, as well as to Caleb's and Nick's mothers, amounts to blackmail." He hadn't meant to sound so harsh, but the truth wasn't always pretty.

To his surprise, Emerald didn't seem the least bit offended by his accusation. "You see it as blackmail. I saw it as protecting my grandsons and their mothers from the hazards of dealing with the paparazzi and a corruptive lifestyle." She sighed. "I was determined to see that you and your brothers didn't turn out to be anything like your father. Owen might be alive today if I had given him more of my time and attention instead of everything he thought he wanted."

Hunter took a deep breath in an attempt to bring his temper under control. "Did he even know that he'd gotten three women pregnant?"

For the first time since meeting the mighty Emerald Larson and learning that she was his grandmother, Hunter watched her lower her head as if she might be ashamed of her philandering offspring. He could almost feel sorry for her. Almost.

"Yes, Owen knew he had three sons. But, as usual, he relied on me to bail him out of taking responsibility for his actions." When she raised her eyes to look at him there was unapologetic defiance in their gray depths. "I'll admit that I've made a lot of mistakes and have more than my share of regrets, but whether or not you approve of my methods to insure you boys were nothing like him, you can't deny that it worked. And I didn't exactly coerce your mother into signing the agreement to remain silent about your father. I just made it clear that should word get out that I'm your grandmother, I would have to deny it in order to protect you from the media frenzy it would create."

Hunter could see her reasoning, but that didn't change the fact that she'd waited thirty-two years before she'd clued him in on who had fathered him or that all that time she'd had private investigators reporting his and his brothers' every move. "Why did you wait so long to tell us?"

"I wanted all three of you to gain some life experiences of your own instead of having to live down your father's reputation of being an international playboy," she said pragmatically. "That would have been a huge burden for all of you. Not to mention how it would have affected you to learn that you had a multimillion-dollar trust fund and would eventually inherit a sizable part of my business holdings."

As Hunter mulled over what she'd said, he couldn't help but agree with her. Handling the knowledge that he'd become an overnight millionaire and owner of his own business was hard enough to grasp at the age of thirty-two. He couldn't imagine the effect it would have had on him at a much earlier age.

But before he could comment, Emerald added, "And before you ask, it was extremely hard for me to read about your accomplishments in a private investigator's report while you were growing up and not be there to see them for myself." She leaned forward as if to emphasize her point. "What I did and the way I went about it I did out of love. Believe me, nothing would have pleased me more than to have had a traditional grandmother's relationship with you and your brothers. But I had to give that up in order to protect you."

Thinking it over, Hunter realized that as difficult as it had been for him growing up not knowing who his father was, it had to have been much harder for Emerald. She'd known all about him and his brothers but hadn't been able to let any of them know how she felt.

"I guess all we can do now is move forward," he said, thinking aloud.

"I believe that would be wise," Emerald agreed. "Taking over the Life Medevac Helicopter Service is a good start for you, and I expect you to do quite well." She surprised him when she rose from the chair and rounded the desk to kiss his cheek. "It's time to get back to what you do best—flying helicopters and helping those in need—and leave the past behind,

Hunter. It's history and can't be changed. But the future is an unwritten page and sometimes found where you least expect it."

Four

"If you don't stop letting Hunter O'Banyon kiss you, you're going to be as big as a barn," Callie muttered, poking another snickerdoodle into her mouth as she measured the ingredients for a double batch of chocolate-chocolate-chip cookies.

The minute she'd arrived back home from her meeting with Hunter, she'd walked straight into the kitchen, put on her apron and started baking. Five dozen snickerdoodles, a double batch of sugar cookies and a pan of brownies later, she still hadn't been able to forget how his lips had felt on hers. Warm, firm and deliciously male, his mouth could very easily be classified as a lethal weapon. At least for her.

Spooning chocolate dough onto cookie sheets, she wondered what there was about Hunter that caused her to abandon every ounce of common sense she possessed. All he had to do was touch her and she clung to him like a piece of plastic shrink-wrap on a hot plate.

She slid the pan of cookie dough into the oven and set the timer. Then, sitting down at the table while she waited on the cookies to bake, Callie stared off into space.

It wasn't uncommon for a woman in her second trimester to find herself feeling more sensual than ever before, but she didn't think her pregnancy hormones could account for the compelling attraction she experienced with Hunter. With just a look he could make her heart flutter. And when he touched her, she practically melted into a puddle at his feet. She hadn't had that kind of reaction to Craig, and he was her baby's father.

Lost in thought, it took her a moment to realize someone was knocking on her door. Hurrying to remove the pan of cookies from the oven, when she walked into the living room and opened the door, she found Hunter squatted down beside the steps. He had replaced the loose board with a new one and was pounding nails into the wood with no more than a couple of whacks with a hammer. She swallowed hard when she noticed how his bicep and the muscles in his forearm flexed with each blow.

"That should last a while," he said, straightening to his full height. "And it'll be a lot safer for you."

When she finally found her voice, she nodded. "Thank you."

He wiped the sweat from his forehead on the sleeve of his T-shirt. "Is there anything else that needs fixing or that you'd like me to take a look at while I'm here?"

"I can't think of anything." She motioned toward the door. "Would you like to come in to cool off and have a glass of iced tea?"

Smiling, he nodded. "That sounds like a winner." He put the hammer and a small sack of nails in the back of his truck, then climbed the steps to Callie's cottage. "It's not as humid here in southwest Texas as it is in Florida, but it's still hotter than hell."

Callie laughed as they walked inside the house. "It's late August. What do you expect?"

"Good point," he said, grinning.

When they walked into the kitchen, she poured them each a glass of iced tea. "Having lived close to the Gulf all my life, I'm not used to all this dry heat."

"Thank God for air-conditioning."

"Amen to that." She smiled as she placed her hand on her rounded stomach. "I've been hotter this summer than I've ever been in my life."

"It's no wonder you're hot, with the oven on all the time." Chuckling, he looked at the plates of cookies and brownies sitting on the counter. "I see you've been at it again."

She smiled wanly. There was no way she was going to tell him that just the thought of him kissing her could send her into a baking frenzy.

He reached for a brownie. "What are you going to do with all this stuff?"

Thinking quickly, she shrugged. "Schools are always having bake sales. I thought I'd donate some of the things I've baked for their fund-raisers. And after the baby is born, I doubt that I'll have a lot of time, so I've frozen a lot of what I've made."

"Good idea." He grinned. "I'm sure Corey will appreciate that."

"I'm sure he will. He eats constantly but never seems to fill up." She frowned. "Do all boys eat like they have a bottomless pit for a stomach?"

"Pretty much." Hunter reached for one of the chocolate-chocolate-chip cookies on the baking sheet she'd removed from the oven earlier. "My mom said that once I hit puberty, I ate everything in sight."

"I guess that's something I have to look forward to." Callie smiled at the fluttering in her stomach. It was as if the baby knew she was talking about him.

"You're having a boy?"

She nodded. "That's what the sonogram indicates."

"When are you due?"

"Around the first of the year." She turned to spoon cookie dough onto a baking sheet. "Of course, that doesn't mean he won't decide to come a couple of weeks early or late."

"That would be anywhere from a week or so before Christmas to mid-January."

She wondered why Hunter was taking such an interest in when she'd give birth, until it occurred to her that he would need to find someone to cover her shifts at Life Medevac. "I'm planning on taking maternity leave at Thanksgiving and being back to work no later than mid-February. Mary Lou suggested that I bring the baby to work with me and she could watch him when I go out on a call. Is that all right with you?"

He nodded. "But are you sure it's a good idea to wait that long to take your leave?" He frowned. "I don't mean to offend you, but won't it be difficult climbing in and out of the helicopter when you're that...far along?"

"No offense taken. I know I'll be quite large." She slipped the pan of cookies into the oven, then turned to face him. "If I see that it's a problem, I'll...take my leave earlier than...I'd planned."

He took a step toward her. "Are you all right?"

Laughing, she nodded. "It's just the baby moving. He seems to be particularly active today."

"Does it hurt?" He looked and sounded genuinely concerned.

"No. If anything, it tickles." She lovingly placed her hand on her stomach. "At this stage of pregnancy it's like having a butterfly flapping its wings inside of me. Later on, I'm told it will feel like I have a prizefighter in there."

"I'll bet that does feel weird." When the timer on the oven went off, he reached for a hot pad. "Why don't you sit down and put your feet up?"

"I'm fine."

Hunter pointed to one of the kitchen chairs. "Sit."

He could tell she wasn't happy about it, but while she sat down and propped her feet up in one of the other chairs, he removed the cookies from the oven. "Damn! That's hot!" he cursed when the back of his hand touched the top of the oven.

She was at his side in a flash. "Let me see."

Reluctantly letting her examine his hand, he tried to ignore how nice her soft palms felt holding his calloused one. "It's nothing."

"It's already starting to form a blister," she said, reaching for a bottle of some kind of clear lotion.

"What's that?"

"Aloe vera. It will stop it from hurting and help it heal faster." She flipped the top of the bottle open, then glanced up at him and grinned. "And don't worry, it won't make you smell like a flower."

As he watched her gently spread the clear gel on the small burn, a warmth began to fill his chest. It had been a long time since he'd had a woman fussing over him. And whether it was wise or not, he liked the feeling more than he cared to admit.

"That should take care of it," she said, closing the bottle.

Amazed at how much better it felt, he flexed his hand. "That stuff really works. Thanks."

"Not…a problem."

She sounded slightly winded, and he figured their close proximity had the same effect on her that it had on him. He was having the devil of a time trying to keep from taking her in his arms and kissing her senseless.

"I think I'd better be going."

"How much do I owe you for fixing the step?" she asked, reaching for her purse on the table.

"I ate enough cookies and brownies to more than pay for the job."

He edged toward the door. If he didn't get out of there soon, he was going to take her in his arms—and that could spell disaster to his good intentions. And he'd have succeeded, too, if she hadn't touched him.

"Hunter, stop being so darned stubborn."

Her small hand resting on his forearm sent a wave of heat streaking throughout his entire body. Without a single thought to the consequences or that he'd promised himself he'd be able to keep his hands to himself, he pulled her into his arms.

"Darlin', friends help each other all the time." He

kissed her forehead. "And they don't ask for anything in return."

She stared at him for several long seconds before she shook her head. "I'm not sure that you and I could ever be just friends. And right now I'm not looking for anything more."

"That makes two of us, Callie." He brushed her perfect lips with his. "But I think as long as we keep that in mind, we'll be just fine." He kissed her soundly, then forced himself to set her away from him and walk to the door. Turning back, he smiled. "I'll see you at work tomorrow evening, *friend.*"

"Where's Corey?" Callie asked when she arrived at work the next evening. "I didn't see his truck in the parking lot."

"He called to say he'd be a few minutes late," Mary Lou answered as she opened the container of brownies Callie had placed on the table by the coffeepot. Removing a double-fudge-and-nut chocolate square, she took a bite and shrugged. "I told him that if we get a call before he reports for his shift, I'd give him a talkin' to he won't soon forget."

Callie frowned. "It's not like Corey to be late. Did he say what's up?"

"He said he and his girlfriend were on their way back from talking to her parents up in Odessa. He should be here in about a half hour or so." Mary Lou lowered her voice and leaned forward. "Can you keep a secret?"

"Of course."

The older woman grinned. "Corey is going to be a daddy in about seven months."

"You're kidding." Callie laughed. "He's not much more than a boy himself."

Mary Lou grinned. "I've always said he's twenty-two going on ten."

"What's up?" Hunter asked, walking into the dispatch room.

Callie's heart came to a skittering halt, then took off double time. If she'd thought he looked good in jeans and a T-shirt, it was nothing compared to the way he looked in his flight suit. The one-piece coverall emphasized the impossible width of his muscular shoulders and narrowness of his trim waist.

"Just some girl talk," Mary Lou said, winking at Callie.

"Which one of us guys are you dissecting?" Hunter asked, grinning.

His comment had been for both she and Mary Lou, but when his gaze caught Callie's, she felt warm all the way to her toes. If he wanted to, she had a feeling Hunter O'Banyon could charm a little old lady right out of her garters with that smile of his.

And he thought they could be *just* friends? She

almost laughed. The way he was looking at her, there was a better chance of elephants roosting in trees.

"Don't worry, big guy." Mary Lou cackled. "We weren't taking you to task for anything. This time."

He arched one dark eyebrow. "This time?"

"We were discussing when Corey would show up," Callie added.

Hunter's skeptical expression turned to one of understanding. "Corey had some important personal business to take care of up in Odessa. He'll be here as soon as he can."

"You know what's going on, don't you?" Callie guessed.

"He came by yesterday evening to ask me and Mike what we thought he should do about the situation," Hunter said, nodding.

"That little skunk told me I was the only one he'd talked to about it," Mary Lou said, obviously put out that the confidence wasn't as big a secret as she'd thought. "Just wait until I—" Mary Lou stopped abruptly when the emergency phone rang.

Callie listened as Mary Lou asked several questions in Spanish. Great. Corey wasn't back yet and on the Evac II team he'd been the only one fluent in Spanish.

"Come on, Callie. We don't have time to wait for Corey," Hunter said, heading for the door. "As it is, we're going to have to race the stork to the hospital."

"Is it Juanita Rodriguez again?" Callie asked,

thankful that Hunter had obviously understood Mary Lou's end of the conversation and would be able to interpret for her.

He nodded as they climbed into the helicopter and put on the headsets that would enable them to communicate over the engine noise. "She's definitely in labor this time. From Mary Lou's questions, I could tell that Juanita's water broke and she's home alone."

"Where's her husband Miguel?"

"He's in El Paso at a National Guard meeting this weekend. We can radio his armory and have him meet us at the hospital."

While Hunter started the engine, Callie strapped herself into one of the jump seats in the back and listened to Mary Lou's voice give the coordinates for the Rodriguez ranch to Hunter. They had about a fifteen-minute flight to reach their destination, then another thirty minutes on to El Paso. Mary Lou was going to stay on the phone with Juanita until they got there, and hopefully Baby Rodriguez would wait to make his or her grand entrance into the world until after they made it to the hospital.

When they lifted off, Callie began to mentally run through emergency birthing procedure on the outside chance that she would have to deliver Juanita's baby, and it took a moment for her to realize Hunter had spoken to her. "I'm sorry. What did you say?"

"I asked if you've delivered a baby before." His

deep baritone coming through the headset was oddly intimate and sent a shiver straight up her spine.

She gave herself a mental shake. Hearing Hunter's voice through the headset was no different than when she'd communicated with George or Corey on a flight.

"I've delivered a few babies—one of them in the back of a taxicab when the E.R. doctors were busy treating victims from a bus accident."

"But you don't speak or understand Spanish?"

She sighed. "No."

They fell silent, and in what seemed record time, Hunter was setting the helicopter down in a field next to the Rodriguez ranch house.

Removing her headset and unfastening her seat belt, Callie grabbed one of the medical cases containing sterile dressings, latex gloves and other medical supplies and hurriedly slid the side door back. She bent slightly to avoid the rotor blades, then, once she was clear of the helicopter, she jogged the short distance to the house. Fortunately the front door was unlocked, and she walked inside without so much as a second thought.

"¡Por favor ayúdeme!"

Callie followed the frantic cries and found Juanita in one of the bedrooms. Drenched in sweat, the young woman was practically hysterical and instead of working with the contractions she seemed to be fighting them.

"¡El bebé está listo!" Juanita repeated, clutching at Callie's hands.

"What's she saying about the baby?" Callie asked Hunter when he appeared in the narrow doorway.

"She said the baby is ready."

"Tell her that I need to check to see how close she is to having the baby," Callie said, slipping on a pair of sterile latex gloves.

While Hunter assured Juanita that everything was going to be all right, Callie checked to see how many centimeters the woman had dilated. "The stork is going to win this one," she said, reaching into the medical case for clamps, a sterile drape and antiseptic. "The baby's head is crowning."

As she arranged the medical supplies she would need for the birth of Juanita's baby, Callie listened to Hunter reassure the woman. She had no idea what he was telling her, but it seemed to calm Juanita as well as send warmth throughout Callie's body. She'd always thought Spanish was a beautiful language and she didn't think she'd ever heard a more sexy sound than Hunter's deep voice flawlessly pronouncing the words.

"Do you have any kind of experience being a breathing coach?" Callie asked as she prepped Juanita for the delivery.

He shook his head. "No. We covered it briefly in EMT training, but that's it."

"You'll do fine." Using the two-way radio clipped to the epaulet on the shoulder of her jumpsuit, she advised the hospital in El Paso of the situation, then turned her full attention on the task at hand. "Tell Juanita to breathe, then show her how. She's tensing up instead of relaxing her pelvic floor and allowing the baby to pass through the birth canal."

"*Respira,* Juanita. *Respira.*"

When Hunter showed the young woman what he meant, she trustingly stared into his eyes and began to concentrate on doing as he requested. Once she stopped fighting the pain, she rapidly progressed to the pushing phase of the delivery. Moving into position to lift her shoulders when it came time to push, he continued to reassure her that everything was going to be all right.

"*Todo será bien,* Juanita."

"Tell her to stop the shallow breathing and start pushing," Callie said, showing the woman how to position her hands on her knees for leverage.

Encouraging Juanita to push with all her might, he supported her shoulders, and after only a couple of tries, the baby's dark head emerged from the young woman's lower body. Hunter watched Callie quickly and efficiently suction the infant's nose and mouth before it was time for Juanita to push the rest of her baby out into the world.

With one more mighty push from Juanita, the baby slid out into Callie's waiting hands. Without being prompted, the baby girl opened her mouth and wailed at the top of her tiny lungs.

"*Mí bebé,*" Juanita murmured tearfully.

"You have a beautiful daughter, Juanita," Callie said, placing the baby on her mother's stomach.

Awed by the miracle he'd just witnessed, the moment was so bittersweet Hunter couldn't have pushed words past the lump clogging his throat if his life depended on it. Although he was happy for the Rodriguez family and their new addition, he'd never know what it was like to watch his own son or daughter come into the world. After losing Ellen and their unborn child, he never intended to put himself in the position of loving someone and taking the risk of losing them. He'd been down that road before and had barely survived. There was no way in hell he could go through that again.

"Hunter, could you please hold the baby while I get Juanita ready for transport?" Callie asked, breaking into his disturbing thoughts.

The last thing he wanted to do was hold a baby. He knew for certain it would only compound his sense of loss and regret that he'd never hold his own child. But before he could protest, Callie placed the baby in his arms. As he stared down at the red-faced little girl wrapped in a soft white blanket, instead of the sorrow he expected, Hunter couldn't help but marvel at how small she was, how perfect.

Gently touching her little hand, he was thoroughly amazed when the baby curled her perfectly formed tiny fingers around one of his. "She's holding on to me."

"Babies do that," Callie said, smiling.

He watched Callie and Juanita exchange an indulgent glance. Apparently there was no language barrier when it came to women's opinions of men. It must be universally accepted that men didn't have a clue about these things. But that was okay with him. Men didn't understand women, so he supposed that made the genders pretty equal.

While Callie radioed the hospital to report a successful, complication-free birth, Hunter contemplated how they were going to get Juanita into the helicopter without Corey. He wasn't about to let Callie lift anything heavier than her nurse's bag or the baby, and the door and hallway were too narrow to get the stretcher into the bedroom. That left only one alternative.

"Are we ready for transport?" When Callie nodded, he handed her the baby. "You take your nurse's bag and the baby while I carry Juanita to the chopper."

"That would probably be best," Callie said, lifting the nylon bag's webbed strap to her shoulder. "You'd probably have to carry her to the front door before you could put her on the stretcher anyway."

Telling Juanita what was taking place, Hunter scooped her slight body into his arms and carried her out to the helicopter. Once he placed her on the stretcher and Callie handed her the baby, Juanita and her new daughter both drifted off into a peaceful sleep.

The flight to El Paso was uneventful, and once they

had Juanita and her new daughter safely checked in to the hospital, Callie and Hunter boarded the helicopter and headed back to the Life Medevac base.

"You did a wonderful job of calming Juanita down," Callie said as she stared through the windshield at the vast blue sky ahead of them. Riding in the front seat next to Hunter on the trip back to Devil's Fork, she enjoyed the view of the rugged Texas mountains that she missed when riding in the back with a patient.

"It didn't show that I had no idea what I was doing?" he asked, grinning sheepishly.

Smiling, she shook her head. "Not at all. Juanita is young and had no idea what to expect when her contractions started. Factor in that she was home alone and miles away from help and it was no wonder she was frightened half out of her mind. You were able to put her at ease and that made it a lot easier for her."

He shrugged. "I just did what I thought would help." They were both silent for some time before he asked, "Who's going to be with you when you have your baby?"

It was the last thing she'd expected him to ask. "Are you volunteering for the job?"

"Hell no."

She laughed at his horrified expression. "But you're a great labor coach."

He grunted. "Only because Corey wasn't there to take over for me. I'm the pilot, remember?"

"You're also a certified EMT."

"Only because my grandmother strongly suggested that it would be a good idea since I was taking over an air-ambulance service." He shrugged. "Besides, whether or not you and the father of your baby are together, I'm sure he'll want to be there when his son is born. He can be your breathing coach."

A cold chill ran the length of her spine at the thought of Craig Culbertson being anywhere near her or her child. "I can assure you, he won't be anywhere around when I give birth."

"Maybe he'll change his mind."

"It's not an issue."

Hunter was quiet for a moment, then turned his head to give her a questioning look. "He doesn't even know he's fathered a child, does he?" His mouth flattening into a disapproving line, he shook his head. "Forget that I asked. It's none of my business."

She hadn't discussed with anyone—not even her mother—why she'd made the decision not to tell Craig about the baby. But she needed to make Hunter understand, without divulging too many details, why she felt she had no choice but to keep her silence.

"Believe me, it's for the best." Placing her hand protectively over her son, she shook her head. "Even if I told him about the baby, he wouldn't care."

"Don't you think you owe him the chance to prove you wrong?"

"No. He's too selfish and self-centered to care about anyone or anything but himself."

Hunter stared straight ahead and she could tell he was thinking over what she'd said. "There must have been some substance to the man or you wouldn't have become involved with him," he finally said.

Callie sighed heavily. "In the past several months I've spent countless hours wondering why I allowed myself to be fooled by his insincerity."

She could feel Hunter's intense gaze as surely as if he'd reached out and touched her. "And?"

"I came to the conclusion that he was the consummate charmer who was more interested in the chase than in a meaningful relationship."

"I know the type," Hunter said disgustedly. "Let me guess—he asked you out several times and you turned him down. That's when he pulled out all the stops and did everything in his power to convince you that he was wild about you."

"That's exactly what happened. I became a challenge that he was determined to conquer." She took a deep breath. "And like a fool, I allowed him to wear down my resistance and charm me into believing that we could have a future together."

When Hunter took her hand in his to give it a gentle squeeze, a warmth like nothing she'd ever known filled her all the way to her soul. "Don't be so hard on yourself, darlin'. It's not the first time a woman has been taken in by a player. And it's sad to say, but it won't be the last."

She knew he was right, but that didn't make her feel any less foolish for allowing it to happen, especially since she was now facing motherhood alone. "Then you understand my reasoning for keeping my pregnancy a secret?"

"Not entirely." He released her hand, then, remaining silent for several long seconds, he finally added, "Don't you think you should at least give him the opportunity to redeem himself? I know if I was in his shoes, I'd definitely be angry if I discovered a woman had denied me the right to know my own son."

Callie knew for certain she couldn't take the chance of telling Craig. But she wasn't ready to outline her reasons to Hunter. "He'd only view the baby as an inconvenience, and my child deserves better than that."

"Do you ever intend to tell your son who his father is?"

"He'll be better off not knowing."

"Every kid has a right to know who they are and where they came from," he said forcefully. His tone left no doubt that he felt very passionately about the subject. "He'll grow up wondering if every man he passes on the street is the one responsible for his existence."

"Why do you feel so strongly about this?"

She watched him take a deep breath, then slowly release it. Just when she thought he was going to tell her it was none of her concern, he spoke. "I grew up not knowing anything about my father, and it wasn't until just recently that I even learned who he was—after he'd been dead for six months."

"Oh, Hunter, I'm so sorry." She began to understand why he felt it was so important that she inform Craig about the baby. "Your mother didn't tell him about you?"

"He knew." There was an edge to his voice. "He just chose to ignore the fact that he'd fathered three sons with three different women." Hunter gave her a meaningful glance. "But the point is, they gave him the opportunity to know about us. He was the one who made the decision to stay out of our lives."

"But she didn't tell *you*," Callie guessed.

He shook his head. "She had her reasons and she knew that one day I would learn who he was. But that didn't make it any easier on me when I was growing up or stop me from resenting the fact that I wasn't given the choice to know anything about the man."

She could understand why Hunter felt the way he did, but her circumstances were different. If she told Craig about the baby, there was a good chance that he and his parents would try to separate her and her son the way they'd done that poor girl and her baby twelve years ago. And that was a chance Callie wasn't willing to take.

"I will tell my son about his father when I feel he's ready," she said carefully. "But until that time we'll be just fine on our own."

Five

For the next few days Hunter couldn't stop thinking about the conversation he'd had with Callie on the way back from El Paso. There'd been something in her voice that had alerted him to the fact there was more to her refusal to tell her baby's father about the pregnancy than she was letting on. He couldn't quite put his finger on what that something was, but it was serious enough that she felt silence was her only option.

Hunter's heart stalled. Could the man have been abusive?

Fury stronger than he could have ever imagined coursed through his veins. He wasn't a violent man by nature, but just the thought that the jerk might have mistreated Callie in any way was enough to make Hunter ready to tear him limb from limb.

Suddenly needing to move before he put his fist through the wall, Hunter grabbed his sunglasses and, taking his ball cap from a hook beside his office door, jammed it onto his head. He felt as if he had enough adrenaline coursing through him to bench-press a 747 fully loaded with passengers and cargo. What he needed was some good, hard physical labor to help him work off his anger. And he knew exactly what he was going to do.

As he drove to the lumber yard, he mentally reviewed all the things in need of repair or replacement at Callie's place. Besides the steps he'd fixed a few days ago, he'd noticed the place could use a coat of paint and a new deck at the back door to replace a badly deteriorating concrete stoop.

Purchasing everything he needed to make the improvements, Hunter scheduled a delivery for the lumber to build a new deck, then loaded his truck with a new extension ladder, several buckets of paint, brushes and scrapers. Satisfied that he had everything he needed, he headed toward Callie's house at the edge of town.

He'd thought about talking to her before he started buying supplies and making plans, but if her protest over the simple repair he'd made to the step was any indication, she would have refused his offer. And whether she liked it or not, he wasn't taking no for an answer. In the case of the back stoop, it was a matter of safety.

When he parked the truck and positioned the ladder against the side of the house, he wasn't surprised when she came out to glare at him. "Why on earth are you making so much noise and what are you doing to my house?"

With her shoulder-length blond hair in delightful disarray, her eyes soft with sleep and her feet bare, she looked as if she'd just crawled out of bed. She also looked sexy as hell.

"Good morning to you, too." He grinned as he grabbed one of the scrapers. "Did you stay up late last night making cookies?"

"As a matter of fact, I did."

"What kind?"

She shook her head. "Don't change the subject. What are you doing here at the god-awful hour of seven-thirty in the morning? And why is that ladder propped against the side of my house?"

"One thing at a time, darlin'," he said, climbing the ladder. "Contrary to popular belief, seven-thirty isn't all that early. Did you know the lumber yard and hardware store here in Devil's Fork open every morning at six?"

Glaring at him, she propped her fists on her shapely hips. "Since I've never had occasion to go into either establishment, no, I didn't know that."

He scraped off a long strip of peeling paint close to

the peak of the roof. "The other day I noticed that the paint on this place had started to crack and peel."

"So you just decided to take it upon yourself to paint my house?" Clearly fit to be tied, she looked mighty damned cute standing there in an oversize pink T-shirt and a pair of mint-green camp shorts, tapping her bare foot against the hard-packed dirt.

"You can't do it," he said as he continued to remove strips of weathered paint from the board siding. "And it needs to be done before winter sets in."

"It could wait until after I have the baby."

He shook his head. "You'll be too busy once the baby gets here. Besides, I might as well do something constructive on my days off."

"But I can't afford this right now."

"You don't have to pay for it."

"Yes, I do."

"I've already taken care of it."

She made a noise that sounded suspiciously like a growl. "Tell me how much you've spent and I'll pay you back."

He grinned. "Nope."

"Are you always this—" she stopped as if searching for the right word "—this meddlesome?"

He stopped scraping to stare down at her. "Are you always this stubborn when someone is trying to help you?"

Rubbing her temples with her fingertips, she shook

her head. "I do appreciate you trying to help. But I can't afford all the improvements right now and I can't let you pay for them."

"Consider it a housewarming gift," he said, sending more flakes of paint falling to the ground.

"That's absurd." She frowned. "You're newer in town than I am."

He chuckled. "Minor technicality."

"I can't let you do this."

"You can't stop me." He climbed down the ladder, then, placing the scraper on the tailgate of the truck, walked over to stand in front of her. "Look, there are things around here that need attention and you're not able to do them in your condition."

She rolled her eyes. "I've told you before, I'm pregnant, not disabled."

"Whatever. You can't do them and I need something to keep me busy on my days off."

He could tell he was wearing down her resistance when she sighed heavily. "Yes, but it isn't fair for you to pay for the materials to make improvements to my house."

Unable to resist taking her into his arms, he smiled as he pulled her to him, then pushed the brim of his ball cap up out of the way. "If it bothers you that much, why don't we strike a deal?"

She looked suspicious. "What kind of agreement are you talking about?"

"I'll do some work around your house and you can make me a few home-cooked meals." He used his index finger to raise her chin until their gazes met. "Does that sound fair?"

"Not really. I still think that I'm getting the better end of this deal."

Her soft body pressed to his was playing hell with his good intentions, and before he could stop himself, he lowered his mouth to hers. "Throw in a couple dozen brownies—" he brushed her perfect lips with his "—some chocolate-chip-oatmeal cookies—" she parted for him on a soft sigh "—and we'll call it even," he finished as he deepened the kiss.

The combination of Callie's sweet taste and the fact that she was kissing him back sent blood surging through his veins and had his lower body tightening with a need that threatened to buckle his knees. Never in all his thirty-two years had he been aroused as fast or as completely as he was at that very moment.

But when she raised her arms to his neck and tangled her fingers in the hair at his nape, her feather-light touch caused a jolt of hunger to fill every fiber of his being and the need to touch her became overwhelming. Sliding his hand beneath the tail of her T-shirt, when his calloused palm met the satiny skin along her side, his heart thumped hard against his ribs. They'd been so embroiled in their argument over him doing repairs to her house that he hadn't paid attention to the fact that she wasn't wearing a bra.

When he cupped her full breast, then gently slid the pad of his thumb over her tight nipple, her moan of pleasure mingled with his groan of frustration. What the hell did he think he was doing?

Not only was he making out with his flight nurse for God and everybody to see, she was pregnant with another man's child. He wasn't looking for a lasting relationship with any woman. And Callie wasn't a woman who engaged in meaningless flings.

Reluctantly removing his hand from beneath her shirt, he broke the kiss to stare into her wide violet eyes. "Darlin', I think you'd better go back in the house and I'm going to get back to work."

Her porcelain cheeks colored a deep rose and she backed away from him. "I'll be…gone for…a little while," she said, sounding out of breath. "I need to go…to the grocery store."

He frowned. "What for? Your cabinets and freezer are full of food."

She took several steps backward. "I have to see if the store carries fifty-pound bags of flour."

Repositioning his ball cap, Hunter watched her turn and hurry around the side of the house toward the front porch. He'd never seen a woman bake as much as Callie. Maybe it was some kind of hormonal nesting thing.

He shook his head as he grabbed the scraper from the back of the truck and climbed the ladder. Whatever it was, as long as she was inside the house baking and he was outside painting, there wouldn't be any more encounters like the one they'd just shared. And if he repeated it enough times, he just might start to believe it.

When she heard someone knocking on the front door, Callie glanced at the clock on the stove. Hunter couldn't possibly have driven out to the Life Medevac hangar, showered and changed clothes, then driven all the way back to her place in such a short time.

After he'd finished the arduous task of scraping away the peeling paint, he'd told her he was going to go back to the hangar and clean up while she finished dinner. Although she couldn't imagine what it would be, he must have forgotten something.

Wiping her hands on a towel, she checked the pot roast she'd put in the oven earlier, then hurried to open the door. "I'm afraid dinner isn't quite…" Her voice trailed off as icy fear froze her vocal cords and filled every cell in her being.

"Hello, Callie." Craig Culbertson flashed his practiced smile as he brushed past her. "Since you didn't know I was coming for a visit, I didn't expect you to make dinner for me. But I'm sure whatever you're cooking up will be delicious."

"Wh-what are you doing here?" she asked, gripping

the doorknob so hard she wouldn't be surprised if she left her fingerprints embedded in the metal.

"I've missed you." He looked around her small, tidy living room. "What were you thinking when you left Houston for this? It's not even as nice as that minuscule apartment you had."

She ignored his insult and repeated her question. "Why are you here, Craig?"

Turning to face her, his charming smile disappeared; it was replaced with an expression of utter disgust. "Good God! You're pregnant."

Drawing on every ounce of courage she'd ever possessed, she squared her shoulders and placed a protective hand on her stomach. "Yes, I am."

"It's mine, isn't it?" he asked, his tone accusing.

Knowing full well that he wouldn't believe her, she shook her head. "No. The baby belongs to—"

"Me."

Callie had never been so relieved to see anyone in her entire life as she was when Hunter walked through the open door and put his arm around her shoulders. Nor had she ever been as shocked when she heard his claim to be her baby's father.

"This is Craig Culbertson from Houston," she said, silently thanking Hunter for intervening. "Hunter O'Banyon is my—"

"Husband," Hunter interrupted, giving her a look that asked for her to trust him.

"You're married?" Craig shook his head. "You can't be. Your mother said you only moved here a couple of months ago. That's not nearly long enough to find yourself a husband and get knocked up."

"I take exception to the phrase 'knocked up' in reference to my wife's pregnancy," Hunter said, his voice hard as granite.

"Sorry." His tone was anything but apologetic, but Craig apparently decided that Hunter meant business and wasn't one to be trifled with, because he immediately began to backpedal. "It was just an expression, no offense intended."

A fresh wave of fear coursed through Callie as she thought about her last conversation with her mother and how she'd tried to get Callie to tell her who the baby's father was. Had her mother inadvertently hinted to Craig that Callie might be carrying his child?

"Why did you call my mother?" she asked, surprised that her voice was fairly steady considering the state of her nerves.

Craig gave her the smile that she used to think made him look endearingly handsome. Now it only made her feel ill.

"When I discovered your old phone number was no longer in service, I remembered your mother's name, looked up her number and called her to ask how to get in touch with you." He shrugged. "She was reluctant to tell me about your move to Texas until I told her that we'd been seeing each other before you left and how much I missed you. That's when she suggested that if I was ever in the Devil's Fork area that I should look you up. I decided to clear my calendar for the rest of the week and make the drive out here to no-man's-land to see how you're doing."

Callie did a slow burn. She wasn't as angry with her mother as she was with Craig. He'd obviously fed her mother a line about how much he cared, and her mother had fallen for it. Unfortunately Nancy Marshall had never met Craig and had no idea what a snake he was. He wasn't interested in how Callie was doing. His ego was still smarting from the fact that Callie had been the one who'd rejected him instead of the other way around.

"Actually your mother and I talked for some time and I found her to be a very nice lady," Craig added solicitously.

"Oh, really?" Callie shook her head. "It's amazing to me that you carried on a lengthy conversation with my mother when you never would take the time to meet her when you and I were seeing each other."

"You've always been close with your mother, haven't you, Callie?" Craig asked.

She gritted her teeth. "You know I have."

"That's the main reason I find it odd that she didn't know anything about your marriage." He rocked back on his heels as he pointed to Hunter. "It seems to me that she would be the first one you told about your marriage to O'Banyon."

When the timer on the stove went off, indicating that the pot roast was done, Callie reluctantly left the two men standing in her living room glaring at each other. She had no idea what was going to take place or how to deal with it. Hunter's expression from the moment he'd walked through the door had been dark and foreboding. And Craig, as was his usual fashion when he felt threatened, had become arrogant and condescending.

Removing the roast from the oven, she hurried back into the living room before punches started flying. "Craig, I'm sure you have better things to do with your time than stand here debating my marital status."

He shook his head. "Not really. But I will take you up on that offer of dinner."

"I didn't—"

Hunter pulled her to his side and pressed a quick kiss to her lips. "I'm sure we have enough for three, don't we, darlin'?"

Had Hunter lost his mind? The last thing she wanted to do was spend more time in the presence of a snake like Craig Culbertson.

"Well, yes, but—"

"Good." Hunter turned to Craig. "Why don't you have a seat while I help my wife finish getting things on the table?"

Craig gave her a triumphant smile as he plopped down on the end of the love seat. "I think I'll do that."

As soon as she and Hunter entered the kitchen, she turned on him. "What on earth were you thinking?" she demanded, careful to keep her voice low. "I want him out of this house, out of this state and out of my life. For good."

Hunter nodded. "That's the plan."

She looked at him as though he might not be the sharpest knife in the drawer. "And having him stay for dinner is the way to do that?"

"I believe so."

Taking in a deep breath, Hunter still couldn't believe that he'd claimed to be Callie's husband and the father of her baby. But when he'd walked up the porch steps and heard the disgust in Culbertson's voice and the fear in Callie's, Hunter had done the only thing he could think of that didn't involve putting his fist in the man's nose.

"Would you care to explain your reasoning?" she asked as she reached for a pair of oven mitts. "Because I'm having a really hard time understanding."

When he noticed how badly her hands trembled, he took the mitts from her and removed a roasting pan from the oven. Placing it on a hot pad, he tossed the mitts on the counter, then cupped her cheeks with his palms. "The first thing I want you to do is calm down, Callie. I give you my word that as long as I have breath left in my body, I won't let him do anything to harm you or the baby. Is that clear?"

She gazed at him for several long seconds, and the fear he saw in her eyes just about tore him apart. "Yes," she finally said, nodding.

"Good." He reached into the cabinet for a platter. Handing it to her, he explained. "It's clear that Culbertson needs some convincing that you and I are married."

"That came as a surprise to me, too," she said, slicing the roast.

He rubbed the tension building at the back of his neck. "Then it's unanimous, because I was pretty damned shocked about it myself. But it's the only thing I can think of that might make him leave you alone. And that's what you want, isn't it?"

"Absolutely." There wasn't even a heartbeat's hesitation in her voice, and Hunter had no doubt that she didn't want Craig Culbertson anywhere near her.

"The way I see it, if we can convince him how happy we are and how much we're looking forward to our first child, he'll get the message, go back to Houston and you'll never hear from him again." He carried the platter of pot roast over to the small kitchen table while Callie set another place. "Now all we have to do is get a few things straight."

"Like what?"

He removed three glasses from one of the shelves, filled them with ice, then reached for a pitcher of iced tea sitting on the kitchen island. "He'll want to know how we met, when we got married and what we're going to name the baby."

She stared at him openmouthed. "We don't have time to coordinate all that."

Thinking quickly, Hunter said, "Just tell me what you intend to name your son and when you discovered you were pregnant. I'll take care of the rest. Just follow my lead and agree with the line I feed Culbertson."

"This is never going to work," she said, plunking a bowl of mashed potatoes onto the table. "There are too many ways he can trip us up."

Hunter caught her by the shoulders and turned her to face him. "Trust me, Callie. Unless you can think of something else, this is the only way."

He watched her close her eyes, take a deep breath, then opening them, she gave him the information he requested. "You'd better be right about this, Hunter. I won't let him take my baby away from me."

"There's no way in hell, darlin'," he said, giving her a quick hug.

Hunter's heart twisted at the fear he'd heard in her soft voice. He wanted to know what had caused her to be so terrified that Culbertson would try to get custody when the man clearly had no use for children. But that would have to wait until later. Right now they had to con the man into leaving Callie alone for good.

* * *

By the time dinner was over, Callie's nerves were stretched to the breaking point. Sitting between the two men, she'd listened to them discuss everything from baseball player stats to the size of engine they preferred in their vehicles. She wasn't sure whether to be relieved or disappointed that the subject of her and Hunter's marriage had yet to come up.

But that hadn't stopped Hunter from playing his part as the devoted husband to the hilt. Throughout dinner he'd given her smiles that threatened to melt her bones and he'd found every excuse imaginable to touch her. She'd caught Craig taking it all in with great interest, but not once had he asked any of the questions she knew for certain had to be running through his mind.

"Why don't we have dessert in the living room?" Craig asked when Callie rose from her chair to slice pieces of German chocolate cake for them.

"Go ahead and have a seat in there while I help Callie clear the table," Hunter said, rising to gather their plates. "We'll join you in a few minutes."

"It's not going the way we planned," she whispered when Craig left the room.

"Be patient, darlin'." Hunter rinsed the dishes to put in the dishwasher, then measured grounds from one of the canisters for a pot of coffee. "If he doesn't get around to asking, I'll bring up the subject myself."

"I should have never let you talk me into this." She shook her head at her own foolishness. "I'm sure he can see right through this little farce."

"Don't worry. Everything is going to be just fine."

As she allowed Hunter to carry the tray she'd arranged with dessert plates, cups and saucers and a carafe of coffee into the living room, she prayed he was right. Her nerves couldn't stand much more. She already had an almost uncontrollable urge to preheat the oven and start measuring sugar and flour.

"I have a question for you two," Craig said when he placed his empty dessert plate back on the tray. "If you're married, why doesn't Callie wear a wedding band?"

Sitting beside Hunter on the love seat, she had just taken a sip of milk from the glass she'd brought with her from the kitchen and it was all she could do to keep from choking at his blunt question. Panic seized her. She'd been right. Craig knew they were only pretending. Now what were they going to do?

"She had to take her wedding ring off when her fingers started getting a little puffy," Hunter said without missing a beat. He took her left hand in his and brought it to his lips to kiss her ring finger. "Once she has the baby, it will be right back where it belongs."

A wave of tingling heat traveled up her arm, then spread throughout the rest of her body at the loving gesture. She was glad that Hunter had been able to think fast because at the moment she wasn't sure she could think at all.

"When and where did you meet?" Craig asked.

Hunter held up his hand. "See that little scar on my palm? I had to go to the emergency room in Houston when I had a run-in with a fish hook. As soon as I saw Callie, I knew she was the woman for me." Giving her a smile that made her insides feel as if they'd turned to warm pudding, he lightly kissed her cheek. "We were married a few days later and pregnant a few weeks after that."

"Why the rush?" Craig asked, sounding more than a little suspicious.

"Once I see what I want, I don't let it get away from me." Hunter put his arm around her shoulders and held her close to his side. "I'm afraid you're going to have to face facts, Culbertson. She's with me now and I'm not about to let her or our baby go."

Callie watched Craig. She knew him well enough to know that he wasn't entirely convinced. There was a huge hole in their story, and although he hadn't asked again why she'd failed to tell her mother about her marriage to Hunter, Callie knew it was on his mind. But gaining strength from the man holding her so possessively against him, she decided that if the matter came up again, she'd simply tell Craig that she didn't have to explain herself to him or anyone else.

"Well, I suppose I should be going," Craig said as

he rose to his feet. "As always, your cooking was delicious, Callie."

When Hunter stood, then helped her up from her saggy love seat, she began to believe they might have pulled off the ruse. Craig would be leaving town and, with any luck, she'd never have to see or hear from him again.

"Have an enjoyable trip back to Houston," Hunter said as they all walked to the door.

Craig shook his head. "Oh, I'm not leaving the area for several more days. While you two were finishing dinner, I checked the phone book and found a little bed-and-breakfast just up the street." His smirk made Callie want to scream with frustration. "I thought I'd stick around for a while and take in the sights." He laughed as he opened the door. "It's been my experience that you can learn a lot from talking to the locals in a town the size of Devil's Fork."

As Craig walked down the steps and out to his sleek red sports car, Callie felt like crying. How could her life have gotten so out of control in such a short time?

Turning to Hunter, she sighed heavily. "Any more bright ideas?"

He didn't look any happier about the turn of events than she was. "The way I see it, we don't have a whole lot of choice. I'm going to have to move in with you until that sorry excuse for a human being leaves town."

Six

Two hours later, after helping Callie clean up the kitchen, Hunter found himself trying to fold his six-foot-three-inch frame into a comfortable sleeping position on her lumpy love seat. Muttering a word he reserved for extreme situations, he sat up, propped his elbows on his knees and cradled his head in his hands. What the hell had he gotten himself into? And why?

If he'd kept his mouth shut, he'd be sleeping on a fairly comfortable, albeit narrow, bed at the Life Medevac hangar instead of torturing himself on the most uncomfortable piece of furniture known to man. And he for damn sure wouldn't be locked into playing house for the next week with a woman that he was already finding it all but impossible to keep his hands off.

But even as he castigated himself for getting involved, he knew he'd done the right thing. After meeting Culbertson and listening to Callie explain how he and his parents had used their money and influence to take the baby away from the first girl Craig had gotten pregnant, Hunter knew as sure as he knew his own name the Culbertsons wouldn't think twice about trying to do the same thing to Callie.

Shaking his head, Hunter couldn't believe how arrogant they were. What gave them the right to take a baby from his mother simply because Culbertson blood ran through the child's veins? What kind of people thought that it automatically made the mother unfit just because their bank account dwarfed hers?

As he sat there thinking about how ruthless and selfish they were, he realized that if Emerald Larson had wanted to, she could have taken him and his brothers away from their mothers at any time. She certainly had more money and power than the Culbertsons ever dreamed of having and she would have had very little trouble gaining custody of her grandsons.

But instead of viewing the three of them as possessions, Emerald had cared enough to content herself with watching Hunter and his brothers grow up in pictures and P.I. reports in order to ensure they turned out to be as normal and well-adjusted as possible. And for the first time since learning the details of his parentage he began to appreciate the sacrifices that had been made by Emerald on his behalf.

Any lingering traces of anger he still carried from being denied the right to know who his father was dissipated. Although Hunter would always have a problem with any man walking away from a woman when she needed him most, he came to the conclusion that Emerald and her philandering son weren't entirely responsible for the anger and confusion he'd grown up with.

It had been Marlene O'Banyon's choice to agree to Emerald's terms. And although Emerald hadn't required that his mother remain single, Hunter sometimes wondered if she'd signed the confidentiality agreement secretly hoping that one day Owen Larson would come to his senses and return to Miami for her and Hunter. But Owen had never laid eyes on any of his children, nor had he seen their mothers again. And with his death in a boating accident somewhere in the Mediterranean eight months ago, it was never going to happen.

Of course, his mother had no idea that old Owen had sown more than just one wild oat. Although she was the first woman he'd gotten pregnant, she certainly hadn't been the last. Hell, Hunter doubted that Emerald was completely certain that he, Nick and Caleb were Owen's only offspring.

But that was immaterial now. The fact of the matter was, in light of the way the Culbertsons had dealt with a similar situation, he understood and could even commend his grandmother for handling everything the way she had.

Lost in thought, it took a moment for Hunter to realize that Callie had gotten out of bed and was tip-toeing her way through the living room into the kitchen. "Can't sleep?" he asked, careful to keep his voice nonthreatening so as not to frighten her.

Her startled cry was loud enough to wake the dead. So much for trying not to frighten her.

"It's just me, Callie."

"Dear heavens, you scared me out of a year's growth," she said, clutching something to the front of her robe.

"I'm sorry." He switched on the lamp at the end of the love seat. "I didn't mean to..." He stopped to stare at her when he realized what she was carrying. "What the hell are you doing with your apron at—" he checked his watch "—midnight?"

"I'm too keyed up to sleep," she said defensively. "I thought I'd find something to do."

He frowned. "So you're going to start cooking?"

She breezed past him to enter the kitchen. "Everyone deals with stress in their own way. Some people drink. Some eat. I bake."

That explained why she'd made enough baked goods to stock a chain of grocery stores, he thought as he followed her. She'd been scared witless since learning she was pregnant that Culbertson would find out about the baby. Now that he had, it appeared that Callie would be making enough cookies to feed every man, woman and child in the whole damned state.

"Our shift starts in a little less than eighteen hours." He yawned. "Don't you think it would be a good idea to be well rested when we go to work?"

She shook her head as she reached for a set of measuring cups and the canister of flour. "Don't worry about me, I'll be fine. You're the one who needs rest to pilot the helicopter. Go back into the living room and get some sleep."

"That's easier said than done," he muttered.

"I promise I won't make much noise," she said, knocking over the cup of flour she'd just measured.

"That's not the problem." He pulled out a chair and sat down at the table. "I'm too tall."

"Excuse me?"

She looked thoroughly confused and so darned cute standing there in her nightclothes and apron, he had to force himself to remember what they were talking about. "The love seat is roughly fifty inches long and I'm six foot three. You do the math."

Her eyes widened. "Oh, dear. I'm sorry. I hadn't thought of it being too short for you." She shook her head. "But it's not a problem. You can take my bed and I'll sleep on the love seat."

"Like hell." He wasn't about to sleep on a comfortable bed while she endured that instrument of torture in her condition.

"Why not?" she asked as she cleaned up the flour she'd spilled. "I'm at least ten inches shorter and shouldn't have nearly as much trouble getting comfortable."

"You're pregnant."

"And you're bossy." She grinned. "But I'm trying not to hold that against you."

Her pretty smile sent a wave of heat straight through him, and he could think of several things he'd like for her to hold against him—every one of them soft, warm and deliciously feminine. He swallowed hard. Thinking along those lines could only accomplish one of two things. It would either get him in a whole lot deeper than he was comfortable with or drive him completely insane. And he wasn't altogether sure that he hadn't already crossed the line in both areas.

"I can sleep in one of the chairs and—"

"Wake up with a terribly stiff neck," she interrupted, dropping an egg on the counter. "Darn." Grabbing a paper towel, she cleaned up the mess. "If I'm going to be flying with you, I not only want you well rested, I'd like for you to have your full range of motion."

"I can manage in the chair." He stood up and started toward the living room, but her soft hand on his back stopped him dead in his tracks and sent a jolt of electric current throughout his system.

"I think we're overlooking the obvious here," she said, turning to measure more flour into a bowl. "I'll probably be up for hours before I'm relaxed enough to go to sleep. There's no reason for you to be uncomfortable when there's an empty bed that you could be sleeping in. And if I want to go to sleep before you get up, I'll be careful not to wake you when I lie down."

She had a point. It was pretty silly for him to try to sleep in the chair when he could be stretched out. But just knowing that she'd eventually be getting in bed with him was enough to send him into orbit.

"I guess that could work," he said, thinking aloud. "And we're both adults. There's no reason we can't handle this." And maybe if he repeated it enough, he'd start to believe it.

"Exactly." She waved her hand toward the other room as she reached for a spoon and promptly knocked over a container of baking powder. "You're distracting me. Now go to bed and let me get started on these cookies."

Yawning, he scratched his bare chest and headed for her bedroom. Hopefully he'd be out like a light as soon as his head hit the pillow. And if he believed that, he was sure somebody had a piece of beachfront property in the middle of Arizona that he'd be fool enough to buy.

* * *

A couple of hours after Hunter went to lie down in her bed, Callie turned off the light in the kitchen and quietly walked into the bedroom. Making several dozen cookies had helped, but her nerves were still on edge and she expected they would remain that way until she was certain Craig was out of her life for good.

As she removed her slippers, then turned to pull back the cover, she forgot all about her current problem with Craig and focused on the sight of Hunter's broad back. From the muted moonlight filtering into the room through the sheer drapes she could see that he was lying on his stomach with the sheet covering him from the waist down.

Her heart stalled and she swallowed hard as the sight of all that delicious masculine skin reminded her of earlier in the kitchen when she'd first seen his bare chest. The play of his perfectly defined chest muscles beneath a light sprinkling of dark hair had fascinated her beyond words and distracted her to the point she'd been about as coordinated as a bull in a china shop.

How on earth was she going to be able to sleep with all that raw masculinity mere inches away? And why did her double bed suddenly seem as though it had shrunk to the size of a cot?

Wishing she had bought a two-bedroom house instead of a charming one-bedroom cottage, she shook her head as she jammed her feet back in her slippers.

She'd go into the kitchen, grab a handful of chocolate chips and lie down on the love seat.

"Are you going to stand there the rest of the night or are you going to get into bed?"

She jumped at the sound of Hunter's voice and her cheeks heated with embarrassment at being caught staring at him. Thank heavens there wasn't enough light in the room for him to see her guilty expression. "I…didn't want to…disturb you."

He rolled to his back and gazed up at her. "I wasn't asleep."

"What's wrong?" The way he'd been yawning before he'd gone to bed, she'd have thought he'd be asleep before he had a chance to close his eyes. "Is the mattress too soft for you?"

"No, it's quite comfortable."

She frowned as she gingerly sat down on the side of the bed. "Then what's the problem?"

"I've been thinking—"

"I'm not altogether sure I want to hear this," she interrupted warily. "The last time you shared your thoughts is what got us into this mess."

"Are you going to take off your robe and lie down?"

She swallowed hard. It would have been hard enough to stretch out beside him if he'd been asleep. But awake? Just the thought caused a tingling sensation to skip over every cell in her body.

"That's what you've been thinking about?"

"No." His deep chuckle sent a shiver straight up her spine. "But you've been going on adrenaline all evening, and I think it would probably be a good idea for the baby's sake if you tried to relax."

Callie knew he was right. But she wasn't sure that was going to be an option, especially with him so close.

"Are you going to keep me guessing or are you going to tell me what you've come up with this time?" she hedged.

He shook his head. "Not until you lie down."

Exasperated beyond words, she shook her head. "I think it would be best if I slept on the love seat."

"Why? You aren't afraid of sleeping in the same bed with me, are you?" She couldn't see much of his expression in the darkened room, but she'd heard the laughter and good-natured challenge in his voice.

"Don't be silly," she lied. "I just think since we're clearly attracted to each other, it might not be a good idea."

"Remember, we're both adults," he said softly. "I give you my word that nothing is going to happen that you don't want to happen."

It shouldn't be a problem, she told herself as she stood up to remove her robe. She wasn't sure why, but she trusted him. And she knew for certain she didn't have to worry about herself. The last thing she wanted or needed was to become involved with another man.

When she slipped into bed, he turned to his side,

propped his elbow on the pillow and rested his head against his palm. His proximity sent a delicious little thrill from the top of her head all the way to the tips of her toes. She did her best to ignore it.

"I think we should get married."

His voice was low and intimate, and it took a moment for her to realize what he'd said. When she did, her heart slammed against her ribs.

"You can't be serious."

When she started to get out of bed, his hand on her arm stopped her. "Think about it, darlin'. It won't take much effort on Culbertson's part to discover that we aren't married or that I've never been to Houston."

"And this just occurred to you?" She rubbed at her suddenly throbbing temples. "Why did I let you talk me into this? I told you it wouldn't work."

"That's why I'm suggesting we get married," he said patiently. "It doesn't matter when we got married, we'll still be husband and wife."

"I can't see where that would do anything but add one more complication to an already impossible situation." A sudden thought caused a chill to race through her, and she had to take a deep breath in order to get words passed the tightness in her throat. "He could ask for a DNA test to prove paternity."

"He might, but something tells me he won't."

Her breath caught on a soft sob. If he and his parents learned that her son had been fathered by Craig, the

Culbertsons were the kind of people who would intervene and take her baby away from her—not because
they loved the child, but because they viewed him as
one of their possessions. They'd find an excuse to find
her unworthy or unfit to raise their heir, the same as
they'd done that poor girl twelve years ago.

"There's no way out of…this." A chill ran the length
of her spine. "They're going to take my child away
from me and there's nothing I can do to stop them."

Hunter reached out to wrap his strong arms around
her and cradle her to him. "Not as long as I'm around
to stop them, they won't."

"I can't see how—"

"Taking a child away from a single parent isn't as
difficult as it is from a married couple."

"Yes, but the Culbertsons are quite wealthy and can
hire the best lawyers. And I'm sure they'll see that the
case is heard by a judge who travels in the same social
circle they do." She placed her hand over her stomach.
"We'd be fighting a losing battle."

"Let them hire whoever they want or get whatever
judge they think will go along with their request." He
kissed her forehead. "It's not like I don't have a few
connections of my own."

Pulling back to look at him, she shook her head.
"I'm not sure who you think you know, but it's going
to take more than a connection or two to keep them
from taking my son."

"You might be surprised." He gently brushed a strand of hair from her cheek with his index finger. "Let me worry about dealing with the Culbertsons and their lawyers. I'm going to do some checking, but I suspect there's more to his visit than what he's saying."

Anger and frustration filled her. "This is the very reason I detest rich people. They think that because they have money it gives them the right to do anything they please."

"Not all people of means are like the Culbertsons, Callie," he said quietly. "My father's family had money, but there was never a threat of them taking me or my brothers away from our mothers."

Remembering their conversation on the trip back from El Paso, Callie bit her lower lip to keep it from trembling as a fresh wave of fear coursed through her. "I'd say your father's family is the exception, not the rule."

"Maybe, but I'm betting it's closer to being the other way around." He lightly ran his palm up and down her arm, sending a wave of tingling warmth to every part of her. "At any rate, I promise you have nothing to fear from the Culbertsons as long as I'm around."

"I hope you're right," she said, hiding a yawn behind her hand.

He kissed the top of her head. "We'll talk more in the morning. Right now we both need to get some rest."

Within moments his deep, even breathing signaled that Hunter had fallen asleep. But, as tired as she was, Callie couldn't stop thinking about the threat that Craig posed or Hunter's offer of marriage.

Everything he said made perfect sense and could very well solve her problem. But friendship only went so far. She couldn't believe he was willing to enter into something as serious as marriage simply to help her. What did he expect to get out of it for himself? And what would happen if they were successful in keeping the Culbertsons from taking her baby away from her? How long before Hunter asked for an annulment or a divorce?

Thoroughly exhausted from the tension of Craig's unexpected visit and the speculation of what would happen if she did go along with Hunter's insane suggestion, Callie felt herself begin to drift off to sleep. But instead of having nightmares of her baby being taken away from her by Craig and his family, she dreamed of marriage to a tall, dark-haired, handsome man with a sexy-as-sin voice and devastating kisses.

The feel of thin, downy-soft hair against her cheek, the steady beat of a heart beneath her ear and the scent of clean masculine skin assailed Callie's senses as she floated in the surreal world between sleep and wakefulness. When a pair of strong arms tightened around her, she smiled and snuggled against the hard male body beside her.

"Good morning, sleepyhead."

The sound of Hunter's voice caused her eyes to fly open and had her tilting her head to meet his incredible green gaze. She was lying with her head pillowed on his broad chest and her arm thrown over his flat belly. But it was the realization that her leg was draped over his muscular thigh—his bare muscular thigh—that sent a shiver of excitement up her spine and had her wondering if she'd be able to draw her next breath.

"H-how long have you been awake?"

"About an hour."

Goose bumps shimmered over her skin at the vibration of his rich baritone rumbling up from deep in his chest. But it was the feel of his hard arousal straining at his briefs that had her gingerly moving her leg away from his. They were treading in dangerous territory and it would definitely be best to put some distance between them.

"Where are you going?" His warm breath stirred the fine hair at her temple and caused her heart to skip several beats.

"I, um, should probably get up and cook something for breakfast."

He held her firmly against him when she tried to pull from his arms. "I've got a hunger, but it's not for food."

A delightful heat like nothing she'd ever known began to flow through her veins at his candid comment.

"I—it wouldn't be a good idea to complicate things more than they already are."

His deep chuckle caused the warmth inside of her to pool in the pit of her belly. "Darlin', kissing isn't complicated." He brushed her lips with his, sending a delightful tingling sensation all the way to her toes. "It's one of the purest forms of pleasure a man and woman can share."

The sound of his voice, his provocative words and the feel of his calloused palm caressing her side through her thin cotton gown were like a drug and she suddenly had a hard time remembering her own name, let alone why it would make their current situation more difficult. But she ceased thinking at all when his mouth settled over hers and he tenderly traced the outline of her lips with his tongue.

"This is…insane," she murmured, trying to draw some much-needed air into her lungs.

He nibbled kisses along her jawline to the sensitive hollow below her ear. "Do you want me to stop?"

"I should demand that you stop and get out of my house immediately."

His lips blazed a trail down her neck to her collarbone. "But you aren't going to do that?"

With a myriad of delightful sensations coursing through her, she had to concentrate on his question. "N-no."

"Why not?" he asked as he ran his palm back down

her side, then slipped his hand beneath the hem of her gown.

His fingers sliding along her bare skin made breathing all but impossible and caused the heat in her lower belly to intensify. "Wh-what you're doing…feels too good."

"Do you want me to stop?"

Unable to think clearly, she shook her head. "Don't you dare."

He caressed her hip, then her ribs as he slowly moved his hand up her body. "Are you aware of what's going to happen if I continue?"

When he covered her breast with his hand, then chafed her puckered nipple with the pad of his thumb, need coursed through her to settle deep in the most feminine part of her. "W-we'll make love."

His hand continued to caress her overly sensitized skin. "Is that what you want, Callie?"

Staring into his dark green eyes, her heart pounded hard in her chest. From the moment they'd first met there had been a magnetic pull drawing them together, a chemistry they'd both tried but found impossible to deny. And with each kiss the tension between them had heightened until it had become a force that was impossible for either of them to fight.

Whether it was her pregnancy hormones that caused a desire stronger than anything she'd ever known or something more, she didn't want him to stop. She wanted to feel the warmth of Hunter's kisses and the passion of his loving touch.

"It's pure insanity. But yes, I want to make love with you, Hunter."

Seven

At Callie's admittance that she wanted to make love with him, Hunter's heart slammed against his rib cage so hard he was surprised it hadn't jumped right out of his chest. Throughout the night he'd lain with her in his arms, and with each tick of the clock her soft body and sweet womanly scent had increased the tension he'd been fighting from the moment he'd laid eyes on her. But when she'd awakened and stared up at him with her sexy violet eyes, he'd become harder than he'd ever been in his life and could no more have stopped himself from tasting and touching her than he could stop the sun from rising in the east each morning.

But as much as he wanted to sink himself deep inside of her, to hear her call his name as he pleasured her, he couldn't bear the thought that she might regret one minute of what they would share. "Are you sure that making love is what you really want, Callie?"

His heart stalled and he found himself holding his breath when she closed her eyes and remained silent for several long seconds. Then, to his relief, she opened her eyes and nodded her head.

"I think I'll go into total meltdown if we don't."

Taking a deep breath, he tried to slow the liquid fire racing through his veins. "I know I should have asked this before things went this far, but would your doctor be okay with our making love?"

Her porcelain cheeks colored a pretty pink as she nodded. "The obstetrician has given me the go-ahead for normal activity with no restrictions. And that includes lovemaking."

Hunter couldn't believe the level of relief that washed over him. If she'd told him there was even the slightest possibility of a problem or the tiniest bit of discomfort for her, he'd have found some way—no matter how difficult—to walk away. But knowing there was nothing to prevent them from having a pleasurable and satisfying experience sent a fresh wave of heat straight to his groin.

Unfortunately it was short-lived. He hadn't planned on spending the night with Callie, let alone making love with her, and protection hadn't even crossed his mind when he'd left the hangar yesterday evening. But he was thinking about it now. Or, more accurately, the lack of it.

But as he gazed at the woman in his arms, he realized there was no possibility of him making her pregnant. And truth to tell, it wouldn't matter to him if she wasn't already expecting a child.

The thought of Callie carrying his baby appealed to him more than he could have ever imagined and should have scared the living hell out of him. It was something he didn't understand, wasn't entirely comfortable with and, at the moment, didn't intend to analyze. All that mattered was bringing her pleasure, cherishing her as she was meant to be cherished.

Without a moment's hesitation he gathered her close and covered her mouth with his. Her soft lips molded to his with a hungry desperation that matched his own and sent fire racing through his veins with the swiftness of a raging river.

When she parted for him to deepen the kiss, Hunter thought his head might come right off his shoulders as she boldly stroked his tongue with hers and engaged him in an erotic game of advance and retreat. She was letting him know that she felt the passion as deeply as he did, that she wanted him as much as he wanted her.

Breaking the kiss, he nibbled his way to the base of her throat as he reached for the hem of her gown.

"Lift your hips, darlin'," he whispered against her satiny skin.

When he'd whisked away her panties and thin cotton gown, he quickly removed his boxer briefs, then tossing the garments to the floor beside the bed, gathered her back into his arms. At the feel of her satiny skin against him, desire raced through his veins, and he had to fight an almost uncontrollable urge to cover her with his body and sink himself deep inside of her.

His entire being pulsed with the urgent need to claim her, but he was determined not to rush things no matter what his body demanded. "You feel so soft...." He trailed kisses down the base of her throat, then past her collarbone to the slope of her breast. "So sweet."

As he teased her with a light swirling motion, the fire of need in his belly grew when she threaded her fingers in his hair and pulled him closer. Arching her back, she gave him better access to the hardened tip, and taking her into his mouth, he chafed her with his tongue and caressed her with his lips.

"P-please, Hunter."

"Not yet, darlin'." Moving his hand down her side to her hip and beyond, he cupped her at the apex of her thighs. "I want to make sure you're ready for me."

"If I was any more ready...I'd burn to a crisp." Her voice sounded wispy and breathless and he had no doubt she was as turned-on as he was.

Parting her, he stroked her, then touched her intimately. Her moist warmth and moan of pleasure assured him that she needed him as much as he needed her.

"I want you to promise me something," he said as he continued to stroke her.

"Anything." He watched her close her eyes and catch her lower lip between her teeth a moment before she whimpered, "You're driving me…crazy."

Her response to his touch heightened his own passion, and he had to take several deep breaths in order to force himself to slow down. "I want you to promise me that if there's even the slightest bit of discomfort, you'll tell me."

"I promise." When she opened her eyes to gaze up at him, the desire in the violet depths robbed him of breath. "Please…make love to me, Hunter."

Unable to deny either one of them any longer, he nudged her knees apart and levered himself over her. As he moved his lower body into position, he settled his mouth over hers at the same time he pressed himself forward.

Slowly, carefully, he pushed into her, and the feel of her tight body melting around him as he sank deeper and deeper had him clenching his teeth as he struggled for control. But when she raised her hips for more of him, the slender thread of his restraint snapped and he buried himself completely within her feminine depths.

With every muscle in his body taut with the need to complete the act of loving her, Hunter forced himself to remain completely still. She needed time to adjust to him and he needed time to savor the feeling of being completely one with the most desirable woman he'd ever known.

Gathering her close, he kissed her sweet lips. "I'm going to try to go slow, but I want you so damned much I'm not sure that's an option."

Her smile caused the fire threatening to consume him to flare out of control. "I want you just as much."

He held her gaze with his as he eased his hips back then forward, thrusting into her again and again. As he felt her respond by meeting him halfway, he increased the rhythm with each stroke, and in no time he felt her body tighten around his, signaling that she was poised to find her release.

When she wrapped her legs around his waist to hold him close, the pressure in his body increased tenfold and it was all he could do to hold himself in check. But he wasn't going to find his satisfaction without her, and sliding his hand between them, he touched her as he thrust into her one last time.

Her moan of pleasure and the quivering of her tiny inner muscles rippling around him as she found her satisfaction triggered his own completion. Heat and light flashed behind his tightly closed eyes as he surrendered to the storm, and feeling as if his world had been reduced to just the two of them, he emptied himself deep inside of her.

As Hunter slowly drifted back to reality, an emotion filled his chest that he didn't dare put a name to. He'd never experienced anything as amazing as what he'd just shared with Callie. Her passionate response to his touch had excited him in ways he'd only dreamed of and he felt more alive than he had in years.

"Are you all right?" he asked when he finally found the strength to move to her side.

"I-I'm fine."

A slight crack in her voice had him rising up to look down at her beautiful face. The tears he saw welling up in her eyes scared him as little else could. If he'd hurt her in any way, he'd never forgive himself.

"Callie, darlin', what's wrong?"

"Nothing. Making love with you was one of the most beautiful experiences I've ever had." She cupped his cheek with her palm, and her smile lit the darkest corners of his soul. "Thank you."

Weak with relief, he shook his head. "I should be thanking you. You were incredible."

When she hid a yawn behind her delicate hand, he kissed the top of her head. "You were up pretty late and it's still early. Why don't we take a nap, then we can talk over breakfast." He hadn't much more than gotten the words out before her shallow breathing signaled that she'd drifted off to sleep.

As he watched the predawn shadows in the room melt away with the light of day, Hunter held Callie close and thought about what they would be talking about later. After the accident and Ellen's death, he'd never intended to ask another woman to marry him. But these were a different set of circumstances. He and Callie wouldn't be marrying for love. They would be doing the only thing he could think of that might discourage Craig Culbertson from trying to take her baby away from her.

He closed his eyes and tried to think of some other way to help Callie. From the time he'd gone to bed until she'd entered the bedroom a couple of hours later, all he'd been able to think about was how they could stop Culbertson and his family.

Hunter had no idea what the man's motive was, but he must have learned about Callie's pregnancy from her mother and shown up to confirm his suspicions that he was the father. Considering the disgust in his voice when he'd accusingly asked her if the child was his, Hunter was surprised that Culbertson hadn't jumped at the chance for someone else to take responsibility. But he hadn't, and Hunter had every intention of pulling out all the stops to find out why. And he knew exactly who to contact to help him start making inquiries into the matter. He'd get the name of a discreet private investigator from Emerald's trusted assistant, Luther Freemont, and see what they could dig up on Culbertson.

If he'd wanted to, Hunter could have asked outright for Emerald to intervene on Callie's behalf and he had no doubt that she would have. But that wasn't his style. Whether it was pride or bullheaded stubbornness, he fought his own battles. He'd offered to help Callie and he'd be the one to see the matter through to the end.

Another reason he didn't want to get Emerald involved was that he wasn't ready for anyone—and especially Callie—at Life Medevac to learn of his relationship to the indomitable Mrs. Larson. For one thing, he had yet to prove himself with the business she'd given him to run. And for another, Callie had trust issues with anyone who had money. If she were to discover that he was Emerald Larson's grandson and had been given a trust fund large enough to make a dent in the national debt, as well as being in line to inherit part of Emerald Inc., she'd automatically assume he was like the Culbertsons and refuse his help. And that was something they both knew she couldn't afford to do.

Gazing down at her sleeping so peacefully in his arms, he fleetingly wondered if getting married would pose a threat to either of their hearts. But he immediately dismissed the concern. They wouldn't be marrying for love, and as long as they kept things in perspective and their emotions in check, there shouldn't be a problem for either of them.

Satisfied that he had everything under control,

Hunter relaxed and closed his eyes. They'd stay together as long as it took to settle this business with Culbertson once and for all, then evaluate the best way to handle the dissolution of their marriage.

An unexpected twinge of regret tightened his chest at the thought, but he ignored it. He and Callie were friends now and they would remain friends once they parted ways. And that's just the way it had to stay.

"Where's your husband, Callie?"

Callie went perfectly still at the sound of the familiar voice. Needing a refill on her prenatal vitamins, she'd stopped at the drugstore on her way to start her shift at Life Medevac. She didn't have the time nor the desire to deal with the likes of Craig Culbertson.

"Not that it's any of your business, but Hunter owns the air-ambulance service and had some paperwork to deal with," she said, heading back to her car.

She could pick up the vitamins another time. Right now she wanted nothing more than to put as much distance between her and Craig as humanly possible.

But before she could get the driver's door open, he caught her by the arm. "What's your hurry? Surely you have enough time to talk to an old friend."

Extricating herself from his grasp, she turned to face him. "We aren't friends and never will be. Now if you'll excuse me, I need to get to work."

His knowing smirk was enough to make her want

to scream. "If your husband owns the business, going in late shouldn't be a problem for you."

She reached for the handle on her car door. "I need to be there on time to relieve the on-duty crew."

He shook his head as he placed his hand on the driver's door to hold it shut. "What you need to do is answer a few questions."

"No, I don't."

"Oh, I think you do." He reached out to trace his index finger down her cheek. "It seems that none of the people here in town knew anything about you and O'Banyon being married. In fact, Mr. Jones over at the grocery store was quite surprised to hear the news."

A cold chill slithered up her spine at Craig's touch. She must have had blinders on not see that his charm was a weapon, not an endearing quality. How could she have ever found herself attracted to such a reptile?

Batting his hand away, she shook her head. "Don't ever touch me again."

"You used to like for me to touch you, Callie," he said, trying to affect an injured look.

"That's ancient history." She tried to remove his hand where he held the car door. "All I want from you now is to be left alone."

His eyes narrowed and a sneer replaced his wounded expression. "Now is that any way to talk to your baby's daddy?"

"Just because you can fertilize an egg doesn't make

you father material. That takes someone special." She jerked the car door from his grasp and started to get in. "Someone who is actually capable of loving a child."

"Like O'Banyon?"

"Yes. Exactly like Hunter."

His sarcastic laugh caused her to clench her fists until her knuckles ached. "Why don't you give up the charade, Callie? We both know you're no more married than I am. If you come back to Houston now, maybe I'll forget that you and O'Banyon tried to dupe me into believing the baby belongs to him." He shrugged. "Who knows? I might even be persuaded to let you have visitation rights."

Fear so strong it threatened to the buckle her knees ran through her. "As long as I have breath left in my body, you won't take my child away from me," she said, doing her best to keep her voice steady.

His knowing smile made her skin crawl. "That remains to be seen, my dear."

As Callie got into the car, her hands shook so badly that it took a couple of tries before she was able to fit her key into the ignition. Everything she'd feared for the past several months was coming true.

As she backed the car from the parking space and drove the short distance to the Life Medevac hangar outside of town, her body trembled and tears ran unchecked down her cheeks. For reasons she didn't have time nor the inclination to analyze, all she could think of was getting to Hunter. She knew it made no sense at all considering the short time they'd known each other, but with him she felt more secure than she had in her entire life. And although she hated being vulnerable and dependent in any way, his reassuring presence gave her strength.

Parking her car at the side of the hangar, she hurried into the dispatch room. Thankfully the on-duty crew and Mary Lou were occupied with a game of Texas Hold 'Em poker. She knew she looked more than a little upset and she didn't particularly want to endure a barrage of questions from Mary Lou.

"Is Hunter in his office?" she asked as she breezed past them.

"He's been in there all afternoon making phone calls," Mary Lou answered without looking up from her cards.

When Callie came to Hunter's office, she didn't even hesitate as she opened the door and walked into the room. Craig might think he had the upper hand, but she wasn't going to stand by and let him take her son away without a fight. And if that meant entering into a marriage with a man she barely knew, then that's exactly what she was going to do.

"If you're still willing to marry me, my answer is yes."

Eight

Hunter was on his feet and rounding the desk in a flash. Callie looked as if she'd seen a ghost, and the tears streaming down her cheeks just about tore him apart.

"What's happened?"

When he took her into his arms, she burrowed into his embrace. As she told him about meeting up with Culbertson and the man's arrogant attitude, pure fury burned at Hunter's gut.

"Do you honestly think we would have a chance of stopping him if we were married?" she asked, trembling against him.

"There's not a doubt in my mind, darlin'."

If he could have gotten his hands on Culbertson at

that very moment, Hunter would have choked the life out of him for putting her through that. The man was without question the sorriest excuse for a human being he'd ever had the misfortune to meet, and it was going to give him great pleasure to deal the arrogant jerk a good dose of reality.

Hunter had spent the entire afternoon on the phone with Emerald's personal assistant, Luther Freemont, and the private investigator Emerald Inc. hired for running background checks on potential employees for Emerald's various companies. After speaking with the man at length, Hunter was confident that if there was anything they could use to combat Culbertson's attempt to gain custody of Callie's baby, the P.I. would find it.

And on the outside chance that Culbertson was squeaky-clean—which Hunter knew damned good and well he wasn't—he and Callie would establish themselves as a married couple with a stable home life that no lawyer, judge or social worker could argue wasn't perfect for raising a child.

"I don't want you spending any more time worrying about Culbertson or what he's going to do," Hunter said as he soothingly rubbed at the tension along her spine.

She leaned back to look at him, and the anxiety he saw in the depths of her expressive eyes caused his gut to twist into a tight knot. "Th-that's easier said than done."

"Do you trust me, Callie?"

"Yes." There wasn't so much as a hint of uncertainty in her answer.

"I give you my word that everything is going to work out." He gave her a reassuring smile. "By the time this is settled, Craig Culbertson will be running back to Houston like a tail-tucked dog."

"I hope you're right."

"I am."

He sealed his promise with a kiss, and by the time he raised his head, his body was as hard as a chunk of granite. Taking a deep breath, he rested his forehead against hers. He had no idea how she'd managed to get under his skin so quickly, but there was no denying that he found her to be the most exciting woman he'd had the good fortune to meet in the past five years. And the thought of making love to her every night, then holding her as she slept, was enough to send a laser of heat straight through him.

"Why…are you willing…to do this for me, Hunter?" she asked, every bit as breathless as he was. "What's in this for you?"

He'd asked himself the same question at least a dozen times and the answer had been surprisingly simple. "Even though my father's family is well off, my grandmother felt that my brothers and I would be much better off being raised by loving mothers who taught us a solid set of values, instead of giving us everything we wanted, like she'd given our father." He grinned. "Her logic must have worked, because we all turned out to be well-adjusted and productive, instead of selfish and hopelessly irresponsible like her son."

"Your grandmother must be a very special, very wise lady."

"She's definitely one of a kind," he said evasively, thinking that was an understatement. "But the point is, I believe every kid deserves the same chance she gave me and my brothers."

"In other words, you're doing this for the sake of my son?"

Hunter nodded. "I know you'll be a great mom and raise him with the love and guidance he needs. He wouldn't get that from Culbertson and his family."

She shook her head disapprovingly. "He'd turn out to be just like Craig—hedonistic, selfish and shallow."

"Exactly." Hunter kissed her forehead. "And to answer your second question, the only thing I expect to get out of our marriage is the satisfaction of knowing that I stopped that from happening."

"How long—"

Placing his finger to her lips, he shook his head. "Let's take it one day at a time. After we take care of this business with Culbertson, then we'll discuss how we want to handle…things." He had no idea why, but he couldn't bring himself to say the word *annulment* or *divorce*.

He watched her nibble on her lower lip as she gazed

at him for several seconds. "Does that mean you'll be moving in with me for a while?"

"Husbands and wives usually live together, darlin'." He grinned. "Of course, you could always move into my room here at the hangar."

For the first time since walking into the room she smiled. "I don't think that would work very well considering you have a twin-size bed."

"Oh, I think it might work out real well." Sharing any bed with Callie sounded good to him. He brushed her lips with his. "When we aren't making love, I can hold you close while we sleep."

He watched a spark of awareness replace the worry in her violet eyes. "That might work for a time. But what happens when my tummy is as big as an overinflated balloon?"

"Good point," he said, wondering what it would feel like to have her baby moving under his hands. A sharp pang of regret that he'd never feel his own child move inside her knifed through him, but he did his best to ignore it. Suddenly feeling as if he might be drowning, he added, "Maybe your bed would be best."

"When do you want to do this?"

He laughed, relieving some of his tension. "If it had been left up to me, we wouldn't have gotten out of bed this morning."

Her cheeks coloring a pretty pink fascinated the

hell out of him. "I meant, when do you think we should get married?"

"I know." He gave her a quick kiss, then stepped back before he gave in to temptation and took her down the hall to test out his narrow bed. "How does tomorrow afternoon sound?"

"Impossible." The sound of laughter in her sweet voice was like a balm to his soul. "Besides the fact that we'll be on duty, there's a three-day waiting period in the state of Texas from the time we obtain a license until we get married."

"I happen to know there isn't a waiting period in New Mexico." He took her by the hand and led her over to the door. "And remember, I'm the boss. I can have the Evac II crew come in on standby for the day while you and I make a trip up to Carlsbad."

She looked a little dazed as they walked out into the hall. "This is all happening so fast."

"Things will slow down after tomorrow." He put his arm around her slender shoulders and held her to his side. "Now put on your best smile, darlin'. We have an announcement to make to our coworkers."

"Do you, Calantha Marshall, take this man to be your lawful wedded husband? To have and to hold..."

The rotund judge droned on, but Callie had no idea if he recited the words of the traditional wedding ceremony or if he was trying to auction off a pile of dirt.

She was way too nervous to think of anything but the fact that she'd not only let Hunter talk her into marrying him, they were actually going through with it.

When the Honorable Juan Ricardo cleared his throat and looked at her expectantly, she swallowed hard and forced herself to concentrate on what he'd asked. "I do," she said, surprised that her voice sounded fairly steady considering the state of her nerves.

Judge Ricardo nodded his approval, then turned to Hunter and asked the same question.

Giving her a smile that curled her toes inside her cross trainers, Hunter's voice was strong and sure when he answered. "I do."

"Do you have a ring?" the judge asked, giving Hunter an expectant look.

Callie's cheeks heated as Hunter shook his head. They were probably the most ill-prepared couple to be getting married that the judge had ever seen.

"As soon as she said she'd marry me, I didn't want to take the time to pick out a ring," Hunter said, giving the man a conspiratorial grin. "I was afraid she might change her mind."

Judge Ricardo chuckled. "Then, by the power vested in me by the state of New Mexico, I pronounce you husband and wife. You can kiss your bride, son."

When Hunter took her into his arms to seal their union, his kiss caused her head to spin and her knees to feel as if they were made of rubber. Raising his head, he gazed at her for several long seconds before he turned and thanked the judge, then took her hand in his and led her out of the courthouse.

As they got into the Life Medevac truck for the drive back to Devil's Fork, she still couldn't believe how quickly everything had taken place. "What in heaven's name have we done?"

When he reached out and covered her hand with his, a sense of well-being coursed through her. It was completely unexpected and caused her to catch her breath. Dear heavens, was her attraction to Hunter more than a case of overactive prenatal hormones?

Being a registered nurse, she knew that due to an imbalance in hormone levels, during the second trimester some expectant mothers felt more sensual and sexy than they'd ever felt in their lives. She'd naturally assumed that was the reason she'd given in to desire and passion when she'd made love with Hunter. But now? Could she actually be falling for him?

No, that wasn't possible. She'd only known him a short time, and although her attraction to him was stronger than anything she'd ever felt, that didn't mean she loved him.

"You're awfully quiet," he said, bringing her hand to his lips to kiss the back of it.

Thinking quickly, she smiled. "I was contemplating whether to keep my last name, hyphenate it or change it to yours."

He nodded. "I did an Internet search this morning and found a Web site with a list of things that a bride needs to do after the wedding. Changing her personal documents and identification was on the list." He gave her a seductive smile. "It's up to you, darlin'. But I think Callie Marshall-O'Banyon or just Callie O'Banyon sounds pretty good."

"Since our marriage is only temporary, I suppose it would make more sense to hyphenate."

"Then Callie Marshall-O'Banyon it is."

"For now."

"Right. For now."

As they rode in relative silence on the way back to Devil's Fork, Callie couldn't help but wonder why the thought that her name change wasn't going to be permanent caused her to feel a deep sadness. She'd known up front that they were only getting married in order to thwart Craig's efforts to take her baby away from her. So why was she feeling so darned melancholy?

But as she analyzed her reaction, she supposed it was only natural to feel a bit depressed. She'd always thought that once she got married and took her husband's name it would be for the rest of her life. Of course, that had been when she'd been idealistic and thought the only reason she would ever marry was for love.

Glancing over at Hunter, she couldn't help but think that he had all the qualities she'd ever dreamed of in a husband. He was kind, considerate and, above all, caring. Very few men would have cared enough about an unwed mother keeping her baby to give up their freedom indefinitely.

Sighing, she stared out the windshield of the truck. She wasn't sure what lay ahead of them once they returned to Devil's Fork or how long they'd be husband and wife. But there wasn't a doubt in her mind that no matter what happened, she could count on Hunter being right there beside her to face whatever Craig Culbertson tried to do.

When Callie and Hunter walked into the Life Medevac dispatch room, Mary Lou and the on-duty crew gave them a standing ovation. "Congratulations!"

Grinning like a Cheshire cat, Mary Lou stepped forward. "We've all talked it over and we're giving you two the night off."

"Yeah, we decided you couldn't have a decent wedding night here at the hangar with all of us hanging around," Corey chimed in. His knowing smile made Callie's cheeks heat with embarrassment.

"I'm taking over for you, Hunter," George said. "And Mark, the Evac III paramedic, is coming in to take over for Callie."

"What about standby?" Hunter asked. "We have to have a crew on call in case we have overlapping runs."

"We've got that covered," Mary Lou said, stepping between them. She slipped her arms through theirs and started walking them toward the door. "The rest of the guys are going to take care of that. Now I think you should go back to Callie's place and spend the rest of the night having a little honeymoon fun."

Callie felt as if the heat in her cheeks would burst into flames at any moment. She might have known that Mary Lou would cut to the chase and tell them exactly how she thought they should be spending the evening.

"Hunter?" She felt bad about everyone giving up their day off to cover for them. The least he could do was put up a token protest.

But his sexy grin sent a streak of heat thrumming through her veins and spoke volumes of what an excellent idea he thought the Life Medevac staff had come up with. "Sounds good to me," he said, nodding. He took her hand in his and led her through the door, then, turning back, added, "We'll be back at eight tomorrow morning to finish out our shift."

When they walked into her house several minutes later, Callie took a deep breath and turned to face Hunter. "I don't feel right about this."

He frowned as he reached to take her into his arms. "We're married, darlin'. Making love is something husbands and wives do."

She shook her head and tried to remember what she'd been about to say. With him holding her close, it seemed to short-circuit her thought process. "I was talking about our coworkers giving up their day off."

"Why?" He bent his head to nibble at the sensitive skin along the column of her neck. "I thought it was a nice gesture."

"It…is." A shiver of excitement slid up her spine when he kissed his way to the wildly fluttering pulse at the base of her throat. "But they have no idea…that we aren't making…a lifetime commitment."

Raising his head, he held her gaze with his as he cupped her cheek with his large palm. "Don't worry about it, Callie. We're committed to each other now and for as long as it takes to make sure Culbertson never bothers you again."

"But—"

"Giving us the night off was something they wanted to do, and they know we'll do the same thing for them when they need time off."

His deep, smooth voice and the look in his dark green eyes quickly had her forgetting her guilt or the reason for it. The feel of his hands sliding the length of her back sent shivers of delight coursing through her, and it suddenly didn't matter why they'd gotten married or that it wasn't forever. God help her, but she wanted to spend the night in Hunter's arms again, wanted to feel his hands on her and the sense of being cherished as he made their bodies one.

She would have told him, but when his mouth settled over hers, the contact was so tender it caused tears to flood her eyes and robbed her of the ability to speak. He deepened the kiss, and as his tongue stroked hers, the mating was filled with promises of things to come. He wanted her and he was letting her know in no uncertain terms how much.

When he swung her up into his arms and walked into the bedroom, their lips never broke contact, and as he gently lowered them both to the bed, Callie's heart skipped several beats. With his legs tangling with hers, the strength of his arousal pressed against her thigh and had her own body responding with wanton pulses of need.

His lips clung to hers a moment before he raised his head to smile down at her. "I want you so damned much I can taste it."

"And I want you just as much." Her body tingled with such need she trembled from it. "Please, make love to me, Hunter."

His slumberous look thrilled her to the depths of her soul as he rose from the bed to remove their shoes and socks, then, taking her by the hand, he pulled her to her feet. Bringing her hands to rest on his chest, he gave her a smile that caused her knees to wobble.

"Let's do this together, darlin'."

Excited by the prospect of removing his clothes, Callie rose up on tiptoes to kiss the skin just above the neck band of his red T-shirt at the same time she tugged the tail of it from the waistband of his jeans. Sliding her hands under the soft cotton garment, she felt his muscles contract as she slowly pushed the shirt up along his lean sides. When he raised his arms to help her, she allowed him to pull the garment over his head and toss it aside.

"Your body is perfect," she said, lightly running her fingertips over his well-defined pectoral muscles.

When she traced circles around his flat male nipples, he sucked in a sharp breath. "As good as having your hands on my chest feels, it's my turn."

Reaching for her, he gently pulled the blue scrunchie holding her ponytail free and threaded his fingers through the shoulder-length strands. "Your hair is like fine threads of golden silk."

He tilted her head for a quick kiss, then with painstaking care worked the three buttons at the top of her oversize polo shirt through the buttonholes. Slowly, carefully lifting it up and over her head, his gaze held hers captive as he reached behind her to unfasten her bra. By the time he slid the silk and lace from her shoulders to toss it on top of their shirts, their breathing sounded as if they'd both run a marathon.

The look in his eyes warmed her all over as he filled both of his hands with her breasts and chafed the sensitive tips to harden peaks with his thumbs. "You're so beautiful, Callie."

He dipped his head to capture one of her nipples with his mouth, and she had to brace her hands on his shoulders to keep from melting into a puddle at his feet.

He teased first one, then the other tight nub with his tongue, and it felt as if her blood turned to warm honey as tendrils of desire threaded their way through her limbs to pool with an aching emptiness between her thighs. When he finally raised his head, the hungry look in his dark green eyes stole her breath.

Without a word, she reached for his belt and quickly worked the leather through the metal buckle. But when she popped the snap at the top of his jeans, she forced herself to slow down. Glancing up at him, she smiled as she traced her fingernail along each metal tooth of his bulging zipper. "This looks a bit uncomfortable. I think you'd probably feel better if we got you out of these."

"I don't *think,* darlin', I *know* I'd feel better," he said, his voice sounding raspy.

Easing his fly open, she pushed the jeans down his lean hips, then past his muscular thighs and calves. When he stepped out of them, she trailed her hands along his hair-roughened skin on her way back up to his navy-blue boxer briefs. She loved the way the sinew flexed and bunched at her touch.

"Is that better now?"

His sexy grin sent heat spiraling straight to her core. "Oh, yeah," he said, reaching for the waistband of her maternity jeans.

His heated gaze held hers captive as he slid his fingers under the elastic. His warm palms felt wonderful brushing against her skin as he knelt to push the jeans down her legs, then slowly skimmed his hands along her legs on his way back to her silk panties. Touching her between her legs, he applied a light pressure against the most sensitive spot on her body, sending waves of pleasure radiating through her.

"Does that feel good, Callie?" he asked when a tiny moan of pleasure escaped her.

Unable to form a coherent thought, all she could do was nod.

When he stood up, his gaze captured hers, and as if by unspoken agreement they both reached for the last barriers separating them. Never losing eye contact, together they disposed of his boxer briefs and her panties.

Callie's eyes widened at the sight of his magnificent body. When they'd made love the other morning there hadn't been enough light for her to see his physique. But as she gazed at him now, she marveled at how perfectly made he was.

His wide shoulders, chest and thighs were well defined by muscles that she somehow knew hadn't been honed by working out at a gym. As her gaze drifted lower, past his lean flanks, her breath caught at the sight of his proud, full erection. He was impressively built, thoroughly aroused and, as she lifted her eyes to meet his, looking at her as if he thought she was the most beautiful creature on earth.

"You're amazing," he said, his voice thick with passion.

"I was thinking the same thing about you." She might have felt a bit unsure about her expanding shape had it not been for the gleam of appreciation in his eyes and the reverence she detected in his voice.

Reaching out, she tentatively touched him. Shivers of hot, hungry desire streaked through her when she circled him with her hand and his warm, thick strength surged at her touch. Measuring his length and the softness below, she glanced up at him when a groan rumbled up from deep in his chest. His eyes were closed and a muscle ticked along his jaw as if he'd clenched his teeth against the intense sensations her touch created.

"Does that feel good, Hunter?"

When he opened his eyes, the feral light in the green depths caused her to shiver with a need stronger than anything she'd ever experienced before. But when he cupped her breasts, then lowered his head to circle each nipple in turn with his tongue, swirls of heat coursed through her and she abandoned her exploration to place her hands on his shoulders for support.

"P-please…"

"What do you want, Callie?" His warm breath on her sensitized skin made her feel as if she'd go up in flames at any moment.

"You."

"When?"

"Now!" He was driving her crazy and he wanted to play twenty questions?

Chuckling, he raised his head and, wrapping his arms around her, pulled her to him. The instant soft female skin met hard masculine flesh, Callie moaned with pleasure.

"Let's get in bed while we still have the strength," he said hoarsely.

When he helped her into bed, then stretched out beside her, waves of sheer delight danced over every cell in her being at the feel of his calloused palms caressing her ribs and the underside of her breasts. Feeling as if she were burning up from the inside out, she pressed her legs together in an effort to ease the empty ache he'd created there. He must have realized what she needed because he reached down to gently cup her, a moment before his fingers parted her to stroke the tiny nub of hidden pleasure. Waves of heat streaked through her and she felt as if she'd go mad from wanting.

Raining kisses along her collarbone, then up the side of her neck, he moved his finger deeper to stroke her inside. "Is this where you want me, Callie?"

"Y-yes."

"Do you want me there now?"

"Hunter...please—"

"Just a little bit more, darlin'," he said as his relentless fingers continued to stroke her inner core.

"I can't…stand anymore."

When he moved his hand away, he immediately nudged her thighs farther apart with his knee and eased himself into position. He covered her lips with his, and Callie closed her eyes at the exquisite feel of his blunt tip against her a moment before she felt him slowly, surely slip inside.

"Look at me, Callie."

When she opened her eyes, his heated gaze held hers as he set an easy pace, and all too soon she felt her body straining for sweet liberation from the tension he'd created within her. He must have noticed her tightening around him because he steadily increased his thrusts until the coil of need within her snapped and she was cast into the realm of intense pleasure. She heard him call her name at the same time his big body stiffened, then quivered inside of her as he found his own release.

Wrapping her arms around Hunter's broad back, she held him close as her body pulsed with sweet satisfaction. When their bodies began to cool, she bit her lower lip to keep from crying. She'd done the unthinkable. She'd fought against it from the moment they'd met, but there was no sense denying it any longer.

She'd fallen in love with Hunter O'Banyon.

Nine

The next morning, when Hunter and Callie walked into the dispatch room, Mary Lou pointed to a slip of paper on her desk. "Hunter, you have a message from someone by the last name of Barringer." She shook her head disapprovingly. "He wouldn't tell me what the nature of his business was. But he said it was important that you call him as soon as possible." She pointed to a huge box over in the corner. "And the new flight suits you ordered were delivered yesterday afternoon."

"Good," Callie said, walking over to gaze into the box. "I can barely zip the one I have now."

Recognizing the name of the private investigator

he'd hired, Hunter nodded. "While I return his phone call, why don't you and Callie sort through the new flight suits and match them against the list of everyone's sizes." He walked over to kiss Callie's cheek. "I'll be back in a few minutes to help."

Her cheeks colored a deep rose and he didn't think he'd ever seen her look prettier. "Mary Lou and I can handle this. Go make your phone call."

"I can sure tell the two of you are newlyweds," Mary Lou said, laughing. "If you can't be away from her long enough to make a phone call, you've got it bad."

Hunter had no idea why, but he couldn't seem to stop smiling as he picked up the slip of paper with Barringer's number on it and walked down the hall toward his office. Maybe it was because the investigator was reporting back so quickly. But he had a feeling that it had more to do with the fact that he'd just spent the most incredible night of his life with his amazing wife.

Callie was the most responsive, sensual woman he'd ever met, and he couldn't wait for the end of the day when their shift ended and they could get back to her place. Unless they were called out for a standby run, they had four days to resume their honeymoon and he had every intention of making the most of their time off. His body tightened at the thought and he cursed the fact that they had eight hours before they were off duty.

When he closed the office door behind him, he took several deep breaths to calm his runaway libido, then walked over to the desk and dialed Barringer's number. He'd no sooner given his name to the man's secretary than Joe Barringer came on the line.

"I've discovered several things about Culbertson that I think you'll find very interesting," he said without preamble.

"You've got my attention," Hunter said, sinking into the desk chair.

"Craig Culbertson is broke. He's gambled away the trust fund his grandfather left him and it appears that he's started siphoning money out of the one set aside for his son."

"But aren't his parents in control of that money?" Hunter asked. He could've sworn that Callie told him the Culbertsons had adopted Craig's son and raised the boy as their own.

"They were," Barringer said. "But there was a stipulation in his grandfather's will that when Craig reached the age of thirty, he gained control of that fund, as well."

"Anything else?" Hunter asked, wondering how he could use the information to help Callie. So far, he hadn't heard anything worthwhile.

"Yes. It appears that provisions have been made for future children."

Hunter sat up straight in his chair. He had a feeling

he was about to learn the motive behind Culbertson's visit to Devil's Fork. "What kind of provisions?"

"Just a second." It sounded as if Barringer was shuffling papers a moment before he added, "Any future offspring of Craig Culbertson will have a million-dollar trust fund set up and—"

"Let me guess," Hunter said. "Culbertson is the administrator."

"You got it." The disgust in Joe Barringer's voice was evident. "His grandfather must have expected Culbertson to sow more wild oats. Instead of leaving him the lion's share of his estate, the old man stipulated that the majority of his money would be held in trust for future heirs." He paused as if consulting his notes. "And Culbertson has to have custody of each child before a trust will be set up in his or her name."

"That explains a lot," Hunter said, thinking aloud.

"Something else you might find interesting—Culbertson has some pretty shady characters breathing down his neck for past gambling debts. I'm not sure he can wait for Ms. Marshall to give birth. He needs the money now," Barringer finished.

"What about his parents? Can't he go to them for the money?" To Hunter, that would be the obvious choice if the man was in that kind of trouble.

"Harry and Alice Culbertson have pretty much washed their hands of their son," Barringer said. "They've bailed him out several times, and from what I can gather, they put their foot down the last time and told him that was it. They wouldn't pay off any more gambling debts."

"In other words, he's desperate for cash and if he can stall his bookies until Callie has her baby, he'll have one more trust fund to steal from," Hunter said, shaking his head at the man's foolishness.

"That's about it. If I find out anything else, I'll give you a call," Barringer added. "But I think you have the most relevant information now."

When Hunter ended the connection, he immediately called the bank, Luther Freemont, Emerald's assistant, then the bed-and-breakfast where Craig Culbertson was staying. Satisfied that he had everything under control, as soon as the fax came in from Emerald Inc. headquarters, he left the office and walked back into the dispatch room.

"I have some business I need to take care of," he said, putting his arms around Callie. "When I get back from town, there's something I need to tell you."

Concern lined her forehead. "It sounds serious."

"Nothing for you to be worried about, darlin'." Not caring that Corey and Mary Lou were avid spectators, he gave her a quick kiss. "I'll be back as soon as I can."

"If we need you, we'll page you," Mary Lou said, pouring herself a cup of her god-awful coffee.

As Hunter drove into Devil's Fork, he couldn't wait to confront Culbertson. He was about to make the man an offer Culbertson couldn't afford to turn down. And within the next couple of hours Hunter fully expected for Craig Culbertson to be headed back to Houston and out of Callie's life for good.

"I have to admit, your demand that we have this meeting came as a bit of a surprise, O'Banyon."

Seated in a booth at the back of the Longhorn Café, Hunter stared across the table at the most despicable human being he'd ever had the displeasure to meet. With his slick good looks, sophisticated air and boyish smile, Hunter could understand why women would find Craig Culbertson attractive.

But Hunter knew the type. Guys like Culbertson used their assets to hide their true nature, and Hunter never thought he'd ever admit it, but the man seated across from him was even lower than Owen Larson. As irresponsible as Owen had been about impregnating women, then leaving them to face single motherhood alone, he'd never used his offspring as pawns to bail himself out of a jam.

"I'm going to make you a one-time offer, Culbertson. And if you're as smart as you try to lead people to believe, you'll take it."

"Oh, really?" The man's sneering expression made Hunter want to reach across the table and grab him by the throat.

"I'm going to write you a check for five hundred

thousand dollars, then you're going to sign a document relinquishing all rights to Callie's baby." Hunter knew the moment he mentioned the money that he had the man's attention. "You'll leave town and never bother Callie or her child again."

"What makes you think I can be bought off that easily?" Culbertson asked, not even bothering to sound offended by Hunter's demands. "And who's to say that once I sign that paper, I won't discover that your check is no good?"

"Believe me, the check is good." Leaning forward, Hunter lowered his voice to a menacing growl. "And I happen to know that if you don't get your hands on some money, and damned quick, your life won't be worth spit."

Culbertson paled visibly. "What makes you say that?"

"It's amazing what a good P.I. can uncover, like the bookies coming after you for your gambling debts." Hunter removed the fax he'd received from Emerald Inc.'s legal department from one of his pockets and shoved it across the table. "This is a confidentiality and custody agreement. Sign it, accept my check and clear out of town or run the risk of not only losing the trust fund that would be set up for Callie's baby but your life, as well."

"Is that a threat, O'Banyon?"

Hunter shook his head. "Not at all. Although I'd like

to take you apart limb by limb, I won't have to do a damned thing. Your bookies will take care of that for me." He held up his hand to get the waitress's attention. "I'm going to order a cup of coffee. By the time I'm finished with it, you'd better have signed that document or the offer is rescinded and you can take your chances with the bookies and the court system."

After the waitress brought Hunter's coffee, Culbertson gave him a cocky grin. "Why should I settle for half a million? If I wanted to, I could get custody of Callie's brat in a heartbeat and end up with a full million at my disposal."

"I wouldn't count on that." Hunter gave the man a confident smile. "For one thing, Callie and I really are husband and wife. That will go a long way in her favor."

"Oh, that's rich," Culbertson laughed. "You own a run-down air-ambulance service in Nowheresville that I'm sure barely makes ends meet and you expect me to believe that my lawyers and good friend Judge Howell would rather see a child raised by you and Callie than in the lifestyle I could provide."

Hunter took a sip of the coffee, then slowly set his cup back on the saucer. "You don't get it, do you, Culbertson?"

"What's to get? I can tie this up in court for years and I know for certain Callie doesn't have that kind of money." His expression condescending, he shook his head. "And I seriously doubt that you do either."

"You might be surprised who could tie who up in court." Hunter laughed harshly. "Besides, I doubt that your bookies would want to wait that long before they start taking their money out of your worthless hide."

Hunter could tell that he'd given Culbertson something to think about. But the man was more arrogant and self-absorbed than Hunter had given him credit for.

"What if I say half a mil isn't enough? What if I want more?"

"It's up to you." Hunter took a healthy swallow of his coffee. "But I'm getting close to finishing this coffee. If you haven't signed that paper by the time I get done, Callie and I will see you in court." He grinned. "That is, if there's anything left of you by the time the case comes up on the docket."

When Hunter started to pick up his cup, he watched Culbertson glance at the contents, then eye the document in front of him. "And you're sure the check is good?"

Hunter nodded. "I can guarantee it."

"How do I know I can trust you?"

"That's something you'll just have to take on faith," Hunter said, lifting his cup. He almost laughed out loud when Culbertson quickly took an ink pen from the inside pocket of his sports jacket and hastily scrawled his name on the designated line of the document before Hunter could take the last sip of the coffee.

Shoving the paper back at him, Culbertson glared at

Hunter as he folded it and put it in his pocket. "You're welcome to Callie and her brat. Now where's my money?"

Hunter removed a check from a zippered pocket on his flight suit, then, before he could stop himself, he reached across the table and grabbed Culbertson by the front of the shirt. Pulling him forward until they were nose to nose, he made sure there was no mistaking the menace in his voice. "Don't ever let me hear you use that tone of voice again when you refer to my wife or our baby. You got that?"

"You really love her, don't you?"

"Yes, I do." When Hunter realized what he'd said, he released Culbertson's shirt and shoved him away. Then, sliding out of the booth, he tossed the check on the table. "Now get the hell out of Devil's Fork and don't let me see you again."

As he walked out of the café and got into his truck, Hunter's heart pounded hard in his chest and he had to force himself to breathe. He loved Callie.

When he'd lost Ellen, he'd vowed never to love another woman and run the risk of losing her. But as much as he'd cared for his fiancée, his feelings for her couldn't compare to the depths of what he felt for Callie. In the past couple of weeks he'd felt more alive than he had in his entire life and he knew for certain that if he lost her he'd never survive.

How the hell had he let himself get in so deep?

When had it happened? And why hadn't he seen it coming?

Somewhere between that wild ride from the airfield when she'd picked him up the day he'd arrived in Devil's Fork and yesterday when they'd exchanged wedding vows he'd let go of the past and reached for the future. A future with Callie and her son.

Steering the truck out onto Main Street, he shook his head. He wasn't fool enough to think that just because he realized he loved her they could work things out and make a go of their marriage. At the time he'd suggested they get married, she'd had just as many reservations, if not more, than he'd had. And the sole reason they'd married in the first place was to keep Culbertson from taking her baby away from her. Now that he was no longer a threat, their reason for staying together was gone.

He took a deep breath as he turned onto the drive leading up to the Life Medevac hangar. He knew that Callie cared for him. Her response to his kisses and the passion they shared when they made love was proof of that. But did she love him?

She'd told him that she trusted him, but that didn't mean she wanted to stay with him for the rest of her life. And he distinctly remembered her telling him the first day they met that she was quite content to remain single.

He also recalled Callie had a problem with anyone

who had money. How would she take it when she discovered that she was married to a man with a multimillion-dollar bank account and who stood to inherit a sizable portion of Emerald Inc., the multibillion-dollar enterprise his paternal grandmother had built from the ground up?

As he parked the truck, got out and walked toward the hangar, he wasn't sure how things would turn out for them. But he had every intention of finding out. He'd tell her how he felt, explain everything about himself and pray that she understood and loved him anyway.

"I was just about to page you," Mary Lou said, hanging up the phone.

"There's been an accident on the Thompson ranch and they need us there as soon as possible," Callie added as she breezed past him on the way out the door.

"Where's Corey?" he asked, following her.

"Right here, boss," Corey called, running after them.

When they were all strapped into their seats, Hunter revved the helicopter's engine and took hold of the stick. He wasn't happy about having to postpone his talk with Callie, but it couldn't be helped. They had an accident victim waiting on them and that took precedence over matters of the heart.

After stabilizing the compound fracture on Carl Thompson's leg and transporting him to the hospital in El Paso, Callie was more than ready to get back to base. It had taken everything she and Corey could do to convince the man that he wasn't on a joyride and couldn't sit up to look out the window during the thirty-minute flight.

"I hope old Carl isn't overly accident-prone," Corey said as they climbed back into the helicopter.

Callie nodded. "If it had taken much longer to get here, I would have radioed for a doctor's order to give him a sedative."

"Well, that's something you won't have to give me," Corey said, taking off his headset and settling back in his seat. "I intend to catch a few winks on the flight home."

When Corey closed his eyes and fell silent, Callie turned her attention to Hunter. As she watched, he put on his headset and flipped switches on the control panel. Her heart skipped a beat and she had to remind herself to breathe. If she lived to be a hundred, she didn't think she'd ever see a man look as sexy as he looked in his flight suit and aviator sunglasses. But then, she thought he was sexy no matter what he did or didn't wear.

She took a deep breath. As hard as she'd fought to keep from loving him, he'd managed to get past her defenses and fill a void in her life that she hadn't even known existed.

Unfortunately that didn't mean they could have a future together. He'd made it quite clear that he was only marrying her to help her retain custody of her son and that once the threat from Craig was over, so was their marriage. Besides, pretending to be happily married and anticipating the birth of a child was one thing. Permanently accepting the role of loving husband and expectant father was something else entirely.

Her chest tightened as she thought of her life without Hunter. She didn't want to think about not being able to see his handsome face every day, hear his hearty laughter or feel the warmth of his touch. But did she have the nerve to tell him how she felt and that she wanted to stay married after her current problems were resolved?

"Damn!" Hunter's vehement curse coming through her headset broke through her disturbing introspection.

"What's wrong?"

"We've got some weather moving in that I don't like," he said, pointing to a bank of clouds.

As she listened to him radio for a weather report from the control tower at the El Paso airport, she was relieved to hear the storm front was moving away from them. She'd never been overly frightened by heavy turbulence in an airplane, but she wasn't sure she wanted to experience it in a helicopter.

"Looks like we're in the clear," he said, lifting off the helipad and steering the helicopter back toward Devil's Fork.

"Did you get your business taken care of this morning?" she asked conversationally.

He nodded. "When we get back to base, we have some things we need to discuss."

"That sounds rather ominous." She wasn't sure from the serious tone of his voice that she wanted to hear what he had to say.

"Don't worry, darlin'. It's not as bad as it sounds."

His endearment reassured her, and they flew in companionable silence for some time before Hunter rattled off a string of blistering curses, ending with a word that most men saved for extreme circumstances.

"I'm almost afraid to ask, but what was that for?" she asked.

"The winds have shifted and we're about to fly right into the middle of that weather front," he said as a gust of wind buffeted the helicopter.

As Hunter fought the stick, Callie tightened her shoulder harness and did her best not to scream when they swayed precariously. Praying they were close to the Life Medevac base, her heart sank when she glanced out the side window and saw the jagged peaks of the mountains.

"I hope like hell I can find a place to set down," Hunter said as he continued to struggle with the controls. "We need to ride this out on the ground."

"That sounds like a good idea to me," she readily agreed.

Glancing over at Corey, she couldn't believe he was still asleep. No wonder Mary Lou complained about trying to wake him up when their crew had a night run to make.

"This is going to be risky," Hunter said, sounding as if his teeth were clenched. "I want you and Corey to hang on tight."

She gripped the sides of the jump seat. "I don't know how, but Corey is still asleep."

"Does he have the shoulder harness buckled?"

"Yes. But he disconnected his headset."

"That's okay," Hunter said tersely. "All that matters is that he's strapped in."

Callie felt as if her heart was in her throat. She knew enough about helicopters to know that landing in a mountainous area was tricky under the best conditions. But during a storm with strong wind gusts it was going to be extremely hazardous.

She felt the helicopter suddenly lurch to one side, and closing her eyes, she prayed as hard as she could while she waited for whatever happened next.

When Hunter spotted a relatively level area at the base of one of the mountains, he clenched his teeth and used every ounce of strength he had to hold the chopper as steady as possible. Fleeting images of another emergency landing and the devastating outcome flashed through his mind. But this time would be different. He was determined that this time the woman he loved and her unborn child would be safe and unharmed.

When the skids bumped the ground hard, then bounced up to come down again with a bone-jarring thud, Hunter killed the rotor engine and released the latch on his shoulder harness. Saying a silent prayer of thanks to the powers that be for a safe, albeit rough, landing, he climbed into the cabin area to check on his passengers.

Taking Callie into his arms, he held her close. "Are you all right?"

She clung to him as she nodded. "Y-yes."

Turning to Corey, Hunter asked, "What about you? Are you okay?"

Pale as a ghost, his eyes wide with shock, the young man nodded. "Wow! That was one hairy landing. Where are we?"

Hunter looked out the starboard windows at the surrounding mountains. "About halfway between El Paso and Devil's Fork."

The adrenaline high he'd been on since realizing they were on a collision course with the storm began to wane, and Hunter felt as if his muscles had turned to jelly. Reaching for the microphone clipped to the epaulet on Callie's flight suit, he radioed Mary Lou to advise her of the situation. Then, after assuring her they were all okay, he told her they would start back as soon as the storm let up.

Unable to stop thinking about how close he'd come to reliving the nightmare he'd been caught up in five years ago and not wanting Callie to see that his hands were beginning to shake, he made up a lame excuse about doing a systems check and climbed back into the pilot's seat.

He was vaguely aware that Callie and Corey were discussing Corey's sleeping habits, but Hunter paid little attention to the conversation. He was too busy thinking about what could have happened if he'd been unable to land the chopper safely.

What would he have done if he'd lost Callie the way he'd lost Ellen? How could he have lived with himself?

He took a deep breath, then slowly released it. The answer was simple. He couldn't. And with sudden insight he knew exactly what he had to do.

As soon as they returned to the hangar, he'd hand Callie the document Culbertson had signed, tell her she was free to pursue an annulment, then terminate her employment at Life Medevac.

Ten

By the time she, Hunter and Corey returned to the hangar, it was time for their shift to end, and Callie was more than ready to turn over the watch to the Evac II crew and go home. Her nerves were still jangled from narrowly escaping a crash landing and she needed to talk to Hunter. He hadn't said more than a handful of words since the incident, and she could tell something was bothering him.

Well, that made two of them. While they'd waited out the storm, Corey had chattered about everything from being hard to wake up to his pregnant girlfriend and their impending wedding, but Callie hadn't paid much attention. She'd been too preoccupied with thoughts of her baby and how close she'd come to losing him.

"I've got a couple of things to take care of here at the office," Hunter said, walking up behind her. "If you don't mind, I'll be over a little later."

Turning to face him, her smile faded at his serious expression. "Is there a problem?"

He hesitated before shaking his head. "No. I'm just not looking forward to the paperwork I have to do."

"We left my car here last night and I need to get it home anyway. I'll see you in an hour or so." When he gave her a short nod and started to turn to walk back down the hall to his office, she asked, "What would you like for dinner?"

"Don't worry about anything for me. I'm not hungry." Then without another word he disappeared down the hall.

She'd only known him for a couple of weeks, but that didn't matter. There was no doubt in her mind that something was terribly wrong, and she had every intention of finding out what it was.

But a hangar full of people wasn't the best place to have a heart-to-heart talk with her husband, and Callie decided that biding her time would be her best option. When Hunter came over, she'd find out what was bothering him, then tell him her news. She was going to grant his wish and ground herself, at least until after her son was born. And, unless she changed her mind, there was the strong possibility that she might give up being a flight nurse permanently.

As she drove the short distance to her house, she placed her hand on her rounded stomach. She knew it would take Hunter some time to find a replacement for her, but that couldn't be helped. Effective immediately, she was resigning her position at Life Medevac to concentrate on becoming a mother and being there for her son as he grew up.

Parking his truck in Callie's driveway, Hunter sat for several minutes staring at her little house. In the past couple of weeks he'd been happier visiting the cozy little cottage than he'd been in five long years, and it was tearing him apart to think that after tonight he would no longer be welcome there.

But what he was about to do was best for all concerned and he knew that Callie would eventually understand that. And even if she didn't, he could at least sleep at night knowing that he'd done everything in his power to protect her and the baby.

When he got out of the truck, he gripped the folder with the papers he was about to give her and slowly climbed the steps to knock on the door. As soon as he got this over with, he had every intention of driving out to that spot he'd found a few days after he'd arrived in Devil's Fork where he could stare at the stars. Maybe if he stayed there long enough, he'd come to terms with the fact that to protect the woman and child he loved with all his heart, he had to give them up.

"Why did you knock?" Callie asked when she opened the door and stood back for him to enter. "Why didn't you just come on in?"

Standing there with her silky blond hair down around her shoulders, flour streaked across her blue maternity top and the prettiest smile he'd ever seen, she was causing his heart to twist painfully in his chest and she didn't even know it.

Walking past her into the living room, Hunter waited until she closed the door, then turned to face her. "We have to talk."

Her smile faded. "Does this have something to do with what happened this afternoon? Because if it does—"

"We were damned lucky this afternoon," he said, cutting her off. He hadn't meant to sound so harsh, but it was taking every ounce of strength he had not to take her in his arms and abandon the course of action he knew he had to take.

"Hunter?"

She extended her hand and took a step toward him, but, shaking his head, he moved away. He knew beyond a shadow of doubt that if she touched him, he'd lose his internal battle. And it was one he knew that he had to win.

"I think you'd better sit down for this," he said, tempering the tone of his voice.

Sinking onto the love seat, she stared up at him with troubled eyes. "You're beginning to frighten me."

"I don't mean to." He took a deep breath and opened the folder in his hand to remove the document that Culbertson had signed earlier in the day. Handing it to her, he explained what he'd learned from the private investigator and about his meeting with Culbertson. "You won't be hearing any more from Craig Culbertson. He's gone back to Houston and won't bother you or your son again."

She gave him a disbelieving look. "You paid him off?"

Hunter shrugged. "I guess you could call it that."

"My God, I can't allow you to do that. That's an exorbitant amount of money."

"Too late, darlin'. It's already done."

Staring at the paper for several seconds, when she looked up at him, she shook her head. "You can't afford this and I can't possibly pay you back."

"I'm not asking you to," he said firmly. "Consider it a baby gift."

"A baby gift is a set of bibs or a high chair. It's certainly not as extravagant as half a million dollars to get someone to leave me alone."

"Don't worry about it. I'm not."

"Hunter, please—"

When she started to rise from the love seat, he shook his head. "I'm not finished yet. Now that the threat from Culbertson is over with, you're free to petition the courts for an annulment."

She sucked in a sharp breath. "Is that what you want?"

It was the last thing he wanted, but he couldn't tell her that. "I believe that was our agreement."

Standing up, she walked over to him. "You didn't answer my question."

"It doesn't matter what I want." He handed her the folder. "After you take a look at this, I'm sure you'll agree that an annulment is for the best."

When she scanned the termination of employment papers he'd drafted and the severance check for a year's wages, she glared at him. "Why am I being fired? And why are you giving me so much money?"

"Because it's the only way I can think of to keep you from flying. There's enough money that you should be able to pay for the birth, as well as stay home with your son for several months." He'd known she wouldn't be happy about it, but that couldn't be helped. It was for her own good and his peace of mind.

"This won't keep me from flying," she said, tossing it onto the coffee table. "I'm an experienced flight nurse. If I wanted to, I could get a job with another air-ambulance service. But I've decided—"

"You'd better not." Before he could stop himself, he reached out to take her by the upper arms. "What happened today was just a glimpse of what could happen every time you climb into a helicopter to make an emergency run. Promise me you'll find a job in a hospital somewhere."

"Hunter, why…are you…doing this to me?" she asked haltingly.

He closed his eyes for a moment, and when he opened them, the tears on her porcelain cheeks caused a pain to knife through him that threatened to knock him to his knees. He didn't like talking about the accident, but he had to make her understand why he couldn't bear the thought of her flying.

"Five years ago I was behind the controls of a helicopter that went down in Central America. It was a mechanical problem and there wasn't a damn thing I could do to stop the crash from happening. I lost my fiancée and our unborn child that day." Wrapping his arms around Callie, he pulled her to him. "I can't and won't let that happen to you."

"That's why you've wanted me to ground myself from the day you got here."

Unable to get words past the cotton lining his throat, he nodded.

Leaning back, she looked up at him. "Why, Hunter? Why can't you let that happen again?"

"Because I love you, dammit." Realizing what he'd said, he immediately released her, stepped back and, reaching up, rubbed the tension gathering at the back of his neck. "Whenever you get ready, stop by the hangar and clean out your locker."

"Are you finished saying what you came here to tell me?"

Fully expecting her to demand that he leave, he started for the door. "Yes."

"Good." She walked up to him and stabbed her finger at his chest. "Now you're going to listen to me."

"I won't change my mind."

Her violet eyes sparkled with anger. "I don't care. You've had your say and I'm going to have mine."

He guessed it was only fair, but it didn't make standing there wanting to hold her and knowing he couldn't any easier. "All right. Make it quick."

"Number one, I'll take as long as I want to tell you what I think. And number two, you need to stop being so bossy and learn to listen." She waved one delicate hand toward the door. "From the minute you walked in here I've been trying to tell you something and you wouldn't let me get a word in edgewise."

"I can't see that it will make a difference."

She folded her arms beneath her breasts and tapped her bare foot against the floor. "Why don't you sit down and hear me out before you start making judgments."

He shook his head. "I don't think—"

"Sit!"

Lowering himself into the armchair, he gazed up at

her. She was working up a full head of steam and he didn't think he'd ever seen her look more beautiful. But then, when a man loved a woman the way he loved Callie, there was never a time when she didn't look beautiful to him.

"If you had let me talk earlier, I could have spared us both a lot of anguish." Standing in front of him, she propped her hands on her hips. "I was going to tell you that after what happened today, I realized that I no longer want to be a flight nurse. So you can take that termination notice and your severance check and stick them where the sun doesn't shine."

Suddenly feeling as if a heavy weight had been lifted from his shoulders, he sat up a little straighter in the chair. "You don't want to fly anymore?"

"No, I don't." She placed her hand on her stomach. "What happened today reminded me of what's important."

Hunter couldn't believe the degree of relief coursing through him. "You have no idea how glad I am to hear you say that."

"And something else." She began to pace. "What gives you the right to tell me what I should do about our marriage? Did it ever occur to you that I might not want an annulment?"

He couldn't believe that she might want the same thing he did—to try to make their marriage work. Almost afraid to hope, he asked cautiously, "You don't?"

"No. An annulment is the last thing I want." She shook her head. "Although, at the moment I'm questioning my sanity and the reason why I love you, you big lug."

Hunter couldn't have stayed in that chair if his life depended on it. Jumping to his feet, he took her into his arms and held her close.

"Thank God!" Giving her a kiss that left them both gasping for breath, when he raised his head, he felt as if his soul had been set free at the love he saw shining in her pretty eyes. "I want to live the rest of my life with you, darlin'." He placed his palm over her rounded stomach. "And if you're agreeable, I'd like to be a father to your baby."

"I'd like that very much." Tears filled Callie's eyes as she reached up to touch his lean cheek. When she'd come to Devil's Fork, she'd had no idea that in running from her past, she'd find her and her son's future. "You're a special man, Hunter O'Banyon."

"I don't know about that, but I promise I'll be the best husband and father I can be," he said, kissing her. "And the first thing I'm going to do for my new family is add a couple of rooms onto the house." He nibbled tiny kisses to the hollow below her ear. "Or, if you'd like, I can build us a new home with lots of bedrooms for babies, as well as guest rooms for grandmothers to visit."

"Could we afford something like that?" Shivering

with desire, she closed her eyes when Hunter cupped her breast to tease her taut nipple through the fabric of her shirt. "You had to spend a lot of money to get rid of Craig."

When his hand stilled, she opened her eyes to look at him. "What?"

"There's something else you don't know about me," he said, looking a bit uncomfortable.

"You mortgaged Life Medevac to pay off Craig," she guessed, hating that he'd put his business in jeopardy for her sake. "Don't worry, I'm a registered professional nurse. After the baby's born, I'll see what jobs are available."

"That won't be ne—"

"I promise I'll make sure the job is on the ground," she hurriedly reassured him.

"But, darlin'—"

"There might be a traveling nurse's position with the tricounty health department. At any rate, I'll be able to help with the loan payments and I can cut a few corners here and—"

His deep chuckle sent a streak of heat straight to her core as he placed his hand over her mouth. "Now which one of us isn't letting the other get a word in edge-wise?"

She playfully touched the tip of her tongue to his palm and watched his eyes darken to forest-green. "I love you," she murmured, letting her lips brush his calloused skin.

He shuddered against her a moment before he took his hand away. "I love you, too, Callie." His expression turned serious. "But there's something more I need to tell you about myself."

Her heart stalled at the apprehension she detected in his voice. "What is it?"

"Remember me telling you about not knowing who my father was until just a few months ago and that his family had money?"

She nodded. "That's when you found out you have two brothers and your grandmother's reason for keeping your father's identity a secret."

"Right." His wide chest rose and fell against her breasts as he drew in a deep breath, and she could tell he was reluctant to say more.

"Surely it can't be all that bad."

He shook his head. "Most people wouldn't think so, but you might feel differently."

"Why do you say that?"

"Because you're not overly fond of wealthy people." He gave her a sheepish grin. "Darlin', I'm rich." He shook his head. "Actually I'm not just rich, I'm filthy rich."

"You're what?" Of all the things that had run through her mind, his being wealthy wasn't one of them. He certainly didn't act like any of the wealthy people she knew.

"When my grandmother finally told me and my

brothers who our father was, she also informed us that we each have a multimillion-dollar trust fund and will one day inherit part of a multibillion-dollar enterprise."

Callie's mouth dropped open and she couldn't have strung two words together if her life depended on it. When she finally found her voice, she asked, "Who is your grandmother?"

He smiled. "Emerald Larson."

"*The* Emerald Larson?"

"The one and only," he said nodding. "I hope you won't hold that against me."

She shook her head. "I can't believe…I mean, you never acted any differently than anyone else and I had no idea—"

He silenced her babbling with a kiss, and by the time he raised his head, she couldn't have cared less how much money he had or who his grandmother was. All that mattered was the man she loved more than life itself was holding her securely against him.

"Hunter, I don't care how much money you have or if you have any at all. I love you and that's all that matters."

"And I love you. Never doubt that." His smile heated her from the top of her head all the way to her bare toes. "By the way, what do you have planned for the end of next month?"

"The same thing I have planned for the rest of my life—loving you." He nuzzled the side of her neck, sending shivers of delight skipping over every cell in her body. "Why?"

When she kissed the strong column of his neck, he groaned and swung her up into his arms. "It doesn't matter. Right now I can't think past taking you into the bedroom and getting started on the rest of our lives."

"I like the way you think, flyboy." Circling his wide shoulders with her arms, as he carried her into the bedroom, she whispered close to his ear, "I love you, Hunter."

"And I love you, Callie." Gently lowering her to the bed, he stretched out beside her, then gathered her into his arms. "And I intend to spend the rest of my life showing you just how much."

Epilogue

As Emerald Larson watched her three grandsons and their wives circulate among the guests at the dinner party she'd put together in their honor, she gave herself a mental pat on the back for a job well done. She'd specifically chosen the companies she'd given each of them to run, as well as arranged for them to meet the women she'd known would be perfect for them, and she couldn't have been more pleased with the results of her efforts.

Glancing at her youngest grandson, Caleb, she smiled fondly. He'd proven to be a genius with his innovative and creative approach to management and had not only improved morale at Skerritt and Crowe

Financial Consultants, he'd increased productivity by fifty percent in just a few months. Along with his wife, Alyssa, he was building a solid reputation as a force to contend with in the financial world.

Turning her attention to her middle grandson, she couldn't have been more proud. Upon his return to the Sugar Creek Ranch, Nick had not only reclaimed his birthright, he'd courageously faced his nemesis and found vindication after thirteen long years. With the help of his wife, Cheyenne, Emerald had no doubt that his plans to turn the cattle company into a free-range operation would meet with complete success. And in the spring, when their first child was born, they'd finally realize their dream of raising a family in that big, charming ranch house under the wide Wyoming sky.

When her gaze landed on Hunter, her oldest grandson, Emerald sighed contentedly. He'd been the one she'd worried about the most. After losing his fiancée and their unborn child, he'd given up flying the helicopters he loved and built a wall around his heart that she'd feared might never come down. But when he'd arrived to take over running the Life Medevac Helicopter Service, he'd not only recaptured his love of flying, he'd met Callie, a young expectant mother whose love had helped him let go of the past and healed his wounded heart.

"You wanted to see me, Mrs. Larson?" Luther Freemont asked, walking up beside her.

As a personal assistant, Luther was highly efficient, his loyalty unsurpassed. But as a man, he was the biggest stuffed shirt she'd ever met.

"I want to thank you for helping me accomplish my goal," she said, continuing to watch her grandsons and their wives. "Our efforts have worked quite well, don't you think?"

"I'd say they've been a resounding success," Luther agreed with her.

"I rather enjoyed watching my grandsons prove themselves with the businesses I gave them to run, as well as helping them find the loves of their lives." She sighed. "It's a shame that I don't have more grandchildren."

Her breath caught and her mood lightened considerably when Luther gave her one of his rare smiles. "Well, as a matter of fact…"

* * * * *

A sneaky peek at next month...

By Request

RELIVE THE ROMANCE WITH THE BEST OF THE BEST

My wish list for next month's titles...

In stores from 20th September 2013:

3 stories in each book - only £5.99!

❏ Wicked Surrender — Sara Craven, Cathy Williams & Daphne Clair

❏ Taken by the Millionaire — Kate Hardy, Robyn Grady & Nicola Marsh

In stores from 4th October 2013:

❏ Payback Affairs — Emilie Rose

❏ Pregnancy Proposals — Rebecca Winters, Raye Morgan & Brenda Harlen

Available at WHSmith, Tesco, Asda, Eason, Amazon and Apple

Just can't wait?

Visit us Online

You can buy our books online a month before they hit the shops! **www.millsandboon.co.uk**

0913/C

Wrap up warm this winter with Sarah Morgan...

Sleigh Bells in the Snow

Kayla Green loves business and hates Christmas.

So when Jackson O'Neil invites her to Snow Crystal Resort to discuss their business proposal… the last thing she's expecting is to stay for Christmas dinner. As the snowflakes continue to fall, will the woman who doesn't believe in the magic of Christmas finally fall under its spell…?

4th October

www.millsandboon.co.uk/sarahmorgan

013/MB435

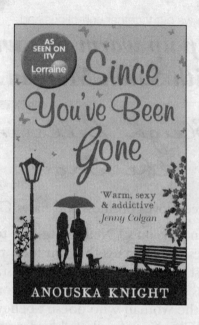

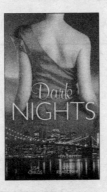
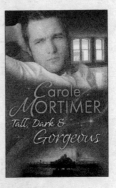

The World of Mills & Boon®

There's a Mills & Boon® series that's perfect for you. We publish ten series and, with new titles every month, you never have to wait long for your favourite to come along.

Blaze®
Scorching hot, sexy reads
4 new stories every month

By Request
Relive the romance with the best of the best
9 new stories every month

Cherish™
Romance to melt the heart every time
12 new stories every month

Desire™
Passionate and dramatic love stories
8 new stories every month

Visit us Online

Try something new with our Book Club offer
www.millsandboon.co.uk/freebookoffer

M&B/WORLD3

The Illegitimate
Heirs: Caleb, Nick
& Hunter

KATHIE DᴇNOSKY

Published in Great Britain 2013
by Mills & Boon, an imprint of Harlequin (UK) Limited,
Eton House, 18-24 Paradise Road, Richmond, Surrey TW9 1SR

THE ILLEGITIMATE HEIRS: CALEB, NICK & HUNTER
© by Harlequin Enterprises II B.V./S.à.r.l 2013

Engagement between Enemies, *Reunion of Revenge* and *Betrothed for the Baby* were first published in Great Britain by Harlequin (UK) Limited.

Engagement between Enemies © Kathie DeNosky 2006
Reunion of Revenge © Kathie DeNosky 2006
Betrothed for the Baby © Kathie DeNosky 2006

ISBN: 978 0 263 90566 3
ebook ISBN: 978 1 472 00139 9

05-0913

Harlequin (UK) policy is to use papers that are natural, renewable and recyclable products and made from wood grown in sustainable forests. The logging and manufacturing processes conform to the legal environmental regulations of the country of origin.

Printed and bound in Spain
by Blackprint CPI, Barcelona